MURDER OF A MESSENGER

Published by Brolga Publishing Pty Ltd
ABN 46 063 962 443
PO Box 12544
A'Beckett St
Melbourne, VIC, 8006
Australia

email: markzocchi@brolgapublishing.com.au

National Library of Australia Cataloguing-in-Publication entry
Grow, Robin
Murder of a messenger
9781922175915 (paperback)
Subjects: Detective and mystery stories, Australian.
Murder--Victoria--Melbourne--Fiction.
A823.4

Printed in Australia
Cover design & typesetting by Wanissa Somsuphangsri

MURDER OF A MESSENGER

ROBIN GROW

CONTENTS PAGE

THE ROBBERY AND GETAWAY

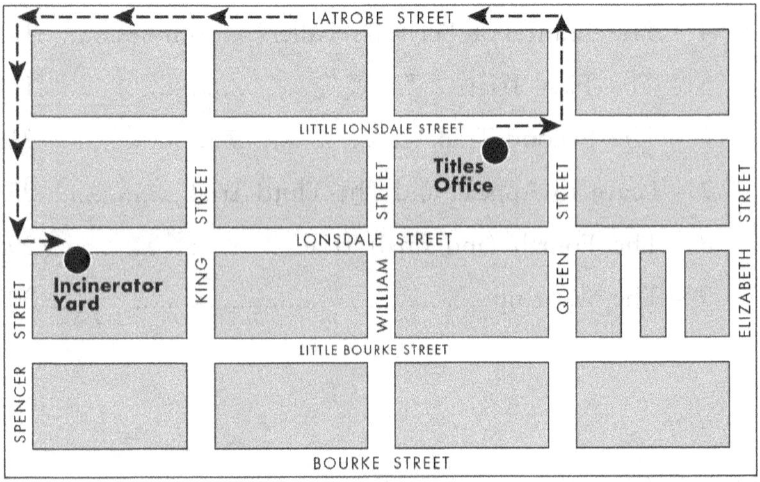

Map by Iconography 2015

PROLOGUE
MELBOURNE IN 1935

It was early 1936 when a group of over 100 well-travelled American tourists, mostly retired businessman and their wives, landed in Melbourne. They found the city to be gracious and enjoyed visiting its beauty spots and the nearby Dandenong Ranges. They regarded the local people and the hospitable atmosphere as particularly charming and compared it to cities in Southern California. They were impressed by Melbourne's homes, gardens and shops, but less impressed by the flies, which they described as 'so much more affectionate' than any others around the world. The only regret they expressed was that they could not stay long enough. [1] Pacific cruises and ports in Australia had benefitted as an alternative for the American market as tours to the Mediterranean had been curtailed due to the war in Abyssinia. [2]

Melbourne was a city in transformation. The Centenary of the city in 1934 had freed up capital and property owners and investors were busily developing (or redeveloping) city properties.

1 *The Argus*, 1 February 1936

2 In 1935 the Italian Fascist government, led by Benito Mussolini, invaded the North African state of Abyssinia. The move was widely condemned around the world and sanctions were imposed by many countries on trading with Italy. It resulted in major tensions across the Mediterranean and North Africa.

A number of stunning new buildings were appearing, using the latest in design – now referred to as Art Deco – and colourful finishes. Queen Street, running from south to north, was lauded from 1928 as the new financial centre of Melbourne. By the mid-30s it contained some of the best examples of this new style. Alkira House (1936/7) provided Melbourne with a touch of Gotham City (albeit a scaled-down version), whilst the new headquarters of the Australian Catholic Assurance Company (1936/7) demonstrated the use of pink synthetic Benedict stone. On the corner of Queen Street and Lonsdale Street, on the edge of the legal district, Rigbys City Family Hotel had been replaced by the Hotel Cecil. The government was determined that sub-standard hotels be eliminated from city streets and remaining hotels be brought up to date in terms of styling and facilities, particularly concerning dispensing equipment, bathrooms and sanitary conveniences. The design of the Cecil, by noted architect Frederick Morsby, was a showpiece of new styling. Finished in materials such as flush panelled walnut, sand-blasted glazing and chrome-plated fittings on all doors and railings, the Cecil offered modern kitchens and food preparation areas, gas appliances throughout and hot water in every bathroom. Importantly it was directly opposite the Titles Office, which guaranteed a steady stream of drinkers from customers and staff of this important government building.

The Titles Office ran along an entire city block, one of only two similar buildings in the central city; the other was the Supreme Court in William Street. It had been designed by JJ Clark and constructed in 1877, with modifications in 1891, 1911 and 1931, when the front door was re-located to face Queen Street. The office was responsible for maintaining all of Victoria's land titles, in paper form, and carried out the tasks of registering transactions on land, such as transfers, mortgages and plans of subdivision, as well as providing access to those seeking to 'search' a title prior to a sale. It also contained departments responsible for the payment of Stamp Duty and Betting Tax.[3] It was a busy, bustling place, frequented daily by clerks searching land titles, solicitors and banks lodging dealings and applications, and those paying Stamp Duty or purchasing duty stamps. Payment for its services was generally made in cash, resulting in a regular accumulation of thousands of pounds at the end of the day. As was common in those days, and for many years after, a staff member had the task of physically transporting the cash to a nearby bank at the end of the day. [4]

Hotel Cecil, 1935

The American visitors did not go anywhere near the legal precinct and the Titles Office during their visit. There were no

3 Stamp Duty is a tax that levied on documents, such as cheques, receipts, and land transactions. A physical stamp (a revenue stamp) was attached to or impressed upon the document to denote payment.

4 For a full history of the operations of the Titles Office, see Robin Grow, *Safe as Houses*, 2013

tourist sites to be found there. Nor did they go anywhere near suburbs such as Fitzroy and Collingwood, regarded as the centres of Melbourne's criminal activity. Melbourne had become an increasingly violent city in which the citizens were scandalised by multiple armed robberies and murders. There was much dissatisfaction with the police force and its Chief Commissioner, Sir Thomas Blamey. Great animosity had been caused by the dispossessing of registered guns and revolvers from 'honest citizens,' which some people interpreted as meaning that armed criminals could operate with impunity.

Titles Office, 1963, John Collins, Pictures Collection, State Library ofVictoria

The suburb of Collingwood plays a major role in this story. It was the centre of many workshops, tanneries, foundries and other industrial buildings. It also included many factories associated with the boot and shoe trade (which relied on a large unskilled workforce living close by), as well as 'slum pockets' hidden away in right-of-ways and small back streets. Living conditions were sometimes sub-standard, with many large families crammed together in small houses that lacked basic facilities. Many houses consisted of only two rooms. One study revealed a population density of 250 people to the acre (0.4 hectare), compared with 5.9 in middle-class Camberwell.[5] The lack of planning controls over land outside the city centre was a major contributor to the physical conditions, with much of Melbourne's populace apparently unaware of the level of 'narrow, evil-smelling streets' and the sub-standard dwellings that characterised a number of the industrial inner suburbs.[6] The streets of Collingwood (along with Carlton, Fitzroy and North Melbourne) were regarded by the government of the day as slums that bred crime, drunkenness, poverty, slovenliness and immorality, and were prime targets for the program that led to the creation of the Housing Commission of Victoria in 1936.

As the Depression had worsened, unemployment rates soared – as did crime. Collingwood had been the centre of scandals associated with S.P. (starting price) betting in the 1880s, when local businessman John Wren initiated a large, heavily fortified backyard totalisator behind a shop in Johnston Street, the main east-west thoroughfare. Children in suburbs like Collingwood generally left school as soon as possible to try and earn some money, although there was little work available. Many families relied on the distribution of food and firewood (together with small amounts of cash) organised by the local Council, or on jobs provided by the Council for civic works. Life was tough for those in the suburb and many took the opportunity to pick up a quid any way they could and put some food on the table.

5 *The Argus*, 29 June 1934
6 *The Truth,* 9 March 1935

Many young men turned to crime and gambling rather than try and subsist on the meagre dole then being handed out. Some in the business community in Collingwood were of the opinion that they could no longer rely on the police to protect them, particularly when carrying large sums of cash at the end of a day's trading. Nightwatchmen were particularly vulnerable to armed thieves and safebreakers and began to organise patrols and to seek licences to carry guns. When John Fitzgerald, a nightwatchmen from Collingwood, sought a gun licence in 1935, he told the Collingwood Court that he belonged to a group called the Returned Soldiers Vigilant Patrol. If he had a pistol, he argued, he would be able to apprehend wrongdoers. Not surprisingly, the police opposed the application on the grounds that if he were allowed to carry a gun, night watchmen all over the suburbs would also want to be armed. However, the Court sympathised with him and granted a licence. [7]

For their part, the local police often dispensed summary justice and felt justified in using threats, violence and coercion to obtain confessions from suspects. Police officers often testified in court that no threats were made towards a suspect and that he had made admissions of his own free will. But when the accused took the stand, it was a different story, particularly if he showed signs of physical injury, like having a head wrapped in bandages. Suspects claimed that they were threatened with 'a belting' if they didn't tell the truth. A favourite technique was to grab a suspect's ear and bang his head against the wall. Faced with such violence, suspects claimed that they made statements admitting guilt only to avoid being knocked around.

The irony of the grim social and employment conditions in Collingwood was the outstanding success of its local football

---

7 *The Argus*, 15 November 1935

team, nicknamed the Magpies because of their black and white striped jumpers. Australian football has long been the glue that holds Melbourne together. The people of Collingwood took great delight in passionately supporting their team as it won six Victorian Football League premierships in the decade between 1927 and 1936, including four in a row from 1927 to 1930 (a record unequalled since, and unlikely to be).

In a city obsessed by sport, the perennial subjects of football, cricket and racing were widely discussed in pubs, clubs and workplaces – including the Titles Office. Much discussion centred on the past (and next) football seasons, but at the end of January, cricket was the dominant topic, as the English team was touring Australia for an Ashes series. In a best-of-five competition, England already had a 2-0 lead. Could the Australian captain, Don Bradman, lead Australia to a recovery in the next Test, to be played soon? From Sydney came the news that Victoria's cricket team had been defeated by the NSW team. Matches between the two states (for the Sheffield Shield) provided the greatest sporting rivalry in Australia, attracting large crowds in both capital cities. Set a massive score of 442 runs in the last innings to win, the Victorians came agonisingly close, losing outright by just 26 runs. In the District Cricket competition in the suburbs of Melbourne, good crowds turned out regularly and close finishes were common.

During January, a sombre note took over the country (and the British Empire) with the death of King George V. His funeral was scheduled for Tuesday the 26th, which threw into doubt the observance of the statutory public holiday (Australia Day) scheduled for Monday, the 25th. Whilst the government could have invoked emergency powers to delay the holiday, it chose not to, leaving decisions about activities to the discretion of citizens. Many sports meetings and picnics were cancelled. The Tuesday was appointed as a day of national mourning, to be observed in a manner befitting a solemn occasion. Hotels were instructed not to open by the Licensed Victuallers Association, whilst cinemas could open if they chose to. Many factories decided to close on the Tuesday. No deliveries would be made to butchers' shops on either Monday or Tuesday, whilst bread was to be delivered on Monday but not on Tuesday. Public servants had the Monday off, but worked on the Tuesday. For those in the Titles Office, which included the Stamps Office, it turned out to be a dreadful week.

CHAPTER 1

THE ROBBERY AND SHOOTING

It was late on Friday afternoon at the end of January 1936 in the Stamps Office, located in the Titles Office building in Queen Street. The week was nearly over, officially at 5.06 p.m., although many of the public servants would be required to work on the Saturday morning. But there was one job to finish on the Friday. The important function of preparing the day's takings for transport by cab to the Bank of Australasia in Collins Street was underway. A sum of £1758 in cash, mostly consisting of small bills from payment of receipts for betting tax, was to be banked. It had been sorted into piles, secured with rubber bands, placed in a locked cash box tied with red tape, and packed into a bag marked Stamps Office in gold leaf.[1]

The money was to be carried by a messenger, Herbert Hervey Gillbank, a slightly built 17 year old. He had been employed at the office as a clerk for over three years and had performed this dangerous function at the same time each day (about 4.45 p.m. during the week and 11.55 a.m. on Saturday), for the last nine months. He was accompanied by an escort from the office staff, Ted Scriven. Aged 64, Scriven was a former soldier and prison warder who had been employed in the Stamps Office

1 According to one newspaper, the sum also included receipts from the Titles Office. *The Advocate, Burnie*, 1 February 1936

for 14 years and was only a few months away from retirement. But things were delayed on this day. The cashier, John Ryan, was having trouble balancing his day's takings. Eventually, the calculations were finished, the money had been counted and stacked in the bag by Gillbank, who was ready to take the money to a waiting taxicab. Scriven was supposed to be armed, but on this day, he had left his pistol in the drawer.[2] It would turn out to be a fatal mistake.

As he had done each day for the last three months, Reg Pullen idled his Yellow Cab[3] outside the door on Little Lonsdale Street, facing west towards William Street, waiting for the messenger and his escort. The street, two-way in those days, generally carried little traffic, and the taxi followed the same daily route. Near the idling taxi, two men were loitering, apparently examining the spare wheel and petrol tank of a car parked behind the taxi.

Herbert Harvey Gillbank, *The Herald,* 1 February 1936

Emerging from the laneway, Gillbank entered the cab first and placed the bag of money between his legs for safety. He saw the two men (one tall and the other of a stocky build) standing on the footpath. Suddenly one of the men began to wrestle with Scriven as he stooped to enter the cab. The other man, holding an automatic pistol, told the taxicab driver, Pullen, to 'sit where you are' before grabbing the bag of cash from Gillbank's grip.

2 *The Argus* reported that Scriven was unable to draw his pistol during the struggle, which was incorrect. He was not carrying a gun. *The Argus,* 1 February 1936

3 Yellow Cabs had the government contract.

Then the unthinkable happened. The tall man, who had part of his face covered by a handkerchief, grabbed Scriven's arm. As Scriven struggled and shouted, the bandit shot him in the forehead. Badly wounded, he dropped to the road beneath the running board of the taxi. Gillbank got out of the car and began struggling with the shorter man who had grabbed the bag. As the man wrenched the bag away, Gillbank was sent staggering back towards the taxi. At the sound of the shot the taxi-driver had stalled the car.

The tall shooter dropped the gun onto the footpath. He ran across the street towards a black Hudson sedan waiting 25 to 30 yards down the street, with its engine running and a third man in the drivers seat. Calling out, 'He's got the bag!' he jumped into the back. The shorter man, carrying a bag on his shoulder and with a gun in his hand, piled into the car. With the engine roaring, they sped off and swung left into Queen Street. With Scriven lying in the gutter next to his taxi, Pullen picked up the gun and ran towards Queen Street, yelling and waving the gun around. He tried to fire at the fleeing bandits, but nothing happened. The gun would not work. He then tried to commandeer a car parked near the corner of Little Lonsdale Street and Queen Street, which would not start, before climbing onto the back of the motorcycle travelling north along Queen Street, yelling out 'chase that car, he has just shot my cobber!' The bike was very slow, only able to go at about nine to eleven kph with two on board. 'Go faster to catch that car,' cried Pullen, only to be told by the owner that 'the bike cannot go any faster' and could not

Ted Scriven,
Sun-News Pictorial,
4 February 1936

keep up. Pullen dismounted at the corner of Latrobe and Queen Streets and returned to where Scriven was lying in the street, waiting for an ambulance. [4]

The robbery scene, *The Herald,* 4 February 1936

Another driver was sitting in his car in Queen Street when the bandits' car roared past, doing about 40 miles per hour (65 kmh) and heading towards the left turn into Latrobe Street. He took off in pursuit, but could not catch the car and lost it at William Street. The speeding car turned left at Spencer Street, zigzagging all over the road, and entered the gate of the City Council Destructor Yard at the southeast corner of Spencer and Lonsdale Streets. The superintendent of the Yard, John Boadle, watched the car enter. [5] He saw a stocky looking man get out

4 PROV,VPRS 00030/P0006, Unit 000004, 1936/777, *Proceedings of second trial*, 15 February 1937

5 Boadle later developed innovative garbage destructors, in conjunction with architects Walter Burley Griffin and Eric Nicholls, such as the one that remains in Holmes Street, Moonee Ponds. The City Destructor was installed at the corner of Spencer Street and Lonsdale Street, later to be the site of the massive electricity generation plant maintained by the City Council. Its massive furnaces generated enormous amounts of noise in this location. *Newcastle Morning Herald and Miners' Advocate (NSW)*, 10 May 1934

and inspect the bonnet, as if he was going to examine the engine. Then he walked back through the gates that the car had driven through. At that time two men came from the rear of the car, a tall man and a short man. The shorter one was carrying a bag in his left hand, against his body, with the top turned over in his right hand. They were stopped by Boadle. While suspicious, he was still unaware of the events from a few blocks away that afternoon. In a dramatic encounter, Boadle backed away from them as they approached him, asking questions. He entertained the idea of detaining them but let them pass through the gate to Lonsdale Street. All up, they were at the Yard for about five or six minutes. [6]

Incinerator Yard, 1936, PROV, VPRS 00030/P0006, Unit 000004, 1936/777

When Boadle learnt about the robbery soon after, he immediately contacted the police who took possession of the car, as well as taking Boadle's account and description of the men. He described the two men – one tall, one short. The tall one was

6 PROV, VPRS 00030/P0006, Unit 000004, 1936/777; *Report of Inquisition by Coroner*, 7 July 1936

slim, with a slight build, and about 6' (182 cm) tall. Importantly, he said that this man had dark, wavy hair with a parting high on the right side and no hat. The shorter man was described by Boadle as of medium build, light fair complexion, fair skin and a rather long rounded face. [7]

Officials at the Incinerator Yard, 1936, PROV, VPRS 00030/P0006, Unit 000004, 1936/777

Back at the crime scene, shocked and dismayed staff from the Stamps Office were gathering. The Deputy-Comptroller of Stamps, William Carnier, was standing near a window facing Little Lonsdale Street when he heard the shot. He cried out, 'It's a hold up!' and dashed out to the street, where he was confronted with the grisly sight of Scriven lying in the gutter, blood coming from the wound in his head. When the taxi-driver

7 PROV, VPRS 00030/P0006, Unit 000004, 1936/777; *Report of Inquisition by Coroner*, 7 July 1936

Pullen returned to the scene, carrying the pistol, he looked at it for a few seconds and then showed it to Gillbank, and asked if 'it was one of ours' (i.e. one that had been issued to the escort) and was told that it was not. He then put it down on the ground at Scriven's feet where it was taken into the possession of Carnier and later handed to the police, along with a discharged cartridge shell picked up from the road by the young cashier, John Ryan.[8] The police now had the pistol, the magazine (containing seven bullets, with one in the chamber), and the shell ejected from the pistol.

Scriven was rushed to Royal Melbourne Hospital in Carlton in a critical condition, arriving just after 5.00 p.m. He never regained consciousness and the doctors decided against trying to remove the bullet from his brain. His wife, Elsie Scriven, had been informed of the shooting at about 6.00 p.m. by an official of the Taxation Department, and she and her son John (known as Jack) hurried to his hospital bed. Gillbank was not injured but, not surprisingly, was badly shaken.

At this stage it was regarded as another well-organised and audacious robbery, but one with fatal consequences. The police were confident that the information they had received would lead to an early arrest. No one could foresee that it would result in four trials, a major re-organisation of the Victorian Police Criminal Investigation Branch (CIB) and a shoot-out on a tram involving a future Deputy Prime Minister of Australia. It would all end in a hail of bullets in the Exhibition Gardens. Around the same time, the chief detective in Victoria would be nearly fatally shot, resulting in an official cover-up and a Royal Commission that led to the sacking of the Commissioner of Police, a hero

---

8 PROV, VPRS 00030/P0006, Unit 000004, 1936/777; *Report from Senior Detective W. Davis*, 10 December 1936

from the Great War, and his replacement by the chief of the famous Flying Squad from Scotland Yard in London! Whew!

The laneway, 1936, PROV,VPRS 00030/P0006, Unit 000004, 1936/777

The laneway, 2015

CHAPTER 2
AFTER THE ROBBERY

In today's world, a major armed robbery occurring late in the afternoon in a large city would be the lead item on the evening television news. It would immediately be posted on web-sites across the internet where it would be instantly available around the globe. But in the mid-1930s, most people in Melbourne found out about the robbery and shooting in the next morning's newspapers. The Saturday *Argus* led off with 'ARMED MEN STEAL £1800 IN CITY', the *Sun* ran the headline of 'BANDITS ESCAPE AFTER SHOOTING MAN IN CITY HOLD-UP', whilst the *Age* headline read 'GOVERNMENT MESSENGER SHOT' (*Age* readers had to go to page 19 to read about it as the *Age* printed the classified pages before any news items in those days). The articles were re-printed by syndicates of newspapers around the country.

The police kept in constant check with the hospital in the hope that Scriven would regain consciousness and they could have a word with him – but he never did. Scriven died at ten to three in the morning with his wife Elsie and son Jack by his bedside. When the news of his death came through, the CIB was faced with its ninth murder investigation in three months. As Ted Scriven's workmates at the Stamps Office turned up for work on the Saturday morning, the word of his death quickly spread through the office. It must have been a sorrowful (and fearful) workplace. The mood of the staff wouldn't have been improved when they observed the Saturday takings from the Stamps Office being transferred to the bank under the protection of two armed constables, one uniformed and one in plain clothes. This time the taxi pulled into the lane behind the office, rather than waiting in Little Lonsdale Street, seen by the staff as closing the barn door after the horse has bolted – the damage had been done! As the editor of the *Argus* stated, 'such a precaution should have commended itself to the authorities earlier.'[1] However, some staff at the office thought that having the taxi in the lane would have made it easier to commit a robbery, because the view of the driver and staff would have been obstructed. Their solution was to have men in the street watching to see that there was no-one hanging about.

The police were looking for three men. The early witness reports said that the man who fired the fatal shot was aged about 40, about 5' 6" (160 cm), of stout build, clean shaven, fresh (approaching red) complexion, round, determined-looking face, bald halfway back of his head, well-dressed in a blue suit and wearing a grey hat. The driver of the car was aged about 24, about 5' 6" (160 cm), of medium build dressed in a fawn or light brown suit and wearing a felt hat undented at the top but dented on both sides. The third man was aged between 23 to 25, about 6 ft (180 cm), with dark wavy hair and a sallow complexion, clean-shaven and with an oval-shaped face. He walked with a slight stoop, was wearing a blue coat, grey Oxford 'bags' (trousers) and a grey felt hat.[2] But the descriptions would vary as time went

1 *The Argus*, 3 February 1936
2 *The Herald*, 3 February 1936

on and positive identification would prove to be the biggest challenge for the police in gaining a conviction. Realising that the three men had probably acquired another vehicle or were leaving the State by other means, the police began checking departures of trains and steamers and calling on their colleagues across the state to watch the roads. Descriptions of the men were circulated by telegraph to police stations throughout the state, to NSW and South Australia. Believing that they were heading to Sydney, one report gave some hope, stating that a stolen light delivery truck, carrying three men believed to be the bandits, was spotted heading north through Kilmore towards Seymour, on the Albury Road. They stopped at Adamson's garage at Kilmore at about 6.00 a.m., telling the garage attendant that the truck needed some repairs. They had left Melbourne at 4.00 a.m. but engine trouble had caused them to take over two hours to drive the 70 kilometres from Melbourne. Later, after the news of the hold-up became common, the attendant recalled that they had told him that they had to make Sydney in ten hours. He had also become suspicious of the numberplate where the registration number consisted merely of figures chalked on a blackboard. Believing that they would abandon the car before reaching the border of NSW, a squad of 25 detectives was engaged in the hunt. When three men in a light delivery truck approached the border town of Albury, they were pulled over by local police but were able to give satisfactory explanations and were allowed to continue their trip. The Melbourne police must have been disappointed when they received advice from Albury police that this promising lead had come to nothing. [3]

Out on the street, the afternoon *Herald* carried the headline of 'CITY BANDITS' VICTIM DIES'. A post mortem was

3 *The Sun*, 3 February 1936

carried out immediately by Crawford Henry Mollison, surgeon, of 41 Spring Street, Melbourne. His examination revealed marked bruising above the right eye. On the midline of the front of the head, about ten centimetres above the base of the nose, there was a lacerated wound, measuring nearly four cm by one cm in diameter, triangular in shape. The bullet had shattered the vault of the skull, leaving the skull above the right ear and lodging in the scalp. Mollison noted that the right hemisphere of the brain had been 'ploughed up by the bullet' and concluded that the weapon had been fired when in contact with the skin. The bullet was handed to Detective Tremewen, in attendance at the post mortem. [4]

Detective O'Keeffe, *Sun News Pictorial,* 1 February 1936

The police now had eyewitness accounts and descriptions of the robbers, clues from the getaway car that had been quickly moved to Russell Street for thorough examination, and a pistol used in the robbery. They also had a bullet, removed during the post-mortem, together with the empty shell from the gun. A massive effort went into checking police records and cross-referencing the descriptions of the suspects. The files contained the names, descriptions and the activities of convicted and suspected persons. There was a flurry of activity in the criminal world as police led by Detectives 'Scotty' McKerral and O'Keeffe spent the weekend

4 PROV,VPRS 00030/P0006, Unit 000004, 1936/777; Report of Inquisition by Coroner, 7 July, 1936

checking the movements of possible suspects. The police Wireless Patrol, carrying squads of detectives, burst into known haunts of criminals. They moved about the city and suburbs such as Abbotsford and Fitzroy, rousting out their underworld contacts as they sought a name (or names). They interviewed every reputed gunman and associate of hold-up men in Melbourne – well, the ones that they could find. The word was out amongst criminal circles and many had gone to ground, not necessarily because they knew details of the murder but just to avoid being questioned. Many gambling halls and inner suburban pubs were suddenly disrupted by the appearance of grim-faced police, who probably used methods that would not be tolerated today. Whilst these methods were often effective, in this case they led to nothing. One set of leads took them to Geelong, where four detectives raided a number of houses in North and West Geelong, and visited a number of mills at Geelong known for criminal activities. Once again, nothing eventuated. [5]

Within a few days, the prospect of a reward was being openly discussed but no recommendation had been made by the Commissioner of Police (Sir Thomas Blamey). The police were particularly interested in a bloke called Doug Brown who they suspected of being involved in a robbery with striking similarities to

Detective Scotty McKerrall, *Journal of Police History*, Summer 1996/7

5 *The Argus*, 6 February 1936

the Scriven hold-up. In April 1935, two armed men robbed a staff member of the Bank of Australasia, Alan Lindsay, who was carrying a bag containing £1725. When Lindsay alighted from a tram in Collins Street in front of a companion, Eric Lyne, he was confronted and told to drop the bag by a man carrying a revolver. As Lindsay did so, the man picked up the bag and ran to a car stationed near the kerb and threw it into the open window. Another man pointed a revolver at Lyne before dashing to the car and jumping on the running board as the car sped away. Criminals of this era must have loved having running boards on cars. In June 1935, Doug Brown's younger brother David, a 20-year old butcher from Brunswick, was charged with the robbery after being captured in Sydney and transported back to Melbourne. The police thought that Doug Brown was in Sydney and were convinced that David had been accompanied by Doug during the robbery and later on when the car collided with a butcher's truck in Richmond. The car had been found in a garage at Boronia, an outer eastern suburb of Melbourne, and still had red paint in the dents on the car, apparently from the truck. But the victims could not identify Doug as one of the robbers. David admitted his guilt but refused to give his brother up, claiming that he was driving the car and the robbery was carried out by two men known to him as Harry and Jack. He had met them at a pub in Brunswick – the revolver found on him when arrested had been given to him by Harry. He had no idea where Doug was currently living. In an illustration of police questioning methods, David appeared in court with a black eye and bruises on his face, head, left hand and body, claiming that he had been assaulted by detectives in Sydney by being been knocked down and kicked until he agreed to make a statement. The Victorian policeman, Detective Halsall, who had accompanied a handcuffed Brown from Sydney, gave evidence that he did not notice any bruises on his prisoner. [6] Allegations of mistreatment of suspects at Russell Street had emerged in a number of court cases in these years, such as the trial of Albert Brooks in March 1935. Charged with shooting at a police constable in Auburn, he claimed that at an interview detectives pushed him around the body, hit him in the face with the heels of their hands, kneed him in the genitals, and then tried to obtain a confession by producing an automatic pistol and juggling it around. Later he was again punched and ill treated until he could stand it no longer and signed a confession prepared by the police. [7]

These were desperate times for many, and the criminals were ruthless. One set of court proceedings gives us an insight into the mentality of those who were prepared to use weapons to rob government offices and payrolls from commercial firms. Thomas Croft was charged with the murder of a stationmaster at Carnegie railway station in 1934 after the stationmaster attempted to use the telephone during an attempted robbery. Hunting for information that could assist him in a very profitable robbery, Croft tried to recruit Kenneth O'Connell, the owner of a business that provided a lot of escort work for government offices. When he was told that payroll parties had armed escorts with them, Croft replied that he would be armed himself and would take care of any escort. O'Connell was worried by the prospect that shooting might occur and one of the men might be killed. Croft said: 'You shouldn't let that worry you, as they only get hurt if they fail to do the right thing. If they hand over the money there is never any shooting, but if they won't hand over the money they deserve all they get. It's either you or them.'[8] It

6 *The Argus*, 5 June 1935

7 *The Argus*, 22 March 1935

8 *The Argus*, 16 June 1945

provides a chilling explanation of the risks that criminals were prepared to take and the way they justified their actions.

In the Scriven case, neither Gillbank or Scriven was asked to hand over the money – it was grabbed and the escort was shot. In a letter to the *Argus* in 1935, a former courier recalled that he had carried tens of thousands of pounds around the city in the course of his banking duties. He had been given wrist strapping but rarely wore it. In his opinion bank robbers would not hesitate to mutilate or cut off the arm or wrist of a courier to obtain a haul, although there had never been evidence of such behaviour in any robbery in Melbourne. Other parties were calling for the introduction of armoured cars to pick up and transport money, as were appearing on the streets of Los Angeles. [9] The licensing of escorts and messengers to carry guns whilst taking money to the bank was sometimes queried. In 1933 a theatre commissionaire, Percy Barnard, told a trial court that he was licensed to carry a pistol but had only ever fired it once – at his married lover's husband, fatally wounding him. He claimed self-defence after the husband discovered the affair and attacked him, and was convicted of manslaughter.[10]

Nevertheless there were many businesses and government offices who continued to tempt fate by carrying large sums of money in Gladstone bags, by the same route, and at regular times. A sub-group existed in the criminal world – the shadowers, who followed them, mapped their actions, looked for 'blind spots' on their routes and also gauged their likely reaction to armed robbery. The shadower then passed on the information to the 'big shots' – the men who carried out the robberies. [11] A key piece of information used by the 'big shots' related to those

9 *The Argus*, 11 April 1935
10 *The Argus*, 9 December 1933
11 *The Argus,* 10 December 1949

transporting money and who had previously used armed police escorts, but had discontinued the practice – as at the Titles and Stamps Offices. They were clearly much more vulnerable than previously.

An obvious option was to pay employees by cheque but employers preferred payment by cash, even if the fear of hold-ups was a very real one. In the 1930s, many workers did not have cheque accounts so payment by cheque was decidedly inconvenient for many. A good example of the inconvenience came from miners (and their wives) in Bendigo. The banks were invariably closed when the cheque was received, so the miners had to visit hotels or stores to have the cheque cashed, often in company of many others looking to do the same. If they took the cheque to the pub, they were expected to buy a drink and shout their mates – even if they did not want to. If they went to a store, the shopkeeper could tell from the cheque just what the miner had earned, and might expect payment of an account when other creditors had prior claims. In addition, payment by cash was set out in the industrial awards, and a move to payment by cheque required a ruling to vary the award to be made by the Arbitration Court. [12] In the Titles Office, where the Scriven shooting had occurred, employees were paid in cash until the late 1960s, queuing up every second Thursday for their pay packets and then heading off to the bank.

There were also many men responsible for carrying money (either payrolls or the takings from their bank or business) who were prepared to take risks when confronted by armed robbers, or to give chase after a robbery. They often displayed extraordinary braveness (or stupidity?) in their actions.

In 1936, the police were still seeking Doug Brown for the

12 *The Age*, 8 July, 1936

bank robbery in 1935. They thought he might be involved in the Scriven killing and were very keen to talk to him about it, issuing a statement that they would be 'pleased to hear from anyone knowing his whereabouts.' [13] It would be a major (and much-needed) victory for the police if they could nail a person for two armed robberies. His description was somewhat similar to one of the Scriven killers, being described as 5'10 (178 cm) tall, with a fair complexion and fair hair that he wore brushed back. He usually wore horn-rimmed glasses with thick lenses but sometimes wore rimless glasses. However, none of the witnesses at the Scriven shooting reported that any of the bandits was wearing glasses that day. [14] The police issued circulars showing Brown and asked the theatres around Melbourne to screen photographs of him, a common practice, and were heartened when they received information that Brown was seen near the Council Incinerator a week before the murder of Scriven.[15]

The police had also formed the theory that there was a fourth man helping the gang and were convinced that he was from the 'southern suburbs'. If so, it was possible that he had disposed of the bag at Brighton Beach. On the Sunday after the Scriven murder, George Theodore, a tailor from Kew, was walking on the beach at low tide when he saw a padlock protruding from the water. On investigation he saw that it was attached to a kit bag adorned with Stamps Office in gold lettering. The bag contained a number of stones (to assist it to sink) and had been slit with a sharp knife. Inside was the cashbox that had contained

13 *The Argus,* 28 February 1936

14 The police never did track Brown down. In 1941, they received unconfirmed information that Doug Brown, still wanted for the 1935 bank robbery, had been killed while serving under an alias with the A.I.F in Libya, North Africa.

15 PROV,VPRS 00030/P0006, Unit 000004, 1936/777; *statement by Detective William Davis,* early December 1936

the money, which had been forced. Speculation was rife as to how the bag was found in shallow water. One view was that one of the robbers had intended to toss it into the deep water around Brighton Pier, but was put off by other people on the pier. Was it then tossed into the water from the beach when the tide was high?[16] Was this an indication that the robbers had not attempted to leave Melbourne immediately after the robbery? Or did it mean that someone else from the criminal underworld was used to dispose of the bag? Some boys had been seen on Brighton Beach on the Friday evening, between 7.30 p.m. and 8.00 p.m., playing with their Cocker Spaniel. Had they seen anyone throwing a bag into the water? And would they come forward? The next Monday morning, the third of February, the headmaster of Brighton State School in Wilson Street addressed the boys at the school to determine if any of them had seen the man. None of the boys came forward with any information, despite an assurance that the names of any boy with information would be kept secret. The Brighton connection was extended, although tenuously, when the police noted that the handkerchief found in the car had been weighed down with 'slit shot', frequently used by anglers and other fishermen for sinking their lines. [17]

That Monday morning also saw the Scriven family, shocked and bereft, preparing to bury Ted (also known as Jim). Born in Gisborne in 1872, Ted had married a girl from Portarlington on the Bellarine Peninsula, Elsie Priddle, in 1898. Within a year they had a son, John Edward George, called Jack, born in Hawthorn, who would be their only child. At the time of the shooting, the family had been renting 10 Addison Street, Elwood, for a number of years. It was a neat 'one of a pair' brick

16 *The Argus*, 5 February 1936
17 *The Argus*, 6 February 1936

Edwardian home, now highly regarded as a desirable property. Elwood was an interesting area. Much of the suburb had been developed in the early 1920s, following the draining of a swamp and the creation of the Elwood Canal. It was popular due to its proximity to tram services, picture theatres, dancehalls and the nearby St Kilda Gardens. Addison Street ran between Dickens Street (to the north) and Glenhuntly Road (to the south) and crossed the canal. Despite the smell of the canal on hot days, the street was popular, particularly with single women, ex-servicemen and with Jewish families, who could easily walk to the St Kilda Synagogue. In some ways it was a typical inner-suburban street, with a mixture of houses, blocks of flats and a small shopping centre that contained a hairdresser, cake maker, physician, butcher, greengrocer and grocer. Not surprisingly in times of depression, life wasn't always stable for those living there. It had its share of divorces, bankruptcies, mortgagee sales, petty thefts, bag-snatchers, and disputes between residents. It had achieved notoriety in 1930, when a schoolteacher, Mary Dean, aged 25, was brutally murdered and her body left in a lane off Addison Street. Mary, whose 'Bohemian' lifestyle was deplored by her mother (she had literary and artistic friends!) had been to a show at the Victory Theatre in St Kilda and was attacked by a 'sex pervert' after she alighted from a tram at the corner of Dickens and Mitford Streets.[18] The street was in the news again in the middle of January in 1936 when a resident, a 21-year old painter who was unhappy that his romantic intentions were not reciprocated, shot a female acquaintance in the St Kilda Gardens. He then shot himself dead – thankfully the girl survived.[19] There was certainly a lot for the locals to talk about in this street. When

18 The tram from St Kilda to Brighton ran through Elwood, along Broadway, until 1959.

19 *The Argus*, 16 January 1936

Ted Scriven was shot, there was another topic of gossip and speculation.

We don't know how Ted got on with the other people in the street or with the local shopkeepers or what his hobbies and interests were. By all accounts he was a loving family man, of solid British stock, and a member of the Church of England. He had been in dangerous occupations before, as a prison warder and while serving in the military during and after the Great War. He had begun work at Pentridge Prison as a warder Grade Four in 1901, with an annual salary of £135, and was still employed at the notorious gaol when he decided to join the Army. In late July 1917, at age 44, [20] Ted and his son Jack headed off together to the enlistment bureau. Jack had just turned 18. Whilst there were numerous examples of sets of brothers enlisting on the same day, it was less usual for father and son to do so. We can only wonder at why Ted joined up at this

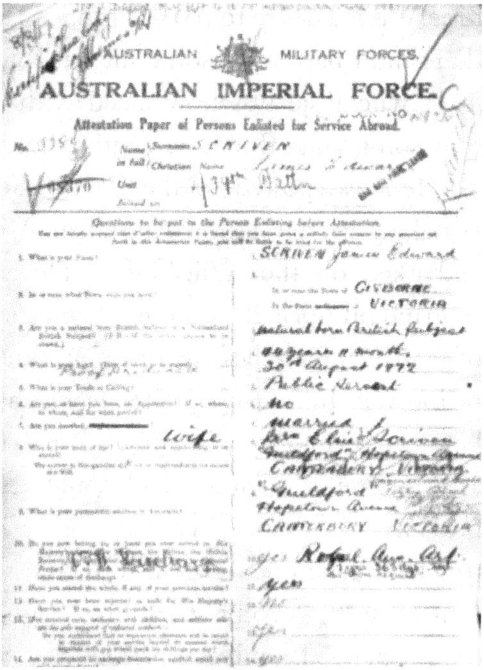
AUSTRALIAN MILITARY FORCES.
AUSTRALIAN IMPERIAL FORCE.
Attestation Paper of Persons Enlisted for Service Abroad.

SCRIVEN James Edward
Gisborne
Victoria
natural born British subject
30th August 1872
Public Servant
No
married
Wife

Ted Scriven, Military Records of Australian Military Forces, National Archives of Australia

20 He probably would have been too old to be accepted in the early days of the war but by 1917, as the war dragged on and Australian casualties were heavy, the rules relating to age had been relaxed.

time. Was it a desire to try and protect Jack? Whatever the reason, there must have been some interesting dinner table discussions. Ted's wife Elsie was now faced with seeing her husband and only son going off to a war with a horrific casualty rate.

Ted was posted to the 8th Reinforcements, 39th Infantry Battalion in the Royal Australian Artillery as a private and embarked on the 'Wiltshire'. [21] He arrived at Southampton, England on April 20 (via Egypt) and soon left for the battlefields of France at Rouelles, the scene of some of the heaviest fighting of the war. In October 1918 he was attached to Headquarters before returning to his unit in April 1919. Assessed medically at this time as having a bad cough, as a result of picking up bronchitis in France, Ted left France soon after. He returned to Melbourne on the 'Wiltshire', the same ship that had taken him to Europe some 18 months ago, and was discharged in September 1919, still as a private.

Ted had survived where many hadn't, and even received two medals – the British War Medal, awarded in December 1921, and the Victory Medal, awarded in December 1922. [22] He also survived the other source of mass death – the Spanish Flu. On his return to Melbourne he had found city in the grip of the pandemic, misnamed as it had originated in the USA. The particularly virulent and rapid disease was transmitted by

21 *The Adelaide Advertiser,* 23 February, 1901; the 39th Battalion was an infantry unit of the Australian Army. It was originally raised in February 1916 for service during the Great War as part of First Australian Imperial Force. Making up part of the 10th Brigade, it was attached to the 3rd Division and served on the Western Front in France and Belgium before being disbanded in March 1919. Following the re-organisation of the Australian Army in 1921, the battalion was raised again as a unit of the Citizens Force, known as the Hawthorn–Kew Regiment. In 1937 it was amalgamated with the 37th Battalion to become the 37th/39th Battalion. See http://en.wikipedia.org/wiki/39th_Battalion_(Australia)

22 *Military Records of Australian Military Forces,* National Archives of Australia

contact and was capable of killing healthy persons within a day. In response to the disease, Victoria was placed in quarantine and steps taken to contain its spread. People were encouraged to wear masks in shops, hotels, churches and public transport. Authorities also banned meetings of more than 20 people and closed places where people would congregate, such as theatres, schools, racetracks and billiard halls. It is not known how these restrictions affected the operations of the Titles and Stamps offices, where there was constant interaction between staff, legal practitioners, business proprietors, bookmakers, and the general public. [23]

While Ted was on active service, he remained in the 'establishment' of the warders at Pentridge. Promotion was by seniority in the Public Service, so it was important to retain one's 'place' on the list. When he enlisted he was second on the list of warders at Pentridge. But life amongst warders was extremely difficult at this time. After an inquiry into the running of the prison in 1919, a series of recommendations were made. Fifteen months later, the prison warders stated that not one had been carried out. They were inadequately paid and understaffed – a common complaint amongst public servants. Given the increase in the cost of living after the war, which had risen by 60% since 1912, [24] the pay packet of a warder was often not sufficient to meet household expenses. One report described life as a warder as 'devoid of all amusement and a continuous struggle to supply himself and his family with the bare necessities of life.'[25] In addition they were regularly criticised for their activities, including charges of trafficking goods to the prisoners. With pay rates clearly inadequate, this activity can be understood, if

23 Robin Grow, *Safe as Houses*, 2013, p. 81
24 Robin Grow, *Safe as Houses*, 2013, p. 82
25 *The Argus,* 19 May 1920

not condoned. Many of the prison's problems arose from the decision to close some country gaols, for economy measures, and to place all the prisoners at Pentridge into the general prison population, instead of grouping them into first-timers, model men, refractory, etc. Following an over-zealous search for contraband in October 1921, prisoners in the brush-ware shop refused to work and were soon joined by about 70 other prisoners. When the ringleaders were punished, the whole prison population refused to work and they were subsequently placed on 'probation'. When they put a list of grievances in writing to prison authorities, they were promised that they would be placed before the Government. But this did not happen, a move that was regarded by the prisoners as a breach of faith. The rebellion simmered for a few weeks until a further revolt broke out in the wire-netting factory. It soon escalated, resulting in furniture being smashed. The reaction of the prison authorities was to put those involved in straightjackets, but they soon realised that they had insufficient straightjackets, so handcuffs had to be used. In reprisal, prisoners set the wire-netting factory alight. [26]

Not surprisingly, given the poor rewards and great responsibility of a prison warder, Ted decided to leave Pentridge, where his salary was £180 p.a. He wanted to stay within the Public Service and in 1922 he took up a position at the Stamps Office, located within the Law Department. The move was a result of a combination of more money, less responsibility and a more benign environment. It was a relatively small office, with a staff of 15 men, located within the Titles Office building that ran along Queen Street between Lonsdale and Little Lonsdale Streets. He began as a Machineman's Assistant and Packer, at an annual salary of £204, which was about a third of that paid

26 *The Argus*, 16 November 1921

to the head of the office, the Comptroller of Stamps. In 1925 he had changed his role to that of an Embossing Examiner (remembering that duty stamps were embossed on documents to denote payment) and was now earning £304 p.a. It was probably a nice quiet life in the Stamps Office, particularly in comparison to the confines of Pentridge prison. An important meeting occurred in 1934 when a young messenger, Herbert Gillbank joined the staff, earning a salary of £91 p.a. Neither would realise how their lives would be intertwined soon after.[27]

Outside the office Scriven appeared to lead a quiet life, described at the Coroner's Inquest as a 'powerful, active man'.[28] He was looking forward to retirement in a few months and had gone off to work as usual where he was shot down in the street whilst doing his duty. According to his mourning relatives, he was without an enemy in the world and they discounted a report that he had spoken before his death of threats that had been made against him. One theory bandied around was that Scriven had been shot as the bandit had served time in Pentridge and Scriven may have been able to identify him.[29] His former fellow warders at Pentridge, together with some who had served sentences during his term there, spoke of him always in terms of the highest respect. His brother-in-law told the *Herald* that 'two men who had served sentences whilst he was at Pentridge told me that he had been a good friend to them, and whenever they needed a shilling they knew where they could get it'.[30] The funeral service, conducted by the Reverend P W Robinson, of St Mathews Church of England, Prahran, was held at the

27 *Victorian Government Gazette*, for 1901, 1922, 1925, 1934, accessed at http://gazette.slv.vic.gov.au/
28 *The Age*, 8 July 1936
29 *The Herald,* 2 February 1936
30 *The Herald,* 1 February 1936

Scriven family home at Addison Street before heading for St Kilda cemetery and another service at graveside.

The chief mourner was Ted's son Jack, aged 36 at the time. He was also a returned soldier, who had seen war service in the same battalion as his father. He had trained as a fitter and turner, but was attracted to a military life, and joined the Army as a fresh-faced boy on 31 July 1917, the day he turned 18. To join the AIF young Jack needed to provide a letter from his mother giving her permission. We can only wonder how Mrs Scriven must have felt when her husband and only son decided to enlist for service in Europe. At this stage, the people in Australia were under no illusions about the ferocity of the war and had grown used to seeing reports of numerous casualties from the Somme in the newspapers each day. His enlistment papers stated that he had been in the Cadets for four years. With brown eyes and black hair, young Jack was a centimetre taller than his father.

The young private was attached to the 8th Reinforcements, 39th Battallion, the same unit as his father. He embarked for Europe in February 1918, via Egypt, joining the 9th Training Battalion at Fovant in England before being sent to France in August 1918. But he didn't spend long in the field, as he was soon wounded in action by being gassed. Chemical weapons such as gas were used on the battlefield for the first time in this war, firstly by the Germans and then by the Allies. It inflicted terrible wounds on those who ingested it but did not necessarily kill those affected, particularly after gas masks were introduced. Jack spent time in a hospital for gas victims in Rouen [31] before returning to his unit and carrying out escort duties and returning to England,

---

31 Rouen was the centre of the southern line of British hospitals in France, which served as receiving stations for the wounded mainly from the area of the Somme.

and then to Australia, in August 1919. He was discharged in September 1919 and, like his father, received the British War Medal and the Victory Medal. But despite his ordeal on the battlefield, he received no military pension. Victims of gassing and shell shock were generally refused military pensions, on the grounds that any illnesses and subsequent health problems could not be deliberately attributed to the events on the battlefield. However, bombardment with gas often occurred before a major battle, so those who were overcome were often spared an actual combat role. Being gassed, whilst horrible, may have saved the lives of some of the soldiers who were subjected to it. One who did survive it was a German infantryman of Austrian descent called Adolf Hitler.

Mrs Scriven must have been overjoyed to have her husband and only son back safely from the war, even if Jack still suffered the after-effects of gassing. Who would have expected that, having survived the battlefields of France, Ted would be murdered whilst working in the benign world of the Stamps Office.

Funeral procession, *Sun News Pictorial*, 4 February 1936

The funeral service was a tragic and sombre event, attended by many of Ted's work colleagues and former Army friends. Floral wreaths arrived from the State Government, the Taxation Department, the St Kilda Army and Navy Club, the Titles Office, the Stamps Office and the 39th Battalion, where both Ted and Jack Scriven had served. Senior government officials acted as pallbearers, including the Chief Clerk of the Treasury, the Director of Finance, the Comptroller of Stamps, a representative of the Commissioner for Taxation, the commanding officer of the 39th Battalion and representatives of the Betting Tax branch and the Master in Equity. [32] A solemn line of returned soldiers formed a guard of honour for the hearse. The Scriven family placed an ad in the newspapers as follows:

> Mrs James Edward Scriven and Mr Jack Scriven desire to convey their sincere and heartfelt thanks to all who sent floral tributes, letters, telegrams, cards, and personal messages in their recent bereavement. They would specially thank the nurses of No. 1 ward, Royal Melbourne Hospital, Colonel Paterson and members of the 39th Battalion, and members of the staff of the Stamps and Titles office, also Messrs Drayton and Garson. Will all concerned please accept this intimation of the gratitude and appreciation of those bereft towards those who contributed in any way to mitigate the sorrow caused by the passing in so tragic a manner of a loved husband and father (10 Addison Street, Elwood).

Scriven's widow, Elsie Theresa, was known to the family as Sass. Living up to her nickname, she took time before the funeral to angrily attack the Law Department for their penny-pinching

32 *The Argus*, 4 February 1936

attitude to paying for police escorts.[33] 'My husband's life was sacrificed through the petty cheeseparing policy of the Public Service,' she said. 'I always knew something like this would happen, and he feared it too. If an adequate guard had been provided, the bandits would not have dared to molest Jim. He asked time and time again for protection but each time was turned down. Now that my husband has been murdered and the danger of the practice has been brought under the notice of the government, I suppose they will decide to do something about it, but it's a bit late for us.'[34] This was but one example of Treasury refusing to spend money on the buildings and services provided by the Titles Office and Stamp Duties Office, which received massive amounts in revenue but attracted the bare minimum in expenditure to maintain their businesses.[35] Elsie Scriven went on to express the hope that the Government would protect its employees more effectively in future to prevent a repetition of the shooting. This would reveal to the public the true conditions under which public servants handling large sums of money are expected to work.[36] Things looked bleak for her, as her son Jack, who would now be her only support, had been unemployed for some time. However, she would be eligible for a payment of £680 in Workers' Compensation (based on a sliding scale relating to Scriven's earnings at the time of death) and a superannuation payment of £1 a week from the government – half the payment to which Scriven would have been entitled after he retired. Many thought that this was insufficient for the widow of a person slain whilst at work. The Secretary of the

33 Elsie's sentiments were correct but she had the wrong target – in 1936 the Stamps Office was under the control of Treasury, having moved from the Law Department in 1935.

34 *The Mirror (Perth, West Australia)*, 1 February 1936

35 See Robin Grow, *Safe as Houses*, 2013

36 *The Sun News Pictorial,* 3 February 1936

Superannuation Board, Mr L G Wilson, explained that under the Superannuation Act there was no authority for any variation of the rate payable from the fund, made up of contributions from Government employees. Whilst this approach seems fair enough for those who retire, it seems a particularly harsh way to treat a widow of someone shot to death whilst serving the Government.

Various groups expressed their support for Mrs Scriven. [37] The National Council of Women of Victoria and the Business and Professional Women's Club scheduled a meeting with the Housewives' Association, whose President, Mrs A Thomas, had gone into bat for Mrs Scriven as soon as she became aware of the Government's position, stating that the indignation of women generally has been already voiced at this proposed niggardly treatment by the Government. The circumstances of Mr Scriven's death were unusual, and the case for compensation should have been treated unusually. She flagged future representations to the Premier, who was interstate. No official move for payment of a further compassionate amount could be made until he returned to Melbourne. At Trades Hall, headquarters of Victoria's union movement, trade union officials claimed that special insurance policies should be applied to special risks, such as those who had to carry large sums of money between business establishments and banks. After all, said Albert Monk, the Secretary of the Trades Hall Council, others in dangerous occupations (such as jockeys, aviators and motor car and cycle race drivers) all had to be covered by special policies. The President of the Trades Hall Council commented that compensation in such a case should not be based on the legal obligations under the Workers' Compensation Act or the Superannuation Act. In his view,

37 *The Argus*, 6 February 1936

a dependant of an employee killed in the execution of their duty should be compensated by the State Ministry in a more generous and broader way. He was sure that this approach would meet with the approval of the community. But the matter wasn't closed, with the Director of Finance for the government flagging it to be considered by the State Cabinet at its next meeting. [38]

When he heard of the killing whilst visiting Canberra for a meeting of the Australian Loan Council, the Victorian Premier, Albert Dunstan, expressed his regret and indicated that he would order an inquiry into the question of providing armed guards for State officers carrying large sums of money. No time would be lost in considering the provision of armed guards, he said – a standard response from a politician.[39] However, Dunstan was widely regarded as an extremely niggardly Premier and had regularly refused to spend money on improving the conditions of public servants. Would this promise be any different?

Albert Dunstan, Victorian Premier, Pictures Collection, State Library of Victoria

Elsie Scriven, who had little money at this point, was forced into court to apply for early payment of her Workers' Compensation Fund entitlement. An immediate payment of £200 was granted in late February – with the balance in three months. Cabinet then decided that she should receive her husband's full salary until the date of his scheduled retirement in 1937, and his full pension of

38 *The Argus,* 6 February 1936
39 *The West Australian (Perth),* 4 February 1936

£2 per week after that date.[40] As it turned out, Elsie did not require the pension for very long as she passed away in August 1943. She had moved to 50 Southey Street, Elwood, in 1941, and John had taken up residence there upon his return from active service in 1946, following WWII.

Whilst the pension received was good news for Scriven's family, there were still major concerns for other public servants required to transport money. The secretary of the Victorian Branch of the Australian Public Servants' Association, Mr J McKellar, called for the government to acquire an armoured car, with an armed 'crack' shot as escort, which could collect money from all government offices. Failing that, all public servants who acted as escorts should be allowed to become accustomed to firearms. He also asked questions about whether government departments had made requests for armed or police protection and whether such requests had been declined, and what compensation was being provided for injured officers or the relatives of those killed on official duty. Certainly, officers were inadequately paid to undertake the responsibility of protecting large sums of money.[41] There did not appear to be any payments made to Gillbank, the young messenger who had been carrying the money.

The police continued their examination of the major clues – the gun, the car and the items found in the car. The pistol was a .32 calibre Webley Scott, able to carry seven cartridges in the magazine. But it had certain characteristics that distinguished it from other guns.[42] The butt of the gun was made of vulcanite, a hard black rubber produced by vulcanizing natural rubber with

40 *Townsville Daily Bulletin, Queensland*, 20 February 1936

41 *The Argus*, 9 July 1936

42 Guns were numerous in Melbourne at the time. Many soldiers had brought handguns with them when they returned from the Great War, and there appeared to be few prohibitions in place.

large amounts of sulphur, and also used for items such as chemical containers and electrical insulators. Whilst vulcanite could be found on many Webley pistols, this one was distinguished by a long curved crack from the shoulder to the heel of the butt. Across the top and the bottom of the butt were two metal bands, made of German silver, each held in place by four metal studs and obviously intended to hold the cracked handle together. The gun would still work without the vulcanite being held in place by the bands, but the spring that controlled the inner workings may not have operated effectively.[43] In the view of the police the repairs must have been made by an expert craftsman. Naturally, they were keen to interview anyone who may have made the bands for the butt. A leading gunsmith explained to the *Herald* that stocks of back plates for this type of pistol were kept by all vendors, and cost about 5/- each. Anyone taking a gun to a reputable gunsmith for repairs would have to show a police license for the weapon before the job would be accepted. It seemed likely that the pistol was unlicensed and had probably been stolen. The repairs could have been carried out by a watchmaker or silversmith, who may have been unaware of the need to see a license and was not aware of the availability of the back plates. Alternatively it could have been the work of a fellow criminal who was handy with tools. In an age where the value of finger-printing was still questioned by many, there was no joy from the finger prints on the gun, mainly because they had been smudged by the hand of the taxi-driver Pullen who had picked up the gun in the street and tried to shoot at the fleeing bandits.[44]

43 PROV, VPRS 00030/P0006, Unit 000004, 1936/777; *Proceedings of trial,* 14 February 1937

44 Victoria Police lagged behind many other police forces in the introduction and acceptance of fingerprint technology, as well as a number of other scientific advances. Fingerprints were also mistrusted by the legal profession.

AUTOMATIC PISTOL used by the bandit who shot Mr J. E. Scriven in the hold-up at the Titles Office, Melbourne. A crack in the stock had been repaired with two metal bands, riveted by an expert craftsman. The police wish to discover the man who did the repair work.

Guards To Be Considered

CANBERRA, Monday.—Consideration would be given by the Victorian Government to the provision of guards for State officers carrying large sums of money, the Premier (Mr. Dunstan) stated today.

This action is being taken following Friday's fatal hold-up.

Gun used in the robbery, *Sun News Pictorial*, 4 February 1936

The examination of the pistol continued – the police realised that until it had been tested with the bullet extracted from Scriven's skull and the breech markings compared by microphotography with the markings on the bullet, it could not be assumed that the pistol was the actual murder weapon. However it was the best piece of evidence available to them at the time as it was not often that a weapon used in a robbery was left behind, even if doubts emerged about whether it was actually the gun used. According to a specialist gunsmith, 'ruthless criminals determined on crimes of this kind invariably use a heavier weapon'. A number of theories emerged, such as the lightweight weapon being used to put the police off the scent and to make them think the criminal was not accustomed to firearms. Or perhaps the pistol was deliberately left behind as a 'blind', with the fatal shot coming from another, heavier-calibre weapon. [45]

45 *The Herald*, 5 February 1936

The police now realised that there was a real chance that the gun they were examining may not have been that used to shoot Scriven.

Like many other aspects of this case, the results of the examination of the pistol provided baffling and contradictory outcomes. By February 10 police had determined that it had never been registered in Victoria, and had never been reported as stolen.[46] One report said that the pistol and bullets were sent to Sydney for testing on February 11.[47] It was a comparatively simple ballistics test, consisting of examining the gun and the fatal bullet in a special microphotographic machine operated by the NSW police. A cast was made of the inside of the barrel and photographed, and the rifling marks enlarged from the photograph and compared with those on the bullet. If they coincided, the original assumption that the pistol was the actual murder weapon would be confirmed. These methods relied upon primitive equipment and methods but were regarded as technologically advanced in the mid-1930s.

The leading technical expert and photographer for the CIB, Frederick Hobley, was requested to examine the pistol and magazine, together with eight cartridges on February 12. The cartridges were Remington, U.M.C., .32 calibre and nickel-plated. Hobley had been carrying out studies of bullets and shells for purposes of comparison for the last three years and had developed tests that could determine whether a bullet and a shell were fired from the same weapon. He later described how the pistol worked to a Courtroom. When the trigger is pulled, if there is a bullet in the chamber, that bullet is fired. The recoil ejects the empty shell, and at the same time allows a bullet to come up from the magazine. As the slide comes up

46 *The Argus,* 10 February 1936
47 *The Canberra Times (ACT),* 11 February 1936

again it brings the bullet from the magazine into the chamber. 'It is actually a self-loading pistol,' he said. The gun will carry eight bullets in the magazine, and one in the chamber.

Hobley carried out his own tests (with help from William Allen, a city gunsmith) by firing a shot from the pistol, using the same type of ammunition that killed Scriven. A careful examination of this bullet and one recovered from the body of Scriven was carried out using a microscope. The two bullets were aligned and the scoriations corresponded, leading him to conclude that they were both fired from the pistol recovered from the scene. [48]

A fortnight later, on February 26, it was reported that Senior Detective Delmenico and Detective West had travelled to Sydney and were working with their colleagues in Sydney on the results of the tests. But in early March the Victoria Police were reported as stating that Scriven was NOT killed by the revolver dropped at the murder scene, but was shot with a Colt automatic pistol. [49] None of the newspapers of the day questioned the police about the turnaround in their story. In early June, Hobley travelled to Sydney and used a microscope to compare the bullet taken from Scriven with the test bullet. He concluded that they had been fired from the same gun, the one dropped by the killer at the murder scene. [50]

Frederick Hobley, courtesy Victorian Police Museum

Late in February, the government (acting on the advice of the Chief

48 PROV, VPRS 00030/P0006, Unit 000004, 1936/777; *Proceedings of trial*, 14 February 1937

49 *Daily Advertiser (Wagga)*, 5 March 1936

50 *The Daily News (Perth)*, 26 November 1936

Commissioner) advertised a reward of £250 for information leading to the arrest and conviction of the murderer(s) of Scriven. With this in their pockets, the police were able to up the ante and increase pressure on the services of their informers – a tactic seen as legitimate and used by police forces around the world. Payment to informers (referred to as phizzgigs) came in the form of direct cash payment from monies held within a central fund or through holding something over an informant that could then be 'forgotten' or minimised. In the world of the 1930s, starting price bookmakers were a regular source of information. The pay-off would generally be assistance with future charges by suppressing details of previous convictions. But relying on informants could be risky if the information turned out to be incorrect (deliberately or not) or was recanted. When they received information from an informant, police resources were often directed at finding material that supported the story rather than finding material that didn't agree with it. If a prosecution case depended upon an informant's story being believed, there was a risk that the case would collapse if the lies of an informant, many of whom may be using rat-cunning to further their own interests, were exposed.[51]

As with all major criminal events the police Publicity Bureau had their hands full dealing with the hundreds of letters received about the case, which included a number from clairvoyants. Four days after the shooting they received an anonymous letter containing information regarding the murder of Ted Scriven that they believed would help them to trace the men responsible. Despite putting out a request for the writer to contact them, including assurances of anonymity and strictest confidence, the writer did not come forward. [52] Was it this letter that caused

51 *The Argus* 31 March 1936
52 *The Argus,* 12 March 1936

police to concentrate efforts on the men later charged?

It was immediately obvious to the police that the car was their most important line of investigation. It was a distinctive 1924 Hudson, square bodied, with two doors and 'bucket seats' in the front that tipped up to let passengers into the rear seats. The police concluded that it may have been stolen some time before the robbery, and soon discovered that it had disappeared from outside the home of a journalist, Edwin Martin Foster, in Grey Street, East Melbourne on the night of January 15; it was there at 11.00 p.m. and missing the next morning at 8.40 a.m. Foster told the police that it had a blue body, black roof and blue wheels. Police quickly realised that the car may have been stolen some time ago and re-painted. Inside the car they found two small paintbrushes, four pieces of sandpaper, a pair of grey trousers (commonly referred to as 'Oxford bags') and a hat. The paintbrushes, with 20 cm (8 in.) handles in bright red, were probably used to paint the car black, and the sandpaper used to remove the lacquer from the car before painting. Police believed that the brushes and sandpaper had probably been bought at the same shop. On the handles of the brushes was the word 'Fitzroy', whilst 'Set in rubber' was on the tin setting. They began an immediate check of sales of brushes in the past few days and within a few days a registered costing code led them to a wholesaler in the city. The distribution records led police to the retailer who sold them, who was soon interviewed. [53]

The car, a 1924 Hudson, No. 86730, *The Herald*, 1 February 1936

53 *The Argus*, 15 February 1936

When Foster next saw his car, on the first of February at Russell Street police station, it had been painted black and the number plates had been altered and given a fictitious set of numbers. But where? Surely someone must have seen it in a shed, garage or backyard in the previous fortnight? Police appealed to any garage employee who could remember supplying petrol to the car. Had it been out on the roads and could anyone remember seeing the distinctive car, remembering that volumes of traffic were quite light in1936? Police believed that several persons had seen the car and two soon emerged, but neither was able to definitely identify the square-bodied car. Another one who saw it and had no problem identifying the car was Rupert Dawborn, the motor salesman who had sold the car to Foster. On January 20 he saw the car in Elizabeth Street in the city and followed it to Fitzroy before losing sight of it. There were two men in the car, one with thick lens glasses and the other with a 'pimplish' face.[54] During their investigations, the police had photographed the car from various angles, and newspapers published close-ups of the upholstery in the hope that someone would remember having seen it. The seat cushions were a distinctive 'fawn moquette' and were torn in a number of places. But no one was to come forward to provide information.

The light-grey hat found in the car had a white lining, partly torn out, so that it could be drawn down over the face as a mask. The lining was also weighted with lead pellets. Witnesses had described one of the bandits (the third man) as wearing a grey hat. The trousers had nothing notable about them and could have been worn over another pair as a precaution against identification and then discarded.

In the following weeks, sensational reports continued to be

54 PROV,VPRS 00030/P0006, Unit 000004, 1936/777, *Report of Inquisition by Coroner*, 7 July, 1936

printed around Australia. Some were appraisals of the facts that emerged – others, particularly the *Truth,* described the shooting as indicators of 'the advent of a new type of criminal, a menace bred by the success of violence and ferocity in crime overseas'. The criminals who carried out the crime were as brutal and vicious as any that that were swept into 'wealth and notoriety' by Prohibition in America. However, Melbourne had been an increasingly violent city for some time, regardless of what was happening in America. Newspapers such as the *Truth* took great delight in reporting on the lawless nature of life and the callous brutality to be found in Melbourne.[55] The threat of violence was ever-present. Newspaper editorials railed that no one can feel safe in a lonely street at night and no householder, particularly women, could leave a house unguarded without misgiving. The difficulties of the Government and the police were recognised but the public was entitled to more protection, according to the *Argus.*[56]

As the end of February 1936 approached, the government was becomingly frustrated by the inability of the police to solve the crime. In mid-March, in the midst of their investigations into Scriven's murder, it was announced that a major change to the structure of the CIB would be instituted at the end of that month. This followed a series of changes made in recent years, including traffic control, enforcement of gaming and licensing laws, plain-clothes patrols, and motor testing and registration. The control of traffic as a result of the extensive take-up of motorcars in Melbourne was now a major component of the activities of the force. A motorcycle squad had been established which had the duty of keeping a special watch for 'road hogs' and 'speed fiends' and motor patrols by the police were replacing foot

55 *The Truth*, 8 February 1936
56 *The Argus* 13 August 1936

patrols. Automobile thefts were rapidly increasing and required increasing levels of resources to track the cars. In one week, three armed and masked men held up a man and stole his car in the Avenue, Parkville. A week later, just outside the Ozone Café in Brighton, a similar scenario occurred when a young man and his girlfriend were robbed by three armed masked men, who then drove away in his sports car. [57]

A major objective for the CIB was to reduce inherent inefficiencies, particularly the removal of the time lag that often occurred between the discovery of a crime and the arrival of an experienced investigator. [58] Some new blood, such as Detective W. (Bill) Davis, joined the Branch. It was to be decentralised into seven new divisions across the metropolitan area, with men living in or near the districts to which they were detailed. This would enable them to be 'readily obtainable' for their special duty. It was hoped that the changes would address the major problem of integration of activities with the wireless mobile patrols. With its headquarters at Russell Street, this group was to remain a separate force. Cars would still operate in the districts (also called divisions, leading to the nickname of 'divvy vans' for their cars) to which they were allotted, from where they were expected to 'co-operate' with the CIB. The No. 1 Division at Russell Street was to be the strongest unit and would assist the suburban divisions when necessary. Each division was to operate independently, but the Sub-Inspector of each division was to be responsible to the superintendent of the Russell Street division.[59]

Regardless of how the CIB was to be structured, police still had their hands full with the Scriven murder. Detectives

57 *The Argus*, 16 March 1936

58 *The Argus*, 29 May, 1935

59 Later events proved that this structure was unwieldy and further re-structuring occurred in 1937.

Delmenico and Davis were busy showing photographs to witnesses. The police also had their hands full with a number of armed robberies around Melbourne. One such robbery had occurred at the Post Office in City Road, South Melbourne on 8 January 1936. Two armed robbers had pointed sawn-off rifles at terrified post office staff, telling them that they would shoot if anyone tried to raise the alarm. They then fled with articles valued at £45, including an automatic pistol. In late March, John Stevens, aged 21 and of no fixed place of abode, was charged. He was later to play a critical role in the events around the Scriven murder. Another armed robbery took place in April, this time at the Hoyts De Luxe theatre in Bourke Street, just east of Swanston Street. Three employees were forced at gunpoint into the theatre's strongroom at about 9 o'clock on a Tuesday morning after the Easter break. The masked bandits then robbed the office and escaped in a car that was waiting in Little Bourke Street. The haul was about £1750, the proceeds from a number of Hoyts city theatres over the busy Easter holiday season, making it the third armed robbery of more than £1,000 in Melbourne within the last 12 months. The bandits had fled at high speed towards North Melbourne in a Buick tourer soon revealed as having been hired by a man identified as Doug Brown, already sought for the robbery of bank officials in April 1935. Following the normal procedure at the time, no information was provided to the press at the daily briefing, and the Chief of the CIB told the press that there would probably not be an opportunity of obtaining an official account. Statements such as this reflected the attitude of the Chief Commissioner Blamey towards dealing with the press. He distrusted reporters and his military background had not prepared him to take advantage of the positive relationship that could be gained from working with the press. At least the journalists got a laugh from the name of the film showing at the theatre at the time – 'Thanks a Million!' [60]

In late April another armed robbery took place when three masked men, all armed with pistols, robbed a grocer in East Malvern of the day's takings, between £50 and £100. The grocer did not get a good look at the men and was unable to tell the police if any of them answered to the description of Doug Brown, who was still sought by the police for the Scriven murder. Soon after, in early June, yet another armed robbery took place (the fifth in less than a week) of a payroll destined for the employees of Messrs Goold Porter Pty. Ltd., boot manufacturers of North Fitzroy. It netted the robbers the considerable sum of £1400 and, once again, one of the robbers was 'small in stature' and was stated to be similar to Doug Brown. [61]

Whilst the team investigating the Scriven murder was still preoccupied, there was about to be a major distraction. When the head of the CIB, Superintendent Culhane, retired in May, his replacement was an officer who would have a profound effect on future operations. He was John O'Connell (Jack) Brophy, currently in charge of the Ballarat police. Brophy had a long history of murder investigations and had worked with the legendary detective Fred Piggott for many years. Piggott had a long and distinguished career, having joined the CIB in 1912 and promoted to Senior Detective in 1919. Although Piggott retired in 1934 and wasn't directly involved with the Scriven murder, he had worked with a number of detectives who were involved in the investigation and what came to be known as the 'Brophy Affair.'

60 *The Argus*, 15 April 1936
61 *The Cairns Post*, 5 June 1936

CHAPTER 3

THE BROPHY AND BLAMEY SIDESHOW

Whilst the search for the murderer of Scriven continued, other issues occupied the minds of senior Victorian police. The working conditions endured by members of the force at Russell Street were deplorable and the buildings were hopelessly out of date. There was an obvious need for a more modern building to replace those built many years ago – one that could provide accommodation and facilities for administrative functions, records storage and spaces for cars. In addition, there was an increasing emphasis by some police officers on the possibilities provided by a more scientific approach to police investigations. This shift in approach required equipment and specially designed facilities that would best be provided by a new building. The police department was seeking extensions to the existing building. However, some in government felt that a more comprehensive plan was required. The Public Works department was asked to prepare a report, which would probably require an outlay of £30,000 for a building that would include extensions on land acquired by the Police department on Latrobe Street.

In addition, Chief Commissioner Blamey's office occupied space in the Magistrates Court building, opposite the Police buildings. A new building would enable him and his staff to move across the road and would free up space for a desperately needed new courtroom.[1] Located on the corner of Latrobe and Russell Streets, the brick and stone Court building dated from 1910. Designed in Romanesque style, it was characterised by gables, turrets and arches, together with a large arched entrance facing the corner. It was generally referred to as the City Court, but the actual City Court was Courtroom One, reserved for cases from within the boundaries of the city. The courtroom was beautifully fitted out – spacious, with high ceilings, decorative stonework and massive carved wooden panelling for the bench. Lawyers working there regarded it as a rabbit warren. Access to the holding cells was via the dock and lawyers had to make their way through it to confer with their clients in custody. At the rear was an elongated L-shaped courtyard. According to Michael Challinger, in his work on Victoria's historic courthouses, the courtyard never lacked atmosphere. For decades defendants, witnesses, lawyers and police mingled here, pacing out their nervousness and treading underfoot a carpet of cigarette butts.[2]

Despite crying poor, the revenue of the Victorian government had increased by nearly 4% in the first seven months of the 1935/6 financial year.[3] At the start of 1936, the state of Victoria had little money to spend on capital works. It relied on provision of funds from the Commonwealth government in Canberra. After years of trying to negotiate through difficult financial times, relations between the Commonwealth government and the States were extremely strained, with State Treasurers increasingly frustrated by the small amounts allocated by Canberra.[4] When the Victorian Premier, Mr Dunstan, inspected police headquarters in early May

1 *The Argus,* 5 December 1934
2 Michael Challinger, *Historic Courthouses of Victoria,* 2001, p. 127
3 *The Argus,* 1 February 1936
4 *The Argus,* 3 February 1936

1936, he was shocked at the conditions and quickly concluded that large sections of the buildings were totally obsolete. Some rectification work would be necessary but that would depend on the amount of money that was available. But Dunstan's visit had started the process by which the classic Art Deco style Police Headquarters building would eventually be constructed and opened in 1941. The government had already prepared a plan for a reconstruction but the Chief Commissioner, Sir Thomas Blamey, had requested that the 'layout' be amended. [5] The cause of Blamey's dissatisfaction with the plans for the building is not known.

Sir Thomas Blamey, Chief Commissioner

Blamey had been born in Wagga, NSW, in 1884. After five years as a schoolmaster, he joined the Army in 1906 and was the first Australian to pass an examination entitling him to undertake military training abroad. He was in England, with a rank of Major, when the Great War broke out in 1914. By December 1916 he was in charge of the 2nd battalion of the Australian Infantry Forces (AIF), and later worked closely with Sir John Monash, attaining the rank of Brigadier-General.[6] On his return to Australia, he was appointed Deputy Chief of the General Staff. War throws up opportunities for energetic soldiers – peacetime, less so. However, when the

5 *The Argus*, 8 May 1936

6 Sir John Monash was regarded as being superior to other A I F Generals in intellect, articulateness and personal magnetism. http://adb.anu.edu.au/biography/monash-sir-john-7618, accessed 7 February 2015

Chief Commissioner of Police for Victoria, Alexander Nicholson, became ill and entered hospital in May 1925 (never to return to duty), the position became available. Blamey was approached to take on the role and was appointed by the conservative Country Party government of John Allan. After some lean financial years, he would have been grateful for the salary of £1,500 a year, which was £600 more than Nicholson had received. Nicholson had been in the process of reconstructing the Victorian police and had introduced the wireless patrol car network. He had also been in charge of the force during the disastrous year of 1923, when many police went on strike over their conditions and pay. A Royal Commission followed, chaired by Sir John Monash, which called for 'substantial change, including better conditions and pay, modernisation of policing techniques and greater investment in police training and education'.[7]

Blamey was expected to rebuild the force along the lines of the Royal Commission's recommendations and his appointment was well-received by the more conservative and propertied elements in the community.[8] It seems likely that Monash would have put a good word in for him to take on the post. He was appointed for five years but apparently on the unwritten understanding that, in all normal circumstances, he would be Police Chief until he reached the Victorian Public Service retiring age of 65.[9] However, Blamey's tenure would prove to be anything but normal.

Whilst he was regarded as an outsider in the arcane world of police culture, his appointment was sufficient to end moves for an enquiry into alleged police corruption and maladministration, particularly in the Licensing Branch. There is some irony here, as

7 Kevin Morgan, *Detective Piggott's Casebook, 2012, p.* 283
8 Robert Haldane, *The People's Force,* 1986, p. 195
9 John Hetherington, *Blamey, Controversial Soldier,* 1974, p. 51

Blamey often openly flouted licensing laws. Other drinkers at a club or hotel after official opening hours welcomed the presence of Blamey as they knew that the Licensing Squad would not raid a place where the Chief was enjoying a drink. At the same time, he had instructed his officers to prosecute licensing infractions and not to withdraw from prosecutions unless there were very good grounds. The stance did not endear him to hotel owners or investors in hotels.[10] Other criticisms were directed at the proliferation of betting shops all over Melbourne, and the failure to enforce the six o'clock closing of hotels, a law which was introduced during the war years but was now regarded as a joke. Not so funny was the prosecution of boys who kicked a football that came in contact with electric light wires, for which the prosecuting officers received rewards from the State Electricity Commission.[11]

Blamey worked without the support of deputy police commissioners, taking on enormous responsibility.[12] In his early years in the job he received regular reports from Senior Sergeant Fred Piggott, who had been selected to undertake a tour of study police methods in San Francisco, Chicago and New York, before heading to London's Scotland Yard and then Holland, Belgium, Germany and France. Piggott was very keen to study methods of selection and training of detectives, as well as the use of informants, women police, fingerprints, photography and methods of identification. The area of fingerprints was still regarded with scepticism by some in the force and Piggott spent considerable time with Scotland Yard examining their methods and results. He also saw the capacity of ultraviolet light to disclose markings on documents that were invisible to the naked

10 *The Argus*, 15 July 1930
11 *The Argus,* 14 July 1936
12 Robert Haldane, *The People's Force*, 1986, p. 183

eye. In France he saw a 'ballistics machine' which, by testing the interior of firearms and the exterior of bullets, could identify the weapon from which a bullet was fired. [13] A decade later, the use of this technique would be part of the investigative procedures employed in the Scriven murder. He also witnessed the Chicago method of identification – a line-up room where prisoners were paraded on a platform before bright lights beyond which the police audience could remain unseen. A similar method had been introduced into Victoria, but was not always used – another key point in the Scriven investigation. [14]

It must have come as quite a shock to Blamey when he was told in July 1930 that the Hogan Labor government, elected in November 1929, had decided not to re-appoint him. Instead they invited applications for appointment to the post for a three-year term at a salary of £1250 a year. Blamey, of course, was welcome to re-apply, which he did. Blamey had never made any secret of his dislike for the left side of politics, nor had he ever made any effort to encourage Labor Party men to see him in a better light. They were convinced that his police force had been particularly harsh in their treatment of strikers and working-class demonstrators. When a conservative government returned to office in 1932, under Sir Stanley Argyle, Blamey's salary was restored to its original level and he was given security of tenure for life.

One of the many pressures that Blamey had to contend with was a lack of confidence in the performance of himself and his police force by many in government (particularly the non-conservative side) and the public. Late in November 1935, the *Argus* reported on a session in Parliament under the heading of 'Conduct of Police Department. Is the public satisfied?' Some

13 Kevin Morgan, ***Detective Piggott's Casebook*, 2012, p. 286**

14 Kevin Morgan, *Detective Piggott's Casebook*, 2012, p. 286

members of the Labor Party alleged that the chief commissioner did not possess the public's confidence and that the police discriminated between gambling games, ethically the same. It appeared that men were fined for playing a game of 'two-up' or acting as starting-price bookmakers, but there was no anxiety by police to raid bridge clubs and parties or clubs in the more respectable parts of Melbourne where gambling was indulged in feely. 'Banker' was a popular game in bowling clubs and was played with impunity. [15] Labor MP (and future Premier) John Cain stated that while Blamey appeared to have the confidence of many in the force, he did not enjoy support in the wider community. In Cain's view, a Chief Commissioner should be above reproach, a man to whom everybody can look up to. Cain also took the view that the government of the day also lacked confidence in Blamey, evidenced by the fact that for the first time in the history of the State, the Chief Commissioner had been sworn in as an ordinary member of the force. He could not be removed by a government and would have the ordinary rights and privileges of a policeman. The government's view was that it sought to protect him from the caprice of a future government and provide him with security of tenure, meaning that he remained there until he reached retiring age.[16] Whilst this debate occupied the minds of members of Parliament only briefly, it was to become hugely important in a matter of months.

One member of the force who fully supported Blamey was James (Jim) Cairns, later to be a Minister in the Whitlam Labor government that swept into office in 1972, and Deputy Prime Minister for a time. Blamey was very keen to recruit men of 'higher intelligence' into the force, not an easy task due to

15 *The Argus,* 30 November 1935
16 *The Argus,* 30 November 1935

the low rates of pay. [17] The two met in 1934 when Cairns, a promising distance runner, was receiving treatment for a torn muscle from a masseur who introduced him to Blamey. With Blamey's encouragement, Cairns joined the force as a constable on 14 January 1935. After six months training, he was assigned to duty at Russell Street and in June 1936 was transferred to the CIB on 'special duty'. He had been selected to become a member of a newly created shadowing squad, which was to conduct surveillance on the movements and activities of criminals and suspects (and which soon earned the nickname of 'the dogs'). He quickly won a reputation as a diligent officer of outstanding potential. [18]

Blamey's major problem was with the metropolitan press. He had a long history of run-ins with newspaper reporters and was firmly of the belief that they should be told as little as possible, being of the opinion that newspaper stories were rarely accurate. He had a particular dislike for the *Melbourne Herald* and refused to let its reporter, Wright, into his office. A few years earlier, he had taken steps to prevent the publication of information about the activities of police, ranging from the apprehension of persons accused of major crimes to the collection of evidence of street accidents. The police refused to disclose the names and addresses of persons injured in accidents or the locality. Officers in the watchhouse were directed to refuse

The young Jim Cairns, 1935, *The Age*, 24 August 2013

17 John Hetherington, *Blamey, Controversial Soldier,* 1974, p. 57

18 Paul Strangio, *Keeper of the Faith,* 2002, p. 29

all information concerning the names, ages and occupations of arrested persons, as well as any charges laid against them. After years of having freedom to wander through the building and talk to whoever they liked, police roundsmen suddenly found that the press room was closed and they were prohibited from entry beyond the public enquiry counter. Any policeman who was detected giving information to the press was to be punished. As a result, members of the force now declined to disclose information, even of the most trivial nature. Only senior officers would be permitted to give information but they were often out on inspections and did not have the information required by the public. Moreover, the official spokesman (generally the superintendent of the CIB) was often either 'delightfully vague' or resented being asked questions at all. [19] It was acknowledged that the press, when previously requested by police not to publish something that might prejudice their enquiries, had generally responded positively and acquiesced. To say that the pressmen were upset about these restrictions was an understatement and, not surprisingly, they reacted badly to the new regime. They argued that the reporting of crimes would serve as a warning to citizens in the localities in which these crimes have been committed and may prevent further crimes. It was an early version of 'the public has a right to know' argument, although not expressed in those terms. The journalists were not reluctant to let senior police know their opinion of Blamey and his bans.

Blamey's preference was to dispense information as he saw fit, which often meant holding back items that he thought the press and the public had little right to receive. According to Blamey, he had a perfect right to evade these people (newspapers) and to prevent them from gaining further information. He was also

19 *The Argus*, 11 February 1950

uncomfortable with the fact that stories went through two or three sets of hands after leaving the typewriter of a reporter and was concerned with the practice of syndication of newspapers, meaning that major stories were reported in newspapers around Australia on the next day. Blamey was a well-known name across the country due to his war service and attracted much more attention than Commissioners of police from other states. His attitude probably reflects the fact that he came from a military, rather than a policing, background, as the police were very much aware of the value of information from the general public in detecting criminals. No such connection was necessary in the military. Veteran crime reporter High Buggy later wrote: 'In my own experience some murder mysteries...would never have been solved without the help of the public. They were solved because the public had been kept fully informed by the Press of all or nearly all the essential facts. Where the people are told little or nothing about a crime they can hardly be expected to rush to the police with information. They are not in a position to appreciate that the information they have might be of value.'[20]

Blamey had also been scarred by a relentless press campaign that began just three weeks after he took office. Known as the 'Badge 80' affair, it centred on a man found naked in a Fitzroy brothel who produced a police badge during a raid on Mabel Tracey's brothel 'Belgrave' in Bell Street. The number on the badge was 80 – Blamey's badge.[21] Although he was able to convince the

20 *The Argus*, 11 February 1950; it was also a view shared by next Commissioner of Police, Alex Duncan, based on his experience at London's Scotland Yard. He told a meeting of business people in 1936 that "the efficiency of the police in London would be impossible without the extraordinarily cordial assistance they received from the public, not only in the control of traffic but in the investigation of serious crime", *The Argus*, 3 December 1936

21 Robert Haldane, *The People's Force*, 1986, p. 198

government that he was not the man at the brothel, the scene was set for a dreadful relationship between the Chief Commissioner and the metropolitan newspapers, as well as between Blamey and some of his senior officers. The years of 1935 and 1936 were momentous for Blamey – his wife died after years of invalidism, he was knighted, and he was involved in a full-blown altercation with a newspaper. Following publication of an article in the *Star* newspaper on 10 December 1935, Blamey had launched a libel action against the newspaper in February 1936. The article had referred to three violent deaths that had occurred in Victoria and the failure of the police to communicate to the public news of the deaths or any of the circumstance of their investigations. It went on to state that Blamey had written a statement that was read in parliament stating that there had been no increase in serious crime in Victoria. According to the *Star*, Blamey was careless whether people disappeared in Melbourne as a result of criminal acts and rarely made their disappearance known to the public. He was also accused of administering the police force according to a policy of silence and had formed the intention to conceal permanently in all circumstances from the public information of the death of one of the three dead men. Not surprisingly, Blamey decided to sue, alleging that he had been greatly injured in his credit and reputation and in his character as holder of his office and that he had been brought into public scandal, hatred and contempt.[22] He sought a trial before a judge without a jury, which was set down for July 1936.

Other events soon were to occupy his mind and actions. As well, the issue of a new building soon took a back seat. Within a few weeks of the visit to inspect the police accommodation, the Premier (and his government) had a major crisis on their

22 *The Argus,* 8 February 1936

hands, centring on a senior policeman and the Commissioner of Police. As expected, John O'Connell (Jack) Brophy had become Officer in Charge of the Criminal Investigation Branch (CIB) and inherited responsibility for the Scriven murder and a number of other still unsolved high-profile cases. Brophy was described as 'jovial, well-rounded, a cheerful personality and easy to get on with...(who)... wore a black Homburg and a heavy gold watch chain across his egg-shaped middle'. [23] Son of a mounted constable, he joined the force in March 1900, conducted himself very well and was accepted into the CIB in 1912. He was promoted to Senior Detective in February 1921 and gained prominence the next year during the murder investigation and trial of Colin Campbell Ross. In what came to be known as the 'Gun Alley' murder, Ross was accused of the murder of Alma Tirtschke, aged 12. There were serious accusations of the conduct of the investigating police, principally Brophy and his long-term partner, Piggott.[24] Ross was convicted and hanged in April 1922. The hanging (and the very real miscarriage of justice) disgusted many observers in Victoria, including a young lawyer called John Vincent Barry, who was later to play a key role in the trials associated with the Scriven murder. Following the hanging of another convicted murderer (Angus Murray, an accomplice of Les 'Squizzy' Taylor) in 1926, Barry would play a prominent role in campaigns to end capital punishment. [25] Brophy also played a major role in the investigation of the Irene Tuckerman murder and later the mysterious Pyjama Girl murder. In a break from his investigative work, he was seconded to the squad providing protection for the Duke of York in 1927

23 Kevin Morgan, *Gun Alley,* 2012, p. 264.

24 Members of the Melbourne underworld had a saying: "Ashes to ashes, and dust to dust; if Brophy don't get you, well, Piggott must."

25 Mark Finnane, *JV Barry: a life, 2007,* p. 41

when the royal visited Australia to 'open' Parliament House in Canberra. As well as a citation (one of a number in his career), he received a medal – the Royal Victoria Medal, presented to him by the Duke. In addition, the Prince presented Brophy (and all the other men on the security detail) with a gold tiepin bearing the prince's plumes and the letter 'E' in enamel.[26]

The job of Chief of the CIB was one that Brophy had long coveted and he was pleased to be back in Melbourne after a stint in Ballarat, a major regional city in the middle of Victoria. He clearly intended to make a name for himself – which he did, but perhaps not in the way he had imagined. A week after he started in the job, on Friday May 22, Brophy was admitted to St Vincent's Hospital at about 11.00 p.m., suffering from four bullet wounds. When he was brought in he told doctors he had been shot by bandits in Royal Park after receiving a telephone message to investigate a crime there. This statement was made immediately after the shooting and before he had any time to invent anything. The next morning, the police and hospital authorities combined to surround the shooting with 'a rigorous girdle of secrecy'. The police Publicity Bureau

John O'Connell Brophy, *Journal of Police History*, Summer 1996/7

26 Victoria Police, *Record of Conduct and Service of John O'Connell Brophy*, courtesy, Victoria Police Museum

released an official statement at 11.00 a.m. Saturday morning at the daily press briefing, stating that 'Mr Brophy, while examining a pistol, was shot in the right arm when it accidentally exploded.'[27]

The wound was not serious, said the police. By Sunday, the initial report was 'cancelled' and replaced by another statement that gave a totally different account of the incident. The official story now was that Brophy had received a phone call from 'informants' at home on the Friday night and had gone to Royal Park to meet the caller. Whilst sitting in a car, he was approached by two men who shot him four times. The scene had been set – a pattern of lies, claims, counter-claims, unconfirmed reports and cover-ups that would dominate the news stories for the next few months. It could only end badly and it did – with a Royal Commission. As often happened, the attempts to cover up the circumstances assumed much greater importance than the original crime.

So what really happened on the night and the following days? Newspaper reports, personal recollections and evidence provided to a subsequent Royal Commission tell us the story and the details.

The immediate question to be asked was why Brophy went to Royal Park? On Friday afternoon, he apparently received a phone call at the office from a known informer saying that he may have some information about recent hold-ups. At this stage, a number of major crimes remained unsolved and Brophy, as the new head of CIB, was very keen to gain any information. Brophy gave him the phone number of his home in Alma Road, St Kilda, telling him that he would wait for a call at home and then meet the man in Royal Park. The area, in Melbourne's inner west, had become notorious for car-thefts

27 *The Argus*, 25 May 1936

in recent months. Brophy was later very reluctant to reveal the identity of the informant, fearing that such disclosure may result in reprisals from the underworld. He had met him there several times before.

The other question raised was why the head of the CIB was dealing with this sort of job. Surely meeting informants was the role of Brophy's subordinates? Not necessarily, as senior police were frequently approached by informers. Whilst not improper for Brophy to meet them, junior men were available and in the circumstances would have been advisable. [28] Brophy later stated that he could have sent O'Keeffe, a senior detective, who also knew the informer. This was one of a number of aspects of the whole sorry affair that could have (and perhaps should have) been handled differently.

Brophy elected to meet his informant by having a friend drive him to the spot. He had an arrangement with Mrs Madeline Grace Orr, a widow and the licensee of the nearby Tattersall's Hotel in Russell Street, whereby he could use her Daimler car when he needed it for personal or police business. If he needed the car, he would ask her, her brother or the barman Meagher for it. Meagher (also known as Maher) was a former military man who was colloquially known as a 'boots' in the hotel. [29] Orr had been a friend of Brophy's for 23 years and was friendly with his wife, as was her late husband. She was a regular in the social pages, as was her daughter (also Madeline) who became a well-known stage and film actor. Tattersall's, on the corner of Russell Street and Little Lonsdale Street, was close to the police headquarters – but not the closest. The Continental Hotel, on the corner of Latrobe Street and Russell Street, had that honour. Also known as the City Court Hotel, it was jokingly referred to

28 *The Advertiser (Adelaide),* 12 June 1936
29 *The Examiner (Launceston),* 12 June 1936; *The Truth,* 13 June 1936

by police as the 'fourth court', before it was demolished in 1988. Because of the proximity to the city court, Tattersall's Hotel was often used by jurors for overnight stays during trials. No longer operating as an hotel, the building remains as one of a number of decommissioned hotels in the city that were turned into shops. Given its proximity to police headquarters, it attracted a lot of custom from members of the force and Mrs Orr was well known, as her late husband, Charles, had been. [30] Like many inner-Melbourne hotels, it had an interesting history. Orr took it over in 1925, renaming it from the City Court Hotel. Charles Orr sold Richmond beer in his hotel and became caught up in the war between Richmond Brewery and Carlton and United Brewery (CUB) in 1930. [31] He was also the licensee of the bar at the Carlton Football Club, located at Princes Park, as well as several other football clubs, Flemington racecourse and a number of coursing and racing clubs throughout Victoria. In 1930 he assumed the role of President of the Hotelkeepers' Association of Victoria, an organisation recently formed by those hotelkeepers that sold beer supplied by the Richmond brewery. Soon after, at half time of a football match between Carlton and Geelong, a quantity of foul-smelling gas was released into the bar of the members' pavilion. It cleared the bar and gave Orr a message about his choice of beer. [32] The well-known hotelkeeper and caterer died in September 1932 after being found in his car in a state of collapse, following a stroke. Mrs Orr gained acclaim as a heroine in 1934 when she dragged a man from his burning bed.

---

30 *The Argus*, 30 April 1925

31 Richmond Lager and Richmond Bitter were produced from 1928 and soon became extremely successful, due to the perceived quality of the products – 'absolute purity, wholesomeness, and delicious flavour', according to the *Sporting Globe* on March 4, 1931. It held about 6% of the Victorian market when it was sold to CUB in 1962.

32 *The Argus,* 22 July 1930

Former Tattersall's Hotel, Russell Street, 2015

Victorian hotels were required by law to provide accommodation and most had a number of long-term lodgers. On a Wednesday night in July 1934, she was awakened from her sleep at 3.00 a.m. by the smell of something burning, and ran up a flight of stairs to find that the bed occupied by George McDonald, a boarder, was on fire. Placing a towel over her face, she managed to reach the bed on which he was lying unconscious in a state of suffocation. Opening the window, she flung a pillow that had burst into flames into the street, where it landed on the head of two constables who were passing. Having attracted their attention, they responded to her shouts, but by the time they reached the room she had half-dragged the unconscious man to safety. A doctor was summoned and fought to save the life of McDonald for more than an hour. The doctor said that the man would have suffocated if it weren't for the prompt action of Mrs Orr. He had fallen asleep and dropped a lighted cigarette on the bedclothes. [33] Mrs Orr remained as a publican, taking over as

33 *The Argus,* 19 July 1934

licensee of the historic MCG Hotel in Wellington Parade, East Melbourne in 1939. It was in this hotel that the first rules of Australian Football were written down in 1859.

Why did Brophy travel in a private car to supposedly meet police informants? One simple answer may have been that the CIB did not have its own cars at that time. Brophy could not have simply conjured up a car for CIB business, as all requests for cars had to be approved by the Officer in Charge of the Wireless Car group. This may have been impossible on a Friday night. The Wireless Car Group only operated during daylight hours and was famous for a retort to a request for a car: 'No cars, no drivers!'[34] In addition, Brophy later stated that he preferred to use private cars or taxis for this sort of work, as the police cars were too well known. Not long before this event, the numbers of all the cars in the police fleet had to be changed as the underworld had a full list of them.

On Friday evening, Brophy left the office at about 5.00 p.m. and headed to Tattersall's Hotel where he met the barman Meagher. Brophy arranged for him to drive him to a job, if it worked out, telling Meagher that he would call him later if he needed him.[35] After receiving a call at home from his informant,[36]

---

34 The Wireless Patrol used a series of Daimlers, which replaced unreliable Lancias. The first Daimler was purchased in 1926 – it was yellow and was christened the 'Yellow Peril'. It was followed by the 'Grey Streak', 'Brown Terror' and 'Red Streak.' By 1933 the force possessed 12 Daimlers, which then began to be replaced by English-built Alvis vehicles in 1937. As with the Daimlers, the bodies were built in Melbourne and each was a different colour. Hence they were called the 'Red Cherry', 'Blue Bird' and the 'Wombat', which was Brown. J R Stewart and K A Humphreys, *No Cars, No Drivers*, 1997, p.67

35 *The Truth*, 13 June 1936

36 At a later time, during the Royal Commission, McKerral was asked whether Brophy had received a telephone message on the Friday. He replied definitely 'no', one of many inconsistencies in evidence from senior police at the Commission. *The West Australian (Perth, WA),* 19 June 1936

he arranged to meet him at Royal Park, near a large black stump. The informant was to walk past Brophy's car on the left, light a cigarette and proceed to the black stump, where Brophy would meet him. Brophy then arranged with Meagher to meet him at the tram stop at the corner of Lonsdale and Swanston Street at about 9.30 p.m.

Brophy was not aware that Mrs Orr had her own plans for her car that night. She and a friend, Mrs Phillips,[37] had been intending to visit St John's Church in Clifton Hill, to see some friends who had died and whose bodies were lying at the church. She had not known that Brophy intended to use the car until Meagher had told her and she was a bit annoyed. 'Dash him,' she said. When they picked Brophy up, Mrs Orr asked him if he was in a hurry as she wanted Meagher to drive her and Mrs Collins to the church in Clifton Hill. It was then that Brophy suggested that they come with him to Royal Park. 'I won't be very long,' he said, without saying what he would be doing. [38] When they arrived at the church in Clifton Hill, they found it was locked, so Orr and Phillips decided to go with Brophy to his meeting at Royal Park.

Arriving at Royal Park, with Orr and Brophy in the back seats, they sat in the car with the lights turned off for ten minutes. This did not seem to worry the two women and they had not questioned Brophy. Blamey later defended Brophy's decision to use a private car. He thought it would have inadvisable for him to have used a taxi, and risky to have used a car with a policeman as a driver. Risky? Isn't that what the members of the police force were trained to deal with? And how could it be any riskier than a car with three civilians? Nor did Blamey see

37 Mrs Phillips was a close friend of Orr (and also a friend of Brophy and his family), and was living on good terms with her husband.

38 *The Truth,* 13 June 1936

any impropriety in the fact that Brophy had taken the women to the meeting – it was just one of the 'accidents of life which most people experienced'. [39] He also discounted any suggestion of immoral or improper actions between Brophy and Orr, one of the scurrilous rumours that later circulated.

Everything changed dramatically about 10.00 p.m. when two masked men suddenly appeared and approached the car, one on either side. Orr cried out 'Who's this alongside the car?' The man on left shone a torch in Brophy's face, which also illuminated the man on the right, showing that he had a gun in his hand. He opened the door of the car and pointed the gun at the driver, Meagher. 'Hands up. Don't make a noise and everything will be all right,' he said. While the gunman was doing this, he looked in the back and saw Brophy. 'Christ, it's Brophy!' he exclaimed. Brophy made a dive for his gun, a .25 calibre pistol, which he kept in a right hand vest pocket, where it was easy to obtain. The gunman saw the movement. 'Don't you shoot, Brophy', he said. Brophy ignored this and immediately fired at the gunman. Brophy had fired first. The gunman returned his fire and Brophy got off another shot before the assailant fired four shots at him, wounding him in the arm, face and chest. Brophy was certain that one of his shots had wounded the gunman before his gun jammed. Many guns were unreliable in these days – sometimes jamming or going off unexpectedly. The gunman's companion had bolted at the first shot and started the engine of his car to drive off, already revving the engine. The gunman fired several shots from a .32 pistol into the back of the Daimler. Luckily for him, one of the shots punctured a tyre. Brophy later recalled that the man who had fired the shots was about 5'10" (180 cm) in height and about 40 years old. He was masked up to the eyes

39 *The Argus,* 25 June 1936

with a dirty white handkerchief, his collar was turned up and he wore a brown hat. Brophy couldn't see the man on the left as he was shining a torch into his eyes. Most people would have expected that these events would have produced a good deal of screaming but Mrs Orr later stated that this wasn't the case. She just asked Brophy whether he was badly hurt – there was very little said. After the shooting the men roared off in a dark-coloured car, with Brophy's car following. [40] The shots had done their damage and Brophy's car had a flat tyre and couldn't keep up with the other car. Perhaps this was a good thing, as the gang reputedly had a sawn-off shotgun and a rifle in the car's dickey seat, with ammunition.

Meagher drove along Royal Parade and into Sydney Road before the wounded Brophy and the driver jumped out of the car and hailed a passing motorist. Fred Millard, a wireworker from West Coburg, was driving along Sydney Road toward the city on the night of May 22. Suddenly he saw two men on the road immediately in front of him. As he slowed down, someone opened the door of the car. According to Millard, he heard someone say something about a hospital and saw a man covered with blood. The other man then asked him if he would take the injured man to hospital to which he agreed. The injured man got into Millard's car and he drove off. Millard initially thought that there had been a motor accident but on the way to the hospital Brophy told him who he was and that he had been shot in Royal Park. Millard was never under the impression that it was a gun 'accident'. He drove to the casualty entrance of St Vincent's hospital in Fitzroy, deposited Brophy and waited there until police arrived. The next day he saw Detective Carey at

40 *The Truth,* 13 June 1936

Russell Street. [41]

Meanwhile, Meagher changed the tyre on the car and then drove the two women back to the Tattersall's hotel. They were probably very much in need of a brandy at this stage. On the way they passed a police station, but Orr chose not to make a report, apparently acting under Brophy's instructions. As she later stated, she did not want her name mixed up in it. The four of them had agreed that the events were to be a 'dead secret' as far as the world was concerned. Meagher later gave evidence that Brophy had not wanted him to report it to police, but he would have done so if Brophy had died. After he dropped the two women back at the hotel, he then proceeded to the hospital, presumably to check on Brophy's condition. It is not known if he was able to gain entry to see Brophy. He then decided to take his employer's car to a repair shop in North Melbourne to be repaired as quickly as possible. He told others at the garage that the car was damaged by someone larking about with a gun when after rabbits - despite the holes obviously not originating from a shotgun. In fact the panel beater (John Albert Young) recovered two bullets that were later handed to police – but not until some months later. [42] The question remains (and was asked at the Royal Commission): why wasn't the car impounded immediately, given that it had been the scene of a major crime. After all, there was no doubt about the car being involved. Was it because the police knew that they were not going to catch anyone for this crime? It added to the confusion in the minds of the public as no official statement contained any reference to the whereabouts of the car. [43]

Saturated in blood and suffering greatly from shock, Brophy

---

41 *The Western Argus (Kalgoorlie, West Australia)*, 23 June 1936

42 *The Argus,* 25 June 1936

43 *The Advertiser (Adelaide)*, 28 May 1936

was admitted to hospital by Nurse Moya Irene Hanlon, the night superintendent at St Vincent's. She later recalled that he 'seemed steady, and said that he had been shot'. He then instructed her not to give information to anyone. Dr Francis Cahill examined Brophy when he arrived. According to Cahill, he seemed slightly excited, but not shocked. He said he had been shot and asked them not to say anything to the press. He then operated on Brophy, removing the bullet from his arm, but Brophy reacted badly to the anaesthetic and was 'difficult' so he decided to delay the bullets being removed from his neck until the next day. Cahill considered that Brophy was exceedingly lucky to be alive and Brophy had thought that he was 'done for'. As he went under the anaesthetic, he told the medical team that 'If there are any inquiries about this, please say it was an accident.' [44]

The medical registrar, Dr O'Loughlin, also saw Brophy soon after his arrival. He thought that his mental condition was quite clear and when Brophy asked him to keep the press away, he replied, 'Certainly, I will.' Although he felt that Brophy was not in a fit condition to be interviewed by anybody, somebody from the Police department did interview him on the Friday night – Detective Bolton. He was on duty at the detective's office at Russell Street police station on Friday night when he received a phone call at around 11.00 p.m. from St Vincent's Hospital, informing him about Brophy's shooting and asking him to call in to the hospital. When he arrived Brophy told him that he had met with an accident and asked him to contact Superintendent McKerral and pass on the news to Blamey, but not to make any reports as nothing could be done that night. Nor was he to bother notifying his home. It was later suggested that Bolton did not make any more enquiries beyond what Brophy had told

44 *The Truth*, 13 June 1936

him, as Brophy was his superior officer. He contacted McKerral late on the Friday night. By all accounts, Bolton was an able and conscientious policeman, if a little unimaginative, but he must have been feeling that he was caught up in something that was about to spin out of control. [45]

When McKerral received the news at home late on Friday night, he knew that he would have to report the events to Blamey that night. He immediately headed off to the hospital, seeking to gain something to tell Blamey that was more than Bolton had told him. Brophy was still very excited and was attempting to leave the hospital, but was restrained from doing so by Dr Cahill. The doctor spoke to Detectives McKerral [46] and Bolton after midnight on the night of the attack, as they sought information to provide to Blamey. Nurses, doctors and hospital authorities at St Vincent's knew that Brophy had achieved a remarkable escape from death. He had suffered four bullet wounds - one of the bullets had inflicted a superficial wound near his heart after being deflected by the buckle on his braces whilst another had entered his cheek and emerged at the back of his neck, narrowly missing a large blood vessel. Two other bullets fractured the bones of his right wrist. The hospital authorities had volunteered to McKerral an exact description of Brophy's wounds and handed him one of the bullets taken from Brophy. McKerral had asked nothing about what Brophy had said about the cause of the 'accident', although the doctors and nurses could have told him. McKerral then went back to Police headquarters to ring Blamey.

The conversation with Blamey must have been difficult. McKerral apologised for the time and told him that he needed to

---

45 *The Argus,* 24 June 1936

46 Brophy and McKerral had worked together for some years, including investigation in 1932 of a woman brutally murdered with a hammer in Albert Park. *The Argus*, 28 July 1932

see him about a matter that he would rather not discuss over the telephone. Bolton drove him to Blamey's house in the prestigious suburb of Toorak at about 1.00 a.m. and waited outside whilst McKerral went inside for about 20 minutes. Blamey and McKerral were fully aware of how the shooting had occurred – at the very least they had grave doubts about it being an accident. Blamey later claimed that, when McKerral arrived at his house, he told him that Brophy had been accidentally shot at Royal Park. No inquiries had been made that night but full information would be available in the morning. This claim stretches credulity – this was a senior detective and the Chief Commissioner discussing how the State's top detective had nearly been murdered and they were leaving it until the morning. Blamey was later asked to compare this reaction to that of a recent holdup of a Coles store in Flinders lane, where a constable was shot and wounded. In that case a large section of the police force was out on that within a few minutes. Blamey's explanation was that the matters were entirely different – the Coles shooting was a definite hold-up and a large sum of money had been stolen. [47]

On the Saturday morning, the first face that Brophy saw when he woke up was that of Blamey, who had telephoned and arranged to see Brophy at 9.30 a.m. Brophy later claimed that he could not remember their conversation that morning – 'not a lot was said, I was not feeling too good at the time', he recalled. Blamey had a different recollection, whereby Brophy told him that he had been in the car at Royal Park with Meagher, Orr and Phillips and had an accident with a revolver. Blamey claimed that he accepted Brophy's version of the story at first but must have had serious doubts as to its truth, and intended to assign two senior men to investigate it. His war experience as part of an

47 *The Truth,* 13 June 1936

intelligence division in France had involved questioning disabled soldiers, and he had found them invariably inaccurate.[48] In the view of some, Brophy had obviously deliberately misled his chief, which was a very serious allegation. When Blamey spoke to the medical staff, he requested that, in the interests of justice, no information about the shooting be released. The *Age* reported that they had made routine enquiries between 11.00 p.m. on Friday and 2.00 a.m. on Saturday but the enquiries 'elicited no word of the outrage', as police and hospital authorities combined to keep the details secret. This implies that the *Age* was tipped off as soon as Brophy arrived at hospital, or that the *Age* reporter, writing a few days later when there was information available, was retrofitting events.[49]

As always when Blamey was involved, stories emerged about his bullying behaviour. Blamey was reputed to have visited the hospital a number of times and told members of the medical staff not to give out any information about Brophy. Whilst he denied the number of visits, he later conceded that that he might have told a doctor not to let the press worry Brophy.[50] Another report was that the medical staff did not take kindly to Blamey's behaviour. Eventually the Medical Registrar told Blamey that HE was running the hospital, not Blamey.[51]

Later that Saturday morning, Brophy received a visit from Detective Sergeants Carey and O'Keeffe, seeking an account of the incident. Whilst he did not tell them everything, he asked them to get in touch with the informer that he had been going to see to find out details of his information. Brophy was convinced that there was no connection between the informer and the

48 *The Truth*, 13 June 1936
49 *The Age*, 25 May 1936
50 *The Mercury (Hobart)*, 12 June 1936
51 *The Truth*, 13 June 1936

gunmen, although one of the theories later tossed around was that he had been set up by the informer and lured to Royal Park by a false telephone message.[52] Brophy had two major concerns that, despite his injuries, he was keen to have addressed. The first was to conceal the presence of Mrs Orr and Mrs Phillips in the car in an attempt to preserve their 'reputations'. The second was to protect his family. His wife had been unwell for some time and he was fearful of the effect on her if she was to discover that he had a close brush with death. His son-in-law, James Hugh Redmond, later claimed that he was told on the night of the shooting by Mr Meagher that Brophy had been shot by bandits and was asked to break the news gently to Mrs Brophy by telling her that it was an accident. On the Saturday morning, Redmond drove his wife and Mrs Brophy to the hospital to see Brophy, who said he had been shot by bandits. He was very excited and they told him to lie still and not to talk. Then they left and went to see Mrs Orr at the Tattersall's Hotel, staying for about half an hour. What was discussed between them is not known but, according to Orr, nothing had been concealed. Not surprisingly, when they returned home the telephone went all day as they were pestered by inquiries from reporters and other people.[53]

On the Saturday Brophy underwent surgery to remove the bullet from his neck. The doctors and nurses at St Vincent's must have been incredulous at the wording of the statement issued by the police on the Saturday that claimed that Brophy had shot himself. Once perhaps would be plausible, but not four times. The Chief Commissioner was later asked if, in his experience at war, he ever came across a man who had peppered himself four times, to which he responded 'no.'[54]

52 *The Argus,* 25 May 1936
53 *The Argus,* 17 June 1936
54 *The Sydney Morning Herald (NSW),* 12 June 1936

At this time few other members of the force were aware of what happened and it was denied that any great stir had been created at headquarters by the occurrence. It didn't take long for questions to be asked by those officers on duty at Russell Street on the Friday night and the Saturday. One question was why Brophy had taken the two women with him on an operation – even if one did own the car. Was there something untoward between Brophy and Mrs Orr or Mrs Phillips?

The other question was whether the entire story was a cover-up for the behaviour of Blamey, an opinion strongly held by some police from Russell Street. In his book called *'Gun Alley'*, based on the story of Colin Ross, author Kevin Morgan provided a startling theory. His source was ex-superintendent, H R (Bill) Donelly, a former chief of the homicide squad. Donelly had worked as a detective under Brophy's control in the 1930s and knew him well. Before his death in 1996, he recounted his story to Morgan, asserting that his information came from 'a senior source in whom I have the utmost confidence'. Donelly explained that the road around the zoo was notorious as a 'lover's lane', but was also gaining a reputation for thuggery and for car-thefts. On the night in question, said Donelly, who was on duty at Russell Street, Blamey had compelled Brophy to drive him to the zoo. Blamey and a prostitute were in the back of the Daimler, Brophy and Mrs Orr were in the front. Blamey was drunk, had 'stripped off' the prostitute and was performing cunnilingus on her when three men appeared around the car. One man threatened Brophy through the open window on the driver's side. When Brophy pushed him away, the man fell to the ground and Brophy wound up the window. The man on the ground 'growled like a dog', Donelly said, and pulled out a gun, shooting Brophy three times. At Russell Street, a telephone call was received from Mrs Orr, asking to speak 'to someone senior'. In the opinion of Donelly, Brophy was made to wear the blame for the dishonourable conduct of his superior officer. [55] The story that Blamey was in the car also had currency in the criminal world. Career criminal Geoffrey Davies later told police that he had heard from a group of men that Blamey was in the car. [56] What do we make of this account? The introduction of a story woven around drunken public officials, prostitutes and sexual antics will always titillate and intrigue readers, but there just seemed to be too many people involved who would have needed to perjure themselves at a later Royal Commission (and risk a gaol term) if this was really true.

After seeing Brophy at the hospital, Blamey met McKerral at Russell Street. Blamey instructed him to go and see Meagher, Mrs Orr and Mrs Phillips, now that they had a point to start from in the investigation. They then concocted a statement to be released to the press later that morning with Blamey's full approval. Blamey (and McKerral) now knew the truth but, jealous of the reputation of the force he commanded, Blamey instructed McKerral to issue a statement that it was an accident. The cover-up had begun. Like many such events, it was to prove disastrous for its architect and gave the enemies of Blamey and the Police Department a perfect opportunity to make the most of the situation.

At 11.00 a.m. each day, the police held a briefing with reporters from the metropolitan press, referred to as the 'hand-out.' The regular procedure was for a member of the force to go through the crime reports, take out the information considered suitable to go to the press, and then give it to the newspaper representatives. No doubt Blamey took a very disparaging view

55 Kevin Morgan, *Gun Alley,* 2012, pp. 265/6

56 *The Argus,* 28 November 1936

of the 'hand-out' as he had little time for the press. This would probably prove to be Blamey's most significant tactical error and certainly contributed greatly to his eventual downfall.

Blamey instructed his detectives, Carey and O'Keeffe, to release the report at the briefing. He left Melbourne about midday and returned that night at about 9.00 p.m. It is unclear whether Blamey had seen the statement that was released by Detective Sloane of Russell Street and provided to representatives of the *Argus* (Doug Gillison), *Herald* (Whitehead), the *Sun* (Robinson) and *Australian United Press* (unnamed).[57] The four reporters were taken into a male witness room at Russell Street. When one of them asked for information, Sloane produced a piece of paper which he placed on the table. It was scribbled in pencil (apparently hurriedly), unsigned and undated. It was very brief: 'Mr Brophy, while examining a pistol, was shot in the right arm when it accidentally exploded.' [58] The reporters then perused the statement before Sloane took it away, but they were not convinced about its veracity. They were annoyed that the police would not answer any questions about where the shooting had occurred and to which hospital Brophy had been taken. All the police would say was that Brophy's wound was only superficial – which was a blatant lie. It was inferred that Brophy had dropped his own pistol, which then discharged, and that the accident occurred at police headquarters. All of the reporters were highly suspicious about the statement. The recollections of the police and the reporters about the statement were later to be crucial but at the time, there was such little information contained in the statement that the *Argus* reporter, Gillison,[59] did not even

57 *The Argus*, 17 June 1936

58 *The Argus,* 26 May 1936

59 Douglas Gillison was later an Australian official war historian and author of *Royal Australian Air Force 1939-42*

write a note about it, although he did leave a note about its contents to a fellow reporter (Lionel Luxton) when he went off duty. Gillison's note to Luxton was an understated comment that 'I think there is something more to it than that', causing Luxton to then ring Gillison at home to ask whether he could recall the exact words of the statement. [60] Luxton then tried to see Brophy at the hospital. The word had got around about where Brophy was – Blamey obviously could not contain that detail for very long – but could not see him. He did however see Brophy's son-in-law, Jim Redmond. [61]

The *Truth* was later to state: 'It must have surely occurred to somebody in authority long before that statement issued to the newspapers and to the public of Australia at 11.00 a.m. on Saturday that a proposition that a man should accidentally shoot himself in four places was utterly ridiculous.' [62] Blamey was later unrepentant about the wording of the statement. He was asked later if he, as Commissioner of Police, was justified in making statements to the press that he knew were not proved to the best of his knowledge. Blamey replied that he was justified in everything he said. He maintained that the statement had been released 'in good faith' and was not intended to suppress information to the press. 'Nobody seems to know anything about it,' he said. 'It was accepted as correct in the first place, but Superintendent Brophy was suffering from shock and I would not allow anyone to interview him for some time after he had

60 *The Argus,* 17 June 1936

61 In December 1941, the *Argus* reporter Lionel Luxton, ofVenus St., Caulfield, was reported missing after beginning a hike in the coastal area between San Remo and Kilcunda. Police located clothes and a tent on the 18th December 1941. Luxton was a member of the *Argus* editorial staff and a keen naturalist. It is thought that he may have slipped on the rugged cliffs in the area or had been bathing and was carried out by the strong undertow. *The Argus,* 19 December 1941

62 *The Truth*, 30 May 1936

been admitted to hospital.' This was another blatant lie. The reporter Tilley from the *Herald* later recounted how McKerral had told him that 'if we had told you the facts you would have interviewed everyone and gone around with photographers and hindered our inquiries'. [63]

Late on Saturday afternoon, Brophy was visited by reporters Reg Warren (the *Sun*) and Stan Wright (the *Herald*), who were told another version of the story – that Brophy had gone to Royal Park on an official mission. He was standing alone in the street with his automatic in his left hand. When his hand became sweaty, he was transferring the pistol to its right hand when it exploded twice, wounding him in the right forearm and the right cheek. Obviously sceptical, Warren asked Brophy why it went off twice, only to be told that automatics were very finely set and he had always been afraid of them! When Wright asked if the gun had gone off four times, Brophy declined to reply. No wonder the press was suspicious and the *Herald* had been so determined to blow the story open.

This was a huge story for crime reporters, with a range of larger-than-life characters. The new head of CIB, previously prominent in the 'Gun Alley' murder and the pursuit of Les 'Squizzy' Taylor. The Chief Commissioner of police – a war hero, but not highly regarded by much of the community and at odds with the press for years. A prominent city hotelkeeper whose car was being used by senior police to meet informers. And all played out against a background of disbelief about how the head of CIB managed to shoot himself four times. Not surprisingly the newspaper offices were soon buzzing when the reports of the police statement began to get around. Rumours and unsubstantiated information started to swirl around in the

63 *The Argus*, 19 June 1936

afternoon as the reporters began to write their stories. The *Herald* broke the story in its later editions on the Saturday. Word was out on the streets that Brophy's wounds had NOT been accidental. The cat was out of the bag and the senior police were starting to look decidedly silly.

So what was Blamey trying to achieve by releasing such an obvious set of lies to the press? His response was that the information in the first statement was given unwittingly in the belief that it was true. He later conceded that he had no intention of being candid. He had intended to convey to the press that it was not known whether the first message handed to the press had come from Brophy or from the young man who drove him to the hospital. He may have been aiming to help Brophy personally but he was never receptive to being questioned about any actions that he undertook. It seems difficult to believe that Blamey accepted Brophy's story so readily, yet that is what he claimed. He would have seen men wounded by gunshots during his war service and must have realised that serious questions would arise. Whatever transpired, the reputation of Victoria Police would suffer. On the other hand, he realised that statements from men who had been shot could not be relied upon for about 24 hours and Brophy was decidedly 'muzzy' (badly shaken) when he saw him in hospital.[64]

According to Blamey, when he returned to Melbourne on Saturday night, McKerral telephoned him and informed him that the first story was incorrect and that the shooting was not an accident after all. The two then began to draft notes about what should then be released to the press, given that the first statement was clearly a fabrication. Many police officers were aware of the shooting after reading about it in the afternoon

64 *Examiner (Launceston, Tasmania),* 12 June 1936

Herald and were also openly sceptical. Blamey took no strong action at that time, arranging to meet McKerral at 10.30 a.m. the next morning (Sunday) where they discussed and drafted another report. McKerral wrote down what Blamey wanted him to say: Brophy, after responding to a message, had gone to Royal Park where he was shot and seriously wounded by two bandits. At the direction of Blamey, McKerral was instructed to 'correct' the accident story when the newspapermen arrived for the daily briefing and to give them the true facts. Carey produced a 'modus operandi' report that was forwarded to the Information Branch to be placed in the 'Police Gazette'. It would be read at the next muster at 2.00 p.m. so that all the police would be apprised of what had happened.

Blamey's laconic action is difficult to believe, given that his most senior detective had just escaped being murdered in a public place. At a later point, this response was viewed by some as evidence that Blamey had known all along of the true nature (and cause) of the injuries to Brophy and was not just guilty of 'inactivity and falsehoods', but had neglected his duty. Blamey was always adamant that he had taken the proper steps to investigate the crime. The police response had been 'inert' but more importantly, there had been a conspiracy to cover up the true cause of the shooting. Failure to take immediate action on major crimes was also one of the deficiencies later identified in a report into the Victoria Police by Alex Duncan from Scotland Yard, who commented that a 'free and easy manner of tomorrow will do appears to prevail'.[65]

On Sunday morning, Brophy was visited in hospital and interviewed by his Deputy, Inspector McKerral, and another officer, Detective-Sergeant Carey, before another visit by

65 *The Argus,* 22 December 1936

Blamey. Brophy had other visitors on the Sunday morning – reporters Luxton (the *Argus)*, Bergin (the *Sun*) and Lawson (the *Age*) had managed to get into the ward. When they approached Brophy and shook hands, Lawson said: 'What did they do to you, Jack?' Brophy replied 'Well boys, Carey and McKerral have been here and will tell you what happened', meaning at the next hand out. [66] Brophy, like his Commissioner, was very wary of the metropolitan press and clearly did not want to talk to the reporters. He was later accused of saying that the objective of the department was to keep the press from getting news. But he liked the *Truth* (and its strong stand in favour of law and order) and often would give it information whilst withholding the same from other papers. The *Truth*, which was very supportive of the police and was a very different paper in the days before it evolved into a sensationalist rag, played up what it considered a 'special relationship'.

There was a flurry of speculation and the town was abuzz with rumours when the reporters turned up at Russell Street on Sunday. Not surprisingly, reporters greeted the second statement issued by McKerral with suspicion. When they arrived at about 1.00 p.m. on Sunday, McKerrall said that he had a statement for them and read it from two sheets of paper. It stated that the accident story was 'not right' and provided the reporters with another statement that was prepared by police and apparently issued with Brophy's approval. Whilst more plausible than the original one, it still stretched credulity. It stated:

> 'Acting on information received, Superintendent Brophy went to Royal Park on Friday night, with the object of catching car bandits who have been operating

66 *The Argus*, 18 June 1936

> in that locality and holding up motorists. Two bandits appeared at the car Mr Brophy was in and attempted to hold him up. Mr Brophy immediately drew his automatic pistol to fire at the bandits, but it jammed. The bandits appeared to recognize Mr Brophy and fired four shots at him. Two bullets struck him in the right forearm, fracturing the bone, one in the face and the other in the chest. Owing to the dragnet being placed round the bandits, who had been operating there for some time, it was considered advisable not to release the true facts of the case at the time (11.00 a.m. on Saturday). But owing to false rumours which got about, and have been published, it is now considered advisable to release the true facts.' [67]

So there it was – the newspapers were to blame! As soon as McKerrall finished reading the statement, he was besieged with requests for more information. The reporters understood that there would be widespread interest amongst their readers. But did the police understand what they had just done and that the statement would become fertile ground for conspiracy theories? The police did not explain why Brophy had gone alone to capture the bandits (as it was then believed) and did not use the resources of the wireless patrol branch and detective force to aid him. Robert Lawson from the *Age* had taken a shorthand note and was pressing him to elaborate – but McKerrall, following Blamey's strictures about providing the press with as little as possible, said that 'that was all he had to give to the press.' Lawson also later recalled that the document McKerrall read from had several items scratched out and a number of interlinings and

67 *The Sun News-Pictorial,* 26 May 1936

differed in a number of ways – the lines were further apart, the paper was larger and the wording was not the same.

Luxton from the *Age* immediately questioned McKerrall about the document, asking the questions that most of the people of Melbourne wanted answered – 'Is that correct? Can you vouch for it?' It soon became obvious that the police had concocted stories. Now they had been found out. There had been massive mistrust of police information by the Melbourne papers that had suffered from Blamey's attitudes towards them for a number of years. This may be a long-awaited opportunity to once again vilify Blamey.

Even after the press had absorbed the second statement, they were still of the opinion that 'almost complete mystery surrounds the circumstances of the sensational attack' on Brophy. This situation wasn't helped by Brophy referring all enquiries to the Chief Commissioner and Blamey, in turn, refusing to see representatives of the press and then sending out word through an orderly that he could say nothing about the shooting. But speculation was rife in Melbourne about the car in which Brophy had been in when shot, with no information available about its location after the shooting. It was becoming a view that the first statement was not just a 'misunderstanding', but was a deliberate falsehood. It was one that Blamey considered he was totally justified in providing – an attitude that foretold of the shape of things to come.

The morning newspapers were full of the case when the next editions came out on the morning of Monday the 25th. *The Age* reported that as soon as the report of the attack reached Russell Street, every available man was concentrated in Parkville, but a most exhaustive search failed to yield any trace of the bandits. But this was totally untrue, as the news of the shooting (and the location) was suppressed (and not available to other police) until Sunday. Did the *Age* reporter make it up? Or was it a supposition inferred from the police spokesman? *The Age* was also laudatory about Brophy, who had been in the job for only a short time and had already made police history by his 'courageous single-handed raid on a gang of car bandits, known to be armed...the first occasion on which an officer occupying his high position in the CIB has taken an active personal part in the apprehension of a criminal'. What a beat-up! No wonder Blamey mistrusted the press when they were capable of printing rubbish like this.

The metropolitan reporters - Gillison *(the Argus),* Aldridge *(the Sun),* Tilley *(the Herald),* and Austin *(the Age)* - finally got to meet with Blamey on the Monday, just before a still-shaky Brophy was discharged from hospital. The meeting was all business and the reporters realised that Blamey had little interest in talking to them. Blamey again stated that 'nobody seems to know anything about it' and described the situation as 'all quite simple'. He would not allow Aldridge to write down what was said. Waving his hand toward him, he said 'Do not take this down.' This time Blamey told the reporters where the attack had taken place. The reporters pressed him about the first statement and Aldridge then asked him whether it was an attempt to suppress information to the press, leading Blamey to state that he did not know where the first statement had come from (clearly a lie) but that it had been issued in good faith (another lie). When he was asked whether detectives would continue an investigation in an endeavour to apprehend his attackers, he retorted – 'what can we do? The men were masked, and the light of a torch was flashed in Superintendent Brophy's face, so that he had no opportunity of identifying them.' The meeting ended when one pressman attempted to put Blamey on the spot by asking what were the chances of catching the assailants and Blamey would not answer. He later stated: 'I had no more information for the reporters, and I evaded the question. My answers were given with the object of not giving information.' [68] As would be expected, each of the newspapers published different accounts of the meeting, leading Blamey to dispute the recollections of the reporters. But it must be remembered that sub-editors often found better ways to express phrases when editing crime stories. In the aftermath of the meeting, there was to be no holding back by the press, and the general feeling around the streets, workplaces and pubs in Melbourne was that the Chief Commissioner had deliberately misled the press and was lying to cover something up.

The headlines and articles kept coming that week. Inevitably, it was revealed in the press that Mrs Orr and Mrs Phillips had been with Brophy in the car when the shooting took place, this causing more speculation around the traps in Melbourne. The *Truth* displayed some insights and probably got it right when they reported on the affair. Describing it as 'one of the greatest public sensations that Victoria has known', they went on to say that 'never has there been so much conjecture, so much rumour, so much vain speculation, and so much public uncertainty as to the motives of the Police department as there has been in this matter…questions being asked by the man in the street must not remain unanswered.' [69] The paper considered Brophy to be the unfortunate victim. Their reporter John Leeming had received a one-on-one interview with Brophy at his home after he was released from hospital, and the *Truth* sought a Royal

68 *The Mercury* (Hobart Tasmania), 12 June 1936
69 *The Truth*, 30 May 1936

Commission, a call that they claimed was supported by Blamey, which seems unlikely.

It wasn't only the press and the people who were unhappy with Blamey's lack of information. Blamey met weekly with the Chief Secretary (Brigadier Murray Bourchier) who was responsible within the Cabinet of the Victorian government for the operations of the police.[70] Bourchier had served at Gallipolli and other war zones in the Great War. He entered Parliament in 1920 and was a leading figure in the Country Party and deputy leader of the party in 1927-30, later assuming the leadership between 1933-35. He was regarded as a principled and predictable man who never lacked a solid bloc of supporters, but he was an uninspiring leader. In 1935 Dunstan replaced him as leader. In the Country Party government formed with Labor support, Bourchier was named Chief Secretary and Minister of Labour and Deputy Premier. One view is that Bourchier had been in Dunstan's Cabinet under sufferance – nevertheless, he served Dunstan's government quite well and displayed sound judgement in dealing with the demise of Blamey.[71]

The weekly meetings were generally informal and did not form part of the public record. According to Blamey, at the meeting on May 27, he told Bourchier the details, including the fact that two women (who he named) were in the car with Brophy. There was later some conjecture as to whether

70 Under the Westminster system, Cabinet is the principal decision-making body of government and includes the Cabinet Secretary and all ministers of the Crown. The Premier leads the government and is the chair of Cabinet. Cabinet ministers are appointed from members of parliament and are responsible for administering government departments http://www.dpc.vic.gov.au/index.php/about/cabinet, accessed 25 January 2015

71 Don Watson, *'Bourchier, Sir Murray William James (1881–1937)'*, Australian Dictionary of Biography, National Centre of Biography, Australian National University, http://adb.anu.edu.au/biography/bourchier-sir-murray-william-james-5303/text8953, accessed 1 January 2014.

this information was actually imparted. The *Advertiser (Adelaide)* reported that the meeting was the usual weekly conference and Bourchier had not received a report of the shooting. However Blamey (under oath) later claimed that he had provided information to the Chief Secretary, including the names of the two women involved.[72] Bourchier told him that there was no intention to appoint a Commission to inquire into the matter and did not require a written report, although these comments were obviously premature. Displaying incredible naivety, it apparently did not occur to Blamey that Bourchier would verbally pass on his comments to the other members of Cabinet.

By Thursday, May 28, things had changed. Government Ministers were furious that Blamey had not furnished a written report to Cabinet about the shooting. The Premier, Mr Dunstan, was on the warpath and wanted a report. He regarded the matter as of the utmost urgency and thought that the public was entitled to complete information. Fully aware of the focus and scrutiny that the government would be subjected to by the press, he intended to ask Blamey for details of the shooting. By this time, Blamey had handed over the investigation to Carey and O'Keefe, who investigated every

Brigadier Murray Bourchier, Chief Secretary 1936, http://www.geni.com/people/Brigadier-Sir-Murray-William-James-Bourchier

72 *Advertiser (Adelaide),* 12 June 1936.

big crime in Victoria, telling them that the Chief Secretary wanted a report. But the written report supplied was confined to the facts of the shooting, and failed to mention the presence of the women in the car. Blamey justified this omission by saying that he had provided the full story in his report to the Chief Secretary, who was 'fully informed of the facts' and putting their names in the written report would have been 'scandal-mongering'. This was not the duty of the Chief Commissioner. It was up to the Chief Secretary to provide information to Cabinet, stating that 'what he did with it was nothing to do with me.'[73]

If the Premier had been undecided about ordering a Royal Commission, this omission probably made up his mind for him. According to Blamey, the intention was to shield the women, as these reports go through a lot of hands. But the names of the women, together with the fact that the car in which Brophy was travelling belonged to one of them, was always going to come out. Perhaps the real entity being protected was the reputation of the police force?

About two-thirds of the Cabinet Ministers were reported as seeking an immediate report and a commission to enquire into the shooting. For those who had been dissatisfied with, and disdainful of, Blamey and the police force for some time, such an inquiry was welcomed and should be wide enough to allow an investigation into the police force generally. Whilst it didn't quite work out that way, significant changes would be made as a result of the shooting of Brophy. Cabinet did not waste any time in setting up a Royal Commission into the shooting. The conservative government of Dunstan was not in a position to shield Blamey from public scrutiny, and Dunstan was dependent

73 *Sydney Morning Herald (NSW),* 13 June 1936

upon Labor Party goodwill for continued political survival. A Royal Commission would ease the pressure on his government and satisfy many of Blamey's long-term adversaries on the left of politics. Newspapers in other states were also joining in the criticism. On May 29 the *News* in Adelaide, under the large headline of 'Victoria's Police Muddle', joined the call for an enquiry, saying that the Victorian public is likely to get what they should have had long ago – a glimpse of what is going on behind the veiled silence.

Cabinet members regarded the position so seriously that a judge of the Supreme Court should be appointed to head up a Royal Commission and the Executive Council appointed Judge Macindoe as the Royal Commissioner 'to inquire into and report upon the shooting of Brophy'. [74] Apart from the public dissatisfaction with the lies and distortions coming from Police Headquarters, often directly from the Chief Commissioner, there was growing public concern about the spate of armed robberies in Melbourne. Whilst the government was finalising the terms of reference for the Royal Commission, another major armed robbery took place – this time at North Fitzroy. It was the fifth in less than a week. What were the police doing?

Royal Commissioner,
Judge Macindoe,
The Truth, 13 June 1936

The terms of reference for the Macindoe Royal Commission

74 Hugh Macindoe was a former Crown prosecutor who had been involved in some ofVictoria's major murder trials in the 1920s.

were announced on Saturday June 6, with a proposed start date on the following Wednesday in the Second County Court. Judge Macindoe was to be assisted by Mr L E B Stretton, KC. It was to investigate the circumstances connected with the shooting of Brophy, the truth or falsity of statements made by Blamey and other police officers and the circumstances around their preparation and issue, and the steps taken by Blamey and his force to investigate the shooting and apprehend the persons responsible. [75] Macindoe was required to not only report his findings of the facts of the enquiry, but also to offer his opinion as to the propriety or otherwise of the behaviour of Blamey and other police officers. He was given a wide range of powers. Frank Brennan represented individual reporters called to give evidence, with the *Herald and Weekly Times* represented by Mr Stanley Lewis and Mr Wilbur Ham, KC. Ham has been described as witty and cultured, though anaemic, with a limp from a cavalry accident in the Great War. Like other members of the Bar (such as Owen Dixon and John Barry), he was a keen member of the Medico-Legal Society of Victoria and had been its President in 1933/4. [76] Blamey, Brophy and other members of the force were represented at the inquiry by Norman O'Bryan, instructed by Mr R H (Ray) Dunn, the son of Blamey's assistant, Tom Dunn.[77]

It was estimated that about 15 police witnesses would be called. The inquiry was the vehicle for which all the answers should come out. But would they? Counsel assisting the Commissioner, Mr Stretton, stated that it was up to the Commissioner to 'lower the bucket into that well where truth

75 *The Argus*, 6 June 1936

76 Phillip Ayres, *Owen Dixon*, 2007, p. 71.

77 Ray Dunn was a pugnacious character. He was not a matinee idol but was regarded as having a brilliant legal mind. He regularly defended the police in court and was on permanent retainer with the Police Association. He later became President of Richmond Football Club.

is said to reside. Perhaps the rope will not be long enough, or perhaps an unexpected and unpleasant liquid will be brought up. We can only hope, however, that what will be brought up will be the pure, clear liquid of truth.'[78] Many people in Melbourne had little doubt about what the Commissioner would find at the bottom of the well.

One thing that was obvious during the conduct of the Commission was the barely-concealed hostility between the Commissioner and his senior officers and the metropolitan newspapers. In front of a packed County Court room, with specially posted police on duty to keep the precinct clear and with many peering in through the glass doors, Brophy took the stand, his arm still in a sling. He took nearly a day to provide his account of the events of that night as he gave evidence that he firstly requested that the affair be described as an accident, as he had a number of concerns. Firstly, he was afraid that Mrs Orr and Meagher might be compromised, as the car was owned by one and driven by the other; secondly because it might upset his wife to know that he had been attacked by a gunman and may have learned about the extent of his injuries; and thirdly, because he was anxious for safety of the informer. Both his wife and his daughter were described as 'practically invalids' and would not have been as shocked by him having an accident compared to being shot by criminals. He was convinced that the gunmen had nothing to do with the informer, whose name he initially objected to providing, but agreed to write it down for the judge. When a sheet of paper was placed in front of him, he suddenly looked up and said to the judge – 'I am frightened of this.' 'You should not be frightened. I am taking the risk, and you are not taking any more risk,' said Judge Macindoe. Brophy then wrote down a name, apparently with difficulty due to his

78 *The Truth*, 13 June 1936

wounded arm, and handed it to the Judge.[79]

The counsel for the newspapers questioned Brophy about the various versions of the shooting, suggesting that the accident theory was first put forward simply as a means to hide the fact that he was out with a woman and that he was ashamed of the escapade he was on. Brophy stated that there was nothing sinister in it. When asked why he did not tell the true story to the press, Brophy replied that if he had it would have been broadcast on Saturday night and Sunday and he would have given the criminal warning to clear out for Hong Kong or somewhere. But counsel kept at him, asserting that there were good reasons why Brophy did not want the assailant to be recognised or apprehended. He suggested that Brophy knew his identity – a suggestion immediately (and forcefully) refuted by Brophy.[80]

Other witnesses included Detective Bolton, who was subjected to a searching cross-examination about accepting without question the story told him by Brophy that it was an accident. Lewis asked him, 'Was it not perfectly apparent to you that Brophy had not been shot accidentally?' He replied, 'No.' Lewis continued, 'You are a detective, and it went beyond your powers of observation as a detective to say whether Brophy had had an accident or not? ' Bolton said Brophy had dried blood on his hands and face but told him it had been an accident and that he believed him.[81] He also denied that any great stir had been caused at police headquarters by the occurrence. When he was asked 'As far as you are concerned, headquarters has just gone along as if nothing had happened?' 'No enquiries have been made,' replied Bolton in a statement that was almost beyond belief. The head of the CIB had just

79 *Cairns Post (Queensland),* 11 June 1936
80 *Cairns Post (Queensland),* 11 June 1936
81 *Report of the Royal Commission,* 2 July 1936, p.6

been shot four times and the place was not in an uproar? [82]

More controversy surrounding the statements provided to the press by the police soon emerged. Two statements were tabled – the first was that handed out by the police information bureau on the Saturday morning, and the second was that read out by Detective-Inspector McKerral to the press representatives on Sunday May 24. It soon became obvious that the documents put before the commission by the police were NOT the documents handed to the press. The copy of the first statement produced at the Commission was different to the one provided at the press briefing on the Saturday, with differences in the writing and the information it contained, with no reference to Brophy's arm being fractured. Remarkably, at the conclusion of the Commission, there was no action taken against the officers for this infraction. After all, misleading a Royal Commission was a very serious offence, particularly for a police officer.

The evidence of reporters in relation to the statements issued by the police became a major point of contention. More acrimony emerged when reporters were questioned and refused to disclose the source from which they had received information. One reporter, John Bergin from the *Sun,* was asked where he had obtained information regarding the arrest of a man who was suspected of having been concerned in the shooting. Despite his counsel objecting on the grounds of the long-established principle that the press should not publish the source of its information, Bergin answered that he had received the tip-off from a policeman. He was also asked where he had obtained the information that a photograph of the suspect had been shown to Meagher, the driver of the car. He refused to answer but denied that it was from a policeman.

82 *The Advertiser, Adelaide*, 13 June 1936

When Mrs Orr entered the courtroom of the Royal Commission with 'a rustle and a stir' to give her evidence, she was noticeably nervous. The press described her as 'a tall, stout woman with aquiline features, dressed in black and wearing a fur coat.' She confirmed Brophy's story of the events of the night and said that, acting under his instructions, she had not reported the shooting. She told the Commissioner that Brophy had said: 'You ladies are not in this at all, leave it to me. It is most unfortunate that you should be here.' Nor did Meagher ring the police when they returned to the hotel.[83] Another issue had raised its head early in the reports of the shooting, when it was revealed that Mrs Orr had accompanied Brophy to Royal Park – a suggestion that Brophy and Orr had been involved in an illicit relationship. The Commissioner found it 'impossible to believe' that Brophy would take any woman with two other people to Royal Park to engage in any immoral or improper conduct. But he went on to say that if there was something between them, there appeared to be no obstacle to his making use of Mrs Orr's hotel if he so desired. This seemed a strange comment for a Royal Commissioner to make. Orr also testified that Mrs Brophy had come to see her at the hotel on Saturday morning, when she had told her everything. She had another visitor later that morning, when Detective Sergeant O'Keeffe came to see her, but he made no attempt to talk to Meagher or to contact Mrs Phillips, who was staying there, she told the Commission. In an extraordinary comment, Phillips told the Commission that this week was the first time that she had been asked for her recollections of the shooting. She also stated that she and her husband were on excellent terms, a statement backed up by him under oath. Meagher told the Commission that the police did

83 *The Advertiser, Adelaide*, 13 June 1936

not interview him until 7.00 p.m. on the Saturday night, nearly 24 hours after the shooting, and that, as far as he knew, the police had not inspected the car, which of course had been fired at by the hold-up men.

The most sensational evidence came from Blamey, who displayed an arrogance that was staggering and moved between a denial of events and a stubborn refusal to admit (or concede) that he had acted incorrectly. Much of his evidence, despite being under oath, was disputed by others and can only be described as bare-faced lies. He said that he had visited Brophy only once in hospital, denying claims that he had 'gone back more than once' to impress upon hospital staff the necessity for not giving out any information.

Curiously, as the details of the 'Brophy Affair' were filling the papers each day, Blamey decided to settle the action with the *Star* newspaper, which, on the face of it, he had a good chance of winning. On the morning of May 28, Justice Gavan Duffy was presiding over a case in the Practice Court. He was due to hear the Blamey libel case in a few weeks. During a lull in proceedings, Duffy was approached by the eminent King's Counsels, Mr Eugene Gorman and Mr Wilbur Ham, still attired in their wigs and silken gowns. Catching the judge's eye, they informed him that the parties had composed their differences and the case would be discontinued. Did Blamey feel that he had enough on his plate, or did he think that the current publicity might affect his chances of success? After all, there were strong similarities between the events that had led to the *Star* article and the current events being revealed. The settlement of the case relied upon an agreement that the terms of the settlement would not be revealed by the parties beyond a statement that the article objected to by Blamey was not intended to reflect on his personal character and any imputation was regretted.[84] The *Star* folded shortly after. It was an interesting case but many people in Melbourne did not need a report in a minor newspaper to be aware of the state of lawlessness of their city or to develop contempt for Blamey.

The Commission finished with an acrimonious exchange between Macindoe and Stretton, counsel assisting the Commissioner. Macindoe had called for certain confidential files from the police which were examined by him and no-one else. Stretton criticised him for receiving documents in confidence, documents which he said could not be tested in the ordinary way. His view was that Macindoe should bring in findings that condemned Brophy's actions and the subsequent inactivity of the police. During his evidence, Brophy did not identify any person as having shot at him. As the Royal Commission approached its end, Stretton was scathing about the police evidence, stating that NO police witness had told 'the truth, the whole truth and nothing but the truth,' including Blamey.[85] In his view, if Brophy's story was taken as true, it should be found that he acted improperly by taking women and a civilian on police duty, exposing them to danger, and withheld information from the police for 12 hours - and had lied to the Chief Commissioner. Overall Brophy had allowed consideration of a personal nature

L E B Stretton,
The Truth, 13 June 1936

84 *The Truth, 30* May 1936
85 *The Argus,* 26 June 1936

to forgo his public duty as a citizen and his professional duty as a police officer. If his story was untrue, Brophy had conspired with certain members of the police force by committing perjury.

Stretton also submitted that the Commission should find that no steps were promptly taken by any member of the police force to investigate the shooting or to apprehend the persons. While there is no evidence to connect Brophy with such neglect or default, other officers gave sworn evidence that was false, including McKerral, O'Keeffe, Carey and Blamey.

The findings of the Royal Commission produced a number of sensations when tabled by the Premier in the Legislative Assembly on July 2.[86] After 11 days and 44 witnesses, Macindoe commenced his findings by acknowledging that he had called for certain confidential files that were examined by him and no one else. The Commissioner found that Superintendent Brophy went to the park on official business. He was exonerated of any wrongdoing and it was found that there was nothing improper in taking women with him to meet an informer. After all, the women could not be exposed to any danger from the informer 'who was obviously friendly'.[87] Macindoe discounted any suggestion that Brophy had been involved in any scandalous conduct which might have led to an enraged husband being responsible for the shooting (one of the theories that had floated around in the streets of Melbourne). Mrs Phillips' husband was certainly not enraged. Brophy's initial reporting of the shooting as an 'accident' was prompted by a desire to protect the women from scandal. However Blamey's evidence was not accepted by the Commissioner who found that, despite knowing the truth about the shooting, he decided not to disclose the whole truth

86 On the following day, the Coroner began his inquiry into the death of Ted Scriven.

87 *Report of the Royal Commission*, 2 July 1936, p.4

about the incident and provided false information to the press in the first announcement on the Saturday. When asked if he was justified in making a statement to the press that he knew was untrue, Blamey replied 'I am not prepared to say yes or no to that.' In addition, the Commissioner could not accept his evidence that he believed it was an accident. After all, if it WAS an accident, it was difficult to understand why he should think it necessary to detail two detective-sergeants to ascertain the facts. The Commissioner concluded that Blamey gave 'replies which were not in accordance with the truth'. [88] According to Robert Haldane, MacIndoe, who had served at Gallipolli and thought highly of Blamey's many achievements in the military and the Victorian police, was impressed with Blamey and, when taking evidence, 'tried to steer him to the true story'. [89] But not even a sympathetic Commissioner could save Blamey from himself.

Nor was another turn of events helpful. During the Commission, Sir Frederick Mann, Chief Justice of the Victorian Supreme Court, denounced improper police practices, known colloquially as the 'third degree', where the police had extorted confessions from suspected persons by coercion and physical violence. Accusations of this practice were regularly made by aggrieved parties but when made by such an 'eminent and competent authority' as the Chief Justice, they clearly deserved deep respect. The problem with these practices was twofold – not only could innocent parties be coerced into a confession, but a guilty party could convince a jury that a confession made to the police had been extorted by violence and is untrue. The use of these methods came to play a major role in subsequent trials concerning the Scriven affair, but, at this time, contributed

88 *Report of the Royal Commission*, 2 July 1936, pp. 7/8
89 Robert Haldane, *The People's Force*, 1986, p. 214

greatly to the criticism of the force being run by Blamey.[90]

The Commissioners' Report immediately went to Cabinet. A week later, Blamey received a letter from the Premier advising him that, in view of Macindoe's finding that he could not accept his evidence, he could not continue to hold the post of Chief Commissioner of Police. He had lied to a Royal Commission

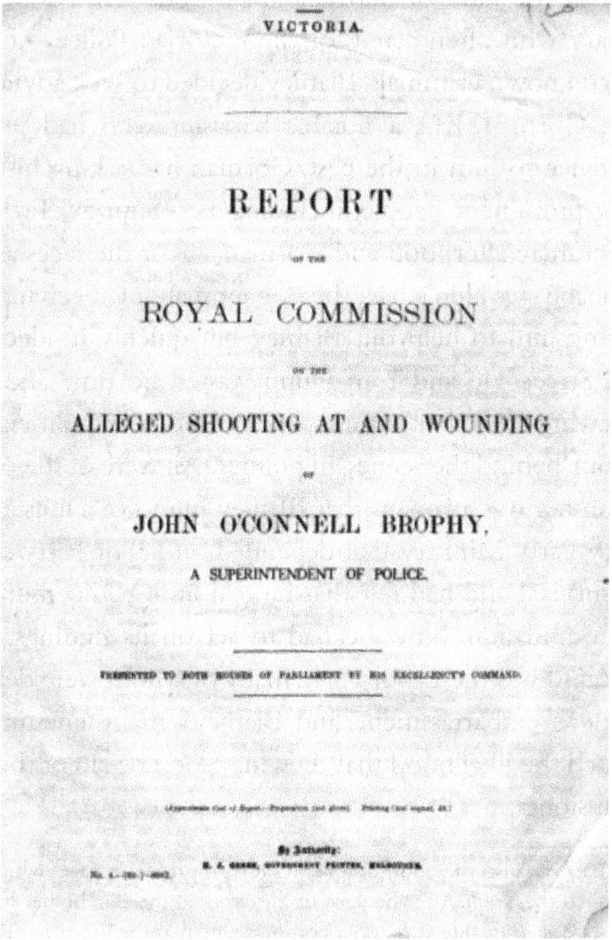

VICTORIA.

REPORT

OF THE

ROYAL COMMISSION

ON THE

ALLEGED SHOOTING AT AND WOUNDING

OF

JOHN O'CONNELL BROPHY,

A SUPERINTENDENT OF POLICE.

PRESENTED TO BOTH HOUSES OF PARLIAMENT BY HIS EXCELLENCY'S COMMAND.

By Authority:

The Report of the Royal Commission

90 *The Argus,* 22 June 1936

whilst under oath. As expected, Blamey initially tried to shrug it off, remarking to his assistant, Tom Dunn, that 'these things are sent to try us.' But the seriousness of the situation was soon pointed out to him. Dunn had been at Blamey's side since he took over the position, acting in effect as Blamey's Chief of Staff. He actually outlasted Blamey in the force, retiring in 1944 with the rank of Superintendent. His son, Ray, became a barrister who often acted for the Victorian Police – but also defended known criminals. Blamey decided to seek advice from Eugene Gorman, KC, a notable barrister who had provided good advice to him in the past. Gorman had a long history of advising prominent people, including Les 'Squizzy' Taylor.[91] It was a Saturday afternoon and Gorman was at the races as usual. He probably wouldn't have been happy about receiving a call requesting him to help out Blamey, but quickly headed off to Russell Street. He and Tom Dunn wasted no time and began interviewing a number of newspaper proprietors, politicians and men from 'behind the scenes' in politics. All were of the opinion that Dunstan was adamant that Blamey must go. Dunstan led a Country Party Ministry that depended on Labor Party support for its survival and had felt that he had little choice but to call for a Commission. Now he had to act on its findings. In the background was the Labor Party, many of whom were delighted at Blamey's embarrassment, and Blamey's many enemies who welcomed the likelihood that they may soon be rid of the Chief Commissioner.

91 Gorman was also the counsel for the Norton press company, which published the *Truth*. After he gave up his work at the Bar, he became an executive at *Truth*. He was also a committeeman at the Victorian Racing Club, and the proprietor of the *Truth* was regularly critical of the management of racing in Victoria. Gorman viewed this as a major conflict of interest and in 1950 the politics of the racing world caused him to resign his directorate at the *Truth*. *The Argus*, 11 October 1950

Blamey was starting to look extremely weary and vulnerable but his demise was by no means a foregone conclusion. Whilst it was becomingly increasingly apparent to everyone around him that he would not survive the battle, he was not prepared to go quietly and fully intended to refuse to resign. Gorman pointed out to him that he would not be entitled to a pension if he were to be subsequently dismissed. Not only that, he would be unlikely to ever be offered another public office, including the military, an important consideration given the massive political unrest in Europe at the time that many thought could quickly descend into war. However, if he resigned the government might be persuaded to grant him a pension. It was a good offer as officers generally only qualified for a pension after serving for fifteen years. Eventually it fully dawned on Blamey that he was in a terrible bind and there was no point continuing with his posturing. He reluctantly agreed to offer his resignation.

Whilst the resignation and transition seemed simple on the surface, it had been the culmination of a week of frantic horse-trading between the Premier (Dunstan), Blamey (and his advisors) and Cabinet. This was clearly a crisis for the government and its integrity was being brought into question and placed under public scrutiny. It was no time for complacency. A series of emergency meetings, both official and unofficial, occupied the time of Cabinet members, together with discussions that involved the Crown Solicitor, Mr Menzies, and legal representatives who had represented the police at the Royal Commission. Blamey's resignation arrived at the Cabinet office about 15 minutes before Cabinet was due to commence its meeting. Cabinet quickly accepted the resignation and passed it on to a special meeting of the Executive Council. [92] Not surprisingly, it was immediately accepted, on the recommendation of the Cabinet, and was announced on July 10 that Blamey would be entitled to superannuation payments, based on his 10 years' service, of about £5 a week. His annual salary as Commissioner had been £1,250 with an allowance of £250. William Walter Mooney, a senior superintendent currently in charge of the Bourke district, was appointed to act in the position until a suitable permanent successor could be found. Mooney was only a short time away from retirement, so would not be considered for the top job. In the meantime, a request was sent to Scotland Yard for a 'high official' to be sent to Melbourne to review and report upon the Victorian Police. Cabinet was seeking to introduce the most modern methods of police and detective work for use in Victoria. It was not a foregone conclusion that the officer investigating the force would become Chief Commissioner, but it seemed like a strong possibility. The officer nominated was Alex Duncan, a successful crime expert from Scotland Yard. The 'Yard', as it was generally known, referred to the headquarters of the London Metropolitan Police, including the Criminal Investigation Branch of the London police. Duncan had been the head of the famous 'Flying Squad' that played a large role in reducing serious crime in London. In 1936, four new groups (called 'S.O.S. Squads') were created, each unit to be fully self-contained and consist of twenty detectives, with a range of

92 *The Argus,* 10 July 1936; The Executive Council comprises the Premier and his or her Ministers who have been sworn by the Governor as Executive councillors, usually at the same time as they are sworn in as Ministers. The Governor, on the recommendation of a Minister and with the advice of the Executive Council, deals with a wide range of matters that Parliament has specified be handled in that way rather than by a Minister acting alone.

expertise. Perhaps their creation led to the decision by Duncan to move to Australia.[93]

The criminal world regarded that Blamey had got the 'sack cold' because he was in the car with Brophy. Career criminal Geoffrey Davies later told the police his version of the shooting, including the names of the perpetrators and, pricked by his conscience, thought of writing to Blamey or Brophy during the Royal Commission to tell them who had performed the shooting. It was the thought that his writing might be traced that stopped him. He also thought of trying to see the premier (Mr Dunstan) but didn't know how to go about it.[94]

Alex Duncan,
Sun News Pictorial,
13 October 1936

In Parliament the resignation was being viewed as a virtual dismissal. In the Legislative Assembly, the Independent member for Gippsland North, Mr McLachlan, asked the Ministry for the reasons for the resignation. The government response was that Blamey had resigned voluntarily and had a perfect right to apply for the position after Victoria Police was re-organised. The response fooled no one. There were still concerns amongst some MPs as to why Blamey had been cast into 'outer darkness… discredited and dishonoured'. After all, he had the 'police force in thorough working order'.[95] This was a view disputed

93 *The Argus,* 25 August 1936; *Cairns Post (Queensland),* 6 June 1936
94 *The Argus,* 28 November 1936
95 *The Argus,* 15 July 1936

by many who had little but disdain for him. Despite his many achievements in reforming the Victoria Police force, there continued to be major problems with the force in areas such as methods of obtaining witness statements, brutality towards suspects, disorganisation between the Wireless car Branch and other Branches, communications between the Police Force and the press and public, and a desperate need for adequate accommodation, particularly at Russell Street. These problems (and more) would soon be revealed by the investigation by Alex Duncan. The investigation was welcomed by members of the Labor Party, which had long clamoured for an impartial inquiry into the failure of the police force to solve serious crimes. Whilst an investigation into a police force by another policeman could hardly be described as impartial, at least it would expose the major shortcomings of the force to a fresh set of highly qualified eyes.

A further result concerned the officers who had testified at the Royal Commission. Despite some concerns expressed by Judge Macindoe about their evidence, Acting Commissioner Mooney recommended to the Chief Secretary that no action be taken against any member of the police force (except Blamey). Mooney did not feel that he would be justified in making any charge of misconduct against Brophy or any other officer. Unofficially, it was expected that this recommendation would be accepted. [96] Was this an example of the Police Force closing ranks around their own, or did Mooney consider that enough damage had been done to the reputation of the Force by the actions of Brophy and Blamey? Or was it just a desire of an officer approaching retirement to avoid major controversy in the final period of his career? Mooney's tenure was soon extended to

96 *The Argus*, 23 July 1936

November, and his salary increased to £1,050 p.a. (compared to the £1,250 that Blamey had been paid). This was almost double what Mooney had previously earned as an inspector (£510 and an allowance of £75). The extension was deemed necessary to enable the arrival of Alexander Duncan, due on October 12.

It was the conclusion of a shocking year in which there had been an epidemic of armed hold-ups in Melbourne, with the proceeds of the robberies running into thousands of pounds. Robberies had occurred in a city theatre, a shoe factory in Fitzroy, a canister factory in North Melbourne, a factory in Prahran, a Maples furniture store in Fitzroy and a bizarre robbery at a post office in Kensington when a robber on a bicycle menaced the postmaster with a pistol and stole £50. The Scriven robbery was the only one where murder was committed and the failure to solve it was a major embarrassment of the Victorian police. The shooting of Brophy was never properly cleared up and remains as one of a number of unsolved major crimes from Melbourne's mid-1930s.

With the advent of World War 11, Blamey was recalled to the military and went on to distinguish himself as Australia's highest ranking military leader, although not without controversy. He earned the enmity of Australian soldiers with some intemperate remarks about their performance in defending the Kokoda Trail in New Guinea. Rumours persisted about his drinking and 'nocturnal appetite'. One report stated that, while on a 1944 trip on the USS Lurline to San Francisco with Prime Minister John Curtin, he insisted on taking on board several cases of spirits for the journey, much to the dismay of Curtin, a reformed alcoholic. Blamey then chose to entertain lonely Australian war brides, heading to life in the USA, in his cabin.[97]

---

97 John Silvester, *The Age*, 24 August 2013

CHAPTER 4

THE HUNT FOR SCRIVEN'S KILLERS CONTINUES

If the people of Melbourne hadn't already been aware of the vendetta between Chief Commissioner Blamey and the press, it became very clear to them after the Brophy Royal Commission. What now became public knowledge was Blamey's direction during the Royal Commission. The special shadowing squad set up by Blamey (containing Constable Jim Cairns) kept a watch on certain reporters from the *Herald* and the *Sun,* including one in particular who was 'suspected in connection with a certain offence', probably Bergin from the *Herald.* Blamey suspected that the reporter was receiving information from a member (or members) of the police force, contrary to an official ban at Russell Street headquarters on the practice.[1] Not surprisingly, reporters had cultivated their own sources, much to Blamey's distress. It was commonly accepted that a great deal of crime information was gathered by the newspapers, despite the ban. Cairns shadowed the reporters for about a month reporting back to Blamey every four or five days. Nothing, it seems, came of the reports. Blamey's obsession with the *Herald* was recognised everywhere. Whilst the purpose of the Commission was quite specific, there was an underlying battle between the police and

1 *The Argus,* 3 July 1936

the press. Blamey and his officers were determined that the Press (and by extension the public) would only receive the information that they deemed to be acceptable. In their view, the press could not be trusted to get it right. Their real underlying objection was that the newspapers were likely to criticize the police. The newspapers were of the opinion that they should be able to report entire stories. For their part, they could not see why the police regarded themselves as immune from questioning and able to control the flow of information.

The revelations of shadowing of reporters became public knowledge following questions in Parliament in early July of 1936. The view from Parliament (well, from the Labor Party at least) was that the public was entitled to correct information. What was revealed was like a script from a Charlie Chaplin or Keystone Cops slapstick film. In late June, when the Royal Commission into the Brophy shooting was still underway, the press had realised that the police were following a car occupied by some journalists and were determined to 'camp on the tail' of their car. The pressmen decided to have some fun and see how far they would go. They drove to Camberwell, made a call, and then drove to Mitcham (in Melbourne's outer suburbs) by an indirect route. The police followed closely. When the two cars passed close to each other near Mitcham, the police officers carefully laid on the floor of their car. Both cars returned to the city and the journalists went to their office, before leaving by the back door to get on with their work, leaving the police watching the empty car in front for some hours. The next day, four policemen in two cars watched the journalists' car all afternoon. The watch continued on the next day, with the press car again being followed. The journalists went into a hotel bar where they were followed by one of the police officers, and then hurried out, so that the police officer had to follow them without having time to finish his drink. They then drove to the seaside suburb of Brighton and lost the police at the New Street railway gates. Enjoying the game, they drove slowly but the police failed to find them. They then drove back to the office, where another police car was waiting. A chase out to Ivanhoe and Heidelberg began. The journalists went down an unmade street and dodged behind some bushes and were greatly amused when the police car following them ran into a bog hole. The journalists waited until the police had extricated themselves from the mud and then drove on, before changing their tactics to a game of 'ring-a-rosy', driving round and round one block with the police after them. Driving faster and faster, they actually lapped the police car, before driving back to the city and going past police headquarters so that the police could return the car to its garage. Whilst this escapade produced much mirth and laughter in Parliament, it was really no laughing matter – particularly when the police were receiving regular demands from suburban and country districts for protection and constantly claimed that they were short-staffed. Blamey had given an assurance that such practices would now cease and the Parliamentarians thought that it was time it did. [2]

But other crimes investigated by Brophy (who was back at work after his shooting) and 'Scotty' McKerrall around this time were no laughing matter, particularly the bombing of the house of Senior Plainclothes-Constable Milne in Newtown, Geelong on July 13. Mrs Milne was killed in the attack and the house badly damaged. [3]

The Coroners Court hearing into the death of Ted Scriven took place in early July, nearly six months after the murder, delayed

2 *The Argus,* 3 July 1936
3 *The Argus,* 15 July 1936

in the hope that police would be able to provide some important evidence. They couldn't and there was little fresh light thrown on the circumstances of Scriven's shooting. The Court building was located in Batman Avenue, next to the City Morgue and close to the original Olympic Swimming Pool, opposite the murky Yarra River. This part of Batman Avenue was a sombre and macabre place, disliked by police roundsmen. A typical day for police reporters included visits to the casualty wards of major hospitals, Russell Street CIB, City Watchhouse, Melbourne Magistrates' Court, Metropolitan Fire Brigade, Civil Ambulance, offices of criminal lawyers (both defence and prosecution) and the one they left to last – the City Morgue. Reporters also attended inquests in the Coroners Court, described as a 'rancid old court, enveloped by a perennial smell of death' by *Truth* reporter Brian Hansen, who attended many such inquests in the 1940s and the early 1950s. [4] The building has since been replaced.

Although neither English law nor tradition required medical coroners, Victoria's coroners had all been medically qualified since 1840. This changed after the retirement of Coroner Cole in 1923, after which no doctor was again appointed as Victorian coroner. The Coroner for the Scriven inquest was the magistrate Arthur Tingate, who occupied the position from 1936 until 1945. The space available for visitors was small and often occupied by the families of the deceased. It is not known how many of Scriven's family attended, but his brother-in-law, Robert Arthur Thomas, a retired public servant from St Kilda, testified that he had identified the body of Scriven at the City Morgue on the first of February 1936. [5]

The surgeon who had carried out the post mortem, Mr

---

4 Brian Hansen, *The Awful Truth*, 2004, p. 124

5 PROV, VPRS 00030/P0006, Unit 000004, 1936/777; *Report of Inquisition* by Coroner, 7 July 1936

Mollison, gave evidence about the fatal wound to Scriven's forehead, and also about the state of his other organs. He had retrieved a bullet from Scriven's brain and handed it to the police.[6]

A number of police officers appeared – all reported their failure to establish the identity of Scriven's attackers. The Coroner also heard from witnesses on matters such as the car used in the robbery. Mr Noonan was granted leave to appear for the Victorian Branch of the Australian Public Servants' Association and told the Coroner that Crown servants had an interest in the outcome as they were doing similar work. It was his view that 'the death was due to the lack of foresight or neglect by the authorities'.

When the messenger, Herbert Harvey Gillbank, gave evidence, he testified that he had been engaged as a clerical officer and received no special allowance for doing the messenger work. He confirmed that he had been escorted daily by Scriven for the last nine months. They took the money to the Bank of Australasia, on the corner of Queen and Collins Streets, by taxicab at 4.45 p.m. each day and 11.55 a.m. on Saturday, and for the last few months he had been driven by Reg Pullen. The taxi always waited at the corner of Little Lonsdale Street and the lane at the rear of the Titles office, never coming into the lane, where it would have been close to the back door and perhaps more secure. Not everyone agreed with this view – the cashier, John Ryan, thought that the lane was congested and that in the street there was a clearer view (as long as all precautions were taken). The office now had men watching to see that there was no one hanging around.[7]

6 PROV, VPRS 00030/P0006, Unit 000004, 1936/777; *Report of Inquisition by Coroner*, 7 July 1936

7 PROV, VPRS 00030/P0006, Unit 000004, 1936/777; *Report of Inquisition* by Coroner, 7 July 1936

It was Scriven's practice to carry his gun, an automatic pistol. Gillbank did not know whether Scriven had been trained, although he probably handled weapons in the army and as a prison warder, nor did he know if Scriven had been given any opportunity for shooting practice. The amount stolen was about £1750. The average amount that he carried was about £1500, whilst the largest amount he had carried over the past year was about £3,500. In a comment directed at Mr Noonan, who was clearly concerned about working conditions for public servants, he told the Inquest that he was 17 years and nine months and weighed about 10 stone at the time of the shooting. No special precautions had been taken on that occasion. The only real instructions that he had received when carrying money to the bank was that he should take all the care that he could, adding that had never had any revolver practice and had not been 'offered or afforded any arms'. He described the robbery and shooting, telling the Coroner that the man who took the bag of money from him as about 5'7" (about 172 cm) and of medium build. The man who shot Scriven was about 5'10" (about 177 cm) and rather thinner than his companion. Another witness, William Thomas Carter, recounted that he had been in Little Lonsdale Street about 30 minutes before the shooting where he saw three men sitting in in a car similar to the getaway car. They hid their faces from him as he walked past. [8]

The cashier John Ryan, told the Coroner that after he heard the shot, he grabbed his gun. When someone called out 'The escort has been shot', he ran out to the street where he saw Scriven lying in the gutter. Next to Scriven's head was an empty shell case that he retrieved, whilst the taxi-driver picked up the pistol. Whilst there were instructions in the office that money

8 PROV, VPRS 00030/P0006, Unit 000004, 1936/777; *Report of Inquisition* by Coroner, 7 July 1936

escorts should be supplied with arms, it was revealed by the Deputy Controller of Imposts (Mr Carnier), that the automatic supplied to Scriven had been found in the drawer of his desk on the day AFTER the robbery. This was obviously a difficult time for Carnier, who had known Scriven since he commenced work in the office in 1920. He also gave evidence that Scriven was an officer of the General Division and it was not part of the duties of General Officers to act as escort. At one time, the escort and custodian of the money had walked to the bank. They used a taxi and then had a police escort. During the Police Strike in 1923,[9] there no policemen available so Scriven volunteered to do the task. When the strike was over the police decided to charge for the service, causing the Controller of Stamps, Mr Metzner, to arrange with the Secretary of the Law Department in 1925 for Scriven to be armed and act as escort. There is no record of Scriven receiving an allowance for the extra duties. Whilst it was Carnier's job to supervise the counting and to despatch the messenger and escort, it was NOT part of his duties to check if the escort was armed. [10] There was no training in the use of weapons for the staff but it was recognised in the Office that Scriven knew more about firearms than anyone else there, and he 'always professed to know all about them', Carnier told the Coroner.[11] In his evidence, Gillbank had stated that no superior officer supervised the arrangements for taking the money away that day – or on any other day – but that arrangement had now changed.

---

9 After years of poor pay, long hours and declining conditions, the grievances culminated in the 1923 Police Strike, when one-third of the Police force refused to go on duty. See Robert Haldane, "Police and Policing", *the Encyclopedia of Melbourne,* 2005, p. 548

10 PROV, VPRS 00030/P0006, Unit 000004, 1936/777; *Report of Inquisition by Coroner,* 7 July 1936

11 PROV, VPRS 00030/P0006, Unit 000004, 1936/777; *Report of Inquisition* by Coroner, 7 July 1936

Aubrey Reeves, *Herald*, 16 December 1936

Major testimony was provided by the closest eyewitness, Aubrey Reeves, a labourer from Kinglake. He had been walking west along Little Lonsdale Street. He saw the yellow cab, with another car behind it, and two men on the footpath behind the car. One was taller than the other. They looked directly at him as he walked past, before stopping to talk to a friend just past the lane at the rear of the Titles Office. Ten minutes later he heard a scrimmage at the car. When he went to approach the men, the taller man, who had a handkerchief tied over his face, pointed the revolver at him. Reeves hopped back a bit, and the man then pointed the revolver at Scriven and shot him. He described the two men as follows: the first was about 28 or 29, about 5'10" or 5'11" (about 178-180 cm) in height, medium build and sallow complexion. He wore a grey hat and a kind of spotted grey suit and his hair was sort of fair. The second man was about the same age, 5'8" or 5'9" (about 175 cm), with a medium build and a complexion similar to the first man, as were his clothes. [12]

The Inquest heard testimony from Reg Pullen, the taxi driver who had bravely chased the bandits. He described how one of the robbers trained his gun on him and told him to 'sit where you are'. When he heard the shot, he got a fright and stalled the

12 PROV,VPRS 00030/P0006, Unit 000004, 1936/777; *Report of Inquisition* by Coroner, 7 July 1936

idling taxi, then saw Scriven lying on the road, with the pistol lying next to him. He jumped out of the taxi and picked up the gun, lying near the front of the taxi, and chased the two men as they ran away and jumped into the Hudson car as it took off. He reached the corner of Queen Street and saw a motorbike coming, so he hopped on the back and told the rider to 'Chase that car, he has just shot my cobber'. But at the corner of Latrobe Street, the car had disappeared because the motorbike was not fast enough. Pullen returned to the crime scene, where they were waiting for the ambulance to arrive, and handed the pistol over to an official of the Stamps Office, saying 'I should not have picked up that gun, I have rubbed all the fingerprints off it now.' Pullen told the Inquest that the man who bailed him up in the taxi (and then shot Scriven) was about 35 years of age, between 5'6" (167 cm) to 5' 9" (175 cm), thick set, broad-shouldered, wearing a sort of grey suit and a grey hat pulled down.

Another witness, Robert Archibald Foy, told the Inquest that he had just parked in Little Lonsdale Street when he heard a shot and ran towards Queen Street. He saw the Hudson go past him, noting that the driver seemed to be having trouble getting the car into gear – it did not seem as if he could get it into second gear. Then he was passed by the taxi-driver, on foot and waving a gun around. When he climbed onto the back of a motorcycle, Foy was certain that someone would get shot. He took the number of the dark blue Hudson, but didn't have a pencil so scratched the number on his hand with piece of a match.

The Coroner then heard from Keith Gruer, who saw the whole thing as he walked along Little Lonsdale Street towards William Street. A motorcyclist, Norman Semmens, told the Coroner that he was riding his motorcycle (and sidecar) west along Little Lonsdale Street. As he crossed Queen Street, he heard a shot and then saw two men (one carrying a bag) run to the waiting Hudson car, which then took off. He noted the number of the car and that the number plate was dilapidated.

William John Smith also described the getaway of the Hudson. He had been travelling west on Latrobe Street, when the Hudson overtook him on the right hand side. He noticed a bit of confusion in the car and the near side door was partly open. There were three men in the car, which turned at Spencer Street and then turned in to the Destructor Yard at Lonsdale Street.

Other witnesses included John Boadle, the engineer superintendent at the Destructor Yard, who had testified about the getaway car being driven into the yard, and Harry Johnstone, the stoker from the Yard. They both described the three men who had driven in. These descriptions would be challenged constantly in subsequent events.

Watching the Destructor Yard from across Lonsdale Street, Leslie Jackson described to the Inquest how he had seen a car containing three men as it rushed around from Spencer Street, zigzagged all over the road and went into the east gate of the Yard. Standing with two other fellows, Jackson made the comment that there must be a job being done. How right he was. He described how the driver came out and stood in front of the gate in Lonsdale Street for about five minutes. Jackson described him as a 'very powerful and big man with a rather sallow complexion and dark eyes, dressed in a blue suit, with a sort of light blue hat'.

The Coroner also heard from George Theodore, who had found the leather bag and cashbox in the sea at Brighton on February 2, and from Joseph Selkridge, a driver from Prahran, who told the inquest that he had seen the Hudson car in Acland Street, St Kilda on January 29, whilst he was assisting the driver of an ice wagon. He also heard from Martin Foster, of East Melbourne, the owner of the Hudson car used in the robbery, and from Rupert Dawborn, a motor salesman who had sold the car to Foster. On January 20 he had been driving along Elizabeth Street on the fringe of the city when he saw two men in the car. He followed them through Carlton but lost them in the streets of Fitzroy.

More evidence about the car came from Albert Gray, a motorman from Caulfield, employed by the Tramways Board. Just after Christmas of 1936 he was painting his front fence when two men approached him on foot and asked whether he could paint a car for them. The next day three men brought a car to his house and asked if he could paint it in six days as they were intended going on a trip to Queensland. The car was in a bad state and he told them it would take a fortnight to paint it, which did not suit them. Two of the men were in their early twenties, slim and with fair hair. The older man was about 40, of stout build and looked like a footballer or fireman, and was called Arthur by the younger men. The next time he saw the car was at Russell Street after the robbery and murder. A police witness, Detective Wightman, testified that he had attended the City Council Destructor Yard, where he saw the black Hudson car, with a number plate of 86730. On the floor he found a grey hat and a pair of flannel sports trousers. The car was then driven to Russell Street.

Further testimony came from William Allen, a gunsmith who examined a Webley-Scott pistol, bullets and shell casings for the police. In his opinion, the bullets were fired from the Webley pistol. But this was hardly conclusive in the emerging world of forensic science and crime. The Official Police photographer, Frederick Hobley, had taken the gun and bullets to Mr Allen, as well as conducting comparison photographs in Sydney at the Police laboratory. His conclusion was also that the bullet produced at the Inquest was fired from the pistol produced at the Inquest.

It was a matter of great concern to the Coroner that large amounts of money were being banked daily and the suggestion that an escort was inadequate was to some extent supported by the evidence. He observed that those departments responsible should obtain the advice of police officials or other competent persons as to the best means of escort, and when suitable instructions are issued they should see that these instructions are carried out. The last comment probably related to the lack of training in the use of pistols. However, as the Coroner had discovered, Scriven was not carrying the pistol provided for escort duty when he was shot. [13] Following the remarks of the Coroner, the cause was immediately taken up by the Secretary of the Victorian Branch of the Australian Public Servants Association, Mr McKellar. He began to push for a Government armoured car, sufficient for all departments, which would avoid much of the risks of violence experienced by escorts. The proposal was not seriously entertained by the government but was later adopted by government departments and the private sector. Today they are common sights on the streets of Melbourne. [14]

Much of the evidence produced at the Inquest would form the basis for witness statements in subsequent hearings and trials. Details and recollections would be challenged and a major characteristic of the whole affair would be a failure to properly identify those subsequently charged.

13 *The Argus*, 8 July 1936
14 *The Argus*, 9 July 1936

On 7 July 1936, the Coroner returned a finding that Scriven 'died from the effects of a bullet wound in the head feloniously and maliciously inflicted on him...by a person or persons to me unknown'. In plain language, he was murdered.[15] Ironically, the day after the Coroners Inquest concluded, a stir was caused in the Stamps Office, still located within the Titles Office, when a report from a pistol rang through the premises. For a few horrifying moments, staff thought that another hold-up had occurred. It was a huge relief to all when it was found that the shot had been fired accidentally from an automatic pistol being taken from a holster by a cashier to place it beside his cash register. Whilst the bullet was embedded harmlessly in the woodwork of a counter, clearly there was still an issue with the use of guns. [16] Pistols were retained in the Office for many years. In 1970 the Registrar of Titles wrote to the Secretary of the Law Department, expressing the opinion that there was no longer any need for pistols on the premises. Despite the opinion of the police that pistols should be retained, the Registrar regarded their retention as useless. In his view, pistols in inexperienced hands could be more of a liability than an asset and their possession could result in physical harm to the cashiers and possibly to other members of the staff or to the public. [17]

The police were still pursuing Doug Brown, but after months of investigating and shadowing, they had three other suspects. William John Cody was a 25 year old labourer and career criminal who also used the aliases of Frank Harsden, William Marston and Mr Rayner. Already balding, he had a

15 PROV, VPRS 00030/P0006, Unit 000004, 1936/777; *Report of Inquisition by Coroner,* 7 July 1936

16 *The Argus,* 9 July 1936

17 Letter dated 8 January, 1970, from Land Victoria archives; see also Robin Grow, *Safe as Houses*, 2013

narrow face with prominent cheekbones. His fellow suspects were the Davies brothers, Rupert and Geoffrey, who were in the illegal starting-price bookmaking business and also operated as stand-over men in Collingwood. Rupert was described as about 5'10" tall (177 cm), of medium build and of fresh complexion, with blue eyes and brown hair which he styled in the fashion of the day – slicked back, with a centre part and cut short above his ears. His older brother Geoffrey was similar in appearance and build and hairstyle – although his was longer.

The three had plenty of form and were enmeshed in the criminal world prevalent in the inner city suburbs of Collingwood and neighbouring Fitzroy. Rupert also had links to the wharves, a hotbed of crime in Melbourne in the 1930s. Cody had been convicted in 1931 of robbery in company while armed with an offensive weapon. He had robbed a woman at an ink manufacturing company in South Melbourne of £100. Cody had meant business, as

William Cody, *Police Gazette, 1937, No. 15,* courtesy Victorian Police Museum

the gun was fully loaded and the safety catch was released. He was currently on parole.[18]

Rupert had left home at age 14 to travel with a carnival. In 1934 he was convicted of stealing wheels from a wagon owned by a coachbuilder in Hoddle Street. He received a two-month sentence, suspended on a bond to be of good behaviour for twelve months. It was his first conviction but he would be a regular visitor to the courts from then on with convictions for larceny, breach of parole and trespass on railways in New South Wales. The Davies family lived in Easey Street, where Thomas Davies was listed as occupying No. 186 in the mid-1930s. The house has gone now, replaced in the 1970s. Leitha (nee Alderson), the mother of Rupert and Geoffrey,[19] ran a small book shop nearby in a two-storey building in Smith Street, Collingwood, one of numerous small shopkeepers trying to eke out a living. The shop was a regular gathering place for her sons and their

---

18 *The Argus,* 2 February 1931

19 There were two other brothers. Cliff had lost part of an arm when riding on a freight train looking for work with his brothers in NSW. He spent much time in his workshop working on devices to help him to overcome his disability. Roy served in the Great War. Living in Lilydale and working as a driver, he joined up on 25 May 1916, aged 19. He went to Signal School at Broadmeadows and embarked for Britain in October 1916, and then to France on 21 December. He was in hospital at Etaples on 26 December, with regular stints in hospital (including at Rouen), before being posted to Belgium in July 1917. He was treated for albuminuria (a kidney disease), advanced cystitis, and an irritable bladder and was probably gassed, as these conditions were associated with gas and Rouen was a centre for gas victims. He transferred to a motorised unit in January 1919 and went back to England, but more illness delayed his return to Australia until October 1919. Discharged in January 1920 as a private, he suffered continual ill health until he died in 1941. Family members recall a large photograph of him in the stairwell at 462 Smith Street. *Records of Roy James Davies, Australian Military Forces,* Australian Imperial Force, Attestation paper of persons enlisted for service abroad, Series B2455, http://recordsearch.naa.gov.au/, accessed April 16, 2015

friends.[20] Another meeting place was the Gasometer Hotel, about a hundred yards away – a regular haunt for criminals such as the Davies brothers, known as 'stand-over' men and SP bookies in the district. Still operating today, as a re-invented (and brightly painted) 'Gastro Pub', it was well known to police and it was no surprise to them when it was bombed in 1951. The chief suspects were two prominent local stand-over men. [21]

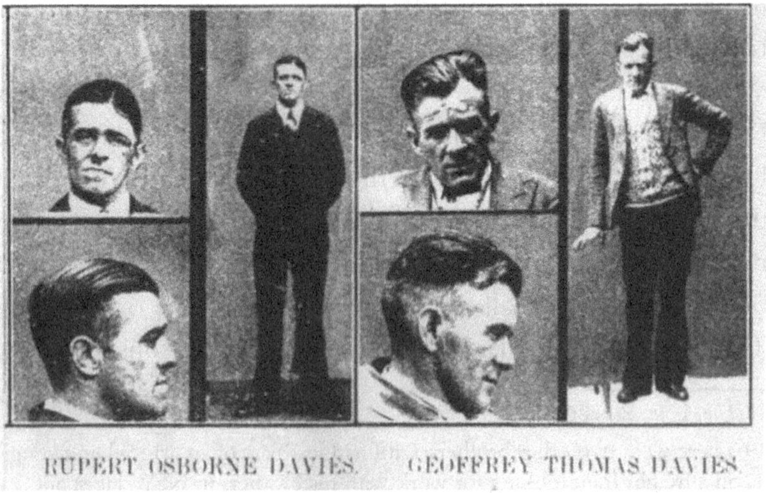

Rupert and Geoffrey Davies, *Police Gazette, 1937, No. 15,* courtesy Victorian Police Museum

Senior Detective 'Bill' Davis later claimed that he first suspected Cody in about March of 1936, just after he was assigned to the case. Davis considered that Rupert Davies had fired the shot that killed Scriven while other police thought that Cody was the more likely murderer. Believing that Cody's mother

20 Rupert's grandchildren recall meetings held under the shop by Rupert and Geoffrey. By candlelight, men (in hats and coats) would come and give money to the brothers. Communications with members of the Davies family, January 2015

21 *The Argus,* 3 September 1951

and sister were going to give evidence for Cody to provide an alibi, Davis, accompanied by Detective Delmenico, interviewed Cody's mother and her daughter Mrs McLaughlin in March 1936 in an attempt to find Cody. When McLaughlin was out of the room, Mrs Cody told the detectives that 'Billy' had left for Culcairn (NSW) a few days after New Year's Day to work on a road contract. He was travelling with a friend of hers called Arthur, who had driven to Melbourne in his truck. Whilst Mrs Cody was obviously trying to provide an alibi for her son, McLaughlin did not appreciate her cooperating with the police. When she entered the room, she turned on her mother and said; 'Why do you talk to them? They only came here to get your bloody guts. Don't tell them where he is.' She soon confirmed the story that her mother had told the detectives. The next day they travelled to Culcairn and interviewed a road contractor named Arthur Patterson. He told them that he had been living as 'man and wife' with Mrs Cody when he was in Melbourne. He then told them that when he returned from Melbourne in early January, Cody was not with him and had never been with him at Culcairn at any time. Cody soon revealed his whereabouts when he sent a letter (in his handwriting) to the Secretary of the Indeterminate Sentences Board, Mr Dicker, on March 31. It was posted from Hamilton, NSW, about two miles from Newcastle. The

Gasometer Hotel, Smith Street, 2015

Board acted as a controller for prisoners on parole and Cody's letter informed Dicker that he was carrying out the conditions of his parole and had been travelling around NSW for the last six months and staying away from trouble.[22] No doubt the Board (and its successors) would have received many similar letters from prisoners on parole. Davis would have been sceptical, at the very least, about its veracity. He was now more certain than ever that Cody had been involved in the robbery and murder. However, none of these suspicions were aired at the Coroners' Inquest in July and did not emerge until November.[23]

The CIB had been in turmoil after the shooting of Brophy and the resignation of Blamey. They were still extremely embarrassed that, by September 1936, no charges had been laid for the murder of Scriven and a number of other serious crimes. A reward of £250 had been offered in the early days after the killing. In September it was recommended to the Ministry that the reward for the Scriven murder be doubled to £500. This time the reward included the offer of a King's free pardon for anyone who gave information leading to a conviction, provided that the informant did not actually commit the crime.[24]

One line of thinking was that the best source of a tip-off would come from an informer within the criminal world, particularly someone involved with the killers, even if on the fringes. Police relied on tips from informers and also made a habit of 'verballing', where they would write a supposed confession on behalf of an accused who would not confess. If they were able to get hold of a signature from the accused, it could be forged

22 PROV,VPRS 00030/P0006, Unit 000004, 1936/777; *undated letter from Detective Davis to Mr Chapple, Law Department; undated letter from William Cody to Mr Dicker at the Indeterminate Sentences Board*

23 *The Argus*, 28 November 1936

24 *Border Watch (Mount Gambier, South Australia)*, 10 September 1936

onto the concocted confession. These documents were often not sufficient to present to a Judge and jury but could be used to convince a co-accused (or informer) that the accused had implicated them in the crime. Whilst the amount of £500 was substantial in those days, the fear of retribution was apparently stronger, as no one came forward to claim the reward. The police failed to convince informers or underworld figures to take the money. During November, Detective Delmenico and other policemen grilled Harold Vivian (Toddy) Rhodes, an associate of the Davies brothers, for two to three hours about painting the getaway car. He denied any involvement, despite being reminded of the £500 reward. 'You wouldn't expect me to get up and give evidence like that in court', he said.[25]

A special CIB squad had been set up, comprising Sergeants O'Keeffe and Carey, Constables Davis, Rickerdick, Sloan, McKeogh, Hogg, Abbott, Delmenico, Tannahill, Tremewen, Simpson, White, Mooney, Guider, Bolton, R. Byrne, H. Byrne, Tauschke, Birrell, Stehn, Batemean, Benton, Fox, Aylett, Suttie, Sweeney and, of course, Cairns. The team was still on the alert for Doug Brown but had also been instructed to watch the Davies brothers and Cody in late August (a job that fell to Cairns). The suspects were shadowed by officers on foot and in cars. Cairns was given no descriptions of the men but was told to watch them. He observed Cody ride his motorcycle to 78 Easey Street and to a house in Wellington Street on a number of occasions in early September.[26] Cody's mother lived at 272 Wellington Street and he had taken a room at 452 Wellington Street when he returned from NSW. His landlady, Maver Gooch, told police

25 PROV, VPRS 00030/P0006, Unit 000004, 1936/777; *Statement by Rhodes,* 22 March 1937

26 PROV, VPRS 00030/P0006, Unit 000004, 1936/777; *statement by Constable Cairns,* n.d.

that Cody's sister had organised the room for him, at 10/6 per week. She described his daily routine – seldom home in the evening, usually came in at 11.00 p.m. or 11.30 p.m., and was always home by 1.00 a.m. He sometimes carried a flat leather case with him. During his stay he rode a motorbike with a NSW number plate and he had an accident with a cab in Johnston Street, Collingwood. In his room he had a pair of rubber gloves and some bottles 'which contained some liquid which smelt funny and had a glass cork or stopper'. He had stayed there for about nine weeks, leaving in September. [27]

Cairns eventually received descriptions that accorded with the descriptions of the Scriven killers. They were vague but were enough to raise suspicions as to why he was shadowing the men. The descriptions were provided via a private police circular, issued only to police working on the Scriven case. [28]

In late September, Constable Cairns, Constable E R Suttie and another constable were following Cody and Geoffrey Davies along Smith Street, in the heart of Collingwood. The talk on the streets was all about the VFL Grand Final between Collingwood and South Melbourne, to be played the following week. Could Collingwood repeat their famous premiership win of 1935? They had seen their champion full-forward, Gordon Coventry, cruelly suspended from playing in the match by the VFL Tribunal and South was playing great football. Despite being strong Collingwood supporters, it probably wasn't football that was occupying the minds of the suspected armed robbers and murderers. They had no illusions about who was following them. After being joined by Rupert Davies, who arrived on his pushbike, they stopped and talked to various men and pointed

27 PROV, VPRS 00030/P0006, Unit 000004, 1936/777; *statement by Maver Gooch*, n.d.

28 *The Sun News-Pictorial*, 28 November 1936

significantly at their shadowers. Finally Geoffrey Davies had had enough – he stopped, turned around and walked back to the police and said: 'We all know you're a bunch of ------- coppers. We know your names and addresses and the names and addresses of the four mugs sitting by the car in Perry Street (close to Easey Street in Collingwood) the other day.[29] We know the registration of every car in Russell Street.[30] My life's not worth anything but I guarantee I get a dozen of you fellows before I go out.' Was this just bluster on the part of Geoffrey Davies, who had no record of shooting anyone? His brother, Rupert, then joined in. 'The next time we see you out here there'll be some cleaning up. You can tell the others that. We will look after them all.' Constable Suttie knew that they were suspects, but did not know what for – or whether their threats were genuine.[31] In fact, the brothers and Cody were often armed – one family member recalls that when they would go to dinner at their mother's, they would take off their guns and give 'ma' a kiss.[32]

This encounter amounted to a declaration of war and the shadowing of the three now intensified throughout October, with Cairns in particular spending time watching the houses of the suspects in Collingwood. Two weeks after the encounter, on October 12, Chief Inspector Alexander Duncan, head of Scotland Yard's famous Flying Squad, arrived in Melbourne.[33] His task was to inspect, report on and improve the Victorian

29 Geoffrey Davies lived in Perry Street, Collingwood

30 The fact that the numbers of all the police cars were known to the criminal world was one of the reasons given by Brophy for taking the car of a civilian to his meeting in Royal Park

31 PROV, VPRS 00030/P0006, Unit 000004, 1936/777; *notes of Constable Suttie,* n.d.

32 Communication with members of the Davies family, January 2015

33 Duncan had been the head of the famous 'Flying Squad' that played a large role in reducing serious crime in London. *Cairns Post (Queensland),* 6 June 1936

Police Force. It is likely that he would have been unimpressed by the progress being made on solving a number of major crimes, including the Scriven murder.

The shadowing soon resulted in the arrest of Cody in one of the most dramatic scenes of a turbulent decade in Melbourne. The first week of November is one of highlights on the calendar of Melbourne. The Spring Racing Carnival starts with the Victoria Derby on Saturday and is followed by the Melbourne Cup on Tuesday and the Oaks meeting on the Thursday. The Melbourne Cup, regarded as Australia's major thoroughbred horse race, is held annually on the first Tuesday of November. For the people of Melbourne, it is a public holiday and a cause of much chattering and betting. The cup is a handicap race open to all horses aged three-years-old and above and attracts huge crowds to Melbourne's famed Flemington Racecourse. It is also the cause of many social events in Melbourne. On a hot day in 1936, over 110,000 racegoers watched a rank outsider from New Zealand, Wotan, take home the Cup in record time and at odds of over 100 to 1, much to the delight of the bookies. The fashion highlight of the Carnival is Oaks Day on the Thursday. In attendance were the Governor-General, Lord Gowrie, and Lady Gowrie, as well as the Governor of Victoria, Lord Huntingfield, and Lady Huntingfield. Oaks Day is traditionally a day for women to dress up and this year was no exception. A huge crowd of fashion-conscious ladies gathered – but Melbourne's fickle weather was a cause of consternation. Would they need to wear a mackintosh by the end of the day? The hot, dusty morning caused many to turn out in white suits of linen or crepe, protected from the sun by white panama hats trimmed with black petersham. Wearing a large hat meant risking losing it to the strong winds. Many carried a fur wrap, suspicious of the notoriously changeable Melbourne weather. The *Adelaide Advertiser* summed up the day as follows: 'Studying the huge crowd of well-dressed women today one could not help noticing that everything in dressing is in the finish and the grooming. The perfectly dressed hair, the perfect shoes and stockings, the restrained makeup and so on.' [34]

But not everyone was at the races on Thursday. Some were about to participate in a frightening cable car tram ride through Fitzroy. Melbourne had a massive cable car network at that stage. Trams operated by being connected to cables laid beneath the road with the connection to the tram being operated by a motorman or driver. The front section of the cable car was called the dummy. This is where the driver (or gripman) stood to control the tram. It was roofed, but not enclosed, and included seats for a number of passengers, generally on outward-facing benches that ran the length of the dummy. There was also space for standing passengers where patrons were allowed to smoke. The second section was like a trailer, called the saloon or 'the car'. It was enclosed, but had windows, and seated 22 passengers on longitudinal seats. Sliding doors gave access to open platforms at each end. [35] Once a cable car had a good speed up, it was difficult to stop – consequently they often sped through intersections (where car drivers were required to stop) without even decreasing their speed. [36]

Cable car, Melbourne, see http://melbourneblogger.blogspot.com.au

34 *Adelaide Advertiser*, 6 November 1936
35 John Keating, *Mind the Curve! A History of the Cable Trams,* 1970, p. 78
36 *The Argus*, 8 February 1937

Constable Jim Cairns, in plain clothes and armed, saw Cody and Geoffrey Davies leave Easey Street at about 1.30 p.m. and walk towards Smith Street. They caught a cable car heading towards the city and Cairns boarded the same tram.[37] Cairns later told an interviewer that his companion, Constable Howlett, didn't catch the tram as he couldn't run fast enough, but he rang Russell Street for assistance. As the tram approached Johnston Street, Cairns saw Davies and Cody move onto the rear platform. The tram turned right into Gertrude Street and then left into Nicholson Street, past the engine house on the corner. Cairns saw a grey police car (the Grey Streak) coming towards them, containing detectives. It passed the tram and then turned back. Cairns, who was in the car of the tram, watched Cody and Davies carefully. When the police car began following the tram, he saw Cody grab Davies' arm and say something, then stiffen and stand up. When Cairns endeavoured to slip his hand into his pocket where he had an automatic pistol, Cody jumped through the rear door of the car and jammed his .32 revolver into Cairns' ribs and fired, but the gun didn't go off. He told Cairns: 'Sit down and drop that rod!' 'All right Bill,' replied Cairns as he complied and sat down. Cairns pushed him aside and Cody backed away, keeping his gun trained on Cairns, before turning and running through the car. He jumped over the division (railing) between the rear car and the dummy, threatening passengers as he waved his pistol around and climbed onto the dummy, before leaping off. Cairns then moved towards Geoffrey Davies, who was still on the rear platform and just about to step off. Cairns jammed

37 Melbourne's cable car network was being electrified but work on the line along Nicholson Street had not yet commenced. There was enormous pressure on the Metropolitan Tramways Board by various municipalities to convert the lines in their district, which often resulted in extension of tramlines and connection with other lines. *The Argus,* 28 November 1936

his pistol into his ribs and said, 'Don't move.' Davies did not appear to be armed and Cairns pushed him off the tram into the arms of Detective Delmenico, who had alighted from the police car. Davies was hustled into a police car. As Cairns jumped from the rear platform of the tram, he saw Cody take off into the Exhibition Gardens in Nicholson Street, running to the west.

Cairns, a champion distance runner and decathlete, then joined in the pursuit of Cody as he ran across to the Exhibition Gardens. There were a number of bystanders in the popular public space. [38] The car containing police had driven into the gardens. Constable Alf Guider had also taken off on foot after Cody, who took aim at Guider and fired at him over his left shoulder. Cairns saw Guider dodge a bullet, and then call out to Cody to stop. When he continued to run, Guider fired three shots at Cody, who turned and fired again at Guider. The pistol jerked down and did not discharge. Increasingly desperate, Cody kept trying to manipulate his pistol with both hands as he ran. Guider's pistol was empty. He yelled out to Cairns, telling him that that he had no more bullets left. Cairns continued the chase, letting off a shot at Cody, who turned to shoot back. But again, his pistol failed. Cairns fired another shot at Cody whilst Guider kept advancing. Cairns later claimed that he had no intention of shooting Cody and deliberately fired into the air. [39] Aware

Constable Alf Guider, *The Herald*, 17 December 1936

38 The Exhibition Gardens was one of a number of sites that had become notorious haunts for robberies in the 1930s. A new 'race of assault and robbery men' had appeared, and prowled regularly in the gardens and the riverside parks close to Melbourne. *The Argus,* 11 February 1950

39 Interview with Robin Hughes for the Australia Biography Project, 22 May 1998 http://www.australianbiography.gov.au/subjects/cairns/interview1.html

that Guider was out of bullets, Cairns cried out, 'Look out Alf, his gun is jammed but he'll probably work it loose.' Cody tried to fire again but his gun was still jammed. He then tried to run backwards to obtain cover from a tree, with Cairns yelling, 'Look out Alf, he's waiting.' Having decided not to continue, Cody stood holding the revolver at his side, about 30 feet (or nine metres) away from his pursuers. Guider approached him from the right and Cairns from the left. Guider reached him first and pulled the gun from his hand. Cairns then arrived and pushed his gun into Cody's ribs. Resigned to his capture, Cody said, 'I have had enough.' According to Cairns at a later time, Guider then said 'Shoot the bastard. No,' replied Cairns. 'He hasn't got a gun.' [40]

Cody later claimed that his gun had gone off by accident and had not been pointed at Guider. He was arrested and placed in a van with Geoffrey Davies and the two were taken to Russell Street for questioning. In the car, Davies told police that he did not know Cody and had not been with him. A

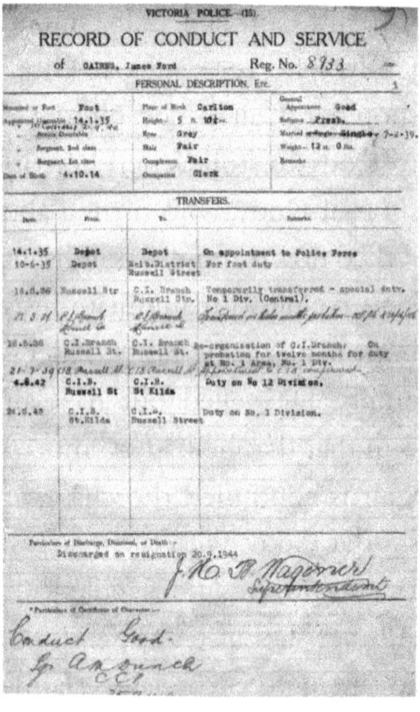
VICTORIA POLICE—(15).

RECORD OF CONDUCT AND SERVICE

of CAIRNS, James Ford Reg. No. 8933

PERSONAL DESCRIPTION, Etc.

Foot
14.1.35
4.10.14
Carlton
5 ft. 10½ in.
Grey
Fair
Fair
Clerk
Good
Presb.
Single
12 st. 0 lbs.

TRANSFERS.

Date	From	To	Remarks
14.1.35	Depot	Depot	On appointment to Police Force
10-6-35	Depot	Melb. District Russell Street	For foot duty
14.8.36	Russell Str	C.I. Branch Russell Str.	Temporarily transferred - special duty. No 1 Div. (Central).
18.5.38	C.I. Branch Russell St.	C.I. Branch Russell St.	Re-organisation of C.I. Branch: On probation for twelve months for duty at No. 1 Area, No. 1 Div.
4.8.42	C.I.B. Russell St	C.I.B. St Kilda	Duty on No 12 Division.
24.8.43	C.I.B. St.Kilda	C.I.B. Russell Street	Duty on No. 1 Division.

Discharged on resignation 20.9.1944

Conduct Good.

Police record for Jim Cairns, courtesy Victorian Police Museum

40 *The Argus*, 28 November 1936; Cairns later recalled that seven years later, after Cody was released from gaol for the shooting offences, he arrived at the Cairns house with a large bunch of flowers for Cairns' wife, Gwen, in gratitude for Cairns not shooting him that day. From John Silvester, *The Age*, 24 August 2013

witness of the chase later told a reporter from the *Age* of 'the hail of bullets that drove card players and park denizens from their seats.'[41] Much of the later evidence showed a large discrepancy in the number of shots fired by both parties.

When Cody arrived at the watchhouse at about 2.30 p.m., he was refused bail and remanded in custody. The police regarded him as highly dangerous and were convinced that he was the man responsible for shooting Scriven. Detective Sergeant O'Keeffe questioned Cody, saying: 'On the 31st of last January James Edward Scriven was held up outside the Titles Office and fatally shot whilst escorting a clerk with £1758 in money. You have been identified by Geoffrey Davies as one of the participants in that crime'. Cody said, 'You are making a mistake'. O'Keefe then told Cody that he had been identified as one of the men seen in the Destructor Yard leaving the stolen Hudson and carrying a bag containing the stolen money. He asked, 'What did you do with the money?' Cody said, 'Why is this all necessary; I have the right not to answer any questions.' When O'Keeffe asked him where he was on January 31, Cody replied that he didn't know. O'Keeffe then asked him about making trips to Brisbane, with Cody admitting that he had made two trips last year, by 'jumping the rattler.' They also questioned him about carrying a fully loaded gun on the tram and shooting at police in the Exhibition Gardens. He had seen the detectives coming up in the car. When he was asked why he would run away and shoot at them, he replied saying that he did not want to go to gaol.[42] He was questioned for hours (until about midnight) about the murder and eventually O'Keeffe told him that he would be charged with murder.[43]

---

41 *The Age,* 24 August 2013

42 PROV, VPRS 00030/P0006, Unit 000004, 1936/777; *notes of Detective O'Keeffe*, n.d.

43 PROV, VPRS 00030/P0006, Unit 000004, 1936/777; *Proceedings of trial*, 22 June 1937

When Geoffrey Davies was questioned about 9.00 p.m. on November 5, he claimed that Cody carried out the Scriven shooting in the company of two men from Sydney – Stan (from Waterloo) and Bill (from Redfern). Stan was to walk up and do the shooting, whilst Cody grabbed the bag of money. Stan was to do the driving with Bill on the running board of the car. They had stored the car in Fitzroy or East Brunswick. They were desperate men who lived in Fitzroy and there will be shooting when you go for them, they have the doors bolted and a wardrobe up against the front door. He described how Cody had come to his home that day, and they had travelled on the tram on their way to the beach. Davies knew that the police were following them.‘ Those bloody fellows follow you and get on your nerves,’ he said, admitting that he and Cody had previously threatened to shoot the police if they were being shadowed. When Detective Carey asked him why he was with Cody on the tram that day, Davies expressed regret that he had been there, but they were both feeling the pressure after having been tailed for some time. Cody was ‘on the key’, meaning that he would not go back to prison and had threatened to give the police ‘a go’ if they go out there to try and take him back. Cody had been warned about continuing to carry his gun: ‘As late as dinner time today (ie the mid-day meal), my old man asked him to dump his revolver, and he would not do it.’ [44] On the tram he told Cody to get rid of his gun but he drew it and went though the tramcar. When police told Davies that they believed that he and his brother Rupert were with Cody when Scriven was murdered, he told them that ‘You need not worry about me. My brother and I were on sustenance work for Collingwood Council on the day that Scriven was shot and we

44 *The Argus,* 28 November 1936

can bring in the foreman and fifty witnesses. You can look up the records and you will find that we were working that day.'[45] Geoffrey had not shown any hesitation about dropping Cody in for the shooting but was extremely concerned about protecting his younger brother.

On the evening of November 5, Senior-Detective F W Rickerdick visited Rupert's house at 78 Easey Street and noted that most of the furniture (bedroom and dining room suites) was new as were the heavy silk carpet and linoleum. The house also contained new women's clothing, including a new fur-coat. Rupert was married to Kathleen Elizabeth (nee Williams) a local girl whose family still resided at 38 Derby Street and would later claim she had bought the coat from her own funds.[46] But Rupert was at his mother's shop at 462 Smith Street, Collingwood when picked up by Detective Tannahill. On the way to Russell Street, Davies asked him 'What is this all about?' 'You will be told later,' said Tannahill, whose job it was to take him to Russell Street, not discuss the case with him.[47] Detectives first asked Davies how long he had known Cody. 'About 12 months', he replied. He was then asked the same questions as Cody about the Scriven shooting. Rupert told O'Keeffe that he was making a mistake. He told police that he didn't know where he was on that day and was told that Geoffrey had said that the brothers were working on sustenance for the Collingwood Council on that day. Davies then responded, 'Yes, I think I was.'[48] Davies was told he would be charged with murder, and he joined his

45 PROV, VPRS 00030/P0006, Unit 000004, 1936/777; *notes of Detective O'Keeffe,* n.d.

46 *The Argus,* 28 November 1936

47 PROV, VPRS 00030/P0006, Unit 000004, 1936/777; *proceedings of trial,* 22 June 1937.

48 PROV, VPRS 00030/P0006, Unit 000004, 1936/777; *proceedings of trial,* 22 June 1937. Davies made no reference to a meeting in a pub with Geoffrey and a friend called Parkes, which would later be relied upon.

brother and Cody in the City watchhouse, a T-shaped building in Russell Street, next door to today's Victorian University. The Victoria Police Gazette on November 19, 1936 lists 27 arresting officers, including O'Keeffe, Carey, Delmenico, Rickerdick, Guider and Cairns, all members of the special CIB squad. The three were also charged with larceny of a motorcar belonging to Edwin Foster from East Melbourne.

The police were now vigorously working with witnesses to positively identify Cody and the Davies brothers as the culprits. Much of the subsequent evidence provided depended on descriptions of those involved. Cody and the Davies brothers were described as follows when they were photographed:

	William Cody	**Geoffrey Davies**	**Rupert Davies**
Year of birth, age	1911, 25	1904,32	1909,27
Height	5'5"	5'7"	5'11"
Hair	Fair	Fair	Dark brown
Eyes	Grey	Grey	Blue
Complexion	Sandy	Fair	Medium
Build	Thin	Medium	Thin
Native of:	Victoria	Victoria	Victoria
Occupation	Labourer	Dealer	Storeman

No rule of law in Victoria laid down what method should be used to identify an accused person. What was needed (and assumed by many to be in place) was a system that was fair and impartial to the suspect and witnesses, while giving the police a system that could not subsequently be challenged (in the Court and on appeal) on the basis of prejudice being shown by officials.[49]

Subsequently, much criticism was directed at the Victorian police for their methods of identification. Two of the major

49 *The Argus,* 15 March 1937

methods generally used were line-ups and photographs. In a line-up, suspects were included in a group of persons of similar age, build, height and body shape, and the witness was asked to select the offender. Sometimes the line-up was conducted under bright lights with the persons identifying them standing in the shadows, a favourite method of American police forces. How were candidates for the line-up selected? Some were approached by plain-clothes constables in the vicinity of Russell Street and asked 'Would you take part in an identification parade?' for which they would be paid an amount of two shillings. They were then taken into the yard and told to stand against a wall. When a suspect joined the group, he would often complain that those taking part were no good to him if they differed greatly from him – perhaps they had a different build or were too skinny and too short, and he would have stood out markedly from the others in the group. Arguments often took place with the officer in charge and a suspect would be told to 'take it or leave it'. They often left it. [50]

The Victorian police were becoming reluctant to use the line-up and often did not use one at all, such as in the Scriven case. However, suspects were sometimes paraded individually. When Cody, who was already in custody, was shown to a witness John Dugan at the police station, singly and not in a line-up, he identified him, both in appearance and by recognising his voice. This led the legal team of the accused to later describe identification methods in this case as of deliberate and calculated unfairness, stating that 'even in the small towns of New South Wales no system other than the 'parade' system was used', a statement that was certainly open to challenge. [51] Never slow at criticising the eastern states, the situation was described in a Perth

50 *The Argus,* 20 August 1938
51 *The Argus,* 29 May 1937

newspaper as 'Victoria's Rafferty Rules for Identification'.[52] The taxi-driver, Reg Pullen, was shown Rupert Davies by himself under lights, but could not identify him. Boadle, the engineer from the City Destructor, was firstly shown thousands of photographs, which included one of Cody, but none of Rupert or Geoffrey Davies. He picked out a number as of interest, including Cody. He was then shown Cody in a group of men, then singly, and positively identified him.[53] Boadle had also been shown a single photograph of Davies. The next day he saw Rupert Davies in a group of about a dozen men, before he was asked to detach himself from the group and walk backwards and forwards by himself in front of the witness. But in no case was the accused presented along with a number of other persons to the view of the witness with a request to say whether any one of them was the person sought. In addition this was ten months after the shooting. It was also two days after Robert Foy, a mechanic from Thornbury, told police that he had seen three men in a Hudson car in Latrobe Street on the day of the shooting, but could not identify them. When he was shown the three accused in the City Watchhouse, he told police that they could have been those he saw in the car, but he could not see enough of them to identify them or anyone else.[54]

The police view of line-ups was supported by some judges who were not satisfied that the line-up was superior to other methods and would not condemn the use of other methods as improper.[55] It was the belief of many that it was the duty of

---

52 *The Daily News, (Perth, West Australia),* 1 June 1937

53 PROV, VPRS 00030/P0006, Unit 000004, 1936/777; *Notes from Snr. Detective Davis,* 3 December 1936

54 PROV, VPRS 00030/P0006, Unit 000004, 1936/777; *statement by Robert Foy,* 11 November 1936

55 Victorian Law Reports, R. v. Davies and Cody (No.2) (1937) Vic Law Report 47; (1937) VLR 226 (11 March 1937) p. 229

trial judges to closely observe the conduct of the police and to reject any evidence that may have been obtained by 'pressure or suggestion or trick'. In some jurisdictions, including England, a trial judge would invariably warn the jury about relying on evidence obtained by showing a suspect singly to a witness, rather than in a 'line-up', and an Appellate Court may even quash a conviction if they thought that evidence obtained in such a way constituted a miscarriage of justice. It was later shown not to have bothered the various judges who would preside over the trials of the three accused. [56]

Photographs were another major method used in investigations. Originally intended to supplement 'line-ups' the method of their use could be problematical in the investigation of crime by the Victorian police. The English police used a system whereby a witness would be shown a collection of about twenty photographs and asked to select one or more that may be a perpetrator of a crime. Photographs were useful where a number of persons of similar size and appearance to a suspect were shown to a witness. The use of a number of photographs introduced the principle of selection, similar to an identification parade.

A practice had developed in Victoria where witnesses in some cases were shown a single photograph and requested to state whether it was a suspect – Yes or No? When a witness was shown a single photograph of an accused, one judge noted that the practice can serve no fair purpose and is certainly improper.[57] The inspection of a photograph of the person in custody before viewing him naturally tends to impress on the

56 Victorian Law Reports, R. v. Davies and Cody (No.2) (1937) Vic Law Report 47; (1937) VLR 226 (11 March 1937) pp. 228

57 Victorian Law Reports, R. v. Davies and Cody (No.2) (1937) Vic Law Report 47; (1937) VLR 226 (11 March 1937) pp. 228

mind the characteristics shown in the photograph. The witness tends to identify the person in custody with the person shown in the photograph rather than with the person whom he saw previously.

At the time of Cody's arrest, other questionable methods were also in place. There was a view in the legal world that submitting a prisoner alone for scrutiny after arrest, pointing out the prisoner as the person suspected or charged, might influence the recollection of a witness and render its independence doubtful and destroy its value.[58] Furthermore, if a witness is shown a single suspect whom he knows is suspected or has been charged with the crime, his tendency will be to think that there is a good reason for his arrest. For their part, the Victorian police regarded their methods as fair 'with honest witnesses'. This is a variation of the argument used by police forces (and totalitarian regimes) all over the world in the face of criticism – that if persons are innocent of crimes, they had nothing to worry about from the police. If only life were that simple.

In this case, some witnesses were taken to the City Court to identify Cody and the Davies brothers as they stood in the dock at one of their hearings AFTER they had been arrested in conjunction with the hold-up and, in some cases, after they had been charged with the murder. For instance, the messenger, Gillbank, was taken to Russell Street on November 12 to see some men who had been arrested. In a room containing powerful lights shining down on the man paraded for view, Gillbank sat in the shadow and could not be seen and was shown Rupert Davies by himself. He stated afterwards that during the robbery he had only a vague impression of a tall man in dark clothes, with a handkerchief over his forehead. The taxi-driver,

58 *The Argus,* 29 May 1937

Reg Pullen, went through a similar process on the next day. After having been shown a photograph of him, he was shown Rupert Davies under the lights after being told that he had been arrested in connection with the hold-up. But he did not identify Davies as the shooter, merely saying that he resembled him. The witness Selkridge was told by police that they believed that Rupert Davies and Cody were the men who had been in the hold-up and that they wanted them to be shown to him. He was taken to the Police Court and shown them in the dock, and then identified them.[59]

In a subsequent trial, it was pointed out that 'the Lord Chief Justice of England had described such methods as indefensible'.[60] The evidence of a witness that he recognised the prisoner as an offender was rendered valueless if it was shown that alleged recognition was made in circumstances that suggested to the witness that the prisoner was in fact the offender or he was believed by authorities to be the offender.[61] When the identification process was regarded as unfair, it followed that the value of the evidence was greatly diminished.

Experience had led the English courts to look for the greatest care to avoid a mistake or prejudice. In their view, a witness, when shown a suspect singly and as the person whom the police have reason to suspect, will be much more likely to identify the man shown as the one in his recollection. On the other hand, if called upon to say whether anyone of a number of persons were the man, his entire mental attitude would be different.

---

59 PROV, VPRS 00030/P0006, Unit 000004, 1936/777; *Statement by Justice Duffy*, no date, concerning the leave to appeal against conviction after the second trial

60 *The Herald*, 18 December 1936

61 *The Argus*, 29 May 1937

William John Cody, aged 25, labourer, was charged with having murdered Scriven on January 31, plus another five charges (having shot at Detective Alf Guider with intent to murder him; having discharged a loaded firearm at Constable Jim Cairns with intent to resist or prevent his lawful arrest; having, as a convicted felon, been in the possession of a pistol; having carried a pistol without a permit; and having consorted with convicted thieves between August 31 and November 6). A number of charges were laid against Geoffrey Davies, aged 32, labourer of Perry Street Collingwood – having shot at Detective Alf Guider with intent to murder him; having discharged a loaded firearm at Constable Jim Cairns with intent to resist arrest; and having consorted with thieves. The first two charges were never going to stick, as Davies had been under the control of detectives whilst the chase through the gardens took place. When the charges were read out, Davies interjected: 'I do not see how I am charged with shooting at Detective Guider when I did not have a gun.' He was told by the magistrate that it was an allegation the police must try and substantiate. His brother, Rupert Davies, aged 27, of Easey Street, Collingwood, was charged with having, at Thornbury on June 19, in company with William Cody and another man, while armed with a revolver, robbed Edward McGuire of £9, together with a charge of having consorted with thieves. They were remanded and the brothers were allowed bail with a bond of £300.[62]

Whilst neither brother had been charged with murder at this stage, the other charges were interesting. All were charged with consorting, defined as being found in the company of criminals four times, a charge used by police to hold criminals in gaol or to add onto more serious charges. In 1931 Chief Commissioner

62 *Chronicle (Adelaide)* 12 November 1936

Blamey had sought to introduce 'a law to regulate the movements of criminals and their associates', such as existed in NSW, partly to deter criminals from other states from taking refuge in Victoria, particularly as Queensland was about to introduce similar legislation.[63] The prominent criminal barrister, J V (Jack) Barry, found himself defending clients arrested for 'vagrancy', which was becoming more popular amongst Melbourne police and was part of the panic which had attacked Melbourne police since the Criminal Consorting Act came into force in NSW.

The new Consorting with Criminals Act was introduced in early 1932 and the first charges were laid under the Act in April 1932. There were concerns in the judiciary about the application of such a law, such as Judge Stretton, the former associate of Judge Macindoe at the Brophy Royal Commission, who had been elevated to the Bench. When he dismissed (on appeal) a three-month sentence for consorting, he expressed the opinion that 'the law against consorting should be construed with great caution, because of the general principles concerning the liberty of the subject'. Other judges supported it. When hearing an appeal against convictions for consorting, Judge Macindoe noted that the provisions of the Act were very severe, but the severity had been taken into account by Parliament when the law was passed.[64] In 1934, when notorious Sydney madam Tilly Devine, accompanied by a friend Dolly Quinn, visited Melbourne, they were charged with consorting, having been seen frequently in the company of undesirable persons. Devine was sentenced to 15 months; Quinn to six. Devine's solicitor asked the court for his client to be discharged if she undertook to leave the State immediately – probably a good outcome for all involved.

63 *The Argus*, 8 July 1931

64 *The Argus*, 24 May 1932

Constable Jim Cairns later joined the Consorting Squad in the early 1940s. He recalled that their job was to go around to hotels and other public places checking whether persons with criminal convictions were associating together. If so they could be charged with consorting. Cairns regarded the Consorting law as 'unjust and discriminatory' as people have certain rights even if they have been convicted.[65]

The Davies brothers engaged Napthali Henry Sonenberg, one of the most experienced criminal lawyers in the city, to represent them. Cody soon followed their lead. He was the obvious advocate for them to turn to. Generally known as Sonny, Sonenberg's path to eminence in his profession had not been easy. Born in Carlton, he had been educated in the State school system before taking the articled law clerks course and being articled to Mr Halsett Dawson. After studying law at Melbourne University, he was admitted to the Bar in 1901 and practiced in all areas of the law. But it was in the criminal law jurisdiction that he was most successful. He made his name with many battles in the rough and tough environment of the Fitzroy Police Court. During the 1930s he defended those charged with a variety of offences, including larceny, those objecting to eviction, consorting, licensing offences, illegal distilling, conspiracy to defraud, indecent assault and malicious wounding, even a tram conductor charged in October 1935 with selling lottery tickets on his tram to try and raise money for the Tramways Cricket Club. More importantly, he accumulated vast experience in the conduct of major trials, many highly dramatic, such as the 1922 trial of Colin Ross for the Gun Alley murder, the trial of Richard Buckley (an associate of Les 'Squizzy' Taylor) for the murder of a bank manager and the

65 Paul Strangio, *Keeper of the Faith*, 2002, p. 43

1928 bombing of the Greek Club in Lonsdale Street.

Sonenberg then began the task of representing the three accused through the process of remand, committal and possible trial. At a remand hearing on November 12, the police prosecutor stated that many charges would be preferred against the three. The next day the Davies brothers were charged with murder in front of a magistrate. The police prosecutor stated that they had been 'identified by a large number of witnesses' as the men who were with Cody when Scriven was shot and later at the Destructor Yard. Not surprisingly, when the magistrate asked if the brothers had anything to say, Geoffrey Davies denied the charges. 'All I have to say is that what they are doing is unjust. As far as my brother and I are concerned, in the eyes of God and the people, we know nothing about it.' Cody objected to the remand, telling the Magistrate: 'I am innocent of the charge. I don't see why I should be held over for longer than is necessary.' Sonenberg protested strongly, saying: 'My clients say that they are innocent and are prepared to go into the box now...there is no reason why there should not be a speedy hearing.' He also pushed the argument that frequent publication of the charges would prejudice public opinion. They had not been able to raise bail and had had not even been served notice of the number of summary charges laid against them. In his view they had been kept improperly in prison. But the magistrate, apparently unimpressed, did not agree and refused bail for Cody and remanded the three once again. A week later, the police were still not ready to proceed, telling the magistrate that they had so many inquiries to make that it was doubtful that they would be ready for the committal hearing scheduled for November 26.

The procedure in Australian courts was for a person accused of a serious charge to face a preliminary (committal) hearing in front of a magistrate, who would determine whether there was sufficient evidence to commit the accused to stand trial and would decide whether a properly instructed jury would convict the accused. Even with a large staff, the police were working day and night on the case. Sonenberg criticised the police strongly, asserting that they should have been able to muster up enough evidence to convince a magistrate that there is a prima facie case, unless it is a very weak case. He continued, 'We are not asking much – we want this trial to come on as quickly as possible, so that these men can be released if they are innocent.' In his view, the police were 'shilly-shallying' and cannot keep three men in custody to suit their convenience. If the charges were not heard soon his clients would likely have to stay in gaol until February. The pressure of the continued delays must have been extremely wearying for the three accused, although perhaps they were content for the process to be drawn out for as long as possible. Another remand was granted.

Finally the committal hearing got under way on November 26 in the Melbourne City Court in front of Mr Freeman, PM. In a sign of things to come over the next 18 months, the committal hearing threw up some sensations. Sonenberg, acting for the three defendants, surprised the police prosecutor by successfully seeking that the witnesses be ordered out of the court at the start of proceedings. The police prosecutor, Detective Sergeant O'Keeffe, caused his own sensation by applying to the bench for suppression of the addresses of the many Crown witnesses who had been subpoenaed. The addresses would not be published or placed in the depositions. Sonenberg protested strongly. 'It would be a scandalous administration of justice if this were allowed,' he stormed, and went on to state 'that the defence case would be jeopardised if representatives were not able to make proper inquiries about witnesses...the accused must have the fullest opportunity of investigating the truth and accuracy of what is deposed to by witnesses.' The Magistrate pointed out that, as a rule, the other side does not attempt to interview the Crown's witnesses. Sonenberg's response was that he may wish to make some inquiries about witnesses and to allow them merely to give names, which may not be their correct ones, amounted to a 'grave injustice' that would not be tolerated in the Supreme Court. In the combative style that characterised many of his court appearances, Sonenberg told the Magistrate that 'We do not care how hard they hit us as long as they allow us to hit back – don't clout us with our hands tied.'[66]

The result was that the Magistrate agreed to the police request. Police need not ask the witnesses their addresses when they gave evidence, but if the defence wished to obtain an address of the witness, application could be made during cross examination. What was the purpose of this application? Were the police concerned that any witnesses would be in danger from the criminal world if their address was disclosed? Or was it a tit-for-tat by the prosecutor after Sonenberg's opening move? Forty-two witnesses were due to be subpoenaed by the Crown and, as it turned out, at least one witness was shot during in the coming months.

The committal hearing showed that Cody and the Davies brothers were now clearly in the frame for the murder of Scriven. A principle in the law saw those involved in armed robberies where murder was committed also charged with the crime, even if they hadn't actually pulled the trigger. A similar situation had arisen in 1923 at the trial of Richard Buckley and Angus Murray, known associates of Les 'Squizzy' Taylor, for the murder

66 *News (Adelaide)*, 26 November 1936

of Thomas Berriman during an armed robbery near Glenferrie Station in Hawthorn. Police were convinced that Taylor had been part of the murder but could not find sufficient evidence to charge him. At the end of that trial, Judge Mann concluded by saying: 'If two men set out in company to rob another, and to do so at all cost, even at the cost of inflicting bodily harm upon the victim, and in the course of their adventure the victim is killed, both the attackers are guilty of murder.'[67] The police asserted that the Davies brothers had been identified by a large number of witnesses as having been with William Cody. Much of the evidence concerned with the charges was presented at the hearing and would again be before the court (and a jury) if the case went to trial. Cody had been identified as the man who, about ten days before the shooting, had engaged James Ezekiel Dugan to repair a pistol for him. Cody offered him £1 to repair a Webley Scott automatic on which the ebonite handle was broken. The next day Dugan repaired the pistol by drilling the handle and affixing two bands of nickel. Cody returned for the gun that night. Dugan did not know that the men wanted him to repair the gun for use in the robbery or for any other unlawful purpose. After he heard of the murder, he was suspicious that he had repaired the pistol used in the offence.

He was reluctant to go to the police because he thought he might have committed a crime in repairing it and was afraid of the whole incident. He was positive that the pistol produced in court was the one that he repaired. But, as it turned out, Dugan had more to worry about from the criminal underworld than from the police.

The clerk from the Stamps Office, Gillbank, gave evidence that he saw Scriven facing two men at the door of the cab –

67 Hugh Anderson, *The Rise and Fall of 'Squizzy' Taylor, a Larrikin Crook*, 1971, p. 166

one put his hand in the cab, grabbed the bag and ran away. At the same time the other shot Scriven. He thought the two men were similar to the Davies brothers but could not positively identify them. As the other key person in the events, his failure to positively identify them must have been a blow for the police prosecutors. The taxi-driver, Reg Pullen, who had a gun pointed at his face, could only state that one of the men 'resembled' Rupert Davies. At least one Crown witness, Aubrey Reeves, would positively identify Rupert Davies as the man who had shot Scriven dead. He gave evidence that he was walking in Little Lonsdale Street near the Titles Office when he saw two men examining a car, who he identified as the Davies brothers. As he was suspicious he walked towards them. But when Rupert Davies pointed a revolver at him, he then tried to get through the gate of a house. Importantly for the prosecution, he was in no doubt that it was Rupert Davies that grabbed Scriven with his left hand and pointed his pistol and fired a shot.

Other witnesses would testify that the Davies brothers resembled men who had taken part in the shooting. The police gave evidence about features of the gun used in the murder that had been subjected to forensic examination. The official police photographer for the CIB, Frederick Hobley, told the hearing that his tests had revealed that the two shells had been fired from the same pistol. The committal hearing also covered the circumstances of the arrest of Davies and Cody, with Constable Cairns recounting the events that led to the arrest of Cody after a wild tram ride along Nicholson Street and a chase through the Exhibition Gardens. But he made it clear that Geoffrey Davies had been arrested and was in a police car when all the shooting took place. 'So he had no part in the mock duel,' said Mr Sonenberg. 'There was no mock duel about it!', Cairns replied angrily. Cairns also gave evidence relating to the recovery of two pistols from the Yarra River at Burnley on August 31 after he had followed the Davies brothers on their motorcycle and sidecar.

When he gave evidence, Geoffrey Davies tried to introduce the shooting of Brophy, in an attempt to be absolved of the charges relating to Scriven, naming Cody, 'Stan and Bill' from Sydney, and another friend of Cody named John Stevens (later to play a major role in proceedings). Stan and Bill 'have supplies of ammunition and Mills bombs and they will use them,' he claimed. Davies claimed that if he received bail on this charge, he could deliver Stan, Bill, and Stevens for the shooting of Brophy within a week. But he made the point to the police that 'there will be some shooting when you go for them!' Sonenberg objected strongly to the introduction of any material not directly related to the Scriven shooting and stated that he would certainly not be asking questions regarding Blamey or Brophy. The magistrate agreed with this stance and ruled this evidence as inadmissible, but not before observing that 'It sounds like Chicago!'[68]

The hearing displayed the tenuous nature of some of the evidence that the Crown intended to call in the event that the case went to trial. The Crown also made a lot of the spending habits of the Davies brothers since the robbery. The clear intention was to demonstrate that men who were on sustenance payments could not have outlaid sums of money.

A pattern of failure by the Crown to positively identify the Davies brothers and Cody as the killers was established at the hearing when the messenger, Gillbank, was unable to confirm them. All he could say was that the men in the dock were similar in size and height to those who had carried out the robbery

68 *The Argus,* 28 November 1936

and shooting. Nor could Pullen, the taxi driver, confirm that the men in the dock were the killers. But the evidence of John Boadle, an engineer and superintendent of the Destructor Yard, was more definite. He was positive that they were the same men that he had seen at the Yard.

The final witness at the hearing was Henry Mutimer, in charge of the sustenance workers engaged by Collingwood City Council, who gave evidence that neither of the Davies brothers was working on sustenance on January 31. But their claim was that Rupert had received payment from the council late on that day, NOT that they had spent the day on a work gang. Geoffrey had certainly been working on the sustenance gang at various times but was not eligible to receive money on the 31st and his name was not on the wages sheet. Evidence was produced from Collingwood Council that Rupert was due for payment on the day of the shooting and that his signature appeared on the pay-roll record. But owing to the number of men paid each Friday, the Registrar of Sustenance was unable to state at what time he picked up his payment that day.[69]

At the completion of the hearing, the combined evidence of Boadle and Reeves, together with that of Constable Cairns about the shootout and the recovery of the pistols, was enough to convince the magistrate, Mr Freeman, that there was sufficient evidence for the accused to stand trial. On Friday November 27 he committed the three for trial. All were refused bail, even

H.M.Prison Pentridge

69 PROV,VPRS 00030/P0006, Unit 000004, 1936/777; *Statement by James Clark,* Registrar of Sustenance, Municipality of Collingwood

though the magistrate made the observation that the evidence was stronger against the brothers than against Cody. Although the evidence was strong, it was clearly a matter for a jury.[70]

So began the long process of trials and appeals of Cody and the Davies brothers. By the end of 1936, they had been remanded six times since first being charged and the whole affair would not be resolved until December 1937. They were placed in the Remand section of Pentridge prison in Coburg. The massive bluestone and iron building was well-known to most Melburnians for its impressive array of walls, towers and gates and heavily barred doors and windows – it was a grim, brutal place. Writing in the *Argus* in July 1934, commentator Bernard Cronin suggested that Pentridge, like other prisons, 'suggests shame and despair, punishment of mind and body.' The layout was 'sternly practical'. In addition to the main administrative block, it comprised A division (for newcomers), B division (for long-sentence men), C division for habitual offenders, and D block for those awaiting trial or on remand.

Remand had separate enclosures for those held those awaiting hearing of charges against them, such as those committed for trial in higher courts and those awaiting sentence. It also housed youths on remand as well as female prisoners (from 1894 to 1956). The prison population in 1935 was 1370 (1315 men and 55 women), and the conditions endured were a matter of concern. Pressure was building at Pentridge after the closure of prisons at Portland, Ararat, Maryborough and Beechworth, and the reduction in status of those at Ballarat, Bendigo and Sale. The Melbourne gaol in Russell Street had also closed. The 'safe housing' of prisoners at Pentridge was a constant concern expressed by the Inspector-General of Penal Establishments in

70 *The Sun News Pictorial*, 28 November 1936

his annual report to Parliament. The economic situation, and the need for rigid management of budgets, had resulted in little money being available for repairs and renovations to gaol buildings and yards. This meant that prisons such as Pentridge were inadequate in conforming to modern methods of prison administration and the application of modern methods for the treatment of prisoners, presumably in the provision of occupational and recreation facilities. Not surprisingly, attempted suicides were common, as were escape attempts including the digging of a tunnel under the foundations of the prison by two prisoners in 1934.[71]

Despite the lack of available funding, there were some attempts to improve the facilities. Plans had been drawn up for the demolition and rebuilding of C and D Divisions but did not proceed. Nothing was done. In September 1936, a group of parliamentarians visited Pentridge and were shocked at what they saw. The administration was praised but they were appalled at the 'appalling ancientness' of the buildings, which were little better than 'bluestone dungeons'. They also expressed dismay at the number of youthful delinquents housed there.[72] In November, two months after this visit, Cody and the Davies brothers were taken to Pentridge in the prison van called the Black Maria. There were two such vehicles, both small and both renowned for the jolting ride that prisoners experienced. When they arrived at Pentridge, they entered a harsh environment. Inside the door, which was now shut and bolted, the prisoners lined up along an asphalt sideway while their charges and sentences were read out. Firstly they were processed at a classification centre – a small but business-like room containing a central table and long shelves

71 *The Argus,* 24 November 1934

72 *The Argus,* 11 September 1936

full of ledgers. Bernard Cronin described the process of arrival and lock-up. Prisoners were photographed, and prison records were updated by 'trusties' acting as clerks. Newly-sentenced prisoners went through the bathroom and received their prison outfits, followed by a 'dixie' of food and then it was off to the cells, accompanied by uniformed warders with jangling keys. 'Doors thud; bolts grind. It is lock-up time.' [73]

Remand prisoners went through a similar process. They were relieved of personal property (which was then carefully 'docketed') but were allowed to retain the clothes they arrived in and then taken to their cells. Did they share a cell? It is not known but unlikely. Life in Remand was harsh. In the daytime prisoners were cooped up in the Remand yard with nothing to do but sit around or pace up and down. It was one of a number that radiated from a central watchtower, enclosed by a high fence topped by iron spikes. If it rained, there was not enough room for everybody to get under the shelter, so some got wet and stayed wet. On hot days the yard was a suntrap. At four o'clock the prisoners were locked in their small cells – without food - for the next fifteen hours. Breakfast consisted of a plate of burgoo stew and a chunk of bread. These were the conditions endured by prisoners who were still innocent in the eyes of the law, who had no crime proved in court but did not have the good fortune (or means and connections) to get bail. Prisoners were allowed visitors, but were separated by a screen with warders close by. Bernard Cronin described the scene in the office of the Remand section, where odd visitors knocked and were admitted – to stand quietly waiting their turn to exchange a few words with friends or relations. As he

73 *The Argus*, 4 August 1934

stated, those who wait also serve sentences.[74]

Remand could be a dangerous place. There was always the possibility of encountering other inmates with a grudge to settle or those looking for scalps to enhance their own reputation. In most prisons there is a pecking order amongst prisoners and a constant threat of violence, with prisoners taking precautions against attacks. The warders would generally let prisoners sort out their own standings, preferring a quiet life. There was also the chance that a fellow prisoner would confess to a crime, which was information that could be traded for advantage. For those like the Davies brothers and Cody, who had been around a bit and enjoyed reputations as hard men, Remand would have been bearable. They could probably talk to each other and others known to them in the yard during the day. But for those who had never been in trouble before it must have been hard. What we will never know is whether they felt any remorse for Scriven and his family, if they had committed the crime. Were they religious? Despite Davies' statement on November 19 about being innocent in the eyes of God, family members recall that they were not particularly religious, unlike their mother, Leitha.

In Remand, they were caged up in circumstances that must have made many wonder about the gaol sentence they may receive - IF they were convicted, and despite the forbidding state of conditions in A Division (for newcomers) or B Division (for long-sentence men). At least convicted prisoners had plenty to occupy themselves with during the day, unlike those in Remand. Their barristers confirmed the complaints of prisoners on Remand. They could read until lights out at 8.30 p.m. (although a cell only had one light

---

74 *The Argus*, 7 July 1934

globe), but there was no other form of diversion. No wireless, no lectures or concerts... just solitude. For men of retiring or nervous natures, the endless hours of waiting in the yard and the long, cheerless nights in their cells must have been a horrifying experience. Escapes (or attempts) occurred occasionally, but this required inmates to climb a high internal wall (such as that separating the hospital from farm paddock) and then the 12 feet high wall around the gaol, all the while eluding armed guards. One such escape by a 16-year old boy in 1938 was successful when the guards chasing him did not shoot because of his age. There had been no such hesitation by guards in 1932 when a prisoner on remand overpowered a warder, stole his rifle and then shot a second warder in the abdomen. The prisoner, Reg Baker (aged 18) was due to be sentenced after being convicted for shooting at a police constable in Richmond. He was poised on the top of a stone wall and about to jump when he was fatally shot by warders, with his body falling back into the Remand yard and landing among other prisoners exercising in the yard.[75]

Prisoners could be held in Remand for several weeks and then acquitted, or a judge may find that some penalty other than imprisonment was adequate punishment for the crime. It was the solitude and the waiting that made their stay worse than actual imprisonment. It was a grim price to pay for the inability to secure bail while awaiting trial. At least they were able to have a Christmas dinner, even if the cost (3/-) was deducted from their 'earnings'.

The weekend after the committal hearing was another of the social highlights in the life of Melbourne – the picturesque river carnival, called Henley-on-Yarra (or just Henley), where

75 *The Argus,* 29 February 1932

rowing crews from around Australia competed through the day for a series of cups. For those in the upper levels of society (including the Governor, Lord Mayor, Archbishop and their parties), it was an opportunity to mingle with other guests and watch the races from one of four gaily decorated houseboats moored at the Henley stage. As well as the social set, large crowds of ordinary citizens turned out to watch the events. A hot start to the day, with the temperature over 94F (31C), looked like it would keep the crowd down. But a blessed cool wind change swept across the city around midday and by two in the afternoon, dense crowds lined both banks of the Yarra from Prince's Bridge to the Morrell Bridge in South Yarra. A notable feature was the large number of family picnic parties who witnessed the triumph of the crew from NSW in the major event, the Grand Challenge Cup for senior eights. Henley was a major event for women who loved to dress up and many chose to wear tailored linen suits, favouring those with a nautical air. A hugely popular colour was Coronation blue, not surprising in the year following the death of King George V and the coronation of Edward V111. As well as the boat races, there was a fashion contest. Sixteen entrants in the Miss Henley 1936 competition paraded before the judges – all wearing simple, charming and well-tailored frocks of linen and sheers, complete with 'correct' accessories. The majority wore white and the prize for the best dressed went to a lass wearing a trim jacket of navy blue atop a white skirt, both of linen, together with a sailor-like blue beret. A large party of soldiers invalided from the Great War (some in cots) watched events from a special reserve, where the Red Cross supplied them with ice creams and cigarettes. If only the crowd had an inkling of the misfortunes that were to befall the Royal

Family within a few months and the world in general in the next decade.[76]

As the crowds made their way home through the gardens and along St Kilda Road, they agreed that it had been a splendid day. But it did not end well for one young man. James Dugan, the 18-year old witness who had testified about the pistol, was shot in the left thigh on the Saturday evening whilst walking alone near the Shrine of Remembrance in St Kilda Road. The fears of the police about retribution by the underworld had been confirmed. Fortunately the wound was superficial and, with a bullet hole in his trousers and blood flowing from the wound, he was able to walk into the casualty section of the nearby Prince Henry's Hospital at about 9.00 p.m. He claimed that he received the wound accidentally but declined to state where the mishap occurred. Ten minutes after the hospital notified police, a carful of detectives (including Detective Davis) arrived to take him away for questioning. The medical superintendent confirmed to reporters that Dugan had walked into the hospital with a bullet wound and had later been taken away by police. The police followed their usual procedure of supplying little or no information to the press on the Saturday night and denied that there was any shooting case treated at the hospital. According to Davis, he and another detective were 'just snooping around' at the hospital. On the following days, Detective Davis was 'too busy' to talk to reporters. When Dugan was interviewed at home, he was uncommunicative, telling reporters (as he was closing the door behind them) that 'it was all a little accident'. The police were obviously convinced that the shooting was not accidental, and were embarrassed about it. According to

76 In January 1936, King George V died. His son was crowned as Edward V111 and abdicated in December 1936, in order to be with his wife, an American divorcee named Wallis Simpson.

Superintendent Brophy, the head of the CIB, 'it had not been thought necessary to give Dugan police protection, but the police now have full details of the occurrence, and expect to clear the matter up in a few days'. They never did.[77]

77 *The Argus*, 1 December 1936; *The Age*, 28 November 1936

CHAPTER 5
THE FIRST TRIAL

The committal hearing had determined that a trial of Cody and the Davies brothers would begin on 16 December 1936, nearly a year since the murder of Ted Scriven. It was expected that it would be over before Christmas. The city was winding down – the property market was quiet and did not expect to pick up until the New Year and numerous Christmas parties were in full swing. In the suburb of Collingwood, where the accused and some of the key witnesses lived, celebrations were continuing after the Collingwood Football Club (the Magpies) had again won the VFL premiership, their sixth in an extraordinary ten years. Ironically, the Davies brothers bore a striking resemblance to the Collier brothers (Harry and Albert), who had been prominent in the Grand Final win, with the Magpies captained by Harry. Melbourne's summer weather, unpredictable at the best of times, was sultry and the city was drenched in a tropical downpour. This caused interruptions to the Victorian tennis championships on the outside courts at Kooyong, the main venue for tennis in Melbourne until 1987.

The trial was presided over by the Chief Justice of Victoria, Sir Frederick Wollaston Mann. Born on 2 May 1869 at Mount Gambier, South Australia, he moved to Melbourne in 1887 to study and was admitted to the Bar in 1896. He fought (and was wounded) in the Boer War in South Africa before setting up as a barrister in 1902. Mann quickly built up a large practice, undertaking both common law and Equity cases and specialising to some extent in patent law. In 1919 he was appointed to the bench of the Victorian Supreme Court before taking on the role of Chairman of the Court of Industrial Appeals in 1931-33. He was knighted in June 1933. When Sir William Irvine, a former Premier of Victoria, retired as Chief Justice in October 1935, Mann succeeded him and also became the Lieutenant Governor in 1936. Standing only 5' 6" tall (168 cm), he was nicknamed the 'Little Gentleman'. Mann was unfailingly courteous in court and helpful to young barristers. He had a reputation for deep learning and was remembered as a patient, careful judge with a strong sense of what the justice of a case required. [1]

The setting for the trial was court three of the City Court, opposite Police headquarters and next to the City watchhouse. The court complex was the venue for many of the State's murder trials and contained a number of courtrooms. Court One was the City Court, generally used for cases from within the city boundaries. It was regarded as magnificent – high-ceilinged and spacious, with decorative stonework, and massive carved wooden panelling for the bench. Court two, the District Court, was used for civil and quasi-criminal cases. Court three (only slightly less imposing than one and two) was used to cope with any overflow from the other two. Like the other courtrooms in the complex, it featured moulded plaster and superb joinery, often in dark polished cedar. The high-set judicial benches and lofty ceilings may have looked impressive but often resulted in uniformly poor acoustics.[2] Other inadequacies in the design of

1 Mann, Sir Frederick Wollaston (1869–1958), Elise B. Histed, *Australian Dictionary of Biography*, Volume 10, (MUP), 1986

2 Michael Challinger, *Historic Courthouses of Victoria,* 2001, p. 133

City Court, 2015

the courts did not assist proceedings. The constant foot traffic provided continual distraction for defendants – and sometimes their counsel.[3] Today the court is acclaimed as Australia's largest and best-preserved nineteenth century court complex, but Cody and the Davies brothers probably did not appreciate the architecture of their surrounds. The prisoners were brought into the court. We don't know what impression the place made on

3 Michael Challinger, *Historic Courthouses of Victoria,* 2001, p. 128

them. Were they subdued and overwhelmed by the surroundings and the cast of characters assembled in the room? Were they quietly confident that their legal team would be able to get them off? Or perhaps they were just resigned to having their fate decided by others? The legal people (both sides) would all have known each other and probably exchanged greetings, despite being on opposing sides. But they were above the proceedings anyway, and all got to go home at the end of the day.

All three were charged with the murder of Scriven. Cody and Geoffrey Davies were also charged with robbery in company. All pleaded not guilty to all the charges. With the trial due to start, the police were taking no chances with security as the accused were brought from Pentridge prison. After all, Alex Duncan from Scotland Yard was taking a keen interest in the case and was a spectator in the courtroom. The accused were regarded as hardened, well-organised criminals with an extensive network of support. There could be no slip-ups in delivering them to court such as had occurred in 1933 when two prisoners bored a hole through the roof of a prison van in Sydney Road, Moreland, on the way back to Pentridge prison from a court appearance, and struggled out through the hole before leaping onto the side of the road. The noise of dislodging the roof of the van was covered by the raucous noise made by the other prisoners in the van singing in very loud voices. After this embarrassment, the locks on prison vans had been strengthened and steel floors introduced.[4] On the trip from Pentridge, the accused were accompanied by three prison warders in the van, escorted by two motorcycle patrols and a police car full of detectives. The prisoners were thoroughly searched before leaving gaol for the courts, were handcuffed

4 *The Argus,* 2 February 1933

inside the van, and then searched again upon arrival at the court. Similar procedures and precautions were made at the end of the day when they were returned to Pentridge.

A large crowd of onlookers and press had gathered in the quadrangle of the City Court to see them arrive. They appeared to be unconcerned, smiling and waving to people in the crowd, including a young fair-haired woman who came close to the wagon and called out, 'How goes it, Johnnie?' [5] Press photographers (particularly the *Herald* and *Sun*) had printed photographs of all the main characters in the drama. The value of including sensational photographs in the selling of newspapers was starting to be realised, and the equipment available to the press was becoming easier to use and lug around. Rolls of film were not used until the 1950s and the press was still relying on the use of glass plate negatives that provided better quality images than the option of sheet film. They were also less likely to bend or distort, especially with large format cameras. The preferred camera was now the large format Graflex Speed Graphic. The rugged and versatile camera weighed in at about 5 lbs. (2.2 kilos) and could be used handheld, with a variety of viewfinders, focus aids and two shutters. A major reason for its popularity with crime photographers (and press photographers) was due to its large attached flash unit that could light up an entire room. [6]

The prisoners watched as the legal teams bustled around, dressed in black cloaks and horsehair wigs. Seated in the dock, on an uncomfortable wooden bench, they heard the charges read out and were asked to stand and state whether they were guilty

5 *The Sun News-Pictorial,* 16 December 1936. One of the accused, William John Cody, was sometimes referred to as John or Johnnie.

6 http://crimephotography.wordpress.com/category/1930s-1940s/; Graflex Pacemaker Speed Graphic by Tim Takahashi, 1996 – see http://photo.net/equipment/large-format/speed-graphic

C H Book, *Table Talk*, 22 March 1928

or not. Each pleaded 'Not Guilty'. In some trials, the practice of plea bargaining (i.e. pleading guilty for a reduced sentence) sometimes occurred. We will never know if Sonenberg ever raised the possibility but it would seem unlikely. Clifford Henry Book, Kings Counsel, appeared for the Crown. In 1928, the society magazine *'Table Talk'* described his rise as a Crown Prosecutor. Born in Liverpool, he migrated to Australia and began a law degree. But like so many others, the Great War interrupted his studies. On his return, he resumed his studies, going into practice in 1920 and then taking up a role as Crown Prosecutor in 1925. The article described him as a man of great courage and a tactician with an excellent voice. 'He can frown suitably and parry the thrusts of the defence that is seeking to pierce his case in a vital organ', said the magazine. [7] By the time of this trial, he had been involved in an enormous range of jury trials. One of his major concerns was for the jury system. In the 1930s there were many questions being discussed about juries, particularly the ability of ordinary citizens to understand complex legal arguments or to disclose other impediments. Some may be too timid or ignorant to speak up in the jury room, or have strong beliefs on some subjects that prevented a clear analysis of evidence. If being unfit to serve did not appear until part way through a trial and a retrial was ordered, great expense was incurred. If unfitness

7 *Table Talk*, 22 March 1928

was not discovered at all, serious injustices could be the result. Arguments were being made for removal of juries from Supreme Court cases and vesting them in 'special tribunals',[8] or for a change to the requirement for a unanimous verdict. Perhaps a ten out of twelve majority verdict should be considered?

The other contentious issue relating to juries was whether women should be allowed to serve. One view was that women around the country would refuse to serve if they were legally compelled to do so, but perhaps they should be allowed to serve on cases relating to women and children, if they applied to do so. Much of Australia's legal system was based on British precedent and it was pointed out that women served on juries in England, with no serious comment or objection. [9] Many judges in England and the United States were of the opinion that the results of trials with women jurors were excellent. If women could be lawyers, litigants, witnesses, legislators and magistrates, then why not jurors? In an attempt to justifying 'keeping them in their place' and not in a jury box, some men objected to women as jurors on the basis that women should be spared the task of sifting objectionable evidence or listening to an unpleasant case. But surely a judge could be given discretion to exempt women jurors in such cases? One view was that women would not make good jurors as they were 'illogical', to which women would be likely to reply that 'men were stubborn and stupid!' [10] Whatever the argument, the jury in this case was all male. [11]

The issue of bribing of jurors (jury squaring) also regularly

8 *The Argus,* 25 September 1936

9 *The Argus,* 26 August 1930

10 *The Argus,* 8 December 1936

11 The irony was that newspapers, such as the *Herald* on 5 February, 1936, ran full-page ads for Ardath cigarettes showing a jury of seven men and five women, all smoking Ardath, beneath the question in bold type – WHO WOULDN'T ACCEPT THE VERDICT OF THIS JURY? Ardath cigarettes were a British product.

raised its ugly head, particularly where a series of trials could not resolve guilt or innocence. The obvious offence was to offer a bribe to a juror to vote for acquittal, but it was also an offence for a juror to incite disagreement in the jury room, which may result in the jury being unable to reach a verdict. Jury squaring had been considerably easier in criminal trials when the officers of the court would produce a list of names and addresses of potential jurors for forthcoming trials. The list could then be purchased, a practice that was discontinued in the 1920s, but not before Les 'Squizzy' Taylor used jury squaring to great effect.

The operation of juries regularly raised a series of questions (and still do). By the mid-1930s, newspapers such as the *Argus* were commenting that a jury would not 'bring in a verdict of murder unless the facts are indisputable and in addition reveal the greatest possible measure of brutality…evidence must be of the most convincing kind and juries, where any opportunity presents itself, add to their verdicts recommendations to mercy.' Newspaper editors represented the views of the propertied middle and upper classes. Not surprisingly they were of the opinion that the scales of justice were 'heavily weighted' in favour of the accused. [12] Alternative views were often espoused by those with a liberal, humanitarian bent, together with those who regularly observed the social effects of long-term poverty, unemployment and lack of education. As we will see, the issue of incontrovertible evidence would come to be a critical aspect of those tried for the murder of Scriven.

When jury selection for the trial commenced, 28 jurors were challenged – 13 by the Crown, 11 by Geoffrey Davies and four by Cody – before a jury was empanelled. All jurors were required to state the oath: 'I swear, by Almighty God, that I shall

12 *The Argus,* 22 February 1935

give true answers to all questions put to me by this honourable Court.' Across the Courts, prospective jurors had many excuses, ranging from hardness of hearing to pressure of business. Those claiming difficulties with their hearing often gave bizarre answers when asked to repeat the oath. Some promised to give true answers to the honourable Lord, another undertook to give 'two answers', and another swore to give the answers to the 'horrible' court. [13] At this trial, one man said that he could not take the oath because he did not believe in the 'Bible and God'. When he was allowed to make a declaration, he then stated that he did not believe in the jury system. It worked, and the judge waived him out of the court. Another did not believe in capital punishment, arguing that the jury might find a man guilty who would afterwards be condemned to death. He was also excused. Not so fortunate was the juror who asked to be excused because he had served on two juries that year. [14]

In major cases such as this one, the jury was sometimes required to stay overnight in a nearby hotel, probably Tattersalls or the City Court, both in Russell Street, with little more than a wireless set to entertain them.[15] In such a prominent case, there must have been a very real fear of recrimination by the underworld if the accused were found guilty. The temptation to find them not guilty (or not arrive at a clear decision) must have been great. Indeed, one of the Crown witnesses (Dugan) had already been shot since the committal proceedings. For their part, the accused must have been worried about the possibility of being found guilty and hanged. There was continual debate about the effectiveness of capital punishment and it still had widespread support in the community. The jurors must have been

13 *The Argus,* 21 July 1938

14 *The Argus,* 16 December 1936

15 *The Sun News-Pictorial,* 16 December 1936

aware that Karl Sodeman, known as the Schoolgirl Strangler, had been recently hanged, the second of 11 persons to be hanged at Pentridge Prison after the closure of Melbourne Gaol in 1929. Surely such an outcome was not possible in this trial? Governments varied in their approach to capital punishment, with those convicted of murdering women or children most likely to be executed. The option existed for the government of the day to commute death sentences to imprisonment for life.

The defence team consisted of J V (Jack) Barry (appearing for Rupert Davies), John A Nimmo (for Geoffrey Davies), and Harry Minogue (for Cody), all instructed by Napthali Henry 'Sonny' Sonenberg, the legendary Melbourne solicitor. He was an admirer of Barry and as far back as 1926 had expressed the opinion that young Jack Barry should read for the Bar, seeing him as one of the most promising of that year's intake.[16] Although adversaries in the courtroom, the Bar was regarded by Barry's biographer, Mark Finnane, as a close-knit fraternity, governed by a set of rules, some almost indefinable, which operate to produce, harmony, friendship and affection amongst its members, though the pursuit of their profession immerses them in their client's bitter conflicts. Other

John Vincent Barry

16 Sir John Vincent Barry (1903-1969). Judge and criminologist, was born on 13 July 1903 at Albury, NSW. Educated at St Patrick's College, Goulburn, and at the University of Melbourne, in 1921 he was articled to Luke Murphy and two years later qualified as a lawyer through the articled clerks' course. Admittted to the Victorian Bar on 3 May 1926, he read with (Sir) Eugene Gorman. Barry progressed rapidly as a barrister He proved himself versatile, initially developing an extensive jury practice, and later an appellate and High Court practice.

writers have a differing, less collegiate view of the relationships amongst senior practitioners of the law.

Before the trial commenced, and in the absence of the jury, Barry raised objections about items in the deposition of evidence to be called. As far as Rupert Davies was concerned, 'certain items should not be opened or admitted…as they were not sufficiently connected with the matter in dispute,' he told the Judge. Barry intended to pick out items in advance of them being presented in court and have them excluded before the trial commenced, rather than objecting and trying to refute the evidence as it was presented in court in front of the jury. It was a novel approach.

One major objection was the inclusion of evidence in relation to the amount of money in the bank account of Rupert and his wife, shown in June 1936. His worry was that an inference would be drawn that this money was the proceeds of the robbery in January. In his view this evidence should not tendered at all. A similar objection was raised about the evidence from Detective Sickerdick about furniture in the house occupied by Rupert and his wife when he was arrested. Again the inference could be drawn that the furniture, which appeared to Sickerdick to be new, was purchased with the proceeds of the robbery. In order to avoid such conclusions, said Barry, the evidence should not be admitted and should not be 'opened to the jury', even if it was not relied on during the trial.

Similar inferences could be drawn from the purchase of motorcycles by the accused. He also objected to the proposed evidence by Cairns that he had observed the prisoners over a period of time, and he had seen them throw something into a river. 'Something is subsequently got up by a diver', which turns out to be two revolvers. But it was not alleged that these revolvers were used in the hold-up, so the only effect of tendering the evidence was to show that by having revolvers they were gunmen. In the view of Barry and Minogue, none of this evidence had anything to do with the charges against the accused. Nor should the evidence likely to be called from Cairns be admitted. His assertion that 'in the months of September and October Cody was associated with the other two accused' was altogether too remote. Other evidence that should not be admitted, argued Minogue, related to Cody's arrest in November in the Exhibition Gardens after the shoot-out with the police. It was nearly a year ago. All it demonstrated was that Cody was prepared to use a gun. It had no relevance to the offence of the robbery and may be extremely prejudicial to him. Barry also told the Judge that notice had just been received that a new witness would be called – Jack Stevens would testify about conversations he had with each of the accused. Barry thought that the statement allegedly by Cody to Stevens that 'one of the other prisoners was in on it is of such a dangerous tendency that it should be excluded'. As it turned out, the testimony by Stevens was incredibly significant.

The Judge was of the opinion that the circumstances of the arrest were generally submitted as evidence of a consciousness of guilt, despite the fact that it occurred nearly a year after the robbery and at no time did the police tell Cody that they wanted to question him about the robbery. Minogue also objected to the evidence of Constable Suttie, the evidence of Constable Guider about the arrest in the Exhibition Gardens and other items of evidence. The Judge was having none of it, stating that he did not propose to adopt this novel practice of going through the case from the depositions and hearing objections in advance. 'I will not do it,' said Judge Mann. 'You can object to specific passages when the time comes, and I will rule on them, either for you or against you.' Naturally, the Crown, when asked for their opinion, fully supported the Judge and expressed the view that all of this evidence was necessary to show that these men were on sustenance shortly before the crime was committed. Within a few months they were buying motorcycles, had money in the bank, and had bought new furniture.[17]

With the preliminary sparring out of the way, the jury was admitted and the main show was underway. Many people had waited for hours to obtain a seat, having been told that seating was generally limited to about four rows, and the room was packed (but orderly) when Crown Prosecutor Book commenced his opening remarks. For those who did gain a seat, there was an expectation of quiet behaviour and minimum of display of emotions. The temperature was around 80.4 F (26.8 C), which must have led to a very hot courtroom. There was no air-conditioning but the windows could be opened for some relief from the heat. The Court would normally sit between the hours of 10.30 a.m. and 4.30 p.m., with an adjournment for lunch. One interested onlooker was Chief Inspector Duncan from Scotland Yard, who had been appointed to investigate and report upon the Victorian Police. [18] Viewers of television programs and film in recent times are used to seeing lawyers (on both sides) leap to their feet and make regular objections to evidence and questioning - but this was not the practice in 1936. Objections could be made (and were) but were generally unusual. They were also couched in terms such as descriptions

17 PROV, VPRS 00030/P0006, Unit 000004, 1936/777; *proceedings of trial*, 15 December 1936

18 *The Herald*, 18 December, 1936; Duncan, Alexander, *Reports of Alexander M. Duncan, Esq., Chief Inspector, London Metropolitan Police, on the police force of Victoria*, Melbourne, 1936-1937

of opposing counsel as 'my learned friend'.

It didn't take long for a major issue to be raised about the charges faced by the three. All were charged with murder, with two of them (Geoffrey Davies and Cody) also charged with 'robbery in company'. The Chief Justice suggested that this second charge be dropped, as it was causing confusion and difficulty in putting the case before the jury. Any evidence, the Judge said, which supported the second count must, under the circumstances, also support the first charge. But Book was not interested. He argued, saying it was for the jury to say whether the men concerned in the robbery had anything to do with the murder. He was not claiming that all three had fired the fatal shot. Whilst it was alleged that Rupert Davies was the shooter, the others might be equally guilty of murder. They were involved in a robbery and as they had made up their minds to carry it out by any form of violence, they were guilty of murder also – in this case a murder of a particularly cruel kind of an inoffensive citizen.[19] It seemed as if Book was hedging his bets. He clearly thought that he could successfully prosecute Rupert Davies for the murder, and told the Court that the Crown would call witnesses who would positively identify Rupert Davies, the tallest of the three accused, as the man who fired the fatal shot. But he appeared to be less sure of the other two. If not successful, he seemed to think that he would obtain convictions for robbery for Cody and Geoffrey Davies, arguing that, after all, the murder arose out of the robbery.

Throughout this preliminary sparring, and for the rest of the day, the demeanour of Cody and the Davies brothers was one of "calm interest...(and)...none showed any trace of nervousness or concern."[20]

19 *The Argus*, 16 December 1936
20 The Age, 17 December 1936

Book outlined the robbery and the shooting to the Court. The first task was to hear from witnesses from the hospital and the morgue, including Crawford Mollison, the surgeon who performed the post mortem on behalf of the coroner. He described the wound that had killed Scriven, fired into the middle of his forehead and either actually in contact with the skin or extremely close to it. He also identified the nickel-cased bullet taken from the head of Scriven. [21]

One of the witnesses called was Henry Nicholas 'Pat' Shea, a licenced surveyor from the Titles Office. He testified that he had prepared a scale plan for the location where the murder occurred and also for the Melbourne City Council Incinerator at the corner of Spencer and Lonsdale Streets. This section of his plan included a description entitled 'Conveyor' which he explained was a track (actually an elevated railway) for conveying rubbish or spoil either into or out of the incinerator. Shea was used to appearing in court and testifying at murder trials, where he often had to prepare detailed plans (to scale) to assist the court.[22] But he had never had to appear at a trial where another public servant, who worked in the same building, had been murdered. We don't know if the two ever met but it still must have been quite unnerving for Shea.

Evidence was given about the theft of the car from outside the East Melbourne home of Edwin Forster, a journalist, on the night of 15 January 1936. It was a two-door Hudson coach, he told the court, with two front seats that tipped up to let passengers into the back. Forster next saw the car, which had

21 PROV,VPRS 00030/P0006, Unit 000004, 1936/777; *Proceedings of trial,* 15 December 1936

22 In 1944, Shea was involved in one of Australia's most infamous murder trials – the Pyjama Girl murder, where Linda Agostini was murdered. See Robin Grow, *Safe as Houses,* 2013, p.66

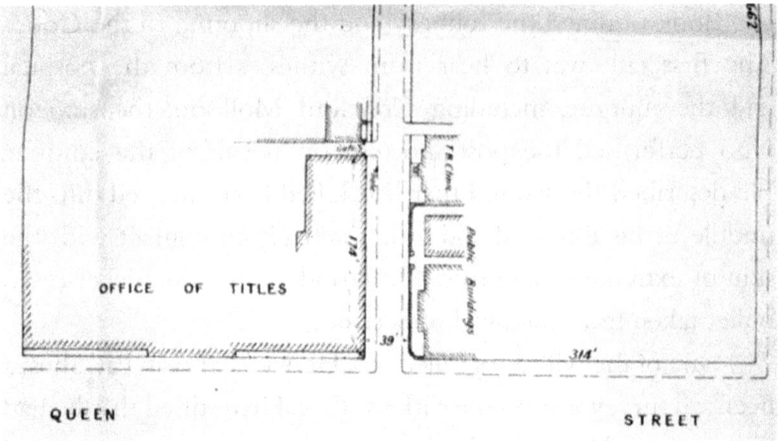

Drawing of scene produced by Pat Shea,
PROV,VPRS 00030/P0006, Unit 000004, 1936/777;

been painted black, at Russell Street on 1 February 1936.[23] The Crown continued its emphasis on the car, calling Joseph Selkridge, a driver from Prahran, who had claimed to have seen Rupert Davies and Cody in a Hudson closed car in Acland Street, St Kilda (near the Village Belle), between 9.00 a.m. and 10.00 a.m. on January 29. He had been sitting on an ice-wagon, stationary at the time, and assisting the driver when he saw the car coming towards him, driving at about 20 mph (32 kph). He noticed that there were four men in the car; he had a quick look at them (for only a flash, about two seconds) and was immediately suspicious. He then wrote down the number of the car. He was certain that two of the men were William Cody, seated in the front next to the driver, and Rupert Davies, in the rear seat. He could not see the driver, who had his arm raised. He had gone to the police and made a statement of his recollections in about the third week of February after reading

23 PROV,VPRS 00030/P0006, Unit 000004, 1936/777; *Proceedings of trial*, 15 December 1936

about the case in the papers, where the number of the car had been frequently published.

Doubts about his evidence emerged when he told the court that he had said in his signed statement that he was driving the cart. The statement was presented at the committal hearing in November. Under questioning by Barry, it emerged that he only had the car under observation for about ten seconds. He maintained that it was long enough to positively identify Rupert Davies in the back seat, accompanied by a man with dark complexion and square shoulders. He had previously described this man as having a 'bull neck' but was no longer prepared to swear to that description. He told the Court that when he was taken to Russell Street in November to identify the men, the police told him that it was in connection with the Scriven shooting and that they believed that Cody and Rupert Davies were the men who had been in the hold-up. He saw the men in the dock at the City Court and observed them for about ten minutes before they were charged. He had originally stated that when he identified the two men he did not know that they had been charged with the murder of Scriven. This prompted a man at the back of the court to yell out 'Good on you, boy'. He was promptly ejected. But as Barry pointed out, it was not until he heard them charged that he decided to make a statement at Russell Street positively identifying them.

The difference between his original statement and his current evidence was explained away by Selkridge - the statement had been written very quickly and he had just glanced at it.

He had also previously said that he was driving the wagon but now was saying that he accompanying the driver, who was serving a customer at the time. When Barry pressed him about whether he was sure of his identification, he hesitated. He told the court that he was no longer prepared to swear that Rupert Davies was in the back seat, saying that it was a man 'like him', but finally said he was sure of Rupert Davies. Was this because he had lived around the corner from Davies for about three years and may have recognised him from the street? Davies later admitted that he knew him.

Much emphasis was placed on evidence found in the Hudson car. Rupert Davies was allegedly wearing light grey trousers during the robbery. When he was approached in the yard of the Destructor he wore dark trousers, but is believed to have changed as they drove along Latrobe Street. But this was a wild swerving ride where changing trousers would have been difficult, to say the least. A pair of light grey flannel trousers was later found in the car, with a waistline within an inch of the waistline of Davies. The trousers had been handed for examination to Charles Anthony Taylor, a medico-legal chemist and the Government Analyst, on December 10. He discovered a bloodstain on the outer surface of the left leg, 17 inches (43 cm) down from the waistband, and another stain about 26 inches (66 cm) down. Both stains were about half an inch (1.2.cm) long and resembled a spot of blood, which he soon determined was human. He also discovered eight small spots of blood on the inner part of the left trouser leg, and nine very small spots on the outside, less than an eighth of an inch (.3 cm) across. He had compared the size of the grey trousers with a pair of blue trousers, also recovered by police. The blue trousers had a waist of 36 inches (91 cm) and a leg length of 54 inches (137 cm); the grey ones were an inch longer and wider at the bottom, but the waist was the same. Witnesses also told the court that the man who fired the shot had something white under his hat and over his eyes. A hat found in the car had the lining cut and weighted to hang down in the front and its size corresponded exactly with the size of the hat that Rupert Davies was wearing when he was arrested. Evidence like this, without the benefits of modern analysis, was at best circumstantial and open to challenges by the defence.

A major witness for the Crown was Herbert Hervey Gillbank, the messenger who was being escorted by Scriven. He described the regular transport of the money; it was locked in a cash box, placed within a leather bag locked with a Yale lock and removed from the office every day at about 4.45 p.m. and 11.55 a.m. on Saturday. He and Scriven were picked up in Little Lonsdale Street near the back door of the Titles Office and taken by a Yellow Cab (regularly driven by Reg Pullen) to the Bank of Australasia on the corner of Queen and Collins Streets. Scriven was generally armed with an automatic pistol. Gillbank described how he had placed the bag on the floor of the cab and sat down, and then saw two men approach Scriven, who was about to get into the cab. As one of the men tried to grab the bag, Scriven tried to stop him. At the same time, the taxidriver, Reg Pullen, tried to start the cab. The other man then shot Scriven from six inches or so from in front of him. The first man (who had a handkerchief hanging down over his forehead and was wearing a hat) grabbed the bag and the two of them ran off, leaving Scriven in the gutter.

Reg Pullen, *The Herald*, 1 February 1936

Gillbank got out of the taxi and ran towards the back of the office. When he was asked whether the men in the dock were those who had carried out the robbery, he could only state that one of them (Rupert Davies) was similar in height, build and general appearance and that the shorter man was not like Cody in build. In an attempt to show Gillbank was unreliable and influenced by what he had read in the newspapers since the robbery, much was made of the fact that Gillbank had not mentioned the handkerchief at either the Coroners' Inquest or the committal hearing. Gillbank admitted that he had read newspaper accounts of the evidence provided by Reeves, the major eyewitness to be produced by the Crown, which referred to the handkerchief.

The taxi driver, Reg Pullen repeated his story that he opened the door of the cab and Gillbank got in. As Scriven was about to enter the cab, a man came and bustled him up against the side of the cab. 'I looked out,' said Pullen, and the man who had pointed the pistol at Scriven pointed it at me and said 'Sit where you are.' Pullen then put the car into gear, and a shot was fired as he was letting in the clutch. The engine stalled as Scriven fell to the ground. Pullen jumped out and saw two men running away and he picked up the gun and from the ground and ran after them. He tried to fire it but the gun would not go off. The two men ran to a waiting car (facing east, on the north side) which swung around into Queen Street, leaving Pullen shouting 'Stop that car!' before jumping on to the back of a passing motorcycle in Queen Street. The getaway car shot away from them, carrying three men – a driver, one in the front seat and one crouched in the back. One was wearing a light grey pair of trousers. He gave chase but lost sight of the car as it went up the hill in Latrobe Street and he then went back to the Titles Office and handed the pistol over to an official from the Stamps Office, Mr Carnier.

It was an incredibly brave attempt by Pullen, but he still could not positively identify the men. The tallest of the three accused, Rupert Davies, 'resembled' the man who had pointed the gun at Scriven. He was 'pretty certain' that this man was Rupert Davies but was not prepared to swear to it. He had never seen Rupert Davies in the street at Collingwood, where Pullen had lived all his life. His house in Oxford Street was not far from Easey Street, where Davies lived. Davies had claimed that he knew Pullen, but Pullen told the court that he was well known in Collingwood but did not know everyone there. Pullen only saw the second man as he was running away and never saw his face at the cab. [24]

Aubrey William Reeves, a labourer from Kinglake, was regarded as a star witness for the prosecution. He told the court that he was walking west along Little Lonsdale Street about 4.30 p.m. when he saw two men examining a car behind a taxi. When the men saw him, they turned and bent down. 'They were Rupert and Geoffrey Davies', he declared. He walked up to the house of a friend, two doors past the lane, talked for a few minutes, and then walked back towards the taxi. He saw Scriven about to get into a taxi and the two men were bustling him. When Rupert Davies pointed a revolver at him, he stepped back, and then kept walking past the lane and the taxi. Geoffrey Davies was leaning in towards the car, and Rupert Davies then grabbed Scriven with his left hand, pulled him towards him, and shot him in the forehead. The two men then ran away. Rupert Davies was wearing a dark coat, grey trousers and a grey hat, dented at the top, and was wearing a handkerchief over his left eye. Geoffrey was dressed in similar fashion. Book again asked him if he was sure it was these two men (the Davies brothers). 'Yes,' he replied. But he was not definite about the time. Having originally made a statement that the events occurred at 4.50

24 PROV,VPRS 00030/P0006, Unit 000004, 1936/777; *Proceedings of trial*, 21 June 1937

p.m., he then changed it to 4.40 p.m. Now he was telling the court that it was 4.30 p.m. The court also heard that he had seen the accused in a street on May 27 but did not go after them or call a policeman. Nor did he volunteer information about the sighting when he appeared at the Coroners' Inquest, stating that he had not been asked so did not give the information. In fact, asked Barry, the first time you have told any tribunal that you had seen the two men engaged in the hold-up was when you came here to give evidence today? Is this correct? 'Yes,' replied Reeves, although he had given evidence at the committal proceeding.

Another witness, Keith Gruer, an insurance agent from South Yarra, described how he walked past a car in Little Lonsdale Street, on the opposite side of the street to the robbery. One man was sitting in the driver's seat, and the engine was running. He had just passed the car when he heard a shot and saw two men running from a taxi to the car. One man, the shorter of the two, was carrying a bag. Whilst the Davies brothers were similar to the two men, he was not prepared to swear it was them. He had run to Queen Street and was followed by the taxi driver, Pullen, who jumped onto a motorbike. Gruer then jumped onto the running board of a car and they followed the Hudson around into Latrobe Street. The getaway car was doing 30 to 35 mph (48 to 56 kph) when it went around the corner. 'By the time we got to the top of the hill at William Street we couldn't see if the car had turned to the right or the left. The driver of our car turned to the right, which was the wrong way,' he told the court. He identified the car in the courtyard of the police station as the one in which the men had disappeared. But the defence was not impressed with Gruer's testimony. Barry pointed out that there were a number of discrepancies between the evidence offered at the trial and that offered at the Coroners' Inquest in July. It had been nearly a year since the murder and Gruer's recollections were imperfect, to say the least, and open to criticism.

Norman Alexander Semmens, electrical mechanic of Malvern, was also called as a witness. He had been riding his motorcycle (with a sidecar) west along Little Lonsdale Street (after having turned from Elizabeth Street) and was doing about 10 mph (16 kph) as he rode towards William Street. The street was two-way in those days. Just over Queen Street, he heard the report of a firearm. The next minute, a man ran across the road to a waiting car on the opposite side. He opened the door of the car, calling out to the driver 'He's got the bag!' and jumped into the back seat. As he rode past the car, he clearly saw that the man in the rear was Rupert Davies. Then another man jumped into the car but he could not recognise him, as he had the bag on his shoulder and his face was covered. Nor could he identify the driver, who was hunched over the wheel, beyond saying that he had light coloured hair and a dark suit on. As it drove away, at a 'fairly fast' pace, Semmens had to give way in the narrow street, and the partially open car door knocked over a safety zone standard, a parking sign that was standing on the kerb. At this time Semmens still had no understanding that there had been a holdup, but he had the presence of mind to record the number plate of the car, 86730. He told the court he knew there was something wrong but did not know what it was. He continued up the street for about 20 yards past the taxicab. Like other witnesses, he was shown the men at Russell Street for identification in November, when the police told him they had arrested the men they believed to be in the holdup. Rupert Davies was first shown to him alone, and then in the company of Geoffrey Davies and William Cody. [25]

25 PROV, VPRS 00030/P0006, Unit 000004, 1936/777; *Proceedings of trial,* 22 June 1936

Another witness, Charles Kirkwood, saw the car turning out of Little Lonsdale Street, carrying three men. The one in the back, wearing grey trousers, resembled Rupert Davies, but Kirkwood had stated that he had hair starting well back from his forehead. When Barry put it to him that Rupert Davies's hair does not start well back, he agreed. Nor was it clear how he could see the colour of the pants worn by someone in the back seat of a swerving fast car. Also giving chase was a car driven by Herbert Gillies Watson, resident of Middle Brighton and a wholesale confectioner. He and a friend were sitting in his car in Queen Street, near the corner of Latrobe Street, when the bandits' car roared out of Little Lonsdale Street, driven recklessly towards Latrobe Street. Watson was surprised at the speed of the car and further surprised when a City Council parking officer, Francis John Dempster, who had been on traffic duty at the intersection, jumped onto the running board of his car and ordered him to follow. 'I lost no time,' said Mr Watson, who took off in pursuit, but could not keep up. 'With a faster car I would have kept up with the bandits,' he said. In an interview on the day after the robbery, he told a *Sun* reporter that he had got a pretty good look at the robbers and would be able to identify them if he saw them again. However, by the time of the trial he was not prepared to swear that Rupert Davies was one of the men in the car. [26]

One of the key witnesses for the Crown, John Boadle (Superintendent of the City Council Destructor Yard), told the court that he was standing in the yard at about 4.45 p.m. when a car pulled up about 60 ft. (18.2 metres) inside the driveway. A man of 'stout build' (also described by the *Sun* as 'a short, fat man') left the sedan and walked to the bonnet as if intending to do something to the engine. Aged about 45,

26 *The Sun News Pictorial* , 1 February 1936

he was dressed in a dark blue suit. Boadle then noticed a tall man wearing no hat and a shorter man carrying a bag come from the opposite side of the car. They went across the yard toward the furnace house but at its corner they made for a gate leading to Spencer Street. (The yard had two gates, one at the east on Lonsdale Street, and one leading onto a right of way leading into Spencer Street). The two men, whom he identified as Rupert Davies and Cody, then made for the gate leading into Lonsdale Street. Davies was wearing a blue suit. Boadle‘s suspicions were aroused, although he had no knowledge of the robbery at this point. Boadle approached the men and asked them what they were after. Cody asked, 'Did you see a short, stout man?' Boadle replied that he had not. Cody then said, 'We saw him come in here and we wanted to see him.' They then left the premises and walked toward Spencer Street. Boadle had not seen the stout man after Davies and Cody left the yard. He then called out, 'Shut the gate and don't let anybody take that car out.' Boadle and the stoker from the Yard, Harry Johnstone, then looked inside the car and saw a pair of grey flannel trousers, a grey hat and some sheets of newspaper. Boadle went and telephoned the police. Subsequently at Russell Street, on February 3, Boadle gave descriptions of the accused that were taken down in writing, but he could not recall signing a statement at that time, although he recalled that he had signed one after the inquest.[27]

Boadle testified that on November 5, the day that Rupert Davies was arrested, he had been shown Rupert Davies at the Detective's office. He did not immediately identify him, but said he was very similar to the tall man. In his own mind, he

27 PROV,VPRS 00030/P0006, Unit 000004, 1936/777; *Proceedings of trial*, 22 June 1937

was satisfied that Davies was the man but he had seen him under artificial lights and wanted to see him in the daylight. He told police in the light of the following day that he recognised Davies. This was disputed by Barry, who put it to him that he did not identify Davies until the 13th, a week later, when he saw him in the dock at the City Court. Boadle had stated this at the committal hearing. More questions emerged about Boadle's evidence. He had stated that Rupert Davies was 'aged about 23 years, about six feet (182 cm), thin build, inclined to be round shouldered, looked like an overgrown boy in build but not in age, round faced, prominent cheek bones which make eyes appear deep set, dark eyebrows, rather dark under eyes, dark wavy hair parted high on right hand side, wearing a dark blue suit. He never spoke.'[28] When Barry asked him if he would say his hair was now wavy, Boadle agreed that it wasn't now, but had been then. 'It looked like as if it had been artificially waved.' Not surprisingly, Davies gave evidence that his hair was the same as it always had been. It had never been artificially waved, nor had the parting been altered. Boadle was also uncertain about the complexion of Davies and had originally stated that he had a ruddy complexion. When asked about it by Barry, he stated that Davies did not have a ruddy complexion now, but he had that day.

These were the first of many contradictions in testimony from Boadle, but the Crown relied heavily on his evidence and the Judge appeared to accept him without question. There had been considerable criticism of the methods of the police in obtaining information for some time, and counsel for one of the accused criticised strongly the methods used by the police in offering the accused for identification. As it turned out, these

28 PROV,VPRS 00030/P0006, Unit 000004, 1936/777; *Proceedings of trial,* 22 June 1937

methods would be a major issue and would haunt the police and the prosecution.

Much evidence surrounded the gun used in the robbery. James Dugan, a ticket writer aged 18 who lived above a florist shop in Victoria Street, West Melbourne, told the court that, ten days before the crime, he repaired an automatic pistol at the request of Cody, who offered to pay him £1 for the repairs. He testified that he did not recollect ever seeing Cody before he appeared with the gun for repair. Dugan, who had been shot since he had appeared at the committal hearing, identified an automatic pistol (alleged to have been the one that killed Scriven) as the one that he repaired. He had placed two German-silver bands on the handle, on which the ebonite plate was cracked. There were about ten different sorts of white metal that could have been used, including German silver and Dabbite metal. Cody also showed him a new Luger pistol (for which Dugan had no ammunition), and another old pattern revolver that he assessed as defective in the trigger. Dugan then stated that he bought ammunition from Hartley's Sports Store and supplied Cody with some nickel-nosed and lead-nosed Remington .32 calibre bullets. Under cross-examination, Cody could not remember where he was that day or the following day or, for that matter, on January 31, the day of the robbery. But he denied that he had seen Dugan on that day, stating that he had never seen him in his life before the case was heard at the City Court. Dugan recalled that when shown a photograph of Cody by police on December 8, as one of six, he picked Cody's photograph as that of the man who had brought the gun to him. The next Thursday, at Russell Street, he identified a man as Cody after he had been shown to him individually under lights, not as part of a line-up. He also told the court that he had repaired a great number (between 60 and 120) rifles, mostly consisting of cleaning and aligning the sights.

Detective Frederick Hobley, the official police photographer, testified about the Hudson car, telling the court that the number plate had been altered by white paint from 60736 to 86730. He also testified that on February 12 he had been handed the Webley Scott automatic pistol and magazine used in the murder. The cartridges were Remington, UMC, .32 calibre, and nickel plated. It was the gun used in the murder, distinguished by two bands of metal. He had made a study of firearms and ammunition over a period of years and told the court that he had fired a bullet from the pistol. He then compared it to the bullet recovered from Scriven's head, using a microscope, to determine whether the bullets were aligned and scoriations correspond. He was of the opinion that the bullet recovered from Scriven's head during the post mortem was fired by the pistol recovered from the scene and produced in court. George Theodore, a tailor from Kew, told the court about finding the bag and cashbox in the water at Brighton Beach.

No wonder Barry was critical of the evidence produced by the Crown, which consisted of discrepancies and imperfect recollections. The fact that the events had taken place nearly a year ago further opened the evidence to criticism. Barry was an early exponent in the overlapping areas of science and the law and would later become a central figure in Australia's first Medico-Legal Society and was intensely interested in the forensics from crime scenes. But Hobley remained adamant about his evidence and Barry was unable to rattle him with detailed questions about the operation of the pistol.

Evidence was given that the brothers had purchased two motorcycles from the firm of 'Stilwell and Parry' in July. Geoffrey had paid £127/5/- and Rupert had paid £124/15/, in three instalments (in cash). The brothers had made the transactions in their names and provided genuine addresses. As was the practice for purchasers of motorcycles, this information was passed on to the police. Again there were no difficulties. A motorcycle dealer from Sydney gave evidence that he had sold a BSA motorcycle to Cody for £47/18/3 on June 27. He paid a deposit and the balance in cash on June 30.[29] The police claimed that Rupert had also bought a fur coat for his wife during this time, a claim disputed by Davies, who told the court that she had bought it out of her own money. Was this consistent with men who claimed that they were receiving unemployment benefits? Not necessarily, but where would they have got this money? Rupert Davies claimed that the money for the motorcycle had come from the proceeds of 'street betting', generally referred to as SP (starting price) betting, and the sale of opossum skins.[30] This was

Walmer Street bridge and bush, 2015

29 *The Age*, 17 December 1936
30 PROV, VPRS 00030/P0006, Unit 000004, 1936/777; *proceedings of trial*, 15 December 1936.

part of the evidence that Barry had tried to suppress before the trial started, realising the inferences that would be drawn about it. But he had made the point that there was no attempt to conceal the purchases, as guilty men may have done.

Police witnesses revealed that the Davies brothers had been followed between August 30 and November 5, with Constable Jim Cairns stating that he had seen the three accused on numerous occasions – sometimes in the company of John Stevens. A major reporting occurred on August 31, when Cairns, dressed in plain clothes, saw the brothers on a motorcycle, with Rupert driving and Geoffrey in the sidecar, holding a small parcel (about 30 cm long) wrapped in hessian and newspaper. He followed them to the corner of Victoria and Burnley Streets, in Burnley, where the Walmer Street footbridge connects Burnley to the suburb of Kew. Watching from about 50 yards away, he saw them walk onto the bridge, look around behind them and then throw the parcel into the river. But a section of the newspaper used to wrap the parcel fell onto the bridge and became caught in the wirework. Cairns recovered it about half an hour later and it was produced at the trial. Soon after, Cairns was present when a police diver, Helmer Pearson, recovered the parcel. It contained two pistols, wrapped in newspaper. One of the pistols was exactly similar to one that Cody had shown to the witness Dugan. Again Barry had sought to suppress this evidence, arguing that it showed no link to the robbery.

Amazingly, given the shadowing that had occurred over some months, Cairns stated (under oath) that August 31 was the first time he had seen the brothers and he did not know either of them before that day. Nor did he know why he was following them. He gave evidence about the dramatic arrest of Cody in the Exhibition Gardens, which accorded with the evidence he had presented at the committal hearing in November.

Waiting room for prisoners, City Court

With the day's proceedings ended, the brothers and Cody were placed in a room awaiting transport back to Pentridge, along with others who had been convicted that day or whose trials were in progress. The next day, December 17, saw the defence counsels begin their case. Not surprisingly, all the defendants denied any association with the crime. In this case the defendants were called on to testify, a move that has traditionally been seen as risky in murder trials, as it exposes defendants to cross-examination. The Davies brothers swore that they were not in the city at the time of the shooting. One of the accused, Cody, swore that in July, Detective Davis (in the company of detective Delmenico) had made comments to his mother and sister that they would shoot him, which had been repeated to him.

Following the account by Cairns of the dramatic arrest on the tram and in the Exhibition gardens on November 5, Cody gave his account of the arrest of himself and Geoffrey Davies. 'I was going into town [31] and he was going to the beach or somewhere. I noticed on the tram a policeman who had been following us around. When we turned into Nicholson Street a car swung around the back of the tram. I could see that it was

31 'Going into town' was used by the people of Melbourne to describe visits to the city centre for business or shopping.

full of police, but it did not approach any closer than 15 or 20 yards (13 to 18 metres). Geoffrey Davies told him that there were police in the car. When I told him I had my gun in my pocket, he suggested that I throw it away. I told him I could not as the policeman (Cairns) on the tram was watching me. I was unable to get off the tram because the policeman stood up and at the same time drew a gun from his pocket. The police in the car had their guns out and were pulling back their jackets. They were not making any attempt to get out of the car. It seemed that they were waiting for me to get out so that they could have a shot at me.' Prosecutor Book sneeringly asked Cody if he was serious when he stated that when he saw the carload of police, he thought that they were going to take a potshot at him. [32] Cody went on: 'I told the policeman in the car (ie the tramcar) to drop his gun and stand back. I jumped off the tram and ran towards the gardens. The police in the car began to fire at me. Ten or fifteen shots were fired at me. I could see two or three policemen running behind me (Cairns and Guider) and firing at me. I turned around and fired into the ground in front of them but they did not stop. Then I saw that the police car had swung right around and was waiting in front of me. The police were not making any attempt to get out of the car – just waiting to get a shot at me. I turned around and ran back toward the other policemen. They were closing in on me so I pointed the gun at the ground and just stood there.' [33] In many details Cody's account was close to that provided by Constable Cairns. Was it reasonable to accept Cody's view that he thought the police were out to shoot him that day, as the police had told his mother? They had been following him around for months and he believed that they had done this sort of thing before. His

32 *The Herald*, 17 December 1936
33 *The Argus*, 18 December 1936

defence was that, although they had fired many shots at him, he did not shoot at them because the odds were too great.

The case against Cody for the murder of Scriven relied on identification by witnesses, who seemed to be able to clearly identify Rupert Davies but were less clear about Cody. The practices of Victoria Police regarding line-ups of suspects were increasingly being questioned and would be reviewed and revised after the delivery of the report by Alex Duncan, brought in by the Government from Scotland Yard to review the practices of the Victorian police. But at the time of Cody's arrest, the methods used were highly questionable.

A sensation occurred during evidence given by John (Jack) Stevens, who had agreed to testify for the prosecution – but only after he had been arrested and charged with consorting. He told the court that, in early February 1936, Cody had called at his home and said he was going to Sydney. He met him again in the middle of March outside the factory in which he was working, where Cody revealed a roll of notes appearing to contain about £20. But the most telling evidence was that in June, having met the Davies brothers through Cody, Geoffrey mentioned the Scriven hold-up in conversation and said with a grin 'that it had been done very nicely – it was a neat job and things went off really well'.[34] On another occasion Cody had said to Stevens that he was in the Scriven business. Stevens asked him what he had done with the money and Cody had said: 'We planted it near the Walmer Street Bridge, took it to Queensland and changed it, and then brought it back to Melbourne'. Geoffrey Davies had said to Stevens that he believed he had been told all about the Scriven affair by Cody. Davies was concerned that Stevens had talked to others about the Scriven affair, telling Cody that he believed Jacky said something about the Scriven case. Geoffrey

34 *The Argus*, 16 December 1936

told him to keep it to himself, which he said he would.

Stevens also told the court that, on about August 1, Geoffrey Davies showed him the revolver with the defective trigger and later told him that he had dumped the weapon, which accorded with the evidence of Constable Cairns. [35] He denied that police had brought pressure to bear on him, stating that after he was arrested he decided to tell the police what he knew about Cody and Davies, and that this occurred before he was charged. Stevens denied that he had agreed to give evidence at the Scriven trial if the police 'treated him decently'. In cross-examination, Barry asked Stevens how he had come to give evidence. 'They (the police) asked me", he replied. 'After you had cheerfully agreed to tell them', said Barry. 'Not cheerfully', he replied. Barry then put it to Stevens that he came here out of a sense of public duty. Yes, he replied, to which Barry asked 'Are you serious?' Barry pointed out that he had previously had trouble with the police and was a man with convictions (criminal, not moral). Stevens maintained that he had never met the Davies' until February 1936, when Cody introduced them. He refuted the suggestion by Barry that he had met and visited the Davies' last year (i.e.1935).[36]

Under cross-examination Cody claimed that the Scriven murder was never mentioned to Stevens at any time and that the whole account given by Stevens was false. [37] The evidence of Stevens came to be one of the most controversial revelations in the first trial. The clear implication was that he had been offered a deal by the police to testify against Cody. The defence counsel for Rupert Davies, Jack Barry, was scathing about the evidence of Stevens, describing him as a Judas and a liar and

35 *The Argus,* 16 December 1936
36 *The Sun News-Pictorial*, 17 December 1936
37 *The Argus,* 18 December 1936

warning the jury about accepting his evidence. This was a man who was arrested first (on other charges) and then decided to tell the police about comments made by his 'friends'. [38]

Rupert Davies was no fashion plate but he appeared in court in a well-fitting grey suit. Not surprisingly he claimed that he had never had the alleged conversation with Jack Stevens about the Scriven murder. [39] He had known Stevens for a couple of years, as he used to bring his girlfriend to Geoffrey Davies' place and had spent a fair amount of time with the three accused. Davies also informed the court that he had been to Brisbane once (in June) since the date of the Scriven murder, travelling by train. But Geoffrey gave evidence that the brothers (together with Cody) had gone to Brisbane twice in that time. It was a discrepancy that would prove to be of enormous importance in the future. Rupert Davies also stated that, on the day of the robbery, he had collected his sustenance payment at Collingwood Town Hall about 4.30 p.m., payments he had been receiving for about three years. [40] He and his brother had then met with a friend, Alexander Parkes, to celebrate his birthday. They met at about 5.15 outside the Abbotsford factory where Parkes worked. From there they went to the North Richmond hotel at 66 Victoria Street but left at about 6.00 p.m. when the pub closed. This evidence was confirmed when Parkes took the stand. He also told the court that he had known Davies for about 20 years and had met Stephens a couple of times. Curiously, Parkes stated that this was the first time he had given evidence, which raises

38 *The Argus,* 18 December 1936

39 *The Sun News-Pictorial*, 17 December 1936

40 At the committal hearing in November, the supervisor of the scheme testified that Cody had not undertaken any sustenance work that day. By the time of the trial, the time books prior to August 1936 were missing. But it was clear that the Davies brothers had worked on one of the gangs of sustenance workers at various times.

the question of why he was not called upon to give evidence at the committal proceedings.

In mid-afternoon of Friday December 18, the prosecution summed up. There was little dispute about what had happened – the question was whether any of the men in the dock were any of those who had carried out the robbery and the murder. Book stated that it was clear that Geoffrey Davies was not one of the men in the robbery and that the jury might well think that it might be dangerous to convict him on the evidence, stating that 'you cannot convict on suspicion'. Given his comments, counsel for Geoffrey Davies, Mr Nimmo, asked the judge whether he needed to address the jury on behalf of his client and was told no. The Judge went on to advise the jury to acquit him. It seemed plain that he was NOT one of the three men who got out of the car. Geoffrey Davies was in the clear for the murder. Counsel for Cody, Mr Minogue, summed up by saying that no one had suggested that Cody had killed Scriven and that no one had suggested that Cody was in the lane at the time. He also attacked the police for presenting a photograph of Cody to the witness Dugan (who was in gaol at the time) and for taking witnesses to the City Court to identify the men who had at that time been charged. According to Harry Minogue, the Lord Chief Justice of England had described such methods as indefensible, which must have raised an eyebrow from Duncan, who was in the courtroom. His report on Victoria Police later proposed many changes to the processes of identification in Victoria.

Now it was time for Chief Justice, Sir Frederick Mann, to sum up the case. He stated the position of the three charged. 'If two or more people agreed together to commit robbery, and further agreed that by carrying it out they would provide themselves with the means of overcoming all resistance, and that they would take steps such as might turn out to be necessary to attain their ends by violence, those persons, if carrying out their scheme, were guilty of murder.' He thought the facts were clear – 'on the first show of resistance by the escort (Scriven), he was murdered… if the jury thought that what those three persons did was what they planned, all three of those persons were guilty of murder; the man sitting in the car as much as the other two.' He went on to remind the jury that the burden of proof was on the Crown, and they should accept nothing but real proof. The case depended principally on the identification of the accused. The Crown, he said, had adopted the policy of bringing into court everyone who, as far as the police knew, had heard or seen anything related to the offence. Four witnesses had sworn to the identity of Rupert Davies. A major consideration was the length of time that had elapsed between the crime and bringing the accused face to face with the witnesses, a period of between nine and twelve months. The Judge noted that 'lengths of time may be fatal to the recollection of one man, and have little effect on the recollection of another'. Another consideration was the circumstances in which each witness made his observations, noting that identification methods employed in this case had been criticised as unfair and improper, but the jury should be solely concerned about how the evidence had been put in this case. Judge Mann was scathing about the evidence provided by John Stevens, advising the jury that they should give no weight to it at all, particularly when the jury had before it 'evidence of men whose character cannot be attacked', presumably Boadle and Reeves. Stevens had been an associate of the accused and had received an admission of them having committed the crime, but 'breathed not a word of it until the time comes when he is arrested himself'. [41] Whilst this was accurate, it would seem

41 *The Herald*, 18 December 1936

an unworldly view about how the underworld operated. After all, Stevens could have come forward at any time to claim the reward but chose not to, obviously in fear of retribution.

The Judge probably favoured the prosecution but appeared to have some doubts about whether the Crown had proved its case. The jury retired to deliberate and consider the evidence presented to them. Were they convinced of the guilt or innocence of the three? More importantly, could they agree on their decision? They were locked away for over five hours and, at about 10.10 p.m., they returned with their verdicts. The result was a sensation. The foreman advised the court that Geoffrey Davies was acquitted of both the murder charge and the charge of robbery in company, but the jury could not agree on the guilt of Cody and Rupert Davies and he told the judge that there was no possibility of an agreement. There was nothing for Justice Mann to do but remand them over for a further trial, probably in next February. The legal profession and Courts traditionally took holidays during January. There is an old saying in legal circles that justice delayed is justice denied. Was it the case here? After all it had been nearly a year since the murder before the trial commenced. And what would the prosecution be able to produce at the next trial that would convince another jury? For the defendants, a retrial was obviously not as preferable as a 'not guilty' verdict, but they were confident that no new evidence would be presented that would result in their conviction at a new trial. How wrong this assessment would turn out to be. A few days after the trial ended, Alex Duncan released his interim report into the Victoria Police. It contained scathing criticism of the Criminal Investigation Branch. He found a grave lack of supervision by the Branch superiors. In fact, there was no supervision at all by senior officers of cases in hand. There could be no efficiency among the rank and file. Whilst the majority of the lower ranks were keen on their job and were doing their best under trying and sometimes difficult circumstances, they were hampered by the lack of training and lack of incentive on the part of their officers. He also found grave neglect regarding prompt attention to requests from the public for the services of the CIB.[42] Perhaps there was no greater illustration of Duncan's concerns than the investigations into the Scriven murder and the Brophy shooting.

But in the meantime there were still other charges outstanding against Cody and the Davies brothers, to be heard in the City Court. They related to the sensational shoot-out on the tramcar and arrest in the Exhibition Gardens on November 5. Geoffrey Davies may have been acquitted of murder but was still facing charges for having shot at First Constable Guider with intent to murder him, as well as the charge of having attempted to discharge a loaded revolver at Constable Cairns with intent to resist arrest. Given that Constable Cairns had described how he had pushed Davies off the tram into the arms of waiting police, and that he had taken no part in the chase through the Exhibition Gardens where the shots were fired, it would seem that the police had no chance of a conviction and the charges should never have been laid. Geoffrey Davies also faced charges of a lesser nature, of consorting with reputed thieves and having been the occupier of a house frequented by reputed thieves. But at least he was able to go home after obtaining bail, set at £500, with two sureties of £250. The police argued that such a high amount was necessary because there were real fears that the witnesses in the Scriven trial would be intimidated. Sureties

42 Duncan, Alexander, *Reports of Alexander M. Duncan, Esq., Chief Inspector, London Metropolitan Police, on the police force of Victoria*, Melbourne, 1936-1937

for bail were often arranged from 'bondsmen' who could be family and friends or clients of solicitors. Sometimes they did not even know the person charged. Many on the bench did not care where the bail money came from; others insisted that the bondsman had sufficient assets to meet any possible contingency, whilst others worried that the money may come from the underworld – what would happen if they began to fight amongst themselves over the amount subscribed? If the charged person was a 'no-show' (i.e. failed to appear), the bondsman would lose the amount that was put up (known as estreating). Cody faced similar shooting charges, whilst Rupert Davies still faced charges of being armed with a revolver and of robbing Edward Maguire on June 19. Both were remanded until the New Year.

Across Victoria, things were looking up at last and the state enjoyed a 'prosperity' Christmas. Holiday resorts reported their heaviest bookings for six years and 'packed out' was the usual comment made to enquiries about accommodation.

The perfect weather attracted thousands to beaches around Melbourne over the Christmas period. In a sign of things to come, the 'drone of airliners arriving at Essendon airport from three states provided a background at the week-end for new records in Victorian commercial aviation'.[43] But the biggest event (and the cause of much speculation in city pubs and workplaces) was the third Test Match of the 1936/7 Ashes series, about to be played at the Melbourne Cricket Ground (MCG). The city was enthralled. England was already two up in the best of five series, so a win for Australia was vital if they were to stay in the competition for the series. The cricket world was certain that the match would be keenly fought out and Melbourne newspapers were confident that Australia

43 *The Argus*, 28 November 1936

could win the test. They boasted the world's leading batsman, Don Bradman, and all its other batsmen were in form. The British press was also confident, regarding that Australia was over-reliant on Bradman. The sensational match began on New Year's Day. Traffic on the roads was quiet (except near the MCG), swimming pools and minor sports were poorly attended, although the New Year's Day races attracted a crowd of 32,000 to Flemington. Those taking their holidays at resorts and camping places were clustered around radio sets. In a weather pattern typical of Melbourne, New Year's Day began with a burst of brilliant sunshine and ended in dismal showers. The match was played in front of 350,534 spectators over its six days, including a crowd of 87,798 on the second day – a world record for a Test match. The massive new all-concrete and steel Southern Stand at the MCG (designed by architects Purnell and Pearce) had just been completed in the expectation of large football and cricket crowds, the latter drawn by the prospect of seeing Australian captain Don Bradman in full flight. They were not to be disappointed in this match, with Bradman compiling 270 in Australia's second innings total of 564. England failed to match Bradman's mercurial efforts, facing a mammoth 689 to win and went on to lose the match by 365 runs and ultimately the series as Australia completed the biggest comeback in Ashes history.

The New Year was welcomed at Pentridge, where each division conducted its own sports meeting. In a major innovation, radio broadcasts of the Test match were played over loudspeakers, with some old-timers blanching when the amplified voice of the announcer shattered the prison stillness. However the prisoners were locked down at 4.00 p.m., and were left wondering about events in the final session of play, although they received a special treat when pudding was added to the menu (normally Friday was a puddingless day). But cricket would have been far from the minds of Cody and Rupert Davies when they appeared in the City Court on the morning of Monday January 4 after the Courts returned from the Christmas/ New Year break. The solicitor acting for Geoffrey Davies, Mr Sonenberg, sought a reduction in his bail surety – from £500 to £300, which was refused by the magistrate. The police sought another adjournment, which was granted. It was the seventh time that the accused had been remanded on the charges. Not surprisingly, the continual delay (even if agreed to by his counsel) was wearing down the nerves of Geoffrey Davies. When he appeared on January 18 at yet another hearing, Davies had had enough and directed an outburst at the police and the court and his own counsel. Alleging that he was being persecuted, he objected to any further delay in the hearing of the charges against him. In his view the police had brought him to court on numerous occasions. He told the court he had done nothing wrong and wanted a chance to clear himself. Sergeant de la Rue, the police prosecutor, explained to the bench that he had an arrangement with Mr Sonenberg, Davies' counsel, to have weekly remands until February 11. When asked by the Magistrate if Mr Sonenberg was still his solicitor, Davies said he did not know. Davies may have been a well-known underworld figure but he had a point about the nature of the shooting charges. As he put it to the Court: 'the police arrested me months ago and charged me with murder. They tried to take my life. They failed in that. Then they charged me with shooting at Constable Guider and brought me here the following day. They admit that I had no gun, that I fired no shot, and that I was not even in Cody's company in the gardens when the shooting took place. The Brophy scandal was put against me here. It was public property outside. Everybody had their own idea what happened. It left a blot on the CIB. That charge was not read out against me because they know they made a mistake. I want these cases heard. I don't want to go on being persecuted.'[44] Davies' reference to the shooting of Chief Superintendent Brophy at Royal Park on May 22, the other sensational shooting of 1936, was timely. It had re-emerged in early January when detectives laid 'informations' against two men who were to be soon charged with shooting Brophy.[45] The two men would be Cody and Geoffrey Davies. The laying of 'informations' described the process whereby an accusation or criminal charge is brought by the public prosecutor. It must state the alleged crimes in writing and be delivered to the defendant at the first court appearance. If the accusation is for a felony, there must be a preliminary hearing within a short period in which the prosecution is required to present enough evidence to convince the judge holding the hearing that the crime or crimes charged were committed and the defendant is likely to have committed them. If the judge becomes convinced, the defendant must face trial, and if the judge does not, the case against the defendant is dismissed. Sometimes it is a mixed bag, in that some of the

44 *The Argus,* 19 January 1937; on the 19th February, Davies was charged with having wounded Brophy with intent to murder him. In the 1970s, Geoffrey Davies was apparently respectable and was a councillor on Fitzroy Council from 1972 to 1978. Another councillor, Tim Harding, recalled recently that Davies had told him the story of being chased and shot at by Cairns in the gardens. But he obviously had substituted himself in the place of Cody. He also claimed to have been a lookout in John Wren's famous tote in Collingwood, which closed in 1913. Davies was born in 1905. He passed away in 1986, aged 81. Communication from Tim Harding, 23 August 2013

45 *Sydney Morning Herald,* 9 January 1937

charges in the information are sufficient for trial and the case is sent (remanded) to the appropriate court, whilst others are dismissed.

Acting for Cody, Sonenberg was outraged that the police should choose to charge Cody and Geoffrey Davies with the shooting of Brophy whilst a capital charge against them was still in abeyance. 'Grossly improper and unfair,' he grumbled. The matter was adjourned for a month. This was a major problem for Davies, who was causing the jail staff distress by continually hammering on the cell door and yelling for bail. Davies claimed that he would just as soon get the trial for shooting Brophy under way, but the police realised that they were in no position to prejudice the Scriven trial by commencing another trial. It must be wondered what the police were trying to achieve by laying charges about the Brophy shooting, as they knew that they had no chance of success with the charges. Was this just an attempt to put Cody under more pressure?

The public was absorbed in reading about the sensational shootout in the Gardens. Who fired first? Cody may have – if so, his justification was that he had been followed for months by police and was certain that they would shoot him that day. The public had to face the real possibility that some armed police were out of control and determined to either frame known criminals, whether they deserved it or not, or were prepared to open fire on them at any time. Their case was not helped by a constable who, in January 1937, fired a number of shots in Swanston Street during the chase by plain-clothes police of a suspected man who had escaped from their custody. This was in a major city street and was obviously very dangerous to citizens going about their business.[46] A few months earlier, in late October 1936, a Police wireless patrol

46 *The Argus,* 17 January, 1937

had fired a fusillade of shots at a man who had broken into the booking office at Flemington Bridge railway station. Responding to an alarm, the wireless patrol discovered a man running along the platform. As he jumped down an embankment they fired several shots but he escaped into a nearby paddock.[47]

In early February 1937, Alex Duncan took up the position of Chief Commissioner. The Scriven case was just one of a number that had been unsatisfactorily investigated and was still unresolved.

47 *The Argus,* 26 October 1936

CHAPTER 6

THE SECOND TRIAL

On February 15, 1937, over a year after the shooting of Ted Scriven, the second trial of William Cody and Rupert Davies began in Melbourne's Criminal Court. C H Book was again the prosecutor for the Crown, whilst the defence team consisted of Jack Barry for Davies together with Harry Minogue and John Nimmo for Cody. As in the first trial, each received instructions from Mr 'Sonny' Sonenberg. This time the judge was Justice Charles Leonard Gavan Duffy, the son of Sir Frank Gavan Duffy who had become Chief Justice of the High Court of Australia. The younger Duffy had been admitted to the Bar in 1908. In 1915 he enlisted in the Australian Imperial Force as a second lieutenant, serving in the Great War at Gallipoli and in France. On 30 May 1933, following the death of Sir Leo Cussen, Duffy was appointed a justice of the Supreme Court of Victoria. His entry in the Australian Dictionary of Biography, written by another member of the Bar, asserts that he proved a competent judge, gifted with keen memory and complete independence of mind and conducting his court admirably. At all times Duffy was courteous, considerate and whimsically good-humoured, but nevertheless dispatched business with firmness. His judgments, though not perhaps as deeply learned as some of his colleagues,

Benches, City Court, 2015

displayed unerring instinct for legal principles and were sound and practical.[1] However, as we shall see, the counsels for the defence, particularly Barry, were highly critical of his performance on the bench in this trial.

Once again, over 30 prospective jurors were challenged before a jury was empanelled. The jurors would have been well aware of the outcome of the first trial and were also aware that one of the Crown witnesses (Dugan) had been shot after he had given evidence at the committal hearing. If the underworld would shoot at a witness, could the jurors regard themselves as safe?

Before the members of the jury took their place, Barry (supported by Minogue) attempted to have the Judge rule that certain evidence that the Crown proposed to lead was inadmissible. They had unsuccessfully tried this tack in the first trial. It concerned the bank account of Davies and his wife and the possession of money in the account in June of 1936, six months after the robbery. Barry was concerned that the Crown would infer that if the couple had money in June, it must have come from a robbery that occurred in January. Another concern was the identification of Cody. It was pointed out to the Judge that a witness, James Dugan, would say that before he was taken

1 Charles Francis, '*Duffy, Sir Charles Leonard Gavan (1882–1961)*', Australian Dictionary of Biography, National Centre of Biography, Australian National University, http://adb.anu.edu.au/biography/duffy-sir-charles-leonard-gavan-6028/text10303, accessed 17 December 2013.

to Russell Street to identify Cody, he was shown a photograph of Cody. Perhaps they thought that a different judge would be more sympathetic. He wasn't and Duffy disallowed the application. In his view the value of evidence given by a witness in these circumstances was reduced considerably but he did not think that the evidence was legally inadmissible. Evidence was later given by Charles Davis, a motor cycle dealer from Goulburn St., Sydney, that he sold a B.S.A motor cycle to Cody, who paid a £5 booking fee on June 27 and the balance of £47/18/3 three days later, all in cash. Cody used the name of Rayner and gave an address in Redfern when he bought the bike. When Davis informed the Court of the sale of a motorcycle to Rupert Davies, it was made clear that he gave his correct name, address and there was no concealment about the sale and he did not act devious in any way. As Barry had asserted, it is difficult to see the relevance of this evidence. [2]

When the jury was brought in and the trial commenced, much evidence was presented about the gun supposedly used in the shooting of Scriven. Dr. Crawford Mollison, the Spring Street surgeon who carried out post mortems for the Coroner, testified that the injury that caused death was from a large wound about four inches from the base of the nose. The pistol was actually in contact with the skin or extremely close to it. The bullet had caused extensive fracturing of the vault of the skull, had passed through the right hemisphere of the brain and out of the skull into the scalp behind the right ear. He had removed a nickel-plated bullet from the head of Scriven and handed it to police after the post mortem. [3]

2 *The Argus*, 16 February 1937; PROV,VPRS 00030/P0006, Unit 000004, 1936/777; *Proceedings of trial,* 14 February 1937

3 PROV,VPRS 00030/P0006, Unit 000004, 1936/777; *Proceedings of trial,* 21 June 1937

Shea repeated his evidence from the first trial, as did most of the other witnesses. But this time Barry put more pressure on Dugan, the young man of 19 who had repaired the gun. Detective Hobley again told the court about the physical appearance of the pistol. The defence team was convinced that Dugan was 'romancing' about a lot of his evidence. Why would Cody have taken the pistol to him instead of a regular repairer of guns? After all, it was a relatively simple job that did not require any repairs to the mechanics of the pistol. Whilst the gun would operate without the plate, it was far more effective with it in place. Under cross-examination, Dugan told the court that he had been repairing guns for about three years and had repaired four or five pistols, as well as between 100 and 200 rifles, usually aligning the sights of rifles for various men in a shooting club. When he told the court that he could not locate a book that recorded all his jobs, Barry accused him of romancing about a lot of things. Dugan admitted that knew he was doing something of which the police would not approve when he repaired the pistol. After he repaired it, he tested the job by firing a full magazine, and recorded its number. He did not have a license to have a pistol in his possession at the time and he knew that it was an offence to be in possession of an unregistered pistol. But the offer of £1 was sufficient for him to overcome his reluctance to do the job. Dugan agreed with Barry that it was good payment for the job.

Dugan also admitted that, after Scriven had been shot, he believed that the weapon used to cause his death was the one that he had repaired. When asked why he did not go to the police until early November, Dugan replied that he did not know where he stood with them, even though he was in possession of knowledge about where the pistol came from.

Book questioned if Dugan were serious. Absolutely serious, he replied. After all, he had been questioned extensively after he had received a gunshot wound on Henley Day, after the committal hearing. Perhaps he was fearful that the police would try and implicate him in the shooting. The smartest thing he could do was to keep quiet. Dugan also told the court that he had been shown about 20 photographs at police headquarters and picked out the one of Cody. But he did not want to rely solely on the photograph. A few days later, on November 12, Cody was shown to him under lights, by himself. He asked Cody to speak, and recognised Cody's voice from his previous dealings with him on the two occasions in January 1936. He had not met him before that date and had not seen him since. For his part, Cody told the court that he had never met Dugan or seen him before he gave evidence at the City Court.

The Stamps Office messenger who had been carrying the money, Herbert Harvey Gillbank, again testified on the events of the day. His evidence was almost identical to that at the first trial. He told the court that the gun used to shoot Scriven was about six inches from Scriven's head when the gunman pulled the trigger. After the shooting, he started to run back towards the Stamps Office, then stopped and ran towards Queen Street, but did not see the escaping robbers. He described the man who fired the shot as a few inches taller than the other one. When asked to look at the men in the dock, he stated that Davies was similar in height, build and general appearance to the man who had shot Scriven, noting that he had what appeared to be a handkerchief hanging over his forehead, down to his eyes, and he wore a hat. Barry pointed out that Gillbank had made no reference to the handkerchief at the Coroners' Inquest in the previous July, nor at the committal hearing in November. But he had recalled this detail at the first trial. What Barry was trying to establish was that Gillbank had not mentioned the handkerchief until after he had read about it in the newspaper reports of the first trial. Despite this minor discrepancy, Gillbank remained a solid witness. It was not unusual for witnesses to recall items and details as they moved through the various procedures leading to a trial, and Gillbank would not be the last. Gillbank also repeated his testimony that the shorter man who had taken part in the robbery was not like Cody in build. [4]

The taxi-driver, Reg Pullen, repeated his testimony about the robbery, swearing that Davies resembled the man who had the pistol and that he was 'rather a square-shouldered built man and rather dark and had a full jaw'. However, he only saw him side face. Whilst Rupert Davies resembled the man, he was not prepared to swear that he was the man. He also told the Court that in November he was shown about half a dozen photographs and asked to identify the men, and then was shown Rupert Davies by himself after Davies was arrested, under the lights at Russell Street. He was one of three men shown to him in this fashion – one at a time. He had read in the newspapers that Davies had been arrested at the same time as Cody, and understood that he was going to be shown a man who the police believed had something to do with the killing. When he was shown Davies, he believed that he was the man the police had arrested in conjunction with the killing. 'Yes', he replied, 'not Cody.'[5]

The witness Aubrey Reeves again told the court of his role and declared that he 'had no doubt at all' that he saw Davies

4 PROV, VPRS 00030/P0006, Unit 000004, 1936/777; *Proceedings of trial*, 16 February 1937

5 PROV, VPRS 00030/P0006, Unit 000004, 1936/777; *Proceedings of trial,* 15 February 1937

shoot Scriven, despite the fact that part of the killer's face was partially covered with a handkerchief over his left eye. However he had seen his full face before the robbery as he walked past the men. He next saw Davies in May in front of the Victoria Market, but he did not report the sighting to the police as he was working and could not leave his truck. His boss was away (he always had a shave at dinner time) and he could not leave the goods. By the time the boss came back it was too late to ring the police, as the men had disappeared. Besides, he was not going to get anything out of identifying the men. He next saw Rupert Davies after he was arrested. However, he was reminded that he had stated at the first trial that one of the men was Geoffrey Davies, who had subsequently been acquitted. The defence was again sceptical of the evidence provided by one of the Crown's star witnesses. Reeves had also changed his mind about the time of the events, now stating that it occurred about 4.30 p.m., not 4.40 p.m. as he had testified in the first trial (which in turn had been changed from 4.50 p.m.).[6] The clear implication was that if it had taken place at 4.30, then Davies would have been able to carry out the robbery and then meet Parkes at about 5.15 p.m. for his birthday drinks.

The superintendent of the Destructor Yard, John Boadle, repeated his evidence that Rupert Davies and Cody were two of the three men who alighted from the car that drove into the yard. He was supported by Harry Malcolm Johnstone, a stoker at the yard, who told the court that he saw two men leave a black car that drove into the yard at about 4.45 p.m. The taller man was Davies and the shorter man, who carried a bag, was Cody.[7]

John Stevens, veneer-cutter, of North Melbourne, and

6 PROV, VPRS 00030/P0006, Unit 000004, 1936/777; *Proceedings of trial,* 15 February 1937

7 *The Argus*, 17 February 1937

commonly known as Jack, said that he had known Cody for four years. He had also gone to school with Dugan but they had not been in contact for years. Cody had told him in February that he was going to Sydney, and when he next saw him in March, Cody showed him a roll of notes. He again swore that he had visited their homes in Collingwood on many occasions. In June, Cody had admitted in conversation with him that he and the Davies brothers had been concerned in the Scriven holdup. Rupert Davies had made a similar admission, he claimed, and the money had been taken to Sydney and changed. Cody had also told him that they had been lucky to get away with the hold-up. Stevens again stated that he was motivated to give evidence (and betray his friends) from a sense of public duty and that he was not stimulated by something the police had done to him, as suggested by Barry. He told the court that at one stage the police suggested that he had been in the hold-up, but he had an alibi for the day as he was working. He told the court that he wanted to 'cut clear' of his old associates. [8] Barry and the defence team were clearly sceptical of his evidence and his motivation. In their minds, there was the real possibility of a deal between Stevens and the police where he would be treated leniently on other matters if he gave evidence against Cody and Davies.

When Barry asked how he had come to give evidence, Stevens said he was taken to Russell Street and charged with consorting. He appeared in court and was remanded for a week. He then appeared in court again and gave evidence at the previous trial of the three men. The consorting charge was adjourned until February 22. 'Did the police at any time suggest that you were in this case?' asked Barry. 'Yes, but I provided an alibi. I was working', replied Stevens.[9]

8 *The Age,* 18 February 1937
9 *The Herald,* 17 February 1937

So Stevens was still waiting for consorting charges to be heard and was not aware that Geoffrey Davies had told police that Stevens' alibi was 'crook'. Despite the fact that Stevens had been in trouble with the police before (he told the court that he had served two and a half years of a sentence of over four years and had been fined), his evidence again appeared to be solid (at least for the moment) and was regarded as damning for the defendants.

The police were again criticised by Jack Barry (for Davies) for their methods of obtaining evidence of identification. The new Chief Commissioner of Police, Mr Duncan, had accepted the position after he had finished his review of the force and made a report to the Chief Secretary. He would take up the position of Chief Commissioner as soon as he had furnished Scotland Yard with his resignation and informed his wife that they were moving to Melbourne. Duncan had made a number of recommendations, mostly direct from the operating procedures of the Metropolitan police in London. He was of the opinion that Commissioners should be practical men, possessing knowledge of all branches of the police service that can be obtained only by experience on the job. Whilst he never outwardly criticised his predecessor, Blamey, he was highly critical of the structure and procedures of the Force, particularly the crude methods adopted early in investigations. He recognised that the force was undermanned and wanted public servants to take over some of the clerical work in order to free up police officers in the traffic and transport sections for active police work. He intended to introduce a new syllabus for the training of police recruits and recognised the need for more police on traffic duty as the motorcar gradually came to dominate the streets of Melbourne. However, despite a spate of holiday casualties on Victoria's roads, he was opposed to the introduction of speed limits on Victorian highways, not wishing to be seen to be tying down the schedules of travellers by a series of regulations. [10] He also saw a solution to Melbourne's growing traffic problems in the introduction of a 'two-storied' approach, with tunnels and undergrounds.[11]

By appointing Duncan to the position, the Victorian government had virtually approved all the recommendations in his reports, including agreeing to the outlay of funds to purchase the 'light' cars that Duncan favoured as substitutes for the heavy patrol vehicles and motorcycle outfits currently in use. He also intended to rectify the practices concerning identification of suspects of crimes, which had attracted major criticism, and intended to extend the British system of an identification parade.[12] A similar system was in operation in the USA, known as 'the line-up.' Barry was able to read out a list of recommendations by Duncan relating to identification in an effort to show up the inadequate methods currently used.[13]

Senior-detective W E ('Bill') Davis suffered some uncomfortable questioning about the procedures, both old and new, but pointed out that the men were arrested before Duncan made his report. When he was asked which would be the fairer system – the one used in this case or the one recommended by Duncan, he replied that both methods would be fair 'with honest witnesses'.[14] Further evidence about identification was provided by Joseph Selkridge, a driver from Prahran, who said that he had been seated on his stationary ice-wagon in Acland Street, St Kilda, on January 29, when he observed a black sedan

10 *Portland Guardian*, 8 February 1937
11 *The Argus*, 3 December 1936
12 *The Argus,* 28 January 1937
13 *The Argus,* 15 March 1937
14 *The Argus,* 18 February 1937

car, numbered 86730, containing four men, two of whom he recognised as Davies and Cody. Davies was in the back seat and Cody was in the front seat next to the driver. He was suspicious of them. The car was coming down the hill towards him, at about 20 mph (32 kph), and he was about 20 yards (18 metres) away from it. Although the car slowed to pass a tram, he only had a few seconds to observe the occupants. When cross-examined by Barry, Selkridge admitted that in his original statement to police (in February), stated that he was driving the ice-wagon and had described Davies as having a bull-neck (short and thick). But now he had changed his story – he could not say Davies had a bull-neck and he would not swear that the man had been Davies. He was now saying that it was like him. He had seen the accused in May but had not reported the sighting to police, as he was on a wagon and his boss was away and he could not leave the goods. But he admitted that another reason was that he was not getting anything from reporting them. In mid-November he had gone to Russell Street at someone's request.[15] Before he viewed Cody and Davies the police had told him that they believed they were involved in the hold-up and murder. He then attended the City Court and saw Cody and Davies being charged with having murdered Scriven. After he observed them for about ten minutes, and they were charged, he told police that 'they were like the men when he first saw them' i.e. in Acland Street. He then went over to Russell Street to make a statement.

In reply to Mr Minogue the witness denied the accuracy of a statement – saying it had been read over very quickly to him by police. [16] Once again the issue of identification became crucial. It had been revealed at the first trial that Selkridge (as well as

15 PROV,VPRS 00030/P0006, Unit 000004, 1936/777; *Proceedings of trial*, 21 June 1937

16 *The Sun News-Pictorial*, 17 February 1937

the taxi-driver, Pullen) had previously lived near to Rupert Davies. Was there a reason for Selkridge to identify Davies, and to lie during his evidence? Was there an element of payback by Selkridge against a notable criminal who lived near him?

When Davies took the stand, he denied ever discussing the Scriven murder with Stevens and could think of no reason why he should give such evidence against him. He stated that he had received his sustenance pay at the Collingwood Town Hall in Hoddle Street (the main thoroughfare in Collingwood) between 4.15 p.m. and 4.30 p.m., talked to some friends for about ten minutes outside the Town Hall and then went with his brother Geoffrey to the Parkside Shoe Factory in Abbotsford to meet a friend. They arrived at about 5.00 p.m. and met Rupert's friend of 20 years, Alexander Parkes, at about 5.15 p.m. Parkes, a bootmaker from Victoria Street, Abbotsford, gave evidence that he met the Davies brothers outside the factory, where he worked, at about 5.15 p.m. and then visited the Victoria Hotel in North Richmond, where they had a few drinks to celebrate his birthday. They left the hotel just after 6 p.m., when all hotels closed. The brothers had arranged on the previous day to meet up with Parkes. But the police thought that it was possible for the two to have carried out the 'hold-up' and still made it to Abbotsford. In evidence, Senior-Detective Davis testified that he had driven from Spencer Street to the factory in about 5 minutes, a distance of 2.6 miles (4.18 kilometres), intimating that there would have been time for the three to commit the robbery and murder and still make it to Abbotsford by 5.00 p.m. But this was a very long bow to draw, particularly as the vehicle used in the robbery was badly damaged in the getaway. A possible scenario was that Parkes was lying. Parkes later stated that when he heard of the date of the murder and the charge against

Davies, he had visited his mother and informed her that Davies was with him on January 31. She then reminded Davies of his whereabouts on that day. When Davies was arrested he could not recall where he was on that day. Faulty memory? Or was it criminal collusion between Parkes and Mrs Davies.[17] Mrs Davies would probably have been capable of such an act to protect her son, but Parkes had a lot to lose – he had not been in any trouble for ten years, had been employed by the same company for seven years, and had a wife and family.

The more telling evidence came from Davies about his trips to Queensland. When cross-examined by Mr Book, Davies said that he had gone to Brisbane only once last year (i.e. 1936), in June. He had gone there to look for a job, but stayed only four days. When Book asked if he had made another trip in September, he replied no. Incredulous, Book asked him if he was serious and then played his trump card - a telegraph money order received in Brisbane in September, transferring £10 from his wife in Collingwood and signed for by him. So he WAS in Brisbane in September. Davies admitted that the money order bore his signature but added that he did not recall going to Brisbane in September. In a pivotal moment for the prosecution, Davies then admitted that he had been there in September for five or six days just for the trip. Realising the importance of this testimony, Book went for the kill: 'When you said a moment ago that you were not in Brisbane in September, you were lying to the jury?' 'No,' he replied, 'I did not want to alter my other statement. I did not want to say I was there because Stevens was with me.' But the damage was done and Davies had damned himself with this admission.[18]

When Cody took the stand, his evidence was similar to that

17 *The Argus*, 23 June 1937

18 *The Argus*, 18 February 1937

at the first trial. He denied having ever met the witness Dugan, who had repaired the gun, and denied any participation in the crime, claiming that he was at Collingwood with his sister at the time of the robbery.

Barry's final address, as in the first trial, concentrated on the methods of identification used by the police, buoyed by the corroboration of his views of the inadequacy of police methods by the new Commissioner of Police, Alex Duncan. However whilst it was certainly improper that suspects were placed under bright lights or that witnesses were asked to identify the men as they stood in the dock at the City Court, charged with murder, it was not enough to sway the jury to find them innocent. Nor was the character of the witness John Stevens, referred to by Barry as 'the horrible spectacle of the informer' who allegedly gave evidence against the accused to protect himself and not because of any sense of public duty. When he addressed the jury, the prosecutor, Mr Book, told the jury that whilst they may have the worst possible opinion of Stevens, they must consider the truth of whether Davies DID tell Stevens that he had taken part in the hold-up of Scriven. Why would Stevens have told the story that he had told against Davies, who had been a friend of his, if it were not true? Judge Gavan Duffy, in his charge to the jury, said that Stevens was a man 'of very bad character', and one might hazard the guess that when he was threatened with a prosecution he thought that it would be a good way out of the difficulty by giving evidence. There was no evidence however that this was his reason. In a somewhat muddled summary, Duffy said that he found it very difficult to understand how it would be possible on the evidence to find Cody guilty of robbery, because if the jury believed the evidence against him it was a clear matter of murder.[19]

19 *The Argus,* 19 February 1937

Barry was later scathing about Duffy's summary, describing it as 'a poor effort, confused and rambling' and it appeared very plainly that he considered the prisoners guilty. Barry was confident that he had shaken 'every Crown witness of importance', and considered that he had nothing to trouble himself about in his performance. But he conceded that he had been outdone by the prosecutor, who showed that Davies had lied over a claim about his trips to Queensland. [20]

Following the summing-up by the Judge to a subdued courtroom, the jury retired to consider its verdict at 5.12 p.m. It was a harrowing time for the families and friends of the accused, who must have realised that the testimony of Davies about his trips to Queensland could condemn him. The jury returned at about 8.30 p.m. to ask a question before returning at 9.25 p.m. to announce the verdicts. The hushed, packed court listened intently as the jury foreman announced the decision. 'Guilty', he stated. Both men had been found guilty of murder. Immediately, a disturbance broke out in the stunned courtroom. Three women seated at the back of the courtroom, relatives of the accused, rose and cried out; 'They are not guilty. They are not guilty. They said they would get him.' Rupert's mother, Leitha, waving her arms in despair, sobbed, 'My son, my son.'[21] Many other women in the court burst into tears amid the frenzied scenes that immediately followed. The commotion was so great that the Associate of the Judge could not be heard when he asked the prisoners if they had anything to say about why the sentence of the Court should not be passed upon them

20 Mark Finnane, *J V Barry: A Life*, 2007, p. 65

21 The Davies family legend is that Leitha supposedly said: 'if my son is guilty may thunder and lightning fill this court room' and apparently the courtroom went dark and sure enough thunder and lightning followed. It is probably apocryphal but makes a good story. Communications with members of the Davies family, January 2015

according to law, and had to repeat the question. Davies replied that he had not had a fair trial and was not guilty. 'I have been framed for this crime from start to finish and what is more, the police know that I am not guilty. We have not had a fair trial and if we had had a fair trial we would not be here now.' One woman in the courtroom began to scream out 'they framed him!' Cody was asked the same question by the Judge and also replied that he was not guilty. But the Judge was unmoved, telling Davies that every point that would tell in your favour had been carefully placed before the jury, and carefully considered by them. Further commotion occurred after these remarks, and a woman was led, struggling and shouting, from the court, whilst other women rushed screaming from the court.[22] Court officials shouted for order and police tried to force the women back into their seats, but were hampered by a group of men, who hustled the police and pushed them aside at the doorways. When order had been restored in the courtroom, a number of women, including Davies' mother, listened in silence. The judge then took over half an hour to read his judgement. Behind the dock a number of women, including Davies' mother, listened in silence. The judge then pronounced the sentence of death in a clear voice at about 9.30 p.m. on Thursday, February 18. When they heard the sentence, Cody swayed slightly and flinched but Davies remained unmoved. Mrs Davies was led from the Court by two women friends. Neither prisoner appeared to be moved outwardly as they were led from the dock, but they knew that they could apply to the full Bench of the High Court of Australia for special leave to appeal against the verdict. Otherwise, their fate would be decided by the Executive

22 *The Albury Banner and Wodonga Express (NSW)*, 26 February 1937; *The Recorder (Port Pirie, South Australia)*, 19 February 1937

Council.[23] Davies immediately stated that he gave notice of appeal. For Barry, an implacable opponent of capital punishment, this was the first time that a client of his had been sentenced to death. As chaos had taken over in the courtroom, the emotions of the moment could have overwhelmed him, but Barry appeared to be 'quite detached and was able to hear the sentence without emotion, and even to watch the prisoners impersonally'. He had now participated in 17 separate murder trials and had become hardened by the system and was unsympathetic to courtroom melodrama.[24] A few days after the trial, Duffy sent for Barry and congratulated him on the effort he had made for the prisoners and for the 'occasional well-turned phrases' in his address, as 'the art of addressing a jury was vanishing.' Following the flattery, Barry found it difficult to retain his resentment of Duffy's 'muddle-headed summing up'. But it must be asked whether his preoccupation with relations at the Bar led to 'an emotional detachment from the fate of his client.'[25]

Outside the Court there was a strong cordon of police around the van that would take them from the cells to Pentridge prison, but there was no demonstration. The next day saw the remaining charges outstanding against Cody and the Davies brothers again adjourned until late February. The police prosecutor must have taken great delight in announcing that Cody and Rupert Davies were not present as they had been convicted of murder on the

23 The Executive Council consists of the Governor and Ministers of the Crown (generally four). In an action such as a hanging, a recommendation (to the Governor-in-Council) would be made to the Council by the responsible Minister. The Ministers would advise the Governor on how to act on the recommendation. It is likely that the sentence of hanging would not have been approved, as this sentence was generally only passed on murderers of children.

24 Mark Finnane, *J V Barry: A Life,* 2007, p. 42, p. 64

25 Mark Finnane, *J V Barry: A Life*, 2007, p. 66

previous day and were in Pentridge under threat of hanging.[26] But the adjournment was clearly upsetting for three female friends of the convicted, who had been in court every day of the trial and again appeared, weeping through the procedures and hurrying from the court as soon as Geoffrey Davies left the dock.[27]

A HEARING SEEKING LEAVE TO HEAR APPEAL

For the people of Victoria, who had followed this case closely for over a year, it appeared to be over – despite the uncertainty relating to identification that had dogged the police case. There was much discussion around the city about the possibility of further appeals and what would happen if they were to be hanged. Would there be mass protests from church groups and union members, as seen before other hangings? Would they repent and confess when faced with the noose, as many others did, or would they go to their deaths protesting their evidence and railing against a police frame-up? Only one of them had pulled the trigger. Despite the legal stricture concerning joint guilt, did the other one deserve to die as well as the shooter? Many women put themselves in the place of their mothers and advocated for mercy. Others placed themselves in the place of Scriven's widow and thought that the sentence was justified for both of the convicted men.

Back in their cells at Pentridge, there was no evidence that Davies and Cody were wracked with remorse or regret or that they sought out the clergy for spiritual comfort. They had other ideas about what would happen next. The ability to

26 *The Argus*, 20 February 1937
27 *The Herald*, 19 February 1937

appeal against a sentence was not automatic. Convicted parties had to demonstrate that there was some deficiency in the legal procedures during the trial that had led to the conviction and a hearing was to be held to determine whether an appeal would be heard. Cody had foreshadowed that he and Davies would appeal against their convictions and, nine days later, this occurred. As this was a capital charge, the appeal had to be dealt with as quickly as possible. As appellants, they were subject to the general regulations applicable to convicted prisoners, but were kept apart as much as possible from other prisoners. [28] In Pentridge, for the first time for 67 years, three men were in the prison at the same time under sentence of death. The third was John Griffith, under sentence for capital offences against two women.

Australian courts can operate in two ways – either in their original form or as a court of appeal. In early March, the hearing seeking leave to appeal the decision began in the Court of Criminal Appeal of Victoria before the Chief Justice (Sir Frederick Mann), Mr Justice James Macfarlan (later Sir James)[29] and Mr Justice Russell Martin. Cody was represented by Mr Wilbur Ham, KC, and Harry Minogue, with Ham and Jack Barry appearing for Davies. Counsels were all instructed by Mr Sonenberg.

The appeal centred on the evidence of Stevens and was based on seven grounds of appeal. The three major grounds were firstly that neither of the appellants was concerned with the killing of Scriven, secondly that the jury's verdict was against the evidence, and thirdly that the verdict was contrary to and wrong in law. Barry also decided to concentrate on the performance of the

28 *News (Adelaide)*, 29 April 1937

29 Macfarlan was regarded as one of the most difficult man on the Bench, given to very cranky moods, and was twice censured by the Bar over his behaviour on the Bench.

trial judge, Gavan Duffy. His appeal cited the following grounds - that Duffy had failed to direct the jury properly or sufficiently as to the care with which it should weigh the evidence of witnesses as to identity; that he did not direct attention properly or sufficiently to the inconsistencies and discrepancies between the statements of witnesses to the police, their evidence at the inquest, and at the first trial; that he did not tell the jury that in the circumstances they should discard the evidence of admissions given by the witness John Stevens; that he did not tell the jury that, apart from the evidence of Stevens, the only evidence implicating the prisoner was that of identity, which should be considered with great caution; and that he did not warn the jury that in the circumstances they should not act upon the evidence of Stevens unless they found some independent fact or facts to support it.[30] Duffy had stated that in his view, the methods of identification used by the police were 'inept, and might properly be considered by the Jury in estimating the weight to be given to the identification.'[31] In Barry's mind, Duffy could have (and should have) been more forceful in his comments to the Jury. Barry further claimed that Duffy had described Stevens as an associate of criminals and a friend of the appellant which conveyed or to the jury that the appellant was a person of criminal character. It was further claimed by Cody's counsel that Duffy failed properly to direct the jury. He did not warn them that the evidence of the witnesses Gillbank, Reeves and Semmens as to the men at the scene of the crime was contradictory with the evidence of Boadle and Johnstone as to the men in the incinerator yard and, taken with Johnstone's evidence as to the driver of the car, tended to exclude Cody from participation in the crime. In

30 *The Argus*, 5 March 1937

31 PROV,VPRS 00030/P0006, Unit 000004, 1936/777; *Statement by Justice Duffy,* addressing the grounds of appeal, n.d.

addition, Duffy did not tell the jury that the evidence of Stevens as to admissions of guilt was worthless by reason of the time at which, the place at which, and the circumstances in which Stevens first informed detectives of such admissions. Mr Ham argued on behalf of Cody that, although the crime took place in the sight of four eyewitnesses, not one of them recognised or described Cody as one of the men present. The evidence of three men directly pointed to the fact that he was not the short man present at the shooting. The fact that he had left a pistol with a man to be repaired was not evidence that he used the pistol in the crime.[32] Duffy wrote a series of statements that addressed each of the grounds. Whilst they obviously defended his actions, he also stated that no witness present at the crime identified Cody as one of the men engaged in it either as the tall man who fired the shot, the shorter man who seized the bag, or the driver of the car in Little Lonsdale Street. But if they believed the evidence of Boadle and Dugan, there was an 'irresistible inference' that Cody was present.[33] Much was made by Mr Ham of the methods of identification employed by the police. In his view it was extremely important that Victoria should not be the only State in which cognisance should be taken of identification gained under conditions that, in England, would be quashed.[34]

Was such a substantial attack on the trial judge unusual? And how was it likely to be received by the appeal judges, all contemporaries of Duffy? Justice Macfarlan's relations with Barry's mentor, Gorman, were hostile although the hostility did not seem to extend to Barry. Nevertheless, Barry found appearing in front of him to be exhausting and told his mother

32 *The Argus*, 5 March 1937

33 PROV,VPRS 00030/P0006, Unit 000004, 1936/777; *Statement by Justice Duffy,* addressing the grounds of appeal, n.d.

34 *The Sun News-Pictorial,* 5 March 1937.

that Macfarlan was the worst tempered man in Melbourne.[35] The public probably assumed that these bastions of law and order would base their decisions and actions impassively on the evidence placed before them. In reality, rumours abounded and confidences were exchanged. Personal qualities of judges played a role in determination of guilt and feuds (often fuelled by alcohol) erupted – sometimes resolved, sometimes not.

ATTEMPT TO APPEAL DISMISSED

On March 11, the Court of Criminal Appeal refused the application for leave to appeal against their convictions. Because of the gravity of the situation, Judge Mann decided to state the reasons for the decisions at some length.[36] The reading of the judgement took over half an hour. Behind the dock a number of women, including Davies' mother, listened grim-faced in silence.

Mann opened his judgement by saying: 'The chief difficulty in the way of the Crown establishing at the trial against either of the accused lay in the fact that no les than nine months elapsed between the prosecution of the crime charged and the identification of the prisoners whose actions had been witnessed on the date of the murder. As was inevitable in these circumstances, the reliability of the identification was attacked both on general and specific grounds which were argued before us with great thoroughness.'[37] Barry had attacked the trial judge for not giving direction to the jury about the effects of the different way of obtaining evidence as to identification. Mann

35 Mark Finnane, *J V Barry: A Life*, 2007, p. 63

36 *Victorian Law Reports, R. v. Davies and Cody (No.2) (1937) Vic Law Report 47; (1937) VLR 226 (11 March 1937) p. 227*

37 PROV,VPRS 00030/P0006, Unit 000004, 1936/777; *Judgement of Chief Justice (Mann), Mr Justice Macfarlan and Mr Justice Martin,* 11 March 1937

commented that he did not think that the trial judge had taken 'a course which in any way affected the fairness of the trial'. It was the duty of the trial judge to closely observe the conduct of the police and to reject any evidence that may have been obtained by 'pressure or suggestion or trick', and the Court could find nothing of this kind in the evidence before them.[38] He went onto support the processes of the police in not using the identification parade, saying that in Victoria 'this method seems now to be rare' and that no member of the Court was so satisfied of the superior methods of the parade method of proceedings as to induce him to condemn the opposing practice as improper.[39] In his opinion, 'no assistance was to be derived from an enquiry as to whether the evidence would or would not have been stronger if other procedures had been followed.'[40] We can only wonder what the judges thought when one of the major reforms later recommended by Alex Duncan, in his report on the Victorian Police, concerned the methods of identification used to identify suspects.

Similar statements were made about the use of photographs in evidence. The witness Dugan had identified Cody as the man for whom he had undertaken the repair of a pistol with which the murder was subsequently committed and to whom he had redelivered it when repaired. He had been shown a number of photographs – about 20 – from which he selected one, namely, a photograph of Cody, as being that of the man in question. After doing this, Cody, who was already in custody, was shown to him at the police station, where he again identified him, both in appearance and by recognising his voice. Mann stated that,

38 *Victorian Law Reports, R. v. Davies and Cody (No.2) (1937) Vic Law Report 47; (1937) VLR 226 (11 March 1937) p.* 228

39 *Victorian Law Reports, R. v. Davies and Cody (No.2) (1937) Vic Law Report 47; (1937) VLR 226 (11 March 1937) p. 229*

40 *The Sun News-Pictorial,* 5 March 1937.

where a single photograph of a man already in custody is shown, 'it can serve no fair purpose and is certainly improper.' But in this case, selection from a number of photographs introduced the principle of selection, similar to an identification parade! Cody's counsel argued that the inconsistency of the evidence meant that the 'evidence as a whole was insufficient to support the case'.[41] The Chief Justice noted that courts in Australia and Great Britain had found occasion to censure abuses in particular cases, it was dangerous to evolve general rules, since to do so might hamper the proper administration of justice.[42] Many observers would have considered that justice had been severely hampered by the actions of the trial judge, an opinion not shared by the Chief Justice.

Mann then addressed the evidence given by the witnesses who were in Little Lonsdale Street and the evidence regarding the men. All agreed that the two men who committed the robbery were different in height – one short, one tall. Gillbank did not see the face of the shorter man, who was not like Cody in build, and only got a vague impression of the taller man. Pullen did not see the face of the man who grabbed the bag. Reeves identified the tall man, who fired the shot, as Rupert Davies, but stated that Cody was not his companion. Semmens described the driver of the car as having light-coloured hair and saw Rupert Davies run across the road and throw himself in the backseat of the car, followed by a shorter man. At the incinerator Boadle saw a stoutly built man get out of the front seat by the door opposite to the driver's seat, and two men emerge from the back seat – a tall man with no hat (who he identified as Rupert Davies) and a short man carrying a bag, who he identified as Cody. Boadle's

41 *Victorian Law Reports, R. v. Davies and Cody (No.2) (1937) Vic Law Report 47; (1937) VLR 226 (11 March 1937) p. 230*

42 *The Sun News-Pictorial,* 5 March 1937.

assistant, Johnstone, identified the two men who alighted as the accused and stated that the stout man definitely got out of the driver's seat. Cody, who could not be described as stout, was clearly not the driver of the car, according to his counsel. Chief Justice Mann discounted it in view of the very clear positive identification made by Boadle and Johnstone. Reeves was the only one who saw the face of the shorter of the robbers and he had said that he was not Cody. According to the judge, it was open to the jury to find that he was mistaken when he said that Cody was not that man, together with considering that Johnstone was in error in stating that the stout man occupied the drivers' seat.

The value of eye-witness identification was questioned, as well as the issue of only accepting evidence that fits the scenario provided by the police and the judges. Further doubt about Boadle's credibility arose when the court was reminded that, on the day of the murder, Boadle had described Rupert Davies as having wavy hair and a ruddy complexion, which he did not have – nor did his companion. The judge then expressed some doubt as to whether he had given these descriptions. Despite the defence counsel placing great emphasis on the statement, the judge again stated that these were matters of credibility of the witness for the jury to decide. [43] No wonder the issue of positive identification was to cause such enormous confusion and disagreement in the courtroom and, obviously, in the jury room. Commenting upon the evidence relating to Cody and Davies having money to spend on motorcycles, the Judge regarded it as admissible if only to meet the comment that would otherwise have been made, that at no time since the robbery had Cody appeared to have money to spend. Given that both the accused

43 *Victorian Law Reports, R. v. Davies and Cody (No.2) (1937) Vic Law Report 47; (1937) VLR 226 (11 March 1937)* p.232

operated as SP bookmakers and standover men at various times, acquiring substantial sums of money was not surprising.

Mann then turned to the evidence of Stevens, 'a man of bad character'. Should his evidence have been submitted or should the judge have directed the jury to disregard it? The trial judge had merely stated that the jury, having been advised about Stevens' character, had only advised the jury to take all that onto consideration before any weight was given to his evidence. Mann noted that it was contended that the facts would have justified a more emphatic warning than this. But Mann defended the actions of the trial judge, stating that there 'is no misdirection, no omission of anything necessary to a fair trial' and 'the learned Judge has stated clearly all the reasons affecting the witness's credibility.' He then went on to recount a mistake made by the trial judge, concluding that 'the jury could not have come to a different conclusion had the mistake not been made.' Mann also defended the contention that the charge of the trial judge was inadequate. The notice of appeal in each case contained allegations of failure to direct and misdirection on his part. The trial judge had not gone into detail about criticism launched against the Crown witnesses for their contradictions and for their false descriptions. To do so would have been a wearisome business to go through again. In his view, the addresses by counsel had laid stress on these issues.[44] To the lay observer, this sounds like being damned with faint praise. When he turned to Cody, he observed that it was contended that in view of the inconsistency of the evidence of some of the Crown witnesses, the evidence as a whole was insufficient to support the conviction. A number of eyewitnesses had sworn that Davies was the man who had shot Scriven, and Gillbank,

44 *Victorian Law Reports, R. v. Davies and Cody (No.2) (1937) Vic Law Report 47; (1937) VLR 226 (11 March 1937), p. 237*

Pullen, and Reeves did not identify Cody. Only Boadle (and his off-sider Johnstone) had identified him, by appearance and by voice. The contention was put very forcibly before the Court and the jury, but Mann did not consider that the jury was bound to accept it against the very positive evidence of identification given by Boadle and Johnstone. This was despite the view by the defence that Boadle was an unreliable witness, as he had described Davies as having wavy hair and a ruddy complexion. But Mann chose to accept that there was doubt about whether Boadle had actually made these statements. Interestingly, the evidence of Dugan relating to the pistol had application only to Cody, not to Davies. Mann addressed the charges from counsel of misdirection by the trial judge and concluded that all the matters that are now complained about were 'dealt with in an exhaustive manner.' He was obviously bristling at the criticism directed at the trial judge. Mann put the view of the Justices that the summing up of the trial judge was 'a fair representation of the defence and in no way violated the rules applicable to a summing up.' [45]

APPLICATION TO HIGH COURT OF AUSTRALIA FOR SPECIAL LEAVE TO APPEAL

Following the refusal of their application to appeal the decision in the Victorian courts, there was only one avenue left to the convicted pair – an application to the High Court of Australia for special leave to appeal from a decision of the Victorian Court of Criminal Appeal, where the High Court would be asked to consider fresh evidence.

45 PROV, VPRS 00030/P0006, Unit 000004, 1936/777; *Judgement dated 11 March 1937*

The families and friends of Davies and Cody were not content to rely on legal procedures. With the boys now sentenced to death, Mrs Davies was frantically trying to discredit the evidence against the pair. A friend of the family, Teddy Rhodes, met with Stevens at the urging of Geoffrey Davies and convinced him to change his evidence. When Stevens old Rhodes he did not want anything to do with the Davies brothers, Rhodes told him that he should think of their mother: 'They helped you once. It's up to you to do something for them now.' [46] When Stevens visited Mrs Davies and her family at her shop in Smith Street, they all put pressure on him to do whatever he could to save Rupert. He was forcefully reminded about how his mother had been supported by the Davies family when he had previously been in trouble and his mother was nearly dead with anxiety. 'That's how my mother is now,' said Geoffrey. In desperation, Leitha asked him to help save her son from the gallows. It could change everything if he would make a statement that the evidence he had given at the two trials was false. 'If you say the police forced you to say these things, that will clear Rupert and Cody,' she said.

She convinced him to retract his previous evidence against Davies and Cody and to make a statement to that effect. They considered visiting the office of Tom Tunnecliffe, Member of Parliament for the Collingwood area, but Mrs Davies then suggested that they go to the office of the *Truth*. When Geoffrey rang the *Truth*, the only person on the premises was the caretaker. They arranged to meet at the *Truth* office the next morning at 9.00 a.m. But Stevens did not make it to the office until late in the afternoon, when he and Mrs Davies arrived to meet a Mr Newman, and he made his statement under oath to a Justice of the Peace. It basically said that everything he had said at the

46 PROV, VPRS 00030/P0006, Unit 000004, 1936/777; *Statutory declaration by Rhodes,* 22 March 1937

trials was a lie. When Newman asked him why he had made the statements in court, he replied that it was because detectives Davis and Delmonico had threatened to charge him with other offences if he did not give evidence. They had also managed to convince Stevens that the Davies brothers were trying to fit him up for the murder and other crimes. As a result he had made the statements that implicated Davies and Cody. Stevens recounted how he had been taken to Russell Street and shown unsigned statements supposed to have been made by Geoffrey Davies that implicated Stevens in a number of crimes. The police regarded these statements as a trump card in obtaining evidence from Stevens. Delmenico said: 'Don't be a fool. They are trying to fit you for it. Think of your mother. You know how your mother was in the last case (Stevens had previously been charged with robbing a post office in South Melbourne). These men are not worth saving. There is a bit of good in you but these men are out-and-out criminals. They are better out of the way. You tell us that these men did the murder and there will be no further charges laid against you. You will go free.' The other officer, Davis, agreed to back up Delmenico, and they told Stevens that they were sure that Mr Brophy, their boss, would go along with it. Stevens then made a written statement as requested. Stevens was very fearful of detectives Davis and Delmenico, as they had framed him once before in the South Melbourne Post Office robbery. He had no doubt that they were capable of doing it again. [47]

Stevens had revealed that he was treacherous and obviously not too bright. Davis went on to tell him that the police had information from friends of his that proved he was in on the murder, and his description tallied exactly with one of the men. 'Tell us who the other men were and we will see that you are

47 *The Argus*, 2 April 1937

not connected in any way with it.' Stevens remained adamant that he knew nothing about the Scriven murder and, as far as he knew, the men accused were innocent. Davis retorted with: 'You can't tell me that. By the time we get through with them they will be murderers. We have got witnesses who have positively identified these men. Unless you talk you will be in with them.' Delmenico had also told him that there was a free pardon going and a reward of £500. If Stevens said that these men did the hold-up, he would see that he would get most of the money. Stevens refused, although fearful as the police had tried to fit Stevens up in the past – 'You tried once before,' replied Stevens. 'We will make sure this time,' said Davis. [48]

Everything had changed by the signing of the affidavit by Stevens that his evidence at the trials was a lie. If Stevens could be believed, he was only trying to help Mrs Davies by making the statement that the evidence he had given was false but he realised that he was committing perjury, a serious offence that could lead to a lengthy sentence. Was this move at the instigation of Soneneberg and his team? Possibly. They certainly understood that its presentation to a court would be a sensation.

As soon as he learnt about the affidavit, Book was on the back foot and realised he needed a strategy to minimise its effect of it. His team swung into action to have Stevens sign another affidavit, contradicting the first one and reaffirming the evidence he had given against Davies and Cody at the first two trials. On instructions from the Chief Commissioner, Inspector Thomas Dunn picked Stevens up at about 2.00 p.m. on March 17. At Russell Street, Dunn said to him: 'I have been told that you were out at Mrs Davies' house in Collingwood on Monday last and made a statement that the evidence you gave in the Scriven case was false. He said 'Yes.' I said 'Was it false?' He said: 'No,

48 *The Barrier Miner (Broken Hill, NSW)*, 2 April 1937

everything I said in my evidence was true.' I said: Why did you tell them it was false?' He said: 'They were all wanting me to do something to save Rupert and I agreed to make the statement.'[49] I said: 'Are you prepared to make a statement setting out the full facts.' He said: 'Yes' and agreed to swear to the statement. Dunn took him to the office of Mr J Evans, a Justice of the Peace, and he swore to the statement being correct. The next morning, Stevens returned to Dunn's office, where Dunn told him that he had re-written the document and that Stevens should read it and check that it is correct. Stevens read the statement over and said: 'That is the truth.' Dunn asked Stevens if he was prepared to make a statutory declaration that it is correct. He said: 'Yes.'[50] The next morning, he signed the statement before a Justice of the Peace that would be relied upon by the prosecution to counteract the effect of the first affidavit.

All these machinations show how underworld characters often had to negotiate their way carefully between the threats presented by the police and those of others in criminal circles. It also highlights the power of mothers in the criminal world.

On Friday March 19, 'Sonny' Sonenberg lodged an application with the High Court. In an affidavit to the Court, he stated that he believed that the application and the grounds of appeal involved matters of grave and substantial concern to the community at large and matters of serious importance in the administration of the criminal law in Victoria. The grounds for appeal were similar to those presented to the Victorian Court of Appeal; principally that the verdict was against the evidence and was wrong in law. The evidence of Selkridge, Dugan and Stevens should not have been admitted and the trial judge

49 The *Herald,* 1 April 1937

50 PROV, VPRS 00030/P0006, Unit 000004, 1936/777; *Declaration by Thom as Dunn,* 24 March, 1937

failed to direct the jury properly concerning pieces of evidence. Special emphasis was now placed on the testimony of John Stevens, together with principles that should govern the Court of Criminal Appeal in the hearing of applications for leave to appeal. Had a substantial miscarriage of justice occurred? [51]

Sonenberg's application contained what he believed would be a major 'game-changer' – the statutory declaration (dated March 16) by John Stevens stating that the evidence he had given at the first and second trials was totally untrue! He had given testimony that Davies and Cody had admitted their complicity in the holdup and murder. The declaration confirmed what the defence team had stated all along; that Stevens' evidence could not be trusted and that he had done a deal with the police in return for perjuring himself at both trials. Surely this new evidence would be enough to get Davies and Cody off death row when it was presented in court at the next occasion! But how could the defence team actually have the new evidence introduced into a courtroom?

Another bombshell soon followed when Book lodged his documents at the court prior to the hearing, including the second affidavit that re-affirmed the evidence Stevens had given at the trials, and declaring that the affidavit presented by Sonenberg (dated the 16th) was totally false. The evidence he had given at the trials was really the truth! The newspaper headlines screamed out: 'Said He Lied At Trial; Now Says He Didn't'. [52] The declaration was accompanied by an affidavit from Thomas Dunn, inspector of police, describing the background to Stevens' affidavit of March 16 including how the family had applied pressure to Stevens that led to the first affidavit and how

51 PROV,VPRS 00030/P0006, Unit 000004, 1936/777; *Affidavit by N H Sonenberg,* dated 19 March 1937

52 *The Daily News (Perth),* 22 March 1937

he had convinced Stevens to recant its contents with another statement.[53]

It was regarded as 'one of the most startling retractions in the history of crime'.[54] Could anything stated by Stevens be relied upon? There was certainly conjecture that Stevens agreed to produce the declarations that supported the case of the police and had been promised some inducements (related to other charges) to do so. But was there any way for the contradictory declarations to be heard in a courtroom?

HEARING IN HIGH COURT OF AUSTRALIA

Things moved swiftly and the hearing in front of the Full Court of the High Court of Australia was scheduled for the following Monday, March 22, for leave to appeal against the convictions in the Victorian court. The Full Court consisted of Sir John Latham, Mr Justice (Herbert Vere) Evatt, Justice (Owen) Dixon (appointed in 1929 and later to become Chief Justice), Mr Justice (Sir George) Rich (appointed in 1913, and now in his 70s), and Mr Justice McTiernan. The Court was not a happy place in the late 1920s and early 1930s. When Owen Dixon joined its ranks, he soon realised that it was a 'bench vitiated by mutual antagonisms and limited by inequality of talents'.[55] However, it improved when Latham became Chief Justice in October 1935. He was an intriguing character. In addition to a distinguished legal and political career, he had a wide range of interests and a keen appreciation of the need for change in society. During the latter part of the Great War he had headed Naval

53 PROV,VPRS 00030/P0006, Unit 000004, 1936/777; *declaration by Thomas Dunn,* dated 24 March 1937

54 *The Daily News (Perth),* 22 March 1937

55 Philip Ayres, *Owen Dixon*, 2003, p. 58

The High Court Building, Little Bourke Street, 2013

Intelligence; following the armistice had been a member of the Australian delegation to the Versailles Peace Conference and in 1926 led the Australian delegation to the League of Nations General Assembly in Geneva. As a Member of Parliament (on the conservative side) from 1922, he became Attorney General of Australia in 1925, combining this role with Minister of Industry from 1928. He led the National Party from 1929, and acted as Leader of the Opposition for 18 months, before becoming Attorney General in the Lyons government. He resigned from politics in 1934 and was appointed G.C.M.G (Grand Cross of the Order of St Michael and St George) before becoming Chief Justice of the High Court in 1935.[56] In the mid-1930s he advocated the construction of a new art gallery on St Kilda road, specifically to hold the works of art acquired under the terms of the Felton Bequest. He was also critical of the dullness of Melbourne, a view expressed by many overseas visitors, and advocated reform of the numerous legislative restrictions that prevented establishment of open-air cafes (similar to those in Europe), tea gardens with orchestras, and the serving of wine with light meals and supper.

56 Stuart Macintyre, *'Latham, Sir John Grieg (1877-1964)'*, Australian Dictionary of Biography, http:adb.anu.edu.au/biography/latham-sor-john-grieg-7104, text12251, accessed on-line 8 July 2014

After a day's submissions, the Court decided that it had no power to take into consideration the circumstances disclosed by the declaration of Stevens. It could not consider fresh evidence in support of the appeals by Davies and Cody. Latham reminded Barry that the Full Court of the High Court was sitting as a court of appeal (and ONLY as a court of appeal) and was not exercising original jurisdiction. Its only power was to consider and determine whether the judgement appealed from is right or wrong on the evidence before the Court at the time. Despite Barry telling the court that Stevens had been shown to have been a witness whose evidence was worthless, the statements by Stevens could not be taken into account as they had not been before the Full Court of the State of Victoria at the time that it entertained and dismissed the appeal to overturn the original conviction. In this case the High Court was invited to consider fresh evidence, but the Court had no power to consider that evidence. Was there any way that they could get the new evidence provided by Stevens into a courtroom? The High Court appeared to be of the opinion that the evidence certainly ought to be considered in relation to the appeal of the two, but Latham summed up by saying that 'We do not think that the Court should proceed with the matter until steps have been taken which will make it possible to have this to have this evidence brought before the Court in a proper manner…this application will stand adjourned'. Importantly he also said that the accused were at liberty to renew it at any time as

Sir John Latham,
High Court of Australia

they may be advised.[57]

But how could that be achieved? Barry stated that if the High Court would not consider fresh material in the present application he would ask it to grant leave on the material placed before the Full Court of Victoria, an approach supported by Mr Minogue. Mr Book, representing the Crown, argued that it was established beyond doubt that the Full Court of the High Court, having purely appellate jurisdiction, would not concern itself with the admittance of material that was not before the Full Court of Victoria. Latham was of the opinion that the fresh evidence certainly ought to be considered in relation to the appeal of the accused to the Full Court of the Supreme Court ofVictoria. The means were provided in the Crimes Act 1928 (Vic) where the Victorian Attorney General has power, on a petition for mercy, to refer the whole case back to the Full Court ofVictoria where it would then be possible to consider the evidence arising from the affidavits provided by Stevens.[58] Latham was undoubtedly worried by the fact that new material should be able to considered before the death sentence was carried out, and asked Book whether he agreed. Surprisingly, Book stated that he was inclined to advise the Attorney- General ofVictoria that this matter should be again referred to the Full Court ofVictoria. Mr Justice Evatt expressed the opinion that one of the new matters to be considered was the credibility of Stevens, which could be considered by the Full Court of Victoria if the case was reconsidered. The Victorian court was not prepared to proceed with the matter until steps had been taken to have the new evidence brought before the Court 'in

57 PROV,VPRS 00030/P0006, Unit 000004, 1936/777; *Affidavit by N H Sonenberg,* dated 23 March 1937

58 *Victorian Law Reports, R. v. Davies and Cody (No.2) (1937) Vic Law Report 47; (1937) VLR 226 (11 March 1937),* p. 237, p. 152

a proper manner'. The Attorney General was then petitioned to refer the matter to the Full Court of Victoria whereby it would then be possible for that court to consider the evidence contained in the affidavits.

BACK TO FULL COURT OF VICTORIA

With the new evidence of Stevens to be considered, the matter was now likely to return to the Full Court ofVictoria, Announcing that the application to the High Court of Australia stands adjourned, Latham noted that if the Full Court ofVictoria considered the question of fresh evidence and again gave an adverse decision, it would be possible to seek leave of appeal from the High Court i.e. the accused persons will be at liberty to revive it at any time. If that were to occur, the High Court would be considering new evidence that it could not consider at this point. It was a confusing scenario for many outside the law, but there still seemed to be a chance for the condemned men.

On March 23, a petition was made to the Victorian Attorney-General to refer the matter to the Victorian Supreme Court under the provisions of the Crimes Act 1928 (Section 610). In the meantime, the threat of hanging still dominated the thoughts of Davies and Cody as they waited out the time in Remand at Pentridge.

CHAPTER 7
LEAVE TO APPEAL & THE THIRD TRIAL

The matter was scheduled to begin in April in front of the Full Court of Victoria, consisting of the Chief Justice (Sir Frederick Mann), Mr Justice Macfarlan and Mr Justice Martin, the three judges who had previously refused leave to appeal. The issue before the Court was based on two matters. The first was a referral from the Attorney General of Victoria on an appeal for the exercise of the King's prerogative of mercy, referred to as 'the petition'. The Court was to 'hear and determine the case as in the case of an appeal by a person convicted'.[1] It was based on the contention that there was now available evidence or material not available or known to the defence at the time of the trial (before Duffy) or at the following appeal.

The second matter, referred to as 'the motion,' was an application by the two condemned men for leave to reopen the appeal that had been dismissed by the Full Court of Victoria. The only power of the Court was to consider and determine whether the judgement appealed from is right. The 'motion' covered the same ground as the 'petition' for mercy and the Court decided to hear the whole case as in the case of an ordinary appeal, acting as a Court of Criminal Appeal for the state of Victoria. If they

1 Victorian Law Report, Supreme Court, R.V Davies and Cody, 1937, P. 154

were successful, a new trial would be ordered.

On the hearing of the 'petition' and 'motion' the court agreed to accept affidavits from a number of involved parties including Stevens, Boadle and certain detectives. Jack Barry again appeared for Davies, Minogue and Nimmo for Cody, with the Crown again represented by Mr Book. As usual in this case, another sensation occurred when the instructing solicitor for the defence, 'Sonny' Sonenberg, died suddenly at his home in Wellington Street, St Kilda. Aged 60, he had been ill for a few days. He left behind a widow, a son and a daughter. Sonenberg was buried in the Hebrew portion of Fawkner Cemetery on Tuesday March 30, with a service conducted by Rabbi Danglow of St Kilda and the Rev W Richter of East Melbourne. The pallbearers were an interesting mix, including Archie Crofts (a leading owner of grocery shops and President of South Melbourne Football Club), H Rockman (whose family owned a department store in Bourke Street and a chain dress store company), Maurice Goldberg (practice partner of Sonenberg) and the entrepreneur and 'sporting identity', John Wren. In attendance were representatives of the Bar and the legal profession, the police and the Salvation Army. In the City Court tributes were also paid; Mr C Barnett spoke on behalf of the legal profession and Sergeant De La Rue (who had experienced some interesting tussles with the deceased) spoke on behalf of the police. [2] Sonenberg was a great loss to his family, the Victorian Bar and to Davies and Cody and their defence teams. He was lauded in newspaper reports for his 'complete and utter honesty, and his tolerance and kindliness' and was regarded as having 'won admiration and trust in a way that few criminal lawyers have ever done'. People trusted him, including many juries. One of his contemporaries said that he

2 *The Argus*, 31 March 1937

always felt that Sonny was in the box with the jury, chatting with them, and he got them in the end. In his role for the defence, he obviously defended many doubtful characters but always believed that even if a man was a villain he had the right of trial, and that everything that could be done for him within the rules should be done. Whilst he normally had an easy-going, smiling manner, barristers who were briefed by Sonny could expect to be driven almost to distraction, with phone calls day or night whenever something important occurred to him. He had been involved in the Scriven case since the accused first sought legal representation. Whilst the loss of such a person may have derailed the defence case for some time, Sonenberg's son (David) was well versed in the case and immediately stepped into the breach. [3]

Court Room 3, 2015

3 *The Herald*, 29 March 1937

When Jack Barry began his defence of Davies, the court was full. Barry was a popular figure around the courtrooms and often drew a crowd. In addition, this case had been around for a considerable time and attracted huge public attention.

At issue was the evidence provided by John Stevens, one of the key Crown witnesses, who had testified at the first two trials that in conversations with Cody and Rupert Davies they had admitted their complicity in the hold-up. Cody had also described how the proceeds of the hold-up (£1758) had been buried near the Walmer Street Bridge, North Richmond and later taken to Queensland and changed.

Stevens had subsequently made a statutory declaration in which he admitted that the evidence he had given at the trials was totally untrue.[4] At last, Barry was finally able to introduce the sensational new evidence in the form of the declaration by Stevens.[5] There was a sense of anticipation in the room as Barry rose to read the document. Stevens was now telling an entirely different story. He had stated that the evidence he had given at the trial and the retrial 'was totally untrue' and made allegations against certain members of the police force as the reason for his having given false evidence, stating that two detectives had threatened to frame him. He later claimed that the affidavit was 'made under the persuasion of the mother and brother of one

---

4 PROV,VPRS 00030/P0006, Unit 000004, 1936/777; *Submission by N H Sonenberg,* 23 March 1937

5 Until the mid-1990s, there was no formal requirement for parties to provide full disclosure of the evidence that they intended to present, although the Crown generally did so. The modern trend in litigation is for both sides to provide full disclosure – a 'hands on the table' approach. Prosecutors are required to disclose to the defence all material which could constitute evidence relevant to the guilt or innocence of the accused, and both the prosecution and the defence are required to make pre-trial disclosure in accordance in accordance with a timetable set down by the court. (see www.criminallawsurvivalkit.com.au/Crime.html, accessed 2 June 2014)

of the condemned men' – Leitha and Geoffrey Davies.

But Book was also able to produce an affidavit that contradicted this declaration, reinforcing that the evidence he had given at the trials was correct and true. Book was trying his best to downplay the effect of the two affidavits that directly contradicted each other. In his view, all that Stevens had done was make a statutory declaration that his trial evidence was false and then followed it with a further statement that it was true. This could not now form part of the appellants' case. In addition the Chief Justice was clearly unconvinced as to whether the statements of Stevens provided fresh evidence.[6] It can only be speculated how Book would have reacted if the defence had produced such evidence.

Minogue submitted that the jury from the first trial might have been profoundly influenced by the evidence now under review. He told the court that 'in a trial so important, that the jury should have before them BOTH declarations of Stevens'. The jury may conclude that the original statement was correct, or that it was impossible to trust Stevens in anything. However, he was present and would, if the Court considered it necessary, go into the box and swear that the evidence he had given at the trial and re-trial was true.[7] There were certainly major doubts about any evidence that originated from Stevens. If he were to go into the box, could the jury believe anything that he said, even under oath?

Barry then told the court that there were a number of other affidavits by police that were concerned largely with denying the allegations made in Stevens' first affidavit. According to Barry, they were designed to clear the police from the accusations made against them. Barry's conclusion was that the police would do

6 *The Herald,* 2 April 1937
7 *The Herald,* 1 April 1937

(and say) anything to swing the focus back onto Stevens' original evidence and to discredit the contents of his first declaration.

Barry wasn't just relying on Stevens to try and discredit the Crown evidence. He produced another declaration from someone who had not given evidence at the previous trials. Harold Vivian ('Teddy') Rhodes, of Flemington Road, Newmarket, a labourer, described how he had been picked up at his workplace and taken to Russell Street by detectives who asked whether he had painted a car. 'I've never painted a car in my life,' said Rhodes. In a room full of detectives clearly trying to intimidate him, Rhodes was told by detectives that Stevens had told police that he (Rhodes) had painted the car. Other detectives had interjected with remarks such as: 'You did paint it, didn't you, Harold? The only thing to do is to save yourself.' This went on for about three hours; Delmenico then told him of Stevens' arrest and his statement naming Rhodes as having painted the car used in the Scriven shooting. Delmenico revealed that: 'We must find a man that painted this car.' Clearly, after two trials and the likelihood of an appeal proceeding, there was enormous pressure on the police to resolve issues such as 'who painted the car?' Rhodes replied: 'You can't expect me to get up in court and give evidence...you know that these men are innocent...you only have to read the daily papers to see that.' These comments enraged the police. Sickerdick said; 'You bastard. A man ought to knock your fucking head through the wall, you liar.' Rhodes again stated that these men were innocent. Delemenico flew into a rage: 'You bastard, you say I am trying to fit an innocent man!' He then punched Rhodes in the jaw. After waiting another hour, Rhodes was allowed to leave.[8]

8 PROV,VPRS 00030/P0006, Unit 000004, 1936/777; *Statutory Declaration by Rhodes*, 22 March 1937

Barry then tried to discredit more of the Crown's evidence by introducing a new witness, a man called Albert Gray, tramways employee, of Webb Street, Caulfield. He swore in an affidavit that 11 days before the shooting, four men had gone to his house in a car similar to that used in the hold-up, which they had asked him to paint. But Gray would not undertake the work. Soon after, at Russell Street, where he was invited to identify the men AFTER they had been arrested, Gray stated that they weren't the men who had driven to his home in the car. The Crown pointed out that the sighting was nearly two weeks before the holdup. Who occupied the car at that time had no bearing on the question of the identity of the murderers.[9]

Barry also attacked the evidence provided by Mr Boadle, the City Engineer at the Destructor Yard. Boadle had been a principal witness for the Crown upon the question of identity and had been unequivocal in his identification of Davies as the taller man in the car that had been driven into the Destructor Yard just after the shooting, and had left hurriedly with a shorter man who Boadle said was Cody. Doubts had been raised at the first trial over Boadle's evidence about Davies' hair style, originally described by Boadle as wavy and parted on the right. But Barry pointed out that Boadle had seen Davies on a number of occasions since he was arrested on November 5, and Boadle was forced to agree that his hair had never been parted on the right, nor artificially waved. Nor did he have a 'ruddy complexion' as originally testified by Boadle.[10]

Barry also used the evidence by Gray to cast doubts upon the evidence provided by Boadle. Gray's evidence stated that when he was invited to Russell Street in early November, soon

9 *The Herald,* 1 April 1937

10 PROV,VPRS 00030/P0006, Unit 000004, 1936/777; *Proceedings of trial,* 22 June 1937

after the arrest of the three accused, to identify the men who had visited his house, he had encountered John Boadle in the office of the Indeterminate Sentences Board (the forerunner of the Parole Board) and that Boadle had identified another man as the taller of the two men who had driven into the City Council Destructor yard just after the shooting – NOT that of Rupert Davies.

Justice Martin queried the introduction of Gray's evidence, stating that it was 'peculiar that counsel for the defence should be investigating the case only two days before the present hearing'. Barry said that the counsel had only received the information during the recent Easter vacation. The comment by the judge seemed to be disingenuous, at the very least – Barry and the defence team were clearly going to seek any new evidence that may help to clear their clients. After all, Gray had given evidence at the Coroner's Inquest in June 1936. The Chief Justice, Mann, was also disdainful of the new evidence, stating that 'numbers of seekers of notoriety would be glad to come into this case.' Barry's rejoinder was that Gray was no seeker of publicity, and it was only with the greatest reluctance that he swore this affidavit and came here today prepared, if necessary, to give evidence. Gray was clearly a frightened witness. He had been scared by an incident after the first trial when a one-armed man on a bicycle, another Davies brother Clifford, turned up seeking his assistance and told Gray's wife that Gray could save his brother and Cody before it was too late. Gray's wife was deeply distressed by this visit. Gray asked Detective Delmenico to confirm that the Davies boys had a one-armed brother, which he did. (Clifford Davies had lost part of his arm in a railway accident when travelling around with Rupert and Geoffrey). When Gray asked him to sit in the next room when Davies returned that night with the women in the family, Delmenico told him that we do not do things that way and assured Gray that he would not be called as a Crown witness.[11]The Chief Justice was clearly unimpressed by Gray's evidence, unlike his laudatory view of Boadle in the witness box. He told the Court that he was able to 'appreciate the great weight that the jury obviously gave to his evidence'. The fact that Boadle was an educated and professional engineer probably helped.[12]

In the first week of April 1937, the Victorian Court unanimously dismissed the 'petition' of mercy and the 'motion' for a new trial. The grounds for both had been based on the assertion that since the trial in February important new evidence had been discovered. It was not uncommon for the Appeal Courts to deal with appeals based on the post-trial discovery of fresh evidence tending directly to establish the innocence or to throw doubt on the guilt of the accused. The Court decided that there was NO fresh evidence of such a kind in this case, concluding that the new material being relied upon solely affected the 'general credit' of Stevens. Barry was of the opinion that the original jury would have based their verdict, to some degree, on Stevens' evidence that the accused had made admissions to him of their guilt. This clearly gave sufficient grounds for quashing the conviction. But the Court maintained the view that Stevens' evidence was 'merely illustrative of the witness's character'.[13] The decision was reached after a few minutes' consultation and the judges did not even leave the bench. The Chief Justice later gave his reasons for the decision. Regarding the 'motion' which covered the first appeal, delivered on 11 March, 1937, Mann said

11 PROV,VPRS 00030/P0006, Unit 000004, 1936/777; *Statement by Detective Delmenico*, 2 April 1937

12 *The Age* 8, April 1937

13 Victorian Law Report, Supreme Court, R V Davies and Cody, 1937, p. 157

that as the judgement 'had been pronounced and entered in the records of the Supreme Court (of Victoria), the Court was of the opinion that it had no jurisdiction, either under its general powers or under the special powers as a Court of Criminal Appeal, to entertain the motion, which was accordingly dismissed'.[14] Nor was the court of the opinion that there was any fresh evidence presented that could establish the innocence or throw doubt on the guilt of the accused, as sometimes occurred in this Court. The new material was relied on solely as affecting the general credit of the witness Stevens. When the Court referred to the conflicting affidavits by Stevens, Mann was scathing about their contents, stating that they showed 'not only a readiness to affirm or deny facts for reasons quite independent of truth, but a readiness to invent false reasons and explanations when required'.[15] Interestingly, there had been no application by either side to either examine or cross-examine Stevens.

Barry was praised for presenting a 'very able and temperate speech', where he had argued that the jury in the original trial had, to some degree, founded its verdict on Stevens' evidence that the accused had admitted their guilt to him, and that the possibility of the jury having done so was sufficient ground for quashing the conviction in the new light thrown on Stevens' character. However, Barry had raised no question of fact on that part of the case. Mann conceded that if the Court had only the first declaration of Stevens to consider, the weight of that evidence may have been seen as bearing upon the rest of his evidence. But this was not the case. It is not the statements of the witness, but their contradictory quality that is here relied upon, said Barry. In addition, the jury had been well aware that Stevens was a man of bad character, who had recently

14 *The Argus,* 8 April 1937

15 Victorian Law Report, Supreme Court, R V Davies and Cody, p. 157

been convicted of a crime and sentenced to four years gaol. He was also the associate and confidant of murderers and gave no evidence until shortly before the first trial when he had been arrested for consorting with thieves. It was up to the jury to decide whether any credence would be given to such a witness, which they obviously had done. In summary, Mann stated that it was clear that grave danger to the administration of the justice must arise if new facts that were merely illustrative of the character of witness at a trial should be accepted generally as a ground for setting aside the verdict of a jury. The new material arising from Stevens contradictory statements did not tend directly to establish the innocence or throw doubt on the guilt of the prisoners. Their request to the Victorian courts for leave to appeal had been dismissed and could not be revived, even if new evidence emerged. The two now seemed destined to hang for the murder. Previous hangings had generated outcries against capital punishment by groups such as the Trades Hall, churches and other organisations concerned with social justice, with large petitions being presented to Parliament, such as had occurred for Angus Murray in 1923. Perhaps if they had been close to hanging, these events would have occurred. The Chief Justice of the High Court of Australia, John Latham, had earlier flagged that the matter could return to the High Court if the Victorian Court would not admit new evidence. With the dismissal of the motion for appeal and petition for mercy, it looked like it was heading there. The Scriven case was no closer to resolution, and Davies and Cody still faced the death penalty.

Just as it seemed that no more sensations could emerge, a hold-up occurred in St Kilda on March 26. John Henry Chapman, a garage proprietor, explained that he had parked his car near the St Kilda Football Ground (near St Kilda junction, to the south of Melbourne) on the night of March 26. At around 9 p.m., he was sitting in the car when two men wearing black silk masks approached him, one on each side of the car. One pointed a pistol at him and told him to get out. When he hesitated he was told 'I'll give you six seconds to get out.' Chapman quickly followed the instruction. When he alighted the two men drove away in the car at a fast speed. But Chapman had a number of brothers who were not having any of this - they intended to recover the car without any involvement of the police. One brother, Charles, telephoned another brother, Frank, who collected two friends, Clegg and Boyden. Armed with a shotgun and a revolver, and having 'heard something,' they drove to Oak Street in Royal Park where they saw the missing sedan. After waiting a few minutes, they drew alongside the car. Boyden flashed a torch on the driver and pointed his revolver at him and told him to put up his hands. When his accomplice began to get out of the passenger's side, Boyden rushed around and found that he had a fully loaded pistol in each hand. He soon dropped them in response to Boyden's command to 'Drop those guns!' A third pistol was lying on the seat of the sedan, and another was later found in a pocket of the car. Two boxes of ammunition were also in the car, and each of the accused had bullets in his possession. Now was the time for the brothers to call the police to collect the thieves. Once again it shows how readily citizens of Melbourne were to take the law into their own hands and provide an armed response when feeling threatened.[16]

The two suspects were taken to Russell Street for questioning. One was James Ezekiel Dugan, the 18 year old commercial artist from Footscray. He had been witness for the Crown at the Scriven trials when he presented evidence about repairing the

16 *The Argus*, 9 April 1937

pistol allegedly used to shoot Scriven, and would again be called on to give evidence against Cody if a third trial took place. The other was McGregor Kean, motor mechanic of Auburn. When he was arrested, Dugan told the arresting officer, Constable Gorey from the Wireless Patrol, that he regretted giving evidence at the Scriven trial and that he would have been better off if he had not done. He could have collected £100 from 'the other crowd' for going back on his original statement and not giving the evidence, even if he faced a charge of perjury. The lawyers representing Cody and the brothers were outraged at the suggestion that Dugan had been offered money not to testify, although such an offer could easily have been made by criminal friends of the accused without the knowledge of their lawyers. On arrival at Russell Street, Dugan would say nothing until he had seen Detective Inspector 'Billy' Davis, but the detective considered that no good purpose would be served by seeing him. However, he saw him the next morning, with Dugan informing Davis that his defence would be that he was going to clean these chaps up that have been following me. Reminding Davis that he had given testimony as a Crown witness in two trials, he tried some horse-trading with Davis, saying that if these charges went against him, which seemed likely, he might take a 'turn of mind' if he had to testify in a future trial of Cody. The clear implication was that if Davis helped with these charges, Dugan's testimony about Cody would be undiminished at a future trial. Davis advised him that he would bring the whole case to the notice of the Crown Law Department, but didn't think that this case would have any bearing on the Scriven trial.[17]

They were then charged with having robbed Chapman of a sedan valued at £750. Dugan was armed with an unregistered

17 PROV,VPRS 00030/P0006, Unit 000004, 1936/777; *statement by Detective Davis,* 27 March 1937

pistol at the time, for which he was convicted and received a suspended sentence. At the committal hearing, Dugan told the magistrate that he had been a witness at the Scriven murder trials and had been followed for months by desperate members of the underworld with guns. Dugan had been shot twice since the trial – once on Henley night and again in January.[18] No arrests had been made for these incidents and there is no official record of the second shooting taking place. Dugan explained that he carried guns because he feared another attempt would be made on his life and told the hearing that threats had been made against his mother. A few days before the incident, Mrs Dugan was in a shop in Footscray and some men had passed and called out a threat against Dugan. The night before the offence Dugan claimed that he had found two men, one of whom he knew to be a member of the underworld, waiting in a car outside his house. Too afraid to go home, he spent the night elsewhere in fear that some of the associates of Davies and Cody would do him some injury. In the morning of March 26 he had gone to Russell Street to seek police protection. Detective Deacon immediately rang Detective Davis, who told him to send Dugan home as he considered that there was no danger of him being attacked. But Dugan thought differently and decided to take the matter into his own hands. He had stolen the car, intending to go to Easey Street, Collingwood, 'to shoot them up.' At the time, Rupert Davies and Cody were still in jail on remand, but Geoffrey Davies was free and lived in Easey Street. Dugan's counsel explained to the court that Dugan had been driven 'almost to distraction…and… terrorised by members of

18 One of Melbourne's high points of colour and activity from 1904 until after WW11 was the annual Henley-on-Yarra regatta, held each Spring between the Caulfield and Melbourne Cups (late October to early November). Attendances peaked at over 300, 000 in 1925. http:/www.onlymelbourne.com.au, accessed 14 April 2015

the underworld, who have been following him since the Scriven trial began...one of his shadowers had a sub-machine gun such as is used by American gangsters, which is capable of holding 150 rounds'.[19] Probably Dugan's mind was deranged on the night of his arrest, stated his counsel Mr Norman Mitchell. He told the court that Keam came from a good family and had an excellent character. Dugan, he said, had been a promising commercial artist who had risen from obscurity as a result of the Scriven trial. His uncle owned a city gun shop and during the trial, the police had given Dugan a permit to carry a pistol. However, recently they had not been so warm in welcoming him. He seemed an unlikely type to be prepared to enter into a gunfight with hardened criminals, as he stated that he intended to do, but there is little doubt that months of pressure from the criminal gang associated with Davies and Cody had affected his judgement, to say the least.

Dugan and Keam were both committed for trial at the Supreme Court later in April on charges of having stolen the car and a quantity of petrol. On Remand in Pentridge, waiting for the trial to commence, Dugan continued to be worried about his safety, fearing that he was at risk from friends of Davies and Cody in the prison. The authorities were not easily scared but, for Dugan's own protection, they saw fit to keep him in solitary confinement during his time on remand.[20] This meant that his contact with the prison officers and his legal representatives was via a trapdoor.

The trial of Dugan and Keam began on Monday April 26. They relied on much the same evidence as presented at the committal hearing. Dugan stated that on the night of March 26, he and Keam were in Fitzroy Street when he saw two men following him and decided that they must get a car. Keam knew

19 *The Argus,* 27 April 1937
20 *The Herald,* 8 April 1937

how to drive and after stealing the car from Chapman, they drove to Hawthorn and then to Royal Park. He submitted that there was no intention to keep the car.[21]

On Wednesday, after a three-hour deliberation, the jury found both not guilty of the main charge but guilty of robbery of the petrol. There was obviously much sympathy for the situation in which Dugan had found himself as a result of the Scriven trial but the jury probably thought that they had to be convicted of something. When they appeared in the Criminal Court for sentencing, Justice Martin took the opportunity to lecture them. 'It is very disturbing to think that young men can procure revolvers and ammunition and hold up citizens in the way,' he stated, adding that he was unable to accept the explanation they both made to the jury of this 'bush-ranging exploit'. Despite a strong recommendation for mercy from the jury, he sentenced Dugan to twelve months imprisonment and Keam to eight months – for stealing petrol.[22] Dugan was released from Pentridge in December 1937, and began to use the name of James Martin. In August the following year, he was acquitted on a charge of breaking into a garage with intent to steal. He was then convicted in November of 1938 for 'breach of recognizance'[23] and received a three-month suspended sentence,

21 *The Argus*, 27 April 1937

22 *The Argus*, 4 May 1937

23 A recognizance (of bail) is a promise that an accused person makes in court, to abide by the conditions that made it possible for them to be released from custody. Those conditions always involve attending court as required, staying out of trouble (keeping the peace) and any other conditions such as staying away from victims, locations, non-communications with people identified by the court etc. The accused person must prove they understand and promise to agree with those conditions to be released from custody. When that accused person is found to be breaching those conditions, they have essentially broken a promise to the court and that results in a further criminal charge along with any other charges stemming from that breach of their promise to the court.

before being convicted in December 1938 for larceny. His punishment was a fine of £23 or 27 days. Failing to pay the fine, there was soon a warrant out for his arrest and he was picked up on 14 December 1938 and sent to Pentridge, to serve the time previously suspended. He was released 'to freedom' on 18 March 1939.[24] But his luck ran out soon after. With the advent of World War II he enlisted in the Royal Australian Air Force in 1940 and soon became a First-class Aircraftman, stationed in Queensland. On duty at Townsville aerodrome on 16 April 1941, a bottle of benzene exploded and he suffered burns on the back and neck. He died the same day, leaving behind a widow in Melbourne.[25]

On the day that Keam and Dugan were found guilty, the Victorian Crown Prosecutor, Mr Book, announced that the Attorney-General did not intend to file a presentment against Geoffrey Davies who had been committed for trial on a charge of having wounded Superintendent Brophy with intent to murder him.[26] In laymen's terms, the charge had been dropped. It had been a ridiculous charge that could never have been sustained.

BACK TO THE HIGH COURT OF AUSTRALIA

In late May, the case of Cody and Davies was again before the High Court of Australia. The matter had been delayed because the Attorney General was not prepared to provide the expenses

24 *Victorian Police Gazette,* for week ending 18 March 1939

25 *The Argus,* 17 April, 1941

26 Presentment refers to a report to a court that a crime has been committed. The Attorney General delivers a presentment on his own initiative without a request or presentation of evidence by the local prosecutor. If, after hearing and reviewing evidence presented to him, the Attorney General determines there is sufficient evidence of criminal activity, the Crown prosecutor issues a written document called a presentment. Not lodging a presentment amounts to the dropping of charges.

of counsel to attend the Court in Sydney, preferring to wait until the matter could be dealt with later in Melbourne. In the meantime, Davies and Cody languished in remand in Pentridge. The Chief Justice was Sir John Latham, assisted by Mr Justice Rich, Mr Justice Dixon, Mr Justice Evatt, and Mr Justice McTiernan. Jack Barry and John Nimmo again represented Davies, with Cody represented by Harry Minogue and John Nimmo. The instructing solicitors were the firm of N H Sonenberg and Goldberg. Mr C H Book and Mr Maurice Cussen appeared for the Crown. It was now getting complicated. There were two motions – firstly for special leave to appeal from the Victorian Court of Criminal Appeal's dismissal of the prisoners' appeal from the verdict of the jury; the second motion was for special leave to appeal from the same Court's dismissal of an appeal constituted by a 'petition' referred to it by the Attorney-General after the first appeal. On that petition the Victorian Court of Criminal Appeal had dealt with new material contained in declarations made by John Stevens, which was not before the Court at trial.

Latham was highly concerned about the delays in this matter, noting that it was now late May and that the court had heard the prisoner's appeal on April 1, had dismissed it on April 5, and had given judgement on April 7. Both legal teams must have been thoroughly weary of this case, having been through a series of hearings, trials and appeals since early 1936. It also raised the issue of how the defendants were able to pay for the continual representation.

The issue regarding identification was set out in the Commonwealth Law Report. The legal principle concerned situations where evidence of the identity of an accused is given by a witness whose previous knowledge has not made him familiar with the accused, and where he has been shown the accused alone and has identified him. This is exactly what happened. Davies and Cody were arrested nine months after the crime. None of the witnesses who identified them claimed any previous knowledge of them. After they were taken into custody, it was desired to find out if the witnesses could identify them. Davies and Cody were not placed in company with other men. They were shown singly to the witness, who was asked to say whether he was one of the men in question. In some cases this was done at the detectives office; in other cases, when Davies and Cody were in the dock at the police court charged with the crime for which the identification was sought. In one case, although Davies and Cody were in custody at Pentridge, the witness was shown some photographs from which he picked out one of them. When that prisoner was brought up to the police station, he was shown him singly for the purpose of identifying him. Legal precedent was that a Court of Criminal Appeal should quash the conviction of the accused unless their identity could be proven by other evidence, direct or circumstantial. This did not occur. At the very least, the jury should be clearly warned of the dangers that exist.[27]

When he addressed the Court, Jack Barry (for Davies) concentrated his arguments on the issue of identification. In his view, submitting a prisoner alone for scrutiny after arrest, pointing out the prisoner as the person suspected or charged, or permitting a witness to see a photograph of the prisoner after arrest and before scrutiny, were all circumstances that might influence the recollection of a witness and render its independence doubtful and destroy its value. The only satisfactory method of identification was the 'identification parade', by which

27 Victorian Law Reports, High Court of Australia, May 27,28,31; June 4, 1937

a suspect was placed amongst a number of persons of similar age, build, and condition of life. The witness was asked to select the offender. That method had NOT been adopted in the case now before the Court, and Barry submitted that the evidence of identification should have been excluded altogether at the trial. Harry Minogue (for Cody) agreed with his colleague and argued that the conduct of identification methods in this case 'was one of deliberate and calculated unfairness.'[28] Regarding the contradictory affidavits by Stevens, Justice Dixon expressed the view that 'the very fact that Stevens had made a second statutory declaration recanting his first statutory declaration seemed rather to strengthen the position taken up by Mr Barry. It indicated that Stevens had made a statement according to the company he was keeping.' The detectives had not adopted the line-up method of identification, but had asked the witness to identify the accused under strong lights. He further submitted that it was the duty of the trial judge to tell the jury that there was a better method for identification than the one used in this case. The critical question identified by the High Court was whether the actual verdict ought not to stand because a miscarriage of the kind described occurred. The judgement of the Supreme Court of Victoria dismissing the appeal, and an order of the same Court on reference by the Victorian Attorney-General, together with the verdict of the jury and the sentence, were set aside by the High Court of Australia – a unanimous decision.

The defence strategy had been successful and the Full Bench of the High Court had upheld the appeals by Davies and Cody. This was a stunning victory for Barry and his colleagues. On a broader level, the judgement was regarded in legal circles as one of the most important on criminal matters ever delivered, as a

28 *The Argus*, 29 May 1937

direction of the High Court of Australia must be followed by all State courts.

In his summary, Chief Justice Latham attacked the methods of the Victoria Police regarding identification, the evidence provided by John Stevens and the performance of Justice Mann. He raised the question of the practice of Victorian police of showing a suspect singly to a witness, rather than in a line-up. The Court held that if a witness, whose previous knowledge of the accused has not made him familiar with his appearance, has been shown the accused alone as a suspect and has on that occasion first identified him, the liability to mistake is so increased as to make it unsafe to convict the accused unless his identity is further proved by other evidence, direct or circumstantial.[29] The Victorian Supreme Court had not regarded this method as so dangerous as to warrant setting aside a conviction based on it, or to require a trial judge to include in his charge to the jury any special warning. Such a warning was often provided in other jurisdictions, including England, and the English Appellate Court would have acted on 'its duty to quash a conviction when it thought on any ground there was a miscarriage of justice' – a duty also imposed on the Supreme Court of Victoria. The trial judge, Gavan Duffy, should have warned the jury of the dangers of the mode of identification adopted in the Scriven case. In this case, he left the matter to the jury without any definite warning of the dangers that such a method of identification might produce.[30] The judge merely said that it was one of the circumstances that the jury might want to look at, a direction that cannot be described as a warning to the jury of the dangers arising from the methods of identification employed by the Victoria Police.

29 Victorian Law Reports, High Court of Australia, May 27,28,31; June 4, 1937, p. 206

30 *The Herald,* 4 June 1937

Most newspapers carried reports of the decision in sober terms, but not in Western Australia, where Perth's *Daily News* took the opportunity to report the decision under a large headline 'THERE WAS NO LINE-UP FOR IDENTIFICATION IN SCRIVEN CASE'.[31]

Barry was not the only one who thought that Duffy's effort at the trial as below par. According to his biography, the decision of the High Court of Australia was a triumph for Barry. He had led the appeal and the judges of the High Court 'cited at some length Duffy's rambling charge before concluding that it was unsafe to convict on the identification evidence that had been presented.'[32]

Latham described how the court would be likely to quash a conviction wherever it appears unjust or unsafe to allow the verdict to stand because some failure has occurred in observing the conditions that are essential to a satisfactory trial. A similar outcome should occur where there is substantial possibility that, in the conclusion itself or the manner in which it was reached, the jury may have been mistaken or misled. Experience had led the English courts to look for the greatest care to avoid a mistake or prejudice. In their view, a witness, when shown a suspect singly and as the person whom the police have reason to suspect, will be much more likely to identify the man shown as the one in his recollection. On the other hand, if called upon to say whether anyone of a number of persons were the man, his entire mental attitude would be different. Similarly with photographs - the inspection of a photograph of the person in custody before viewing him naturally tends to impress on the mind the characteristics shown in the photograph. Given this, the witness tends to identify the person in custody with the

31 *Daily News,* (Perth), 4 June 1937

32 Mark Finnane, *J V Barry: A Life,* 2007, p. 66

person shown in the photograph rather than with the person whom he saw previously. Furthermore, if a witness is shown a single suspect whom he knows is suspected or has been charged with the crime, his tendency will be to think that there is a good reason for his arrest. In cases such as this the jury should be clearly warned of the dangers that exist but the observations of the judge in this trial do not amount to a fulfilment of this requirement. Instead he described the different methods of identification as 'schools of thought', rather than pointing out the dangers of the methods employed.

The evidence of Stevens, if it could be believed, would have carried the case against the accused the whole distance. But he had since recanted by swearing a statutory declaration stating that his evidence was false in every material particular, and had now shown himself to be completely untrustworthy. Whilst the judge had originally warned against accepting the evidence of Stevens, the Crown continued to rely on his evidence and the judge's charge did not advise the jury to reject his testimony. It cannot be known whether the jury gave any weight to Stevens' evidence but, in the opinion of the court, the facts relating to his evidence are sufficient to entitle the accused to a new trial. Latham had identified the key issue for all the trials – that there were a large number of witnesses who were asked to identify the suspects, there was significant doubt about the identity of the robbers, and there was only one witness (Reeves) willing to positively identify the killer at the site of the shooting. The police methods used were highly questionable (and would soon be changed) and the judge had not sufficiently warned the jury about accepting evidence based on these methods. The main provider of supporting evidence, Stevens, had now retracted his evidence and admitted to perjury.

A new trial was ordered and the legal teams on both sides now prepared for a third trial, due to start on Monday June 21. Most importantly for Davies and Cody, the threat of hanging had been removed – at least for the moment.

THE THIRD TRIAL

At the third trial by jury, the presiding judge was Mr Justice Macfarlan. Mr Maurice Leo Cussen[33] appeared for the Crown as the regular Prosecutor, Mr Book, was ill. Barry once again represented Davies, and Minogue and Nimmo appeared for Cody. The opening day was to be difficult for the defendants. Half an hour before they were due to appear before the Criminal Court, they were called into the City Court (in the same building), where Cody was charged with having shot at Constable Guider, with intent to murder, and with Rupert Davies, with having robbed Edward McGuire (while armed) on June 19 at Thornbury. Empanelling a jury again proved difficult – the Crown stood aside 12 jurors, Davies had challenged 20 and Cody had challenged four. It was becomingly increasingly difficult to find members of a jury as there could hardly be anyone in Melbourne who was not aware of the series of court battles and associated issues surrounding this case.

Barry was again subject to attacks from the bench by Justice Macfarlan, recalled later by Nimmo as 'brutal, undeserved and,

33 The Cussens were a famous and distinguished legal family in Victoria. In 1932, State Cabinet appointed Cussen as a Crown prosecutor. He was a son of the Acting Chief Justice (Sir Leo Cussen). Additional Crown prosecutors had become necessary to cope with the congestion that had occurred in the lists of criminal cases. Cussen, who was aged forty, graduated in law at the Melbourne University. After leaving the University be enlisted and served in the Great War with the Second Division Artillery. He was admitted to practice in 1920. *The Argus,* 17 February, 1932.

had any publicity been given to it, ruinous in its consequence.' Macfarlan's court behaviour had become so bad that Barry's mentor, Eugene Gorman, allegedly refuse to appear in a Macfarlan court.[34]

The Courtyard, City Court, 2015

The evidence of the witnesses such as Gillbank, the messenger, Hobley, Keith Gruer, George Theodore, Aubrey Reeves, Francis Dempster (who was on traffic duty at the intersection on the day of the shooting) and police officers such as Charles Taylor, William Davis, Andrew Tannahill, Fred Sickerdick, William Sloane and Fred Delmenico, was largely a repeat of that from the first two trials. Davis again stated that when Davies was arrested he said that he was working for sustenance on the day of the shooting. When Detective O'Keeffe told him that they had checked that statement and found it to be untrue, Davies said, 'If I was not there I don't know where I was.' Davis also repeated evidence

34 Mark Finnane, *J V Barry: A Life,* 2007, p.67

that he had driven from the City Council Destructor Yard to the Parkside factory in Collingwood, a distance of 2.6 miles. Travelling at a decent speed, it had taken five minutes. This was another effort to demonstrate that Davies and Cody could have carried out the robbery and still made it to meet with Parkes for a drink. But presumably the trip by Davis had not been made at 5.00 p.m. on a Friday afternoon after committing a robbery and murder. Davis also confirmed that there was never a line-up of prisoners when Cody was shown to any of the potential witnesses. When Barry asked Delmenico if he was familiar with the practice followed at the gaol when witnesses are asked to identify prisoners in custody there, the Judge said 'What have we got to do with that? I don't think that we have got anything to do with that except as a little demonstration to the jury and to draw a red herring across the trail.' Barry demurred but was clearly frustrated.[35]

When Gillbank was asked about the process of identification at Russell Street, where he had observed the accused under bright lights, his Honour queried the relevance on the basis that Gillbank had not identified the men during this process. But he was prepared to allow this line of questioning for those witnesses who had identified the accused. In response to questions from Mr Minogue, for Cody, Gillbank agreed that he 'never said that Cody was like either man who had taken part in the affray at the taxi cab.' Gruer again testified that one of the men he had seen running from the robbery was similar to Rupert Davies, but could not positively identify him. 'He is about the height, but I could not definitely say about his face,' he told the court. Nor could he recall seeing the motorcycle ridden by Semmens in the street at the time. Dempster again recounted how he had

35 PROV, VPRS 00030/P0006, Unit 000004, 1936/777; *Proceedings of trial*, 22 June 1937

rushed to the driver of a Morris roadster, Herbert Gillies Watson, standing in Queen Street. He climbed onto the running board of the car and they took off after the Hudson, turning left into Latrobe Street. Watson was again able to testify that Davies was one of the men in the car, who was struggling to get the door of the car closed as it headed along Queen Street. However, he would not swear to it, which was consistent with his evidence at the Committal hearing and the first two trials. But Watson and Dempster lost sight of the car as they approached the intersection with William Street. A following witness, Smith, described how he had followed the Hudson along Latrobe Street to Spencer Street, where it turned left and proceeded to Lonsdale Street. It then turned into the gate of the Destructor Yard. After he had seen it turn in, Smith kept driving and went on with his own business. During this time, the front door was open 'about a foot' and the near side mudguard was dented. There seemed to be a lot of confusion in the car, he told the court.

Barry and his defence colleagues spent considerable time probing witnesses about possible discrepancies and inaccuracies between their evidence and that previously given at the Coroner's Inquest, the Committal hearing, and the first two trials. They managed to score some minor points but little of great substance emerged from these questions. It was nearly a year since the Coroner's Inquest; not surprisingly, the recollections of some of the witnesses were starting to fade.

The major issue continued to be about identification. Much attention was directed towards the evidence of the taxi-driver, Reg Pullen, who confirmed that he had been told by police that he was going to be shown men arrested in conjunction with the hold-up. He confirmed that he had seen Rupert Davies under the lights, but could not identify him. He had seen a photograph of Davies two days before that day. The criticism of these practices had been a major reason for the success of the appeal that led to the third trial. The failure of Pullen to positively identify Davies is curious, as Davies lived about 50 yards away and told the court that he knew Pullen slightly.

The Crown was again relying heavily on the evidence provided by Aubrey Reeves, who had witnessed the shooting at close hand and had been consistent in his identification of Rupert Davies as the man who shot Scriven. Although his face was partially covered by a handkerchief, he had no doubt that he was the same man that he had seen hanging around a few minutes before with his face uncovered. Reeves again testified that he did not see Cody, telling the court that Rupert was accompanied by Geoffrey Davies. But Geoffrey had been acquitted at the first trial. His credibility as a witness was called into question when he testified that he saw the men run down Little Lonsdale Street and turn into Queen Street – still on foot. He did not see them get into a car and could not recall seeing a black or dark car on the street opposite the scene of the crime. In his words, 'I never saw no car there at any stage (sic).' This was totally at odds with the evidence given by a number of other witnesses. It was also at odds with his previous evidence. Barry pointed out that he had given different versions as to whether he had seen the men run around the corner into Queen Street or whether they had got into a car. He was also reminded that he had originally told police that Davies' hair 'was sort of fair'. But when it was pointed out that Davies had dark hair, Reeves responded that he 'would not say his hair was fair, because it was dark and I might have just got mixed up with the two hairs'. When he received a message to call in and see the police at Russell Street in November, he claimed to have had no idea what it was about. Nor was he curious, as he told the court that he had nothing to be curious about. He had no other dealings with the police at the time and had not heard of the arrest of anyone in connection with the Scriven murder. He was then driven to the City Court by Constable Fox, but was not told why he had been called in. It wasn't until he went into the City Court that he realised what it was about.

By this time, Barry was becoming incredulous about his answers: 'The constable who called for you took you to the City Court, you did not ask him why he wanted you, and you did not have any idea you were being taken there about the Scriven case. Are you serious?' In the Court that day he saw the Davies brothers and Cody in the dock. When he left the Court, he spoke to Constable Fox outside but he did not say anything to him about recognising them as the men involved in the Scriven hold-up. Nor did he tell any of the number of detectives standing around outside the Court. He saw a number of other witnesses being taken in to the Court to see if they could identify the prisoners. After waiting around for about half an hour, the police took him underneath the court to the cells at the Watchhouse, instructing him to come in 'and have a look at these men'. Again, Reeves did not volunteer to the police that he recognised the men. It was not until he went over to the Detectives' office in Russell Street that he said that he recognised the men - about an hour after he had first arrived at the Court. Reeves also acknowledged that he had told his story in a number of proceedings and that there were various iterations. He told the Court that he had not called police when he had seen the Davies brothers in Victoria Street, West Melbourne in May, as he was working and could not leave the truck he was on. His boss was away, having a shave, and he was alone on the truck, which had valuable goods on it. He had also told the court at the second trial that he did not call the police because he would not get anything out of it. By this time his credibility as a witness (and as citizen) was severely tarnished.[36]

Norman Semmens, who had been riding his Indian Scout motorcycle and sidecar in Little Lonsdale Street near the hold-up, identified Rupert Davies as the man who jumped into the back seat of the car, but he could not identify the other man who was carrying the bag. The only description of the driver that he could give was that he had light hair and was wearing a dark suit. When he was about a yard in front of the car, it took off and he had to give way to it. If he had not swung out of its way, he may have been knocked down. He had not grasped the situation fully at that time but had noted the number of the car, 86730. As the car moved off, the kerb-side door was still open and it knocked over a safety zone standard (a parking sign) in Little Lonsdale Street. Like other witnesses, he testified that when he was taken to Russell Street on November 13, he knew that an arrest had been made for the Scriven shooting and that a charge of murder had been laid. But the police did not tell him that, only that they wanted him to look at some men. This evidence differed from that he had given at the first trial, where he said that the police had told him that they wanted him to see three men they believed were involved in the hold-up.

The evidence of John Boadle, engineer supervisor of the City Council Destructor, was critical. He repeated his testimony from the previous trials, stating that on the afternoon of January 31, his attention was attracted by a large black sedan that pulled up suddenly at the gate facing Lonsdale Street, leading to the Destructor Yard. He saw a man in a dark suit leave the front

36 PROV,VPRS 00030/P0006, Unit 000004, 1936/777; *Proceedings of trial,* 21 June 1937

seat and apparently examine the bonnet. Two other men – one short and one tall – came from the rear of the car, the short man carrying a bag. They ran diagonally to the corner of the furnace house, about 50 feet away, before stopping and then walking toward the gate leading to a right-of-way to Spencer Street. They found the gate locked and turned to the Lonsdale Street gate, near the office, and walked toward him. When he stepped over to intercept them, the short man asked if another short, stout man had been seen in the yard. When he told them that no such man had been seen, the shorter man said that the man he was asking about did not work in the yard but had been seen going into it. The men then edged to the gate and he let them pass through, before slowly heading towards Spencer Street. He was certain that the shorter man was William Cody and the taller man Rupert Davies. He was only about three feet from them and observed them for five or six minutes.

The defence queried him about his supposed signature on a statement he made to police on February 3. The inference was that Boadle had not signed this statement and he would not swear that it was his – all he would say is that 'it is very much like it (my signature) but I don't recollect it being put there'. He also testified that he had no recollection of signing a statement to the police. It was starting to sound like the police practice of verballing where they concocted a statement purporting to be signed by an accused. Boadle had originally stated that Davies had 'dark wavy hair, artificially waved, I should say, with a parting high up on the right hand side…and a ruddy complexion'. Now problems had emerged with these descriptions, leading to doubts about who he had actually seen in the Destructor Yard. Further difficulties with Boadle's evidence arose from the police identification procedures. After the shooting, he next saw the accused at Russell Street police headquarters on November 5, ten months after the events. He identified Cody immediately (he was paraded before him by himself), with identification assisted when Boadle heard him speak to a detective. He recognised the 'peculiar light voice' that he had last heard from Cody in the Destructor Yard. He identified Rupert Davies on the following day, after he was 'walked up and down' in front of him.[37]

His identification was supported by Harry Johnstone, a stoker at the Destructor Yard. He told the Court that he thought the car was bringing something into the Yard. Two men alighted from the car, followed by a third who walked out the gate leading to Lonsdale Street. The two men came straight down towards him, walking pretty fast and went past me and then down to the bottom end of the yard. They had passed about a metre away from him, swearing and muttering 'the bloody bastards'. He had no doubts whatsoever that they were Cody and Davies, he told the Court. He had not seen them stopped by Boadle, although he understood that had happened. Boadle had then joined him, yelling out: 'Shut the gate and don't let anybody take that car out.' When they looked inside the car, they saw a pair of grey flannel trousers, a grey hat and some sheets of newspaper. Boadle then went to call the police.

Johnstone had identified Rupert Davies and William Cody on November 19, knowing that they had been charged with the murder, but not knowing that Boadle had identified them as the men on November 5. Johnstone told the court that, between the 5th and the 19th, he had not heard that Boadle had identified them. He had heard rumours that Boadle had gone to Russell Street, but did not know why. Although Boadle was his Superintendent, he stated that he had never talked fully about the

37 *The Argus,* 23 June 1937

matter with him, and had never talked about the identification of the men. Nor did he talk to Boadle before he gave evidence at the committal hearing on November 26. When Barry attempted to infer that he and Boadle had discussed the appearance of the men BEFORE he went into the box, he attracted the displeasure of the Judge. 'You leave that out, Mr Barry,' he growled. Given that this was a major incident in the lives of two men who worked together, this evidence is curious, even dubious. Perhaps it reflects the divide between a Supervisor and a stoker in those days.

Another problem arose when Johnstone was asked about a statement he was supposed to have made to Detective Sloane on the day of the incident – unfortunately not dated or signed. Johnstone was now saying that he had no recollection of talking to Sloane, but spoke to two other young policemen. By this time, there had been about a dozen policemen milling around. When Mr Minogue, for Cody, questioned him about the identification of the men in the Yard, Johnstone was forced to agree that none of the descriptions he had originally provided could possibly describe Cody. Constable Sloane was also questioned by Barry about the statement he had taken from Johnstone, with much doubt raised by Johnstone about the accuracy of the account that was provided. Sloane could not say that it was definitely accurate, as it was 'roughly taken down' and was more for Sloane's own information than for preparing a case. Johnstone was a workingman, a stoker, with little understanding of legal and police procedures. It seemed unreasonable to expect him to have full recall of what he had said and whom he had spoken to during a stressful incident that had occurred over a year ago. Sloane was questioned strongly about the statement, taken by him about four days after the incident.[38]

38 PROV, VPRS 00030/P0006, Unit 000004, 1936/777; *Proceedings of trial*, 22 June 1937

As he had at the hearing seeking leave to appeal in Victorian Full Court in early April, Albert Gray (a tramway motor-man, employed by the Tramways Board) again testified about events towards the end of April 1936. In company with Boadle, he had examined between 400 and 500 photographs at the office of the Indeterminate Sentences Board. Boadle had identified a photo of a man (not Davies) as the taller man that left the Destructor Yard and was now identifying Davies, a totally different man. Cussen then went on the attack – 'And you did not think it was proper in the interests of justice to mention it for ten months until the defence solicitor came to see you?' Gray responded that he considered it was just a mistake on Boadle's part. He had not brought it to the attention of the police. Although he wanted to see justice done, he had little knowledge of the law and had not been subpoenaed by the Crown or the defence. 'You will not give evidence in the interests of justice unless you are subpoenaed, is that it?, asked Cussen. 'Well, can I?', replied Johnstone.

In another instance of witnesses giving directly contradictory evidence (under oath), Boadle denied having any conversations with Gray about the photograph, which Barry wanted to introduce as evidence. When pressed by Barry, the Judge reacted by having the jury retire and then admonishing Barry about this line of questioning. In his mind he had already stated his disapproval, and it was clear that Boadle's evidence would be believed by the Judge.[39]

This was yet another example of the confusion concerning identification in this long-running saga. Barry also attempted to use testimony from Gray regarding the Hudson car in an effort to clear Davies. On January 20, four men drove up to Gray's

39 PROV, VPRS 00030/P0006, Unit 000004, 1936/777; *Proceedings of trial*, 22 June 1937

house in Caulfield in a Hudson motor car, the one that later was seen by Gray in the police yard and was undoubtedly the one used in the holdup. Gray had previously been asked by the men to paint the car but was unable to do so. He had recognised the car from a photo in the *Herald,* about 14 days after the robbery, and reported it to the police; as well as viewing the car, he was shown the three accused. He was clear that Rupert Davies was not one of the men and he had given similar evidence at the Coroner's Inquest. Barry saw this as evidence that Davies was not connected with the stolen car. The irascible judge asked how it would be evidence to show that five months before, certain people were in a car? When Barry pointed out that it was not five months, the judge conceded that he supposed it was two or three months, but still could not see the relevance. Barry's rejoinder was that the Crown witness Selkridge had testified that he had seen Davies in the car in St Kilda AFTER it had been stolen. It was just as relevant to show that some business was being done in the car, and that it contained four men – none of whom was Davies. He contended that it was a reasonable inference for the jury to draw that after the theft of the car and the commission of the robbery, the car remained in the possession of the people who stole it and they had stolen it for some felonious purpose. The judge disagreed; his view was that those who had stolen the car would then choose someone else to carry out the robbery. He considered the evidence to be entirely valueless and certainly did not assist the prisoners. But Barry continued to press it. Cussen was of the view that it did not prove or disprove anything and the judge stated that he could not see what possible bearing it could have. Cussen was probably right but it seems about as relevant as Davies and Cody having money to spend on motorbikes six months after the robbery, which was again raised. Cody told the court that he had purchased a motorcycle in Sydney 1936 with money (£47) that he had saved up over a number of years from the proceeds of illegal bookmaking and the sale of opossum skins. After an accident in George Street, he had sold the motorcycle for £17 as he had no money for repairs. [40]

Another major difference in testimony came from Davies. He confirmed that he had never had wavy hair in his life, had always parted it the same way 'as it is today' and that his complexion had not altered since January 1936. He testified again about his work record and his negligible earnings from sustenance, from which he could not possibly have bought a motorcycle. The money for that came from 'starting price bookmaking', where his brother was the bookmaker. Both Cussen and the judge seemed to struggle with this idea. Cussen asked if Davies won from his brother. Davies explained that the money was won from other people. The judge then said to Davies, 'I still do not understand. You mean that you and your brother were carrying on a starting price bookmaking business together?' Davies then explained that the brothers did not keep any books, papers or documents.[41] He also testified again about his whereabouts on the day of the robbery and having met Parkes for birthday drinks after he knocked off at the Park Side Shoe Factory in Park Street, Abbotsford, off Victoria Street. The two had been friends for over 20 years. Some years ago (when he was about 16), Parkes had been convicted for housebreaking and stealing, had broken his parole and was sent back to a Reformatory, finally being released when he was about 21. He was now 31,

40 *The Argus*, 23 June 1937

41 PROV, VPRS 00030/P0006, Unit 000004, 1936/777; *Proceedings of trial,* 22 June 1937; an irony is that they would have avoided paying the Betting Tax that made up a lot of the money taken during the robbery.

hadn't been in trouble since he was released, was married with a family and had worked constantly, including the last seven years at the Park Side Shoe Factory, a considerable effort in the days when the shoe manufacturers (and their staff) were ravaged by the Depression. The judge then attacked Barry saying that the address of the factory did not mean much to him. When Barry tried to explain, saying that it was immediately opposite the North Richmond Railway station, the judge stated that he was just as ignorant about the station. 'Is it on the Collingwood line?', he asked. Barry explained that it was near Hoddle Street. Clearly His Honour did not spend much time on trains or in areas such as Abbotsford. Nor did he appear to understand the difference between the Watchhouse on one side of Russell Street and the detective's office across the street where Cody had been taken, until Cussen explained it to him. [42]

Davies had considerable difficulty remembering where he was in the period before the robbery, including the dates when he had been undertaking sustenance work. Nor could he remember clearly where he was on the day of the robbery. It was only about 11 months later that his mother was visited by Parkes who told her that he had met Davies that day. She immediately reminded her sons. Parkes testified that when he had seen in the newspaper that the three had been arrested for events that had happened on his birthday, he immediately got in touch with Rupert's people. During questioning of Parkes, Cussen queried his version of events in relation to the time that he had met the brothers. Rupert had testified that they had met him about a quarter past five, just after the knock-off whistle had blown at the boot factory. Clearly Cussen had no knowledge of factory workers' habits. He put it to Parkes, a finisher of boots, that by

42 PROV, VPRS 00030/P0006, Unit 000004, 1936/777; *Proceedings of trial*, 22 June 1937

the time he had washed off the leather, cleaned himself up and got dressed, it would have been nearer half past five before he was out. Parkes soon put him right, stating that was that it would not take him more than half a minute after the whistle until he was outside on the street. 'I just put my coat on and I am on my way home.' Or, on this occasion, to the pub. Without the jury being present, Barry sought an order from the Judge that the examination of Parkes in relation to his previous convictions should not be published to the world, as he had been out of trouble for ten years. He was now married with children and had been working for the same employer for seven years. But the Judge did not see any reason to make a special order in this case and Cussen raised his previous record during questioning, including clarifying 'misunderstandings' about the extent of his convictions that had arisen during the second trial. However the judge DID recommend to the press that they should not publish the evidence about his convictions, which was observed by the newspapers. The judge continued to attack Barry's questions, telling him on a number of occasions that he rejected his question, that a question in that form was not admissible, and other statements that seemed to call Barry's competence into question.[43]

The major issue was the evidence Davies had given at the second trial. He had testified that he had not been to Brisbane in the previous September, only to admit under cross-examination that this was not truthful and that he had lied to the jury. He had previously told the police that he had visited Brisbane only once in 1936 and decided to stick to his story. But evidence had been produced that he had received a telegram, transferring money from his wife, which he had signed for. However, lying

43 PROV,VPRS 00030/P0006, Unit 000004, 1936/777; *Proceedings of trial*, 22 June 1937

to police is entirely different to lying under oath to a jury. This time he testified that he had gone to Brisbane in June with his brother to look for work and to try and start up a starting-price bookmaking business. Although the bookmaking business 'was doing pretty well' in Melbourne, they were being watched a little bit by the police coming around. But it did not work out and they returned after five days, 'not exactly disappointed'. [44] On his return he paid £124 for a new motorcycle. His brother also purchased a bike, 'just for pleasure' instead of giving the money back to race horses. He soon sold the bike, at a loss of over £50, because he needed the money to open a shop in Smith Street. They returned to Brisbane in September 'for no particular reason', staying five or six days. This did not seem to make any sense to Cussen – an 800 mile (1280 km) round trip for no reason whatever. He questioned Davies as to whether the real purpose was to dispose of the money from the Scriven holdup, a claim denied by Davies. It seems incongruous that if he had taken the proceeds of a robbery with him that he would have been so short of money just after arriving that he needed to write to his wife, Kathleen. He also gave evidence that he had known Cody for about two years and that they were friends. He also claimed that Cody had visited his house, and was also a friend of his brother Geoffrey. But he had not seen him between January and June of 1936. [45]

The evidence previously provided by Joseph Selkridge was also attacked and discredited. He had originally said that he was driving an ice-wagon in Acland Street when he saw a Hudson approaching him, containing four men. Rupert Davies was

44 PROV, VPRS 00030/P0006, Unit 000004, 1936/777; *Proceedings of trial*, 22 June, 1937

45 PROV, VPRS 00030/P0006, Unit 000004, 1936/777; *Proceedings of trial*, 22 June 1937

in the rear seat, and Cody was in the front next to the driver. Selkridge had given evidence that Davies 'had a bull neck.' But the evidence from the second trial was repeated, where Selkridge conceded that Davies is NOT a man with a bull neck. He was also saying that he saw it from 50 yards away, where he had originally testified that he was only 20 yards away. He was reminded that at the second trial it had been shown that he could only have seen the car for up to 20 seconds, rather than the two minutes that he had originally stated. Selkridge was now doubtful that Rupert Davies was the man he saw in the car, testifying that 'I said he was like the man'. Nor was the identification of Cody given much attention, as Selkridge was sitting on a raised ice-wagon, looking down in to the car, and only got a side-view of the man. The evidence of Selkridge was clearly now of little value to the prosecution. It emerged during the testimony of Davies that he knew Selkridge, who had lived around the corner from him for about three years. Not surprisingly, Davies denied being in Acland Street on January 29.

When Cody took the stand, he also denied being in the car in Acland Street. He again told the court that on the day of the robbery he was somewhere in Melbourne but he did not know where he was at a quarter to five. He was living in Collingwood with his sister at the time. He had never driven a car in his life (but had a motorcycle) and had never been in the Destructor Yard. Until November 1935 he had been working in Queensland, just over the border, loading wool on the railways, and had money when he returned. For the next four months, until April 1936, he had been working for his father, a contractor for the Hawthorn City Council, earning about £1 or 25/- a week. He was paying his sister about a pound or 15/- a week for board, which did not leave him much spare money. In April

1936 he returned to Queensland. Whilst the police maintained that he had travelled there with the Davies bothers, he said that he had never admitted anything of the kind. But there was little work this time, only a day on or off, so he went to Sydney at the end of June, only to find there was no work there. He had bought a motorcycle at the beginning of July in Sydney, for a sum of £47, using money that was in his possession – about £60 in total. He did not have a bank account, as he moved around too often. He wanted the motorbike to be able to get to places that he could not reach on the train. He returned to Melbourne on the motorbike and then sold it for about £17, a loss of £30, after he had a smash on it (he ran into a cab) and did not have sufficient money to repair the damage. The bike could not be ridden as the exhaust was off and he would have been fined for riding it.[46]

Addressing the jury for his summation, Jack Barry (for Davies) concentrated on the issue of identification. None of the witnesses could recall any particular gesture by which he could identify Davies. Ten months had elapsed between the commission of the crime and the time when the witnesses were called on to identify Davies. 'The Crown case was so riddled by doubt that little reliance could be placed on it,' railed Barry. At five past six, the twelve jurors filed from the Courtroom to the jury room, watched hopefully by the two strained and haggard defendants. After six anxious hours, they were called back from the cells to hear that the jury could not agree on their guilt. Once again, the Judge had no option but to discharge the jury members and remand the accused for a further trial.[47] Would this case ever be resolved?

46 PROV,VPRS 00030/P0006, Unit 000004, 1936/777; *Proceedings of trial,* 22 June, 1937

47 *The Northern Miner (Charters Towers),* 24 June 1937

With the fate of Davies and Cody not yet sealed, Superintendent Brophy decided to retire on grounds of ill health after 26 years as a detective, many of them turbulent. For many years he played a conspicuous part in numerous police investigations in conjunction with Inspector Fred J Piggott. In early May 1937, a report was sent to the Chief Commissioner of Police, Alex Duncan, stating that Brophy was medically unfit to return to duty. He had never properly recovered from being shot in 1936 and he planned to take a sea voyage for his health. However a series of illnesses followed, including lung cancer and heart trouble – not surprisingly for a heavy smoker. He was to finish his service on September 19.

CHAPTER 8

THE FOURTH (AND FINAL) TRIAL

The Courtroom was again crowded on a wintry day in late July as selections took place for the jury for the fourth trial of Cody and Davies for the murder of Ted Scriven. From a pool of 75 possible jurors, 20 were stood aside by the Crown, with 32 challenged by the defence (20 by Davies and 12 by Cody).[1] So far the three trials had occupied 20 days in five courts, spread over eight months, and Cody and Davies had been gaol since November 6. As in all the previous trials, Jack Barry acted for Davies and Nimmo and Minogue acted for Cody. The judge was Mr Justice Martin, the fourth judge to preside over this saga in Criminal jurisdiction. It was getting towards the end of the football season and many in the city were looking forward to the finals. Geelong was playing very good football – maybe Collingwood, who had won the last two premierships, would meet their match this year. But there was a sense of fear and foreboding in the community, particularly amongst those who were parents. An outbreak of infantile paralysis had occurred in Melbourne, with 31 confirmed cases. Unfortunately, four were fatal. State schools in the affected areas were closed, children were relocated to outer districts, real estate agents were advised

1 *The Daily News (Perth, West Australia)*, 26 July 1937

not to let houses to people from the affected suburbs, and hotels and guest houses were requested to co-operate. The outbreak had brought anxiety and terror into homes, with the spectre of crippled limbs and ruined lives. One newspaper exhorted its readers to 'face the trouble in a true British spirit' and avoid hysteria. When it ran the headline 'No Cause for Panic', it immediately resulted in widespread public alarm.[2]

The Crown case largely consisted of the same evidence as at the previous trials. This caused Mr Minogue to submit that the murder charge against his client Cody should be withdrawn from the jury as Crown witnesses had said that the shorter man seen at the hold-up was unlike Cody. But the Judge thought that there was sufficient evidence to go to the jury.

Much of the prosecution's case was directed at the financial situation of the accused. Cody repeated his evidence from previous trials, telling the court that between November 1935 and January 1936, he had done odd jobs for his father, for which he was paid £1 or 25/- a week. In June 1936, five months after the robbery, he had travelled to Sydney and bought a motorcycle, on which he travelled through western New South Wales looking for work, unsuccessfully. Before he bought the bike he had about £60.[3]

Davies was also again under attack about his finances, telling the court that he had been out of regular employment since November 1935. He had been receiving sustenance on and off for the last two years and continued to do so after the day of the hold-up. As Book pointed out, while drawing sustenance, Davies had to complete a declaration that he was without means of support, which he confirmed he had done. And yet, said Book, Davies had travelled to Brisbane in June 1936 and bought

2 *The Australasian,* 31 July 1937

3 *The Age*, 29 July 1937

a motorcycle for £124. 'So where did the money come from?' asked Book. 'From starting price betting', replied Davies, who also confirmed that he had over £100 in his pocket before heading to Brisbane. Davies also confirmed that he had told the jury in his first trial that he had only made one trip to Brisbane, but had admitted in the second trial that he had made two Brisbane trips that year.[4] This was the key piece of evidence that had resulted in the two being found guilty. Whilst significant, this was old ground and contributed little to achieving a different outcome for the Crown.

Identification was again the main contention with more doubt thrown onto the methods used by the police and the failure of the Crown to definitely establish the identity of Davies and Cody as the guilty parties. Once again, a major Crown witness was John Boadle, superintendent of the City Council Destructor Yard. Again he identified Cody and Davies as the two men he had confronted in the yard on the day of the hold-up and murder. He repeated his evidence that he had a good view of both men. As in the first trial, he stated that Davies had wavy hair – it became a major contentious issue. Davies denied that he had ever had wavy hair in his life. Interestingly, the *Herald* reported the day's proceedings as one concerning hair that was curly, not wavy, beneath a headline of 'Question of Curly Hair In Scriven Trial'.[5] But whether it was seen as wavy or curly did not matter to Davies, who told the court that his hair had always been straight and he had never parted it differently. He was supported by the evidence of Stephen Roberts, who had been been acquainted with Davies for about three years. He had never known him to have fair, wavy hair or to have it combed in any way other than straight back. The prosecutor (Mr

4 *The Age,* 28 July 1937
5 *The Herald,* 28 July 1937

Book) produced a photograph from a newspaper and passed it to Davies, asking 'Is that a photograph of you?' 'Yes,' he replied. 'Have you got wavy hair in that picture?' 'No,' Davies replied. 'Are you serious?' asked Book. 'Yes.' 'You say that the man in that picture has not wavy hair?' 'No, he has not,' replied Davies.[6]

When Davies returned to the stand the next day, Barry said that an examination of the block made from a photograph of Davies, a newspaper copy of which was produced by the Crown on Tuesday, showed that the appearance of wavy hair on the head of Davies was the result of the block maker having 'routed out' the top of the block. Book then stated that he had the original photograph from which the block was made and wanted to reproduce it. Barry then recalled Davies to the stand. He looked at the photograph and said it was a good likeness of him and was taken about eight years ago. After three previous trials where there were serious disagreements about identification, had it come down to this? A dispute about how a photograph had been reproduced.

After Barry and Book addressed the jury for some hours, Minogue delivered his final address and the Judge then summed up for the jury with a two-hour address. [7] He told the jury that one of the main questions it must consider was the identification of Davies and Cody. 'The High Court has laid down principles which are applicable to identifications,' Mr Justice Martin said, 'and you will, of course, accept those principles. The High Court has said that there is a danger when one suspect is shown singly to witnesses; that danger is the power of suggestion to which all men are susceptible. If you see a man in the dock, the suggestion is that he would not be there if he had not done something wrong, and that suggestion tends to pervert the independent

6 *The Argus*, 28 July 1937
7 *The Courier-Mail (Brisbane, Queensland)*, 30 July 1937

recollection which you have. Accordingly, the High Court has said that when a witness is shown to a suspect singly, it is unsafe to convict on his evidence, unless supported by other evidence, direct or circumstantial. In this case, it is clear that every witness of identification was shown the accused men separately, that is to say, not in a group of other men.'[8]

The jury retired at about 1.00 p.m. Earlier, the judge reminded them to banish from their minds anything they had heard outside the court about the case, which had become notorious. For the last 18 months, the whole city had watched and dissected the results of four trials about the case. To expect jurors to follow this direction was fanciful, to say the least. It was expected that a jury would spend at least six hours in seeking to arrive at a decision. Davies and Cody spent the time in trepidation and uncertainty waiting for the verdict.

Finally, the jury returned at 7.15 p.m. The foreman advised the court that they were unable to agree on charges against either prisoner, nor, in the opinion of the foreman, would they be able to agree if further time was allowed. Book asked that the prisoners be remanded for further trial at the August sittings of the Court, which Judge Martin proceeded to do after thanking and dismissing the jury. Would it ever end? This was the first time that any accused person had been tried four times on a capital charge in Victoria. If another trial proceeded it would be the first time in Australia that a person had been presented for a fifth time on a capital charge, and the first time for many years since the Crown proceeded with a fifth trial on any charge. There was no limit in law as to the number of times the Crown may present an accused person for trial after disagreements, but the practice in recent years had been to abandon prosecutions

8 *News (Adelaide),* 29 July 1937

after three abortive trials.[9] Would the Crown continue with what appeared to be an intractable situation? The cost of running capital trials was considerable and there appeared to be little chance of gaining a conviction of either prisoner on the murder charge whilst major doubts about identification remained. The Attorney-General, Mr Bussau, said that he intended to study the transcript of the evidence given at the trial within a few days and would decide whether there was sufficient evidence to justify holding a fifth trial.

In the meantime, changes had occurred at Russell Street, Superintendent Deeley had assumed charge of the CIB and was expecting to be confirmed in the position when Superintendent Brophy was superannuated, scheduled for September 19. Detective-Inspector 'Scotty' McKerrall returned to his former post as officer in charge of the city division.

THE FIFTH TRIAL THAT NEVER WAS

On Monday August 16, the Court convened for the commencement of the fifth trial. But it wasn't to be. The senior Crown prosecutor, Mr Book, dropped a bombshell (but one not entirely unexpected) when he announced to the Court that the Attorney General had entered a 'nolle prosequi' in the charge of murder against Davies and Cody. The Crown had decided that it would not proceed further against Davies and Cody on the murder charges. It was over for Mr Book and his prosecution team and it must have been a bitter pill to swallow. However, whilst Davies and Cody no longer faced the threat of hanging for the murder of Scriven, they still faced a number of serious charges and the police still had an opportunity to see the two

9 *The Argus*, 30 July 1937

career criminals sentenced to substantial gaol terms when the trial on those charges took place, due to commence on August 18.

As well as the shooting and robbery charges faced by Davies, a charge of perjury was laid in the afternoon of August 16. The charges derived from the proceedings of the second trial on December 17, 1936. Davies immediately pleaded not guilty. He had sworn that he had been to Brisbane once in 1936 but was proven to have gone there in June and September of that year. When he appeared before the court on the morning of Wednesday August 18 , Davies sought an adjournment for a month so that he could seek counsel and arrange his defence, telling the court that he had been in gaol for ten months on a murder charge. He claimed he had no time to prepare for this case and had relied on his mother to try and obtain counsel for him. Justice Duffy gave him an adjournment – until the afternoon. The trial continued with Davies unrepresented by legal counsel. In his defence Davies stated that it was unfair that the Crown had not given him sufficient time to obtain counsel, as it was only on the Monday that he knew he was not going to be charged with murder again. On the charge of perjury he stated that he was under great stress at the time. But it was all to no avail and Davies was convicted of perjury and sentenced to imprisonment for two years, with hard labour. The maximum sentence for perjury was 15 years. The perjury was 'of an impudent type', said Justice Gavan Duffy, never one to miss an opportunity to slight a member of the criminal class. Despite his previous six convictions for various offences, the sentence would appear to be excessively harsh. As the judge stated, it was a serious case but there were no special circumstances to make it particularly heinous. The Scriven family may have disagreed. [10]

10 *The Argus,* 19 August 1937

Davies and Cody were still facing charges of armed robbery and Cody, no longer facing the gallows for the murder of Scriven, was still facing charges of shooting at Constable Guider at the time of his arrest. However he was struggling to find the money to pay for his defence team.[11] But at least his shooting charge had been reduced in severity, being amended to read 'with intent to do him (Guider) grievous bodily harm or to prevent your lawful apprehension'. Whilst this was an improvement on the original charge of 'intent to murder', Cody was confused as he was under the impression that he had been found guilty of shooting with intent to evade arrest but not of shooting at any particular person or in any specific direction. Hadn't his legal team told him of the final wording of the charges against him? Cody was being chased by armed police at the time that he fired, after having been shadowed by them for some months. Whilst the police all testified that Cody had fired the first shot, he claimed that he was returning fire against a barrage. A common practice was for police officers to confer before giving evidence and provide almost identical accounts, even if under oath. Was this the case?

On Wednesday the 18th, Cody was found guilty of having shot at Constable Guider 'with intent to prevent arrest'. After being found guilty, he admitted seven convictions, which included larceny, breach of parole and trespass on railways in New South Wales. Two days later Duffy sentenced him to six years imprisonment with hard labour. The Judge again took the opportunity to lecture Cody when he passed sentence. 'Persons who take to a life of crime should remember that although the

11 One of the interesting aspects of a case like this is how the defendants paid their legal costs. The 'Fee Book' of JV Barry shows that his fees for defending Rupert Davies from December 1936 until July 1937 comes to nearly £200. Cody would have faced similar costs for his barristers, and both would have incurred costs for the instructing solicitors.

use of a revolver or pistol may be highly convenient in their profession, it is also liable to be very dangerous to themselves if they are convicted of any offence arising from the use of it.' Duffy also expressed the hope that use of firearms by the police will be as unusual as it is in England. Duffy again revealed his deeply conservative nature by expressing the opinion that those who sit on the bench may do a public service, and should do one, by treating with proper severity crimes of the kind of which Cody had been found guilty. He told Cody: 'your record is not such to entitle you to any consideration and you may consider yourself extremely lucky that your aim was not straighter, and that you are not here waiting to be sentenced for having successfully shot at the constable.'[12]

Cody gave notice of his intention to appeal against the sentence, which he regarded as excessive. Davies had also given notice to appeal against his sentence for perjury. But in early October, both told the court that they wished to withdraw their appeals. [13] It is unlikely that they would have been successful as the judiciary was clearly not about to do Cody or the Davies brothers any favours.

Davies and Cody were career criminals, but it is entirely possible that they had been fitted-up for the murder of Ted Scriven. Of the judges that had participated in the series of trials and hearings, only those at the High Court (Sir John Latham, assisted by Mr Justice Rich, Mr Justice Dixon, Mr Justice Evatt, and Mr Justice McTiernan) appeared to display any compassion towards Cody and Davies. Nevertheless, it was a sensational end to the search for the murderer of Ted Scriven. Whilst some of the police methods were called into question, it could never be said that they rushed into laying charges against the accused.

12 *The Argus*, 21 August 1937
13 *The Argus*, 8 October 1937

The pair was found not guilty on the charge of robbery in Thornbury on the basis of insufficient evidence. The Judge was L B Stretton, who had assisted Judge Macindoe at the Brophy Royal Commission. He had obviously followed the Scriven case closely and was highly conscious of the dangers of convictions without ironclad evidence and therefore directed the jury to find them not guilty. Davies was also charged with another count of armed robbery (with a sawn-off shotgun) of a factory payroll on Wilson Bros. in North Melbourne in October 1936 but the charge was withdrawn in September. Cody would now serve his six-year sentence for shooting at Constable Guider, and Davies would serve his two-year sentence for perjury. Davies was released from Pentridge in March 1939; Cody was freed on14 August 1943, about the same time that Scriven's widow, Elsie, passed away. It had been an extraordinary 18 months in Melbourne. The money from the Stamps Office was never recovered. No one was convicted for the murder of Ted Scriven and no one else was ever accused of the crime. Cody and Davies may have been framed by the police, whilst members of the jury at the first, third and fourth trials may have been 'got at.' No one was ever convicted of the shooting of Jack Brophy and the only people ever charged were Cody and Davies – a clear mistake by the police and one that never proceeded to the courtroom.

CHAPTER 9
THE WASH-UP

And what of some of the players and locations in this game? Where and how did they end up?

JACK BARRY.

John Barry, 1949

If there was a hero in this story, it was certainly Barry. He was a foundation vice-president (1935) of the Australian Council for Civil Liberties (president 1946) and foundation secretary of the Medico-Legal Society of Victoria (president 1948-49). Barry joined the Australian Labor Party in 1939, stood unsuccessfully for the Federal seat of Balaclava in 1943 and was a member of the Victorian central executive in 1945-47. At the Bar, Barry's progress was not diminished either by his willingness to represent unpopular causes, or by his political activism. Appointed Kings Counsel in 1942, he was appointed to the Supreme Court of Victoria in January 1947. In his early years on the court

Justice Barry was the one progressive element on an extremely conservative bench. He had advocated the introduction of the parole system as a means of conditioning the public to accept an alternative to imprisonment, and the lead that he set in parole was substantially copied elsewhere in Australia. He had a greater influence on Australian penological theory and practice than any contemporary. Barry was the co-author of texts on Australian criminal law and on the ethics of advocacy. He received a knighthood in 1961, and died in 1969.[1]

C H BOOK

Clifford Henry Book was the Crown Prosecutor throughout the Scriven trials. Born in Liverpool, he migrated to Australia and began a law degree. On his return from military service during the Great War, he resumed his studies, being admitted to the Bar and going into practice in 1920 before taking up a role as Crown Prosecutor in 1925. In 1939, he was appointed as an acting judge in the County Court for three months, a measure to relieve the pressure in the Victorian courts. The Victorian Bar Association had made representations to the government regarding delays in the hearing of both criminal and civil actions.[2] In 1943 he was appointed as a judge of the County Court. He was also a former president of the Baptist Assembly and an advocate of Freemasonry During World War II, he was a chair of the Aliens Tribunal. [3]

1 See Mark Finnane, J V Barry, and Bernard Teague, *'Barry, Sir John Vincent (1903–1969)'*, Australian Dictionary of Biography, National Centre of Biography, Australian National University, http://adb.anu.edu.au/biography/barry-sir-john-vincent-9442/text16601, accessed 19 December 2013.
2 *The Argus*, 23 August 1939
3 *The Argus*, 16 March 1943

'SCOTTY' MCKERRAL

McKerrall retired from Victoria Police in 1938 with the remarkable record of never having been reprimanded in 38 years service. He had been a detective for 26 years and taken part in the investigation of 44 murders and many other major Victorian crimes. He had gained an extensive knowledge of criminals, not only by experience in the service but also by a great deal of reading and research.[4]

ALEX DUNCAN

Duncan arrived in Melbourne in October, 1936, with a brief to review the Victorian Police. He presented his interim report on December 16 1936 and his final report on January 22 1937. The first report, focussing on the wireless patrol, C.I.B. and plain-clothes branch, made 16 recommendations, including proposals for detective training and the use of forensic science. His second report contained a further 25 recommendations, addressing such issues as traffic control, police transport, the promotion system and deployment of personnel. Both reports were blueprints for change and highlighted the poor state of the Force under his predecessor, Sir Thomas Blamey. The Dunstan government appointed Duncan as Chief Commissioner on 7 February 1937, with a mandate to implement his reforms. Under his control, the detective force was decentralised on lines similar to Scotland Yard. The CIB was augmented by 110 new detectives, the number of suburban detective squads was increased by 11, and ten detectives were stationed in country districts. The Plainclothes Branch was abolished. There was a rush by serving

4 *The Argus*, 25 April 1938

officers to join the Detective force, with about 800 applications received, soon whittled down to 250 to be interviewed. [5]

The CIB also had a new boss. Superintendent Deeley replaced Superintendent Brophy, who finished his career early, after never fully recovering from the shooting in Parkville that led to the downfall of Chief Commissioner Blamey. It was an interesting choice – Deeley was fully immersed in the existing police culture that had been severely criticised by Duncan and was nearing retiring age. Moreover, he was the President of the Victorian Police Association. After being in the position for a year, he retired and handed over to Superintendent Robert Dower.[6]

Realising that many criminals were increasingly employing scientific methods, Duncan's view was that science should be used against them. He introduced new scientific equipment (such as a comparison microscope, binocular microscope, helixometer, analytical lamps, clinical camera, tessar lenses, technical filters, projector lanterns and an electric exposure meter) that he claimed was better than any other force in the world, including Scotland Yard. In a speech to the Insurance Institute in 1939, he told the audience that 'the development of science as an aid to crime detection had led to remarkable results and many crimes were solved because it was now possible to link up the most minute particles left behind and identify them with the criminal.'[7] Another major initiative was the establishment of a training school where detectives would be trained in Chemistry, Physics, Ballistics, and allied subjects of Applied Science that prove useful in the detection of crime.

Duncan was described by the *Argus* as a 'genial, but quiet man, with broad shoulders and thick grey hair'. He was of middle

5 *The Argus*, 25 March 1938
6 *The Argus,* 6 February 1939
7 *The Argus,* 24 August 1939

height and thickset, and spoke with a trace of a Scottish accent. He had moved quickly to improve the force. Despite the added pressures of World War II and his role as chief air-raid warden for the State, he became one of Victoria's most successful (and its longest serving) Chief Commissioners in the twentieth century.

Duncan had married Elizabeth Ann MacDonald on 1 September 1917 at Trinity Presbyterian Church, Lambeth, and they had one daughter. In 1946, he was appointed a Companion of the Order of St Michael and St George. Duncan was active in the Boy Scouts' Association, Melbourne Rotary, the Young Men's Christian Association, the Royal Humane Society, the National Fitness Council and the State Relief Committee. He retired from the force in 1954 and died in Brighton, a suburb of Melbourne, in 1965. His daughter survived him.[8]

JAMES FORD (JIM) CAIRNS

Cairns continued as a member of Victoria Police and was regarded in 1939 as 'a man of superior education…showing promise of becoming a good detective… one of the most promising of the young men.' He gained commendations for the apprehension of factory breaking and shop breaking (1937), safe breaking (1938) expert forgers (1939) and for an extremely difficult observation of an alien suspect (1941). Whilst his record of service and conduct makes no direct reference to the shootout with Cody, in 1937 he was cited by Jack Brophy, head of CIB, for having performed valuable surveillance work regarding notorious criminals. In May 1938 he was commended by the Chief Commissioner 'for outstanding courage displayed

8 See Robert Haldane, adb.anu.edu.au/biography/duncan-alexander-mitchell-10062

in the execution of duty by effecting the arrest of an armed criminal'. (The same terms were used in the record of Constable Guider). Cairns was part of the Special Branch, responsible for surveillance, and was also in the Consorting Squad.[9]

During his police service, he studied at night and completed an economics degree at the University of Melbourne, becoming the first Victorian policeman to hold a tertiary degree.

In 1944, Cairns resigned from Victoria Police and became a lecturer in economic history at the University of Melbourne. He joined the Australian Labor Party (ALP) and became active in its left wing. In 1955 he stood successfully for the House of Representatives in the working-class seat of Yarra. He held the seat until 1969 when it was abolished in an electoral redistribution, and then shifted to the safe seat of Lalor in Melbourne's western suburbs. In 1967, Cairns contested the leadership of the ALP, but was defeated by Gough Whitlam, who appointed him shadow minister for trade and industry. In 1972 he was a member of the Whitlam government which won office after 23 years in opposition and Cairns became Minister for Overseas Trade and Minister for Secondary Industry. After the 1974 election, he was elected Deputy Leader of the Labor Party and thus became Deputy Prime Minister.

In December 1974, Whitlam appointed Cairns to the senior economic portfolio, Treasurer. Whitlam dismissed him from the ministry on 2 July 1975. After the Whitlam

Jim Cairns, 1970s

9 Victoria Police, record of Conduct and Service, of Cairns, James Ford, Reg. No 8933, and of Guider, Alfred Cecil, Reg. No 7307, courtesy of the Victorian Police Museum.

government was defeated in the 1975 election, he remained in parliament until 1977. He died of bronchial pneumonia, aged 89, in October 2003.

RUPERT OSBORNE DAVIES

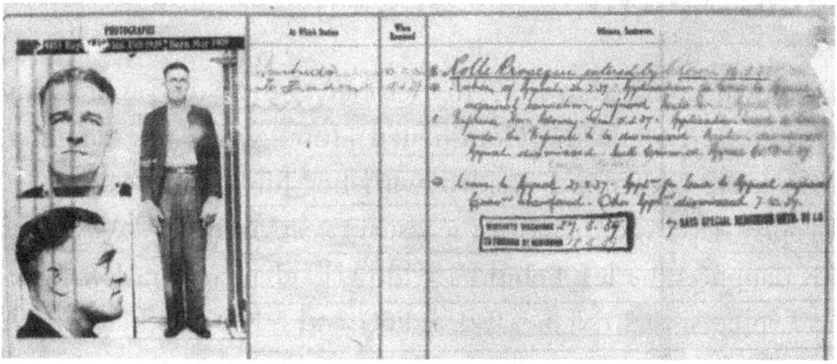

Record of Rupert Davies at time of his release,
Victorian Police Gazette, week ending March 18, 1939

The younger Davies brother was convicted of perjury on 16 August 1937 and sentenced to two years gaol (with hard labour), served at Pentridge. During his term, he gained seven days special remission and was released 'to freedom' on March 18 1939. The Victorian Police Gazette, published weekly, contained details of prisoners released back into the community, including full details of any aliases, nature of conviction (perjury), number of previous convictions (six by the CIB), occupation (storeman) and physical description, such as height (5' 10"), complexion (fresh, which was used for most prisoners, even after spending years in the confines of Pentridge), hair colour (brown) and eye colour (blue), and their docket number (3865/36). Reference was also made if the prisoner's photo had been included in the Photo Supplement to the Gazette. [10] Davies returned to his previous

10 *Victorian Police Gazette,* for week ending 18 March 1939.

haunts in Collingwood. He had married and had one child (a son, Thomas, born 1928) and four grandchildren. There is no record of any criminal charges after his release from Pentridge. He lived until he was 94.

JOHN BROPHY

Brophy had retired in 1937. In October 1946 he died after a long illness, aged 68, at the Continental Hotel, where his daughter, Mrs Jessie Redmond, resided with her husband, the licensee. Brophy had lived there for the last six years of his life. As well as his daughter, he left behind a widow, Evelyn, a grandson Peter, and three sisters (Nellie, Eva, Edith) and a half-brother Tom. A son, Francis, had tragically pre-deceased his father. [11]

HERBERT HARVEY GILLBANK

The whole episode must have been traumatic for the young messenger who had been carrying the funds when Scriven was shot in front of him. Herbert Harvey Gillbank endured the attention of newspaper reporters and investigating police, followed by the Coroner's Inquest, the committal hearing and the subsequent four trials, where he gave evidence. Whether he received any compensation or reward for his part in the shooting is unknown, but unlikely. It was also unlikely that he received any sort of medical attention, and it is unknown whether his health or nervous state was affected. Whilst he was only 17, it wasn't all that long ago that thousands of boys around the same age had been sent off to fight in the Great War. It was not only regarded that young men should do their duty but that

11 *The Argus,* 14 October 1946

they should do it quietly and without complaint.

Gillbank, a member of the Gillbank family from Footscray, had passed his Intermediate Certificate (4th Form) in 1932 and gained his School Leaving Certificate (5th Form) in 1933. He then joined the Public Service and took a position at the Stamps Office. He commenced a Law Degree (LL.B) at Melbourne University in 1939. It is not known what attracted him to the law; perhaps the series of events following the murder of Scriven led him to it, perhaps he had always been interested in it. He enrolled in (and completed) two subjects in 1939 and three more in 1940. He also enlisted in the Army in August 1940 and was attached to the 6 Australian Topographical Survey Company, which provided survey and mapping support to military operations in Victoria, Northern Territory, Western Australia, Queensland, New Guinea, and New Britain. He must have had the opportunity to study during his war service, as he enrolled in three subjects in 1941, four more in 1943, and two more in both 1944 and 1945.

After his military discharge in November 1945, as a corporal, he took advantage of the opportunity for financial assistance under the 'Commonwealth Reconstruction Training Scheme', set up for ex-servicemen starting or returning to university studies in the postwar years. In 1946 he completed four more subjects, together with a further four 'single subjects' in 1947 i.e. not part of the student's degree program. He was a solid, but not spectacular student, with passes in all the subjects he attempted, but no honours.[12] Other ex-servicemen in the Public Service who were married with families rejected the lure of study, feeling that their families had endured enough whilst they were away fighting and it was time to go back to work and

12 Student record of Gillbank, courtesy of Melbourne University

earn a good wage. [13] Gillbank had married during the war, to Norma Elizabeth Halstead, a schoolteacher in the days when women teachers had to resign when they married. By 1948 he had qualified as a solicitor and moved to a position in the Public Solicitors' Office in the Law Department, earning an annual salary of £501. He also took the opportunity to move to the other side of town, leaving his birthplace of Footscray for the more genteel eastern suburb of Carnegie, where he resided in a Californian Bungalow in Neville Street. The Gillbanks had three children - Linden Rae, Peter and Jan. In the early 1970s he had moved again to Ramona Avenue in Chadstone, between the Monash Freeway and the ever-expanding massive Chadstone shopping centre. By the time he retired in 1978, he had risen to the lofty position of Assistant Crown Solicitor. He passed away in the late 1990s. Members of his family remember him as a quiet man who rarely spoke of himself or his work. Not surprisingly, he had not told his children of the robbery and his brush with death. [14]

PENTRIDGE PRISON.

The conditions in Pentridge continued to be a point of concern for many concerned with prison reform. In 1946 it was reported that a number of divisions were still unsatisfactory, with the area used for female prisoners described as 'dank, gloomy and vermin-ridden'. But by this time there were no funds available to resolve overcrowded and unsuitable conditions, as the Cain Labor government decreed that 'more worthy projects, such as providing homes for ex-servicemen and others, would have

13 Robin Grow, *Safe as Houses*, 2013, p.96

14 Thanks to Linden Rae Gillbank and her family for assistance with details and memories of their father.

to come first.' [15] By 1951 it was recognised that a completely new institution was required that would replace the 'insanitary and outmoded' facilities, although there was a stream of society unconcerned about what prisoners had to put up with, arguing that they got what they deserve.[16] Judges did not seem to understand the inadequacy of conditions, with one Judge telling convicted youths that 'gaol is much more severe than the Remand Yard'. Some observers, such as the Anglican chaplain to the gaol, stated an opposing view, based on regular attendance, asserting that the Remand Yard was about ten times worse than the rest of the gaol. [17] By the mid-1950s, criticism of the Remand section was becoming louder, with accommodation being described as 'fowl pens'. In 1955 the government called for tenders to renovate parts of the prison. Female prisoners were to be relocated and part of their former quarters would be used for improvements to the Remand section. [18] The prison was finally closed in 1997 and is slowly being redeveloped for housing.

RUSSELL STREET POLICE HEADQUARTERS, MELBOURNE

In the 1930s, the Victorian Police force was severely under-trained, ill-equipped and struggled to solve (and prevent) serious crime carried out by armed criminals. One of the major issues that became obvious during the investigations into the Scriven murder and the shooting of Brophy was the deplorable working conditions endured by the police, particularly at their

15 *The Argus*, 5 February 1946
16 *The Argus*, 11 July 1951
17 *The Argus*, 15 April 1954
18 *The Argus*, 1 October 1955

headquarters in Russell Street in the north-east corner of the city of Melbourne. The police had occupied this site, opposite the City Watchhouse, since the 1850s. It was recognised in 1934 that the buildings were hopelessly outdated and there was an obvious need for a modern building and facilities that would assist with the introduction of the latest developments in methods of crime detection being used overseas. There was also a need for accommodation and space for administrative functions, records storage and cars. The police department was seeking extensions to the existing building at a cost of £15,000. But some in government felt that a much more comprehensive plan was required and the Public Works department was asked to prepare a report, which would probably require an outlay of £30,000 and would include extensions on land acquired by the Police department on Latrobe Street, to the east of the existing offices.[19]

The year of 1935 saw another proposal to replace the inadequate buildings. This time the estimate was for the expenditure of £75,000. Tentative plans were produced, which included a proposal for a new barracks for single members of the force. It would also enable all the administrative units of the force to be concentrated in one building, instead of scattered across a number of locations.

At the start of 1936, Victoria had little money to spend on capital works. But when the Premier, Mr Dunstan, inspected headquarters in early May 1936, he realised that a large section of the buildings was totally obsolete. Some rectification work would be necessary but that would depend on the amount of money that was available. However Dunstan's visit started the process by which the classic Art Deco style Police Headquarters

19 *The Argus*, 5 December, 1934

building would be eventually constructed. When Alex Duncan, the new Chief Commissioner, arrived in late 1936, a new building became one of his main priorities. He had quickly formed the opinion that the Russell Street building was in a shocking condition. The administrative offices were badly arranged and the part occupied by single members was dilapidated, offering little comfort for the men. Rather than piecemeal additions, based on available budgets, he was convinced that the government had to commit to spending a large amount of money. The solution was to re-build. The Victorian Cabinet was starting to agree with him and in 1937 a Cabinet sub-committee reported on a plan to construct a three-storey building in Russell Street to replace existing buildings. The proposal would allow the Chief Commissioner to move into the building and would be in conjunction with the transfer of the police car fleet to a newly-roofed over former gaol site on the opposite side of Russell Street. A significant event occurred at this point when the Chief Architect for Victoria, Percy Everett, was asked to prepare plans and detailed estimates.[20]

Finally the money was found by the State government. A new building was to replace existing facilities in Russell Street and extend along Latrobe Street. But it would be twelve storeys, not three. Everett's final plan was for a building, in the latest style, to be constructed in three stages (central portion, south wing, east wing). The total cost would be around £125,000 – a considerable amount for a government building in a country that was faced with war. It would be a stepped building constructed in reinforced concrete, clad with face brick curtain walls on a plinth of sandstone. Cream bricks were used, with

20 *The Argus,* 23 June, 1937. Everett left a wonderful legacy for the people of Victoria with many of his designs for schools, colleges, prisons, mental hospitals, police stations, and courts throughout the state.

salt-glazed manganese brown bricks used in spandrel panels below the metal-framed windows, providing contrast. The narrow windows emphasised the verticality of the building. [21] Everett also employed some of his trademark features such as bevelled bricks, as well as moderne styling in the ground floor foyer, terrazzo floors, wood-panelled stairwells and stylised metal balustrades. The symmetrical façade featured central vehicle access, flanked by side pedestrian entrances and flagpoles. In a predominantly flat city, it was located on one of the high spots and became an instant beacon for the people of Melbourne. It included a range of facilities, including a nerve centre for communications (the radio room in corridor D, room 24, which led to the nickname of the building – D24), administrative offices, a gymnasium and recreation hall and accommodation for unmarried policemen who had to spend time living on-site. A major driver was the opportunity to incorporate a large radio communications tower on the building, which assisted the operations of the radio-controlled fleet of police cars, one of the world's first. [22] The massive radio tower served as the aerial for a 2 kilowatt transmitter that marked the change from morse code to voice transmission for the patrol cars. Previously each car was equipped with a morse code transmitter to send messages to headquarters for decoding. As well as vastly improving police communications, it provided a new entertainment forum for the people of Melbourne who were able to listen to police messages on their own domestic radio receivers.[23] Along with the improvements in radio, the police introduced a direct telephone network in December 1939. Direct landlines now connected

21 *Victorian Heritage Register,* H0913

22 It also assisted the war effort when Victoria Police took on the responsibility for providing alerts to the city by way of sirens.

23 *Police in Victoria 1836-80,* Victoria Police Management Service Bureau, 1980 p. 104

police headquarters with 55 metropolitan police stations and fire stations, ambulance depots, vital railway centres, electric power stations, and other points. The system enabled an officer at Russell Street to speak simultaneously to all connected points and for immediate replies to be received. It was developed by the Chief Commissioner with the co-operation of experts from the Postmaster-General's Department.

Police Headquarters, Russell St, Melbourne
From Pictures Collection, State Library ofVictoria

In early 1940, construction began on the first section of the new building – the central block, in which bedrooms would be provided for 150 single men, at a cost of £90,000. This section was completed in 1941, much to the pleasure of Chief Commissioner Duncan, and the other sections were completed over the next two years. When he opened the building in 1943, Duncan used the opportunity to rebuke 'those who spread tales that Melbourne people are living in a city of disorder and disorganisation and that Melbourne is a place full of wrongdoers.'[24]

24 *West Australian (Perth)*, 30 April 1943

The officers who occupied the new building thought that they were in heaven as they enjoyed facilities such as single rooms, hot and cold water, a beautiful dining room, comfortable lounge and reading room, gorgeous bathrooms, superb kitchens, all mod cons, and panoramic views to the sea and the distant ranges. What a dream for a policeman, claimed one report. It seemed too good to be true to have a good clean spacious building for their offices in place of the old, rambling, poky block of buildings that it had replaced.[25]

Police headquarters achieved further notoriety in the 1950s with a weekly radio show called 'D24' on radio 3DB, and as the setting for a long-running (and popular) television show called 'Homicide', which ran from 1964 to 1976. Every week viewers watched as the stars of the show alighted from their Falcon car in front of the building, adjusted their skinny ties and hats and embarked on another day of fighting crime - with everything neatly wrapped up in the next 50 minutes.

Plaque on former Russell Street headquarters, 2015

25 *The Argus,* 9 October, 1943

Numerous social activities took place in the building, including sporting contests, dances, Debutante Balls, etc. The methods of technical investigation improved – as did the training of police. Renovations occurred as required and when the budget permitted. But by the 1980s the building was becoming increasingly tired and there was a feeling amongst many police that it was time to move to a new building. A major event occurred in 1986 when a young police constable, Angela Taylor, became the victim of a carbomb outside the front entrance of the building. For many this demonstrated that the force was vulnerable in its current location.[26] In 1995 Victoria Police vacated the building, causing major angst among many officers who had occupied the building for a large part of their working lives. But what would the government do with it? It was listed on the government's own Heritage Register and protected by legislation, so it couldn't be demolished. Could it be converted to a hotel? Offices? Perhaps apartments? A number of schemes were proposed, all of which fell through. Finally in 2003, developer Max Moar (of Lustig and Moar) presented the government with a proposal to convert the building into apartments. Moar had a great love of the Art Deco style, but in order to pay for the restoration of the existing building and conversion to 80 apartments, he required that a new 27-storey residential tower be constructed at the rear of the existing building. The total cost of the project would be about $160m, of which $5m. was to be spent on restoring the existing building. The new tower required demolition of the gymnasium and an adjacent 1970s office building. Like all conversions of heritage buildings, nothing was easy as the architects (led by Graham Morrison, of Bruce Henderson Architects) dealt with

26 The blast of the bomb also caused some damage to the historic City Court building on the opposite corner, which was vacated in 1994 following the construction of a new Magistrates Court building in William Street.

issues such as pipes, access, lifts, security, power and water, whilst complying with building codes that had not been in existence during the original construction. Much remediation took place on the exterior surface, with repairs to brick work and the replacement of window frames. But the biggest job was to restore the radio tower. The apartments went onto the market in 2005, and have proven to be very successful.

ACKNOWLEDGEMENTS AND THANKS

A number of people and organisations were helpful in providing support, information and recollections about characters and events in this story.

They include members of the Davies family; the Gillbank family (particularly Linden Rae Gillbank); the Victorian Police Museum; Peter Stewart, Victorian Government Solicitor; Katie Wood, Archivist, Access and Outreach and Curator, Malcolm Fraser Collection, The University of Melbourne Archives, University Library; the staff at the Public Records Office, Victoria; Lina Favrin, Information Services Officer, City of Yarra; Mark Finnane; David Sonenberg; Clive Fredman; John Sylvester; Shane Kenna and Tim Harding.

A number read the work in entirety, or chapters and extracts, and made helpful comments. Thanks to Ken Oldis, Reg Egan, Bill Condon, Jan Hatch and Peter Sheridan.

As always, massive thanks to Robyn for her patience and tolerance.

MURDER OF A MESSENGER

ROBIN GROW

ISBN 9781922175915		Qty
RRP	AU$24.99	.....
Postage within Australia	AU$5.00	.....
	TOTAL*	$________

* All prices include GST

Name:...

Address: ....

....

Phone:..

Email: ....

Payment: ❑ Money Order ❑ Cheque ❑ MasterCard ❑ Visa

Cardholder's Name:..

Credit Card Number: ....

Signature:..

Expiry Date: ....

Allow 7 days for delivery.

Payment to: Marzocco Consultancy (ABN 14 067 257 390)
PO Box 12544
A'Beckett Street, Melbourne, 8006
Victoria, Australia
admin@brolgapublishing.com.au